HOBO STORIES

by Patrick & Terence Casey

Off-Trail Publications
Elkhorn, California

*With thanks to J. Randolph Cox, Doug Ellis, John Gunnison,
and Phil Stephensen-Payne*

HOBO STORIES
Copyright © 2010, Off-Trail Publications
ISBN-10: 1-935031-14-7
ISBN-13: 978-1-935031-14-7

OFF-TRAIL PUBLICATIONS
Elkhorn, California
offtrail@redshift.com

Printed in the United States of America
First printing: December 2010

CONTENTS

James Patrick Casey
1892 - 1941

Edward Terence Casey
1894 - 1945

Once Upon a Time in the Pulpwoods
By John Locke

ONE FINE DAY IN 1908, Terence Casey, eighth grader, came across an article by Upton Sinclair in the October 1906 *Cosmopolitan*. Sinclair had quickly risen to renown after the success of his 1906 novel *The Jungle*, which exposed the horrors of the Chicago meatpacking industry; and here he was in a leading magazine talking about his aims and values. But of far greater interest to Terence than socialism and slaughterhouses was Sinclair's revelation that he had sold fiction as a mere teenager:

> I [had] a happy knack . . . of composing (and marketing) boys' adventure stories. For a considerable period I used to talk these off to a stenographer, grinding them out at the rate of six or eight thousand words a day; in which manner I took care of myself from the age of sixteen. I have frequently walked all the way around Central Park, in New York, "thinking story." It was just after the Spanish War, and the scenes of my heroes' adventures were laid in Cuba; so I used to call the work of composition "killing Spaniards." In those days I wrote under the name of "Ensign Clark[e] Fitch," and "Lieutenant Frederick Garrison"; and my productions appeared in brilliant red-, blue-, green-, and yellow-colored periodicals, known as the *True Blue Library* and the *Starry Flag Weekly*.

Terence, and his brother Patrick, older by two years, had grown up on dime novels possessing the same kind of rousing boyhood drama. They particularly enjoyed the tales of Street & Smith's Frank and Dick Merriwell, by Burt L. Standish. Frank Merriwell began his fictional life in a military academy, and then moved on to Yale, where he played football and otherwise confronted the problems of the world.

Amazingly, Upton Sinclair had paid his dues in the world of cheap adventure fiction, then catapulted himself into literary stardom. Well. To Terence, here was the road to glorious success already mapped out.

He shared the article with his brother. Patrick was sixteen, a copy boy for the *San Francisco Examiner*, his toes already wetted in the world of writers. Patrick shared Terence's enthusiasm for Sinclair's article, leading Terence to suggest they collaborate on their own dime novel. Patrick agreed.

Edward Terence and James Patrick Casey were the two youngest of six children. Their parents, Patrick J. (1848-1917) and Catherine (1853-1923), had emigrated to the United States from Ireland in the early 1870s. They undoubtedly met here, and then married in about 1877. Patrick Casey Sr. was a coal dealer in San Francisco, where all six children were born. John Joseph Casey (1878-1930) came first; then three girls: May (*b.* 1881), Margaret (*b.* 1882), and Gertrude (*b.* 1888). Patrick was born on May 12, 1892; Terence on September 29, 1894. The boys grew up in the Mission District, south of Market Street.

John J. Casey was the first of the siblings to make his name in the world. After finishing high school he became an assistant bookkeeper in his father's business. He studied drawing on the side. In 1901, he moved to New York, where he was an illustrator for *The New York American* and *The New York Evening Journal.* He also did magazine illustration. So when Terence and Patrick decided to become writers, there was precedent in the family for artistic success.

Upton Sinclair's boy stories had featured both main branches of the service, using West Point and Annapolis as settings. The Caseys, having grown up in a port city, and having been familiar with ships and shipping, chose the Navy for theirs. Sinclair had been older when he sold his dime novels, but the brothers figured that by working together they could overcome the disadvantage of their youth.

They toiled in secret into the Spring of 1910, by which time Patrick had become a sports reporter and Terence had followed his brother's path, entering newspaper work as an office boy. Terence wrote the first drafts; Patrick edited them. The manuscript ballooned to a ridiculous 200,000 words. The story was finished, but they wisely decided that it was too long-winded. Patrick called in sick for two weeks, stayed home, and slashed the manuscript to 40,000 words. The first publisher they sent it to turned it down as "too exciting," i.e. too melodramatic. So the brothers did what they should have done in the first place, sent it to the old publishing house of Upton Sinclair's dime novels: Street & Smith. Miraculously, it sold and became one of the first serials published in a new pulp, *Top-Notch Magazine.* The story, *Dave Manning, Midshipman,* appeared in five installments, from the issues of August through November 1, 1910 (the magazine switched to a bimonthly in October). It was bylined "Ensign Lee Tempest, U.S.N.," inspired by Sinclair's "Ensign Clarke Fitch" Navy novels.

Some years later, Patrick had a chance meeting in New York with boyhood hero Gilbert Patten, the man behind the Burt L. Standish name, and was astonished to discover that Patten, *Top-Notch's* initial editor, also hidden behind Standish, had been the very person to accept the Caseys' first story. (Presumably, the Caseys had dealt with an assistant editor.)

After that initial sale, the brothers were convinced their writing career was underway. Patrick quit his newspaper job, while Terence finished high school. They never stopped writing. No sooner had *Dave Manning, Midshipman* completed its run, the next issue of *Top-Notch* (November 15) ran an Ensign Lee Tempest novelette featuring a new character, "Bob Storm," in "Bob Storm, of the Navy." Tempest . . . Storm . . . Manning gave way to a grand thematic possibility. Storm, a plebe (freshman) at the Naval Academy, starred in many other Casey *Top-Notch* stories. Storm played football, got in fights, went sailing, liked pretty girls, etc. The December 1 issue started a serial, *Bob Storm in the Line*. In it, Storm gets into a fight with an upperclassman. Later, on the eve of the Army-Navy football game, an anonymous letter is sent to the faculty accusing Storm of the forbidden sin of smoking. Cigarettes are discovered in Storm's room. He faces court-martial and, even worse, missing the big game. The day is saved, he does play and, in fact, performs brilliantly, winning the game for Navy. Later in the narrative, the Caseys contrive to get Storm to San Francisco, to stay at a classmate's home over Christmas holiday. "Enamored with the navy life," the chums visit the battleship U.S.S. *Arizona*, harbored on the bay. The boys emerge on deck in the evening, contemplating a trip back to the city on a launch:

> It was no matter for laughter. It was not that the night was stormy, very windy, or over cold; it was that a thick, impenetrable blanket of fog lay over the bay. So thick that Bob, as he followed right at the heels of Ralph, could just barely make out the black, overcoated figure of his chum.
>
> It was cold, and damp, and clammy. It filled Bob with an eerie feeling as he tried, with his eyes, to pierce its intangible depths.
>
> It filled the commonplace night with unrealities and mystery; the bridge looked like the battlement of a castle on a height; the masts seemed cut off some feet above the deck; the ship's lights flamed out of nothingness; the water of the bay could not be seen; and the only things to be heard were the deafening sounds of the fog siren close at hand on the ship, and the faint tooting now and then of a horn or a siren on a passing boat. It was a first-class San Francisco fog.

The writing is pretty good; at least, the readers wouldn't have suspected they were reading the prose of two teenage boys. In the climactic events of the final installment, Bob and Ralph are shanghaied, then join a band of mutineers, described as follows:

> One was, by his own account, a college boy; another, a former member of the Northwest Mounted Police; a third, an Australian, and a fourth, a wharf rat. They were of the kind of men who await the flip of a card, or the fall of a dice, to bring them fortune—or nothing; who forever trek in the desolate places along the outskirts of civilization; who play, solitary, among black men and yellow at a great risk and for a mere pittance.

One of the mutineers, an Irishman, turns out to be a San Francisco newspaperman—the Caseys took every opportunity to merge the adventure idiom they had absorbed from dime novels with their own knowledge and experience. In the end, they're rescued by the *Arizona* and lament that, back at Annapolis, the fellows weren't going to believe how they spent their Christmas vacation.

Not only had the boys turned into smooth stylists, they learned to work fast, as the pulps demanded. They composed one 80,000-word serial in three weeks. That, too, followed the Sinclair model of efficiency.

After a six-month gap, Storm was back in *Top-Notch*, starting a three-part serial. Another novelette appeared in the September 15, 1911 issue. A three-parter, *Bob Storm on the Bridge*, ended the year, and the Bob Storm cycle.

The capacity of the Caseys to produce saleable stuff quickly expanded beyond the dimensions of Bob Storm's life, magnificently heroic as it may have been. In 1910 they sold stories to *The Boys' Magazine*, which had started publication in January, and included fiction in the same vein as *Top-Notch*. Then, audaciously, they placed an article, "The Juvenile Field," in *The Editor*, also in 1910. They'd gone from never being published to dispensing advice to other writers within months, if not weeks. The article appeared under the byline "James Edward Casey," combining their names to share credit. They would not have wanted to sign an article, Ensign Lee Tempest, U.S.N., which any pro would have recognized as a fake.

They appeared with a short, "Shanghai Tom," in the February 1911 issue of *The Black Cat*, published by another firm, also under James Edward Casey. Whether officially or not, Tempest belonged with Bob Storm and Street & Smith. In the March 1, 1911 *Top-Notch*, they appeared again as James Edward Casey with a novelette, "Stan Hardy of Cornell," which sounds like it may have been an attempt to launch another series. There were additional James Edward Casey stories sprinkled throughout their tenure at *Top-Notch*. None were serials and none, apparently, featured series characters. Curiously, the byline switched to "James E. Casey" for a story in the August 15, 1911 issue, as if a transition was underway, and then to "James *Edmond* Casey" for a story in the September 15, 1911, and that remained their byline for non-Storm stories in *Top-Notch* thereafter. The reason for this transition isn't known, but it was probably the brothers' decision, and not Street & Smith's error, since additional stories in *The Black Cat* (January, April 1913) went out under James Edmond Casey. It may be that a conflict with a real person arose. James Edward Casey is a somewhat common name, while James Edmond Casey is not, and there was a real James Edward Casey in San Francisco at the time. The final Casey story in *Top-Notch*, under any byline, appeared in the March 15, 1913 issue.

Seemingly wise beyond their years, the Caseys were acting in every way like professional wordsmiths. In two issues of *Top-Notch*, they appeared under both the Tempest and Casey names (September 15, December 15, 1911). They had diversified their opportunities within *Top-Notch* and, by selling outside the company, had diversified their markets.

After the last Bob Storm serial concluded (January 15, 1912), there immediately followed three more James Edmond Casey stories (February 1, March 1, April 1). After that, nothing else appeared in print in 1912. In early 1913, one more *Top-Notch* short, and two more *Black Cat* shorts appeared. This period must have been when the decision was made to hop to the next stepping stone along the Sinclair path, and move up to higher ground. They would not appear in *Top-Notch* again until 1919, and in *The Black Cat*, never.

The next story to find print was "The Orchid of Allure," which appeared in *Adventure* for September 1913, under the simple name of "Patrick Casey." The story was about orchid-hunters in Borneo who labored under the threat of the local headhunters. This, indeed, was a move up in markets. *Top-Notch* aimed squarely at juvenile readers; *The Black Cat* was a low-paying bottom rung; but *Adventure* was a magazine of fast-growing reputation. It featured adult fiction with exciting, often violent, stories grounded in authentic detail, frequently written by men who had witnessed the kind of things they wrote about. Other Patrick Casey bylined stories soon appeared in *Adventure*: "Tropics," December 1913, set in Panama; and "A Debt to Pay," February 1914, set in South America. The writing, too, was a step up in quality. Compare, for example, the above description of San Francisco fog with this paragraph from "Tropics" describing a boat trip in the Canal Zone:

> All the tortuous passage up the dismally embowered stream I stood in the bow of the *cayuca* and searched with my eyes the banking walls of morbidly bright-colored jungle-foliage. The air beneath was dank with steam and rancid with vegetable odors that weighed like a load on the lungs. The banks were bloody cesspools of red clay. Back of them great coleus-plants, arching ferns, cannas, and wonderful orchids splashed the eyes with the tints of the rainbow. Over all, in the stagnant heat, draggled the heavy fronds of cocoanut-palms.

The fog description is pleasingly atmospheric, but composed of details easily conjured from the imagination. The jungle description, on the other hand, is not only atmospheric, it amplifies the mood with a depth of specific detail. The use of exotic language gives the passage a strange beauty, the feel of an alien place which permeates the whole story. The detail might lead one to guess, in the absence of contradictory evidence, that during the fallow

1912-13 period, older brother Patrick visited a few of the hostile corners of the world, in that age of exploration. A logical deduction. Once the glow of satisfaction from being published dimmed, the low-paying markets could be seen for what they were: ruts leading nowhere special. To write well and convincingly about the world, mustn't one must first experience the world?

That's how logic might fill in the blanks. But we have "The Playboy of a Back Street."

"Playboy" was a Casey short story that appeared in the pulp *Romance*, February 1920. *Romance* was published by The Ridgway Company, the same firm that published *Adventure*; and shared *Adventure's* editor, Arthur Sullivant Hoffman. The aim of *Romance*, as stated in Hoffman's announcement in the first issue of November 1919, was to address a problem in publishing. The higher-class magazines offered nonfiction alongside literary-quality fiction. But no one magazine published literary-quality fiction as its exclusive domain. *Romance* would do this. Its aim might seem to be a repudiation of *Adventure*, and the other pulps. Reading between the lines, though, *Romance* was intended to be a pulp of *Adventure's* caliber, but with an appeal broad enough to attract female readers. The first issue led off with a Joseph Conrad serial, but many of the authors were established *Adventure* names: Gordon Young, Charles Beadle, S.B.H. Hurst—and Patrick Casey. Casey's story, "Ah, Never Believe Your Eyes," "was built around the history of two mushroom millionaires of the '49 period of California." At any rate, *Romance* folded after twelve issues.

"Playboy," appeared in the fourth issue. Terence reminisced about the story for the *San Francisco Chronicle* (February 5, 1922). Note that the brothers were reasonably well-known writers by 1922, particularly in the Bay Area.

> Our favorite character is one we called the Playboy of a back street. His name was Aloysius Columbkill O'Callahan—he was Irish of the Irish—and although still in his teens, he turned out thrilling serials and 15 cent paper-covered novels by the ream. You never heard of him, of course, as he never signed his name to that stuff.
>
> He lived on Fair Oaks street of San Francisco, which we changed in our story to the name of another battle of the Civil war—Seven Pines. . . .
>
> Never did we know him to write a serial or paper-covered novel about a dark-complexioned heroine. Always he made his heroines blue-eyed and golden-haired. The trouble with O'Callahan was that from making up yarns, move by move, about his dime-novel creatures—about "Bob Storm" and "Dave Manning" and the Lovely Ladies of the Lola Dean Lively Library—he had taken an easy step: a very natural step when you have youth and dreams. He made up stories

about himself, in which he acted like his own dime novel heroes by rescuing a dream girl from all manner of enemies and perils.

That dream girl was, to be sure, golden-haired and blue-eyed—an angel. She it was he attempted to describe in his novels. She was his ideal. The poor, lonely, dreaming boy-man imagined himself in love with her because always in novels heroes love heroines. To Aloysius Columbkill O'Callahan there could be no better nor stronger reason than that such was so in dime novels. . . .

I remember that O'Callahan graduated a year or so later from his dime-novel writing into one of the red blooded magazines. He wrote a novelette called "The Orchid of Allure," which was supposed to be a "free translation of the report of Herr Fritz Hoffrahm, explorer for the Hamburgische Gesellschaft." Sinclair Lewis, not having written *Main Street* as yet, was then acting as assistant editor of the magazine, and perhaps it was he who wrote this announcement:

"This story is splashed with the vivid color of the Orient. It actually makes you feel the moist heat of the silent jungle. You can hear the drums and hypnotic chant of the Borneo head hunters. The mad desire of two men to secure the famous Trevor orchid makes a story as unusual as it is full of color and action."

The trouble with that magazine was that most of its authors claimed to have lived in the strange lands about which they wrote and to have experienced much of the drama they put into their contributions. There was, indeed, a department in the rear given over to the personal experiences of these adventurous adventure writers.

O'Callahan at the time, although he wrote of Borneo, had never been farther east than Shellmound Park, farther north than Monte Rio on the Russian river, farther south than the cemeteries, while the horizon of the Pacific as visible from the Cliff House was to him the end of the western world. But as a dime-novelist he was not to be outdone. Here's what he wrote to the editor-in-chief, which that editor swallowed—hook, line and sinker—and which he afterward published in the rear of the magazine:

"After smoking two Durhams I can think of little to add to the fact that I am just a tropical tramp. I was born on Rincon Hill, in 'the city that was'—that is, San Francisco in the old gone days before the fire. In those strangely remote times it was great to be a little tad on Rincon Hill. From the weed-grown iron dogs of former mansions, the hill fell away to the water front, where the engrossing mystery of the sea lured me ere I was knee-high to a capstan.

"At the stage when most kids are reading Alger and Henty I was living the wanderlust of Stevenson and Louis Becke. I was 'out' on a ship which shall be nameless, as I 'jumped' it at Hongkong. In other words, I went 'topside' on a day I shouldn't—the day she pulled up her mudhooks—and I didn't come down until she was out of sight of the Peak.

"Since then I have been many things in that black and brown and yellow vortex called the South Seas. I gambled in Macao with proverbial 'griffin' luck. I shipped on more tramps than I have fingers on my hands. I met all manner of characters—some strange white men and not a few white Chinese.

"In Manila, where I worked for the Government for a spell, been shanghaied on a ship, that I met a newspaper man who had run the Japanese blockade about Port Arthur. Another newspaper man, who was acting as press agent, scenic artist, stage director and comedian of a troupe of actors, saw possibilities in me for a juvenile part. We played in Manila, Pago Pago, Singapore, Banjermasin, Ho-Ho, Macassar and throughout the South islands.

"After that I was for a year quartermaster on a steamship of the Koninklijke Paketvaart Maatschappij, the Dutch Borneo line which plies between Kuerbing, Sarawak, Banjermasin and Singapore. From this I saved up a tidy sum, and once back in San Francisco I was ready at last for the humdrum prosaic existence of the city dweller. Quien sabe? Any moment I may hear again the call. I know I shall answer it."

The reader may be led to surmise, from all these intimate details, that this character, O'Callahan, is none other than my brother Patrick or myself. There is a bit of truth in the supposition; but the whole truth is that O'Callahan is a composite of certain characteristics and experiences of my brother and myself.

The disorienting aspect of this article is that Terence conflates the experiences of his brother and himself, with the fictional O'Callahan— and attributes it all to O'Callahan. One might assume, for instance, that O'Callahan wrote stories about "Bob Storm" and "Dave Manning," making O'Callahan's disguise completely transparent. But O'Callahan's fictional character was named "Bob Breakaway"; and it's O'Callahan who writes for the Lola Dean Lively Library. Fortunately, we have the text of "Playboy" (included in this volume), to clear up the confusion. Once we strip away the details that apply to O'Callahan, what's left from the article appears to be literal Casey autobiography.

For example, the brothers probably were born on Rincon Hill. Rincon Hill was a neighborhood in the northeast corner of San Francisco that was wiped out by the 1906 Earthquake and Fire; the hill currently provides the foundation for the west end of the San Francisco-Oakland Bay Bridge. Fair Oaks is, in fact, a back street of San Francisco's Mission District where the brothers grew up, although it sounds like the move preceded the Earthquake.

From "O'Callahan's" graduation to the "red blooded magazines" forward, it's all Casey. The "red blooded magazine" is obviously *Adventure*.

"The Orchid of Allure," the Caseys' first story for the magazine, does indeed feature characters named "Hoffrahm" and "Trevor." Sinclair Lewis was in fact Hoffman's main assistant in the early years, involved in many areas of the magazine's production. Lewis left *Adventure* in August 1913, so if he wrote the announcement copy for "Orchid," it would probably have been one of the tasks he performed in his final weeks. The "department in the rear" was *Adventure's* popular column, *The Camp-Fire*, which often featured letters from the issue's authors discussing the authenticity of their stories in that, or previous, issues. First-time contributors to *Adventure* were invited to contribute introductions to *The Camp-Fire* describing their backgrounds. This leads us to the most amusing element of Terence's article: it's a thinly-disguised confession that the Caseys fabricated an adventurous background in order to establish credibility and break into *Adventure*; that, in fact, they hadn't traveled much at all, e.g. "O'Callahan, although he wrote of Borneo, had never been farther east than Shellmound Park. . . ."

The article's obfuscated style, combined with its reluctance to name names, was probably to avoid bringing direct embarrassment to the hook, line, and sinker swallowing editor of the red blooded magazine—Arthur Sullivant Hoffman. Terence reveals that Hoffman initially received *two* stories from the Caseys, "Orchid," and a fake first-timer autobiography. The Caseys must have been delighted when they cracked into *Adventure*, a goal that would elude many fine adventure writers over the decades to come; but they may have been a bit disheartened when they read that second story in *The Camp-Fire*. Hoffman had edited out some of their best fibs. Terence misquotes what Hoffman actually printed; in his introduction to the letter, Hoffman summed up the five paragraphs cited in Terence's article:

> Probably only a comparative few of you know Borneo from personal experience, so that of the large remainder there may be some inclined to think that Patrick Casey has drawn on his imagination for more than the plot itself in "The Orchid of Allure."
>
> Seven years ago he shipped out of San Francisco, his native place, as a cabin-boy on "a liner which shall be nameless, as I jumped the ship at Hongkong." Then he traveled the South Seas and the Far East in general with a theatrical troupe. Then served under the Government at Manila. Then a year as quartermaster on the Borneo Limited Company's steamships that run between Kuching, Sarawak and Singapore. That, and what appears in his letter that follows, are only samples from his wanderings, but the rest we'll save for another time. There are more stories of his to come.

And here following are some of the juicy excerpts that Hoffman did print, which Terence did not quote in the article:

The character of Hoffrahm is drawn from a composite of all those queer sentimental itinerant Dutch and Germans who wander up and down the outer *campongs* of civilization at the beck and call of Amsterdam and Hamburg. As a rule, they are quiet, wordless characters, but do a favor for them, help them out in their slaving business in some slight way and they will open up their homesick hearts to you and you will find that they have lived stories outlandish and fanciful and some, as life will have it, too tragic to be written.

Bourke is a man of the beach. A white man, a cool dicer spun forth from the Foochow Road, a gin-drinking remittance man. His spine is growing flexible and fishy with tropic heat and indolence, at the time Hoffrahm takes hold of him. He has been living on the gin-*pahits* you buy him and in a little while will reach the "mat" stage, and after that—well, he will no longer be a white man. You'll find the graves of him and his kind, marked and unmarked, on the stark beaches of many a South Sea isle. . . .

"The Orchid of Allure" is just a mass of tales and customs and scenes that have come either to my ears or eyes. In the story itself is explained where I saw gaps like the one I describe—in the Patkoi Mountains of Burma and the Himalayas near the Khaiber Pass. I have seen others far in the interior of Borneo in the prodigally vegetated uplands. There are some in Mexico, even, and the Andes of South America. In fact, you'll find them wherever the mountains are high and the process of formation still working havoc. . . .

Throughout the story I have tried to state offhand where I got the basis for each incident. Like the sing-song of the woman. I really was present at Fort Alfred when that old head-hunter was brought in. The sensation Bourke experiences at the sound of the single high shrilling note is my description of just what I felt at the time. . . .

The actual description of the shape of the orchid is drawn from such an one as I saw in my wanderings on the Mahakkam River. It was withered and it draggled in the stifling heat. From far off it looked like some bird's nest as it clung to a huge banyan tree. But when I drew near, its weird form left an indelible impression on my mind. The only color I felt could really bring out that dove shape was a most brilliant bleeding red.

The impressions the orchid causes on Bourke are the impressions these terrible travesties have made on myself and other men. The loss of breath, the subtle perfume, even the sentient faculty of sucking the life-blood from man or animal—all these views have a basis either in tales or still stranger fact.

When "Tropics" was published in the December 1913 *Adventure*, it too was accompanied by explanatory material for *The Camp-Fire*, including more fabrications:

I have come in personal contact with several scourges. Once, down in Panama, at a way-station called Bocas del Toro (The Mouths of the Bull), we alighted to drink from a public fountain. The most distinguishing features of the village were a wooden church painted in exact imitation of Castile soap, with wavy pink stripes through its blank whiteness, and this rude outdoor font. The theatrical troupe of which I was a part found a myriad of red ants forming two lines to and from the basin. We did not drink. On inquiring further in the village for some water, we found the *barrio* visited with smallpox. Overwhelming fear lent wings to our flight and *en masse* we, one and all of us, were vaccinated the following day. Once our arms were bandaged we felt safe, and safe we afterward proved to be. No one of us had contracted the plague.

Still another time, in Singapore, there was an outbreak of bubonic plague. The way I escaped scatheless that time was by keeping my system inoculated to drunkenness with gin-*pahits*. Alcohol and stimulants, in the case of bubonic plague, have proved an infallible anti-toxin. The hired carriers of the dead, old beach-combers mostly, go reeling along the byways under the effect of liquor, hardly capable of upbearing the poor victims of the disease.

While in Panama with the theatrical troupe, I met Colonel Gorgas and Shanton, who was the head of the Zone police. At that time their greatest fight was with the Yellow Jack [yellow fever]. Hence, I laid my story in Panama and at about the time they were engaged in their winning fight. The different aspects of the Jack that came to my notice I have attempted to incorporate into the story.

The brown woman and the indolent degenerating white man have many counterparts in all tropical lands. You will find them especially in Coolie Town of old [Panama seaport] Colón—that filthy negro slum. I remember a case that forced itself on me when I was in the Government service in Manila. A young fellow from North Carolina had a desk next to mine. He had formerly been employed, back home, by a large tobacco concern. One pay-day several of us went out to "do" the town. After an evening at a native theater, we adjourned to a café. The fellow drank heavily and then all of a sudden burst into copious tears. He was thinking of the girl he left behind him. He was living "without benefit of clergy" with a mestiza woman in the walled city. I heard, some time afterward, that he committed self-destruction. The animal life, at the outset so novel and fair, had sickened him.

"A Debt to Pay," in the February 1914 *Adventure*, was published without accompanying *Camp-Fire* material.

At this point, we can revisit the issue of the Caseys' bylines. Heretofore, all their published work had gone out under "Lee Tempest" or "James Edward/E./Edmond Casey." Now the three stories for *Adventure* were published using a new name, Patrick Casey. In the absence of other evidence, a natural conclusion would be that Terence had thrown in the towel and that Patrick was forging ahead on his own as a writer, using his middle name to make a clean break from "James Edward/Edmond." (The boys may have been known by their first names early in life, then switched to their middles during their writing days.) Terence's *Chronicle* article on "Playboy" could be read to imply that "The Orchid of Allure" was a joint effort, but the conflation of O'Callahan and Casey prevents the point from being explicit. However, there's ample other evidence to show that "Patrick Casey" was, in most cases, two people. The *Chronicle* article included a sidebar with a long list of the brothers' collaborations. Of the initial three *Adventure* stories, only "Tropics" is cited, but that too had a Patrick Casey byline. Another valuable source was a profile of the brothers' career published in the *Oakland Tribune*, February 24, 1918. It quotes Patrick: "Then, in 1913, I took particular pains on a story of head-hunting and orchids and Borneo, which resulted in my selling to the *Adventure* magazine 'The Orchid of Allure.' " But wait. After the three *Adventure* stories, the next Casey publication was "The Gay-Cat," which will be discussed in due course. Later, in the same *Tribune* article, Patrick said: "In the latter part of 1913 my brother and I wrote a story of a hobo kid entitled 'The Gay-Cat,' which ran in the *Saturday Evening Post*." "The Gay-Cat" appeared in the April 14, 1914 issue of the *Post*, only two months after the third *Adventure* story, and it, too, was published under the Patrick Casey name alone. Both quotes point to the same fact: that in 1918, the Caseys were still protecting the subterfuge. The first quote reinforces the ruse for 1918 readers; the second quote shows that, in 1914, the ruse had to be carried forward to the *Post*. It wouldn't have taken much detective work in 1918 to uncover the Caseys' little secret but, pre-1922, they weren't going to tip anyone off to the hunt. Not in print, anyway. Any of their San Francisco acquaintances who had read the *Camp-Fire* letters would have been in on the joke.

Why did they use a single name for the early *Adventure* stories, instead of sharing a byline? With the context of the fabricated background, the likely explanation is that it increased the credibility of the lie, as if two brothers traveling to the many distant places described in the fake biography added a touch of fairy-tale togetherness that might have exposed the truth. They were probably that finely-tuned to the sense of reality in their words. Reading the fake biographical passages, it's clear that they'd become highly skilled in the *art of lying*—which is an uncharitable description of the art of storytelling. Additionally, "Patrick Casey" didn't bear enough of a resemblance to "James Edward/E./Edmond Casey" to tip off any New York editor who hadn't already had contact with the brothers. "Patrick Casey" could come to town with no past to contradict.

Another question is why Patrick won the prize of the byline in preference to Terence. This point is never addressed in any documents we've discovered. Perhaps Patrick pulled rank as the eldest. Perhaps the idea of the fake biography had been his; perhaps he did more than half the work. At any rate, after the fiendish chortles of glee had died down, and the checks had been spent, Terence may have been a bit disgruntled that his name was getting left out of their joint triumphs. Their next story for *Adventure*, and their next dispatch to *The Camp-Fire*, show the brothers taking the first steps toward correcting the injustice. The story was a four-part serial, *The Story of William Hyde*, which ran from December 1915 through March 1916. They'd apparently taken most of 1914 and '15 to write it, as evidenced by a dearth of other published work during the period. Sam Moskowitz mentioned the novel in his survey of the Munsey magazines, *Under the Moons of Mars* (1970), in a brief digression on *Adventure*:

> One of the better lost-race stories published by *Adventure* was *The Story of William Hyde*. . . . William Hyde, the narrator, tells of his discovery of a "lost race" in Borneo who are the descendants of an army of Tartars sent there by Genghis Khan to conquer the land. Hyde resembles the ancient Khan, so he is accepted, and marries, but is finally driven out, partially through the vindictiveness of a jealous queen who also loves him. Extravagantly promoted as "One of the Greatest Romantic Stories Ever Written," *The Story of William Hyde* rates fourth among all stories published in 1916 by a vote of the readers, but the editor confessed that its publication received some of the most vigorous protests in the history of the magazine. This acted to tighten still further *Adventure's* restriction on fantasy.

Hyde was the first story signed by both brothers under their real names, and finally brings us to the names that they are known under. Thereafter, "Patrick and Terence Casey"—or "Terence and Patrick Casey"—became their common byline. Both forms were used, perhaps in alternation. The letter to *The Camp-Fire* was signed by Patrick, but identifies Terence at the end of the note, almost as an afterthought: *"William Hyde* is not dead. My brother and I are at work, right now, writing of his further adventures and tragic end." Of course, we have no way of knowing what Hoffman may have edited out of the letter before printing it.

In comparison to the previous *Camp-Fire* letters, this one downplays "Patrick Casey's" fictional past as a source for the work:

> *The Story of William Hyde* is almost unalloyed fiction; but no man ever yet wrote without some basis of fact. For instance, I could not write about imaginary inhabitants on the planet Jupiter without giving

them some far-fetched characteristics of human beings, because human beings are the only type of living, breathing persons that I know. Again it is well known how impossible it is to imagine heaven because so few, if any of us, ever have come back to give us some basis of fact.

He seems to be suggesting—if, like *Adventure's* readers, we were to assume the sincerity of his words—that he's no longer storytelling from personal experience; he's now become a creative writer, free to wander where his imagination takes him, including places—Jupiter—that he's never been. This is an especially important point when we consider the timing of this letter. It was not published in conjunction with any of the four parts of *Hyde*. It appeared in the July 1916 *Adventure*, which published "To Crack a Safe," the first of the hobo stories to appear in the magazine. The letter seems to be preparing the reader for the possibility that the Casey who wrote so knowledgably of the tropical jungles was now writing about America's hobo jungles, two worlds alien to each other. There was a paragraph of whoppers in the letter, but they eschewed the exotic in favor of drawing our fictional author back to the continent and domestic matters:

> And *William Hyde*—I never met him, but many and many a man I have met of his ilk. Once, in working my way down to Honolulu, I chanced upon a fellow-workaway who had not even to his credit so much as a change of socks. But the stories that man could tell! He'd been graduated from a law college in Albany, New York. He'd been in Alaska, rich now, then broke. He said he had a letter from the then new President, Woodrow Wilson, a pal of his! Surely enough, when I met him the day after we landed in the Islands, he was all togged out in new regalia: a straw hat, tan oxfords, silk socks. He was a member of the bar. He introduced me to senators and princes and influential half-breeds of the territory. And it is he, and such happy-go-lucky, take-a-chance, bull artists as he, that have gone to make up the character of *William Hyde*.

Perhaps the letter was intended primarily for the reader-in-chief, that is, the editor-in-chief, Arthur Sullivant Hoffman. We have to wonder what *he* was thinking. It must have dawned on him at some point that Patrick Casey may not have been the brave yet humble man he pretended to be. Now he has a brother who writes? Now he's writing about common hoboes? Assuming he did get suspicious, we have to believe he would have cared—some. *Adventure* had a reputation to uphold. Readers loved it for its fact-based fiction. Frauds would not have been welcome. But, in the end, the Caseys delivered the goods—entertaining stories—and maybe that's what mattered most.

There may be a postscript. The Caseys' last story for *Adventure* was "Children of the Road" (July 18, 1921), the last of the hobo stories. Terence's *Chronicle* article explaining "Playboy" was published February 5, 1922. Did word of the article find its way back to Hoffman, thus causing him to blackball the brothers? Or were the brothers simply moving on of their own accord? Probably the latter; but it's a mystery.

The *Hyde* serial became the Caseys' first book, published by the Hearst International Library in 1916 as *The Strange Story of William Hyde*. The sequel, *The Chase of the Four Fools*, appeared in *Adventure* from November 1916 through January 1917.

To reiterate, after the first three stories in *Adventure*, the Caseys hit the April 4, 1914 *Saturday Evening Post* with "The Gay-Cat."

Soon after, they appeared in the August 8, 1914 *Collier's* with a short, "Thief of the World," about a newspaper copy boy. This pair of publications represented yet another step up in prestige and exposure. The *Post* at the time was publishing popular authors like Mary Roberts Rinehart and Ring Larder; *Collier's* was home to Sax Rohmer's Fu Manchu. The westerns of fellow San Franciscan Peter B. Kyne appeared in both. For the Caseys, however, these magazines were pinnacles to be visited infrequently. The bulk of their work would appear in the better pulps.

"The Gay-Cat" describes the experiences of a twelve-year-old runaway, stricken with wanderlust, who travels as the virtual slave of an older hobo, and adopts a stray dog. We would assume that the starting point for the story was the main character, the boy, known as the Frisco Kid. There were many "road-kids" wandering around in that era and the Caseys may have seen some. But in fact the triggering inspiration was the dog. The brothers used to frequent a San Francisco police station in search of story ideas and authentic street lingo. One day in late 1913, a kind-hearted policeman brought in a puppy that had been rescued from a raid on a "Chinatown resort." The boys adopted him, affectionately naming him "Gay-Cat," a hobo term. But the call of the road proved too strong for Gay-Cat and, after several absences, he ran away for good, to be reborn as the dog of the story.

The story represents a merger of sorts. The Caseys had written boyhood fiction for *Top-Notch*; then moved on to more adult topics for *Adventure*. In "The Gay-Cat," those two thrusts came together. It took a boyhood theme and gave it a literary roundness. The Frisco Kid's wanderlust is presented as a psychological crisis and taken by steps to a resolution which returns him to domestic tranquility, and mitigates reader discomfort with the perilous life of a boy on the road.

The term "gay cat" dates from the late 19th Century and had several meanings. It was a derisive term among hoboes for an inauthentic hobo, that is, a hobo who worked instead of begging, or was otherwise not completely committed to the freeloading hobo lifestyle. It also was a name for the young companion of an older hobo; the youngster making a more effective beggar because of his sympathetic appearance. "Gay cat" also had meaning in the criminal world, referring to a member of a bank-robbing or safe-cracking gang, "yeggmen"; the gay-cat, with his innocent appearance, scouted out easy places to rob but didn't take part in the actual crime. In Arthur B. Reeve's Craig Kennedy story "The Yeggman" (*Cosmopolitan*, April 1912), which may have been known to the Caseys, the yeggman says: "Now here's the Gay Cat—that's what we call a fellow who is the finder, who enters a town ahead of the gang." The Caseys utilized all these definitions in the series, but clearly the primary meaning was in regards to the authenticity of a hobo, and the affectionate use of the word as a name for the dog. The Frisco Kid starts the story as a gay-cat to the older Frisco Red, but is his own man through most of it.

The term also implied a homosexual relationship between the older hobo and his underling which, of course, is absent from the Caseys' stories. Theories on the origins of "gay" as slang for "homosexual" cite the hobo "gay cat" as an influence. It's certainly plausible; the only weakness in the argument is that "gay cat" appears to have dropped out of common knowledge from the '30s to the '60s, when "gay" was redefined.

A related term which is used heavily in the series is "blown-in-the-glass," as in "blown-in-the-glass stiff." A "stiff" is a hobo, and "blown-in-the-glass," or "blowed-in-the-glass," is another measure of authenticity. In the 19th Century, some commercial bottles were manufactured with the brand and product names shaped into the glass to guarantee against knockoffs.

The Caseys received fan mail on "The Gay-Cat" from authors Fanny Hurst and William Wallace Cook. Peter B. Kyne was so impressed that he tried, without success, to meet the authors, as he revealed to them years later. The favorable response led the Caseys to continue the Frisco Kid and The Gay-Cat as a series:

> We recognized that we had found something in that story. It was a Celtic symphony composed of gray dawns and empty crimson sunsets and weeks of brooding persistent rain. Through it burly tramps and wistful road-kids trudged along brown rutted roads to knock at forbidding back doors in wintry gloamings.

Before proceeding to the further adventures, they produced *The Story of William Hyde* for *Adventure*. Having then established themselves as *Adventure* stalwarts, it became the natural home for the first series-installment of the hobo stories, "To Crack a Safe," which appeared more than two years after "The Gay-Cat." Whether they attempted a return to the *Post* isn't known, but that would have presented a problem. "The Gay-Cat" resolved the Frisco Kid's crisis of conscience; it didn't leave an opening for a sequel. Moving to *Adventure* discarded that burden for a fresh start elsewhere. It also gives us a rare opportunity to read the same milieu and characters as they were slanted for different tastes and markets.

The hobo stories in *Adventure* were structured as standalone episodes, in contrast to the paradigmatic structure of the *Post* story. Each story put the Frisco Kid in a new place, introducing him to new characters. The *Post* story has a poetic quality, whereas the *Adventure* stories shift to plot and happenstances. The *Adventure* stories also deemphasized the dog, who is central to "The Gay-Cat." The hobo stories are not really dog stories. The Gay-Cat never displays the kind of heroism we expect from dog heroes like Rin-Tin-Tin and Lassie. He really is never given much of a personality or much to do, a weakness in the series. The character of the Frisco Kid has a weakness, too, the detriment of his youth in being surrounded by often violent adults. He's not always central to the action, and even passive at times in regards to his own destiny.

Another advantage of *Adventure* was the possibility of writing longer works. "The Gay-Cat" was 11,000 words. "To Crack a Safe" (July 1916) jumped up to 14,000. The next in the series, a year later, was "According To His Caste" (July 1917) which took a big leap to 25,000 words. That was soon followed by "The Phoney Man" (January 18, 1918) at 22,000 words. "Children of the Road" (July 18, 1921), which completes the series, was a short novel of over 48,000.

In 1921, part of the series was published as a novel by The H.K. Fly Company, *The Gay-Cat: The Story of a Road-Kid and His Dog*. The novel reveals how the Caseys intended the stories to fit together. It opens with the first two-thirds of "The Gay-Cat," up to the point where the Frisco Kid breaks free of Frisco Red. Then "To Crack a Safe" and "Children of the Road" are inserted. The novel ends with the final third of "The Gay-Cat," in which the Kid finds his way back home to California at last. "According To His Caste" and "The Phoney Man" were omitted from the novel.

There were only minor changes made to the magazine texts in producing the novel. A little stitchery was required to blend the separate stories together. Some of the dialogue was tweaked. Some names were changed, e.g. Cincie Shorty and Albany Joe became Pittsburgh Shorty and Cheyenne Joe. One curious change was in moving the Kid's starting age from twelve, as it is in the individual stories, to ten in the novel. Ten percent more poignant, maybe.

A central character in "Children of the Road" is the benevolent old maid,

Miss Heffernan. Her surname, not terribly common, is of interest. There was an author named John L. Heffernan who appeared ten times in early issues of *Adventure*, including the first issue of November 1910. We can assume from their knowledge of *Adventure* customs that the Caseys' were fans of the pulp before they were contributors; therefore, it may be that the use of "Heffernan" is a tribute or an in-joke of some sort.

There were never any accompanying *Camp-Fire* letters to explain the roots of the series. The letter that was published with "To Crack a Safe" only referred to *The Story of William Hyde*. Perhaps the Caseys, in not saying anything about the origins, or Hoffman, in not publishing such comments, were seeking to obscure "Patrick Casey's" past as a jungle adventurer, which would have added a discordant footnote to a tale of American hobo life. Then again, perhaps Hoffman didn't want to draw attention to the fact that *Adventure* was taking up characters started in the *Post*, as if that might make the magazine appear to be a follower, or a home for *Post* rejects. "According To His Caste" included the only *Camp-Fire* notes for any story in the series. "Caste" was a boxing story, and Patrick's letter (reprinted in this volume) recounted interesting incidents he'd witnessed in matches as a sports reporter in 1909-10. It may have been the first true thing they'd sent to Hoffman.

By the time the Caseys wrote "The Gay-Cat," there was already a small body of hobo literature for them to draw upon as research material. There's no evidence they ever took to the roads, or the rails, to experience Hoboland firsthand; they certainly would have mentioned it if they had. Two books, in particular, rank as probable sources because of the number of specific items which found their way into the Caseys' stories.

The first is *Tramping With Tramps: Studies and Sketches of Vagabond Life* (1899), by Josiah Flynt, assembled from 1890s magazine articles. Most appeared in *The Century*, but one key chapter from the book, "The Children of the Road," came from the January 1896 issue of *The Atlantic*. It discusses the kind of road-kids that feature in the Casey stories. It talks at length about the *"Wanderlust"* that serves as the Frisco Kid's motivation, e.g.:

> I knew in New York State a boy . . . who had as comfortable a home as a child could wish, but he was cursed with this strange *Wanderlust*, and throughout his boyhood there was hardly a month that he did not run away.

The chapter goes on to describe how some of these runaway boys fell into the clutches of older hoboes, who enticed them with fanciful tales of the adventure of the open road; and how the boys would be steadily drawn into virtual slavery, the same relationship that the Frisco Kid has to the older

Frisco Red as "The Gay-Cat" opens.

Tramping With Tramps also contributed a lot of incidental flavor to the Caseys. The similarities between hoboes and the Romany—gypsies—are described. Romany characters turn up in the Caseys' "Children of the Road." Flynt described the "fawny man," a peddler of cheap jewelry, who becomes the central character of the Caseys' "The Phoney Man." Many other bits of hobo terminology and lore can be absorbed from the book.

Tramping also discusses the importance of San Francisco in Hoboland:

> San Francisco and Denver are the main dependence of tramps in the West. . . . " 'Frisco" is even better [for begging] than Denver, furnishing districts in which tramps can thrive and remain for a longer time unmolested. There are more low lodging-houses, saloons, and dives; and there is also here a large native class whose character is not much higher than that of the tramp himself, so that he is lost among them—often to his own advantage.

This section may have prompted the Caseys to be more observant of their own surroundings.

The second important source was Jack London's *The Road* (1907), dedicated to Josiah Flynt, in which London wrote of his own experiences in hoboing as a teenager, in the time before he went to sea. London discusses the importance of "monicas" (monikers, or nicknames) in Hoboland, an important element for the Caseys. In particular, London's own moniker became " 'Frisco Kid," after he had crossed the Rockies and was far enough away from San Francisco where the name would have meant something.

A key chapter for the Caseys was "Road-Kids and Gay-Cats." London writes in the opening paragraph: "I became a tramp—well, because of the life that was in me, of the wanderlust in my blood that would not let me rest." He defines the difference between a road-kid and a gay-cat. He describes the "strong arm," a choking technique used by road-kids in subduing a robbery victim; the very same technique used by the Frisco Kid in "The Gay-Cat."

In another chapter, London describes a technique used by railroad brakemen to dislodge hobos who were "riding the rods" under a boxcar. The brakeman attached a cord to a coupling-pin and played it out under the moving train until the pin was in position to bounce off the wooden ties and strike the hobo. London noted: "Every blow of that flying coupling-pin is freighted with death, and at sixty miles an hour it beats a veritable tattoo of death." In the Caseys' "Children of the Road," this nasty bit of business becomes Frisco Red's reminiscence of what Strong-Arm did to him. It's one of the few times the Caseys drew rail-riding lore into their series.

A 1973 film, *Emperor of the North*, was based primarily on *The Road* and an anonymously published memoir, *Life and Adventures of A-No. 1: America's Most Celebrated Tramp* (1910). Though updating the setting to the Depression, the film memorably depicts hobo jungles, road-kids, rail-riding, the coupling-pin assault, the spectrum of hobo life. Of note, the film has a character named "Gray Cat," an obvious attempt to use the colorful term "gay-cat" while avoiding the homosexual connotation which would have been inferred by a 1973 audience. *Life and Adventures of A-No. 1*, which has an international scope, and is as much a travel memoir as a hoboing guide, doesn't appear to have been an influence to the Caseys.

Although the Caseys' hobo series was based more on research than experience, we would be remiss in leaving the impression that they cobbled the stories together from their background material. They steeped themselves in the atmosphere, lore and lingo of Hoboland, then used it as a setting for original fiction. In fact, all of the probable sources were nonfiction memoirs. It was left to the Caseys to create a fictional milieu, and invent characters who live and breath through their actions more than their profiles.

Several topical elements in the Caseys' stories are worth noting, such as the unexpected presence of "Hindoo" farm workers in "To Crack a Safe":

> Drawn up before the door of the kiln was a two-horsed farm-wagon and behind that, down the dust-carpeted road, strung farm-wagon after two-horsed farm-wagon. Each wagon was crowded with men. They were brown men. They were brown men, long and starveling of limb, with heads wrapped in red and yellow and white turbans.
> "Th' ragheads!"
> "It's the ragheads, all right—a whole army of Hindoo laborers. Old man Haines has imported them to finish harvesting his crops!"

In 1882, the U.S. Congress passed the Chinese Exclusion Act, which barred immigration from China. As an unintended consequence, cheap labor came into the country from Japan, Korea, and India—the "Asiatic Peril," as it was known in the labor movement. From 1900-17 approximately 7,000 workers, primarily from India's Punjab region, came into British Columbia and the western U.S. Though paid less than American workers, they received considerably more than they would have in their impoverished homeland. Many were migrant workers in California's San Joaquin Valley where the Frisco Kid is from and where "To Crack a Safe" takes place. The vast majority were Sikh, however, not Hindu. In 1917, the Chinese Exclusion Act was expanded to include most other Asians, and this marks the end of Indian immigration. Most of the Indian immigrants were men, and, if they married here, they tended to marry Mexican women who were part of the migration fleeing the turmoil of the Mexican Revolution in the teen years. Punjabi-Mexican families still exist in the central valley, though the numbers are relatively small.

More topical references turn up in "Children of the Road" with the character of Strong-Arm:

> "Strong-Arm's got his own pertic'lar line. He's a gun-man, yer kin see; but he's kinder quieter and less wiciously murderous than most. I've heard him called various monikers—Strong-Arm, an' the Black Finn, an' even the Big Sab-Cat."
>
> "What! A Wobbly?"
>
> "Sure," he whispered guardedly; "an I.W.W. I think he's a quick-limer er a bomber fer the Wobblies."

The Industrial Workers of the World (IWW), founded in Chicago in 1905, was an international union that was still on the rise when "Children of the Road" was written. Its goal was to unite workers as a class independent of their trades. Their nickname was "the Wobblies"; the origin of the term is unknown. Finns were a sizable contingent of the IWW, thus the nickname "Black Finn." From 1915-17, the IWW often recruited migrant farm workers in railway yards and hobo jungles; workers and hoboes both rode the rails; thus the group became closely associated with hoboes. Frisco Red says to Strong-Arm: "Yer ain't—yer ain't toined Salvationist, has yuh, Strong-Arm?" This is probably a reference to the practice of employers using Salvation Army bands to drown out union events.

The IWW was involved in numerous labor disputes, which provoked a strong reaction from the government, which in turn provoked an increasing militancy within the IWW. They became associated with sabotage and other criminal activities. One of the group's symbols was a black cat. Thus the term "sab-cat," used frequently in the story, is a reference to an IWW saboteur.

Returning to literary matters, the hobo stories, particularly "Children of the Road," evoke the use of children in Charles Dickens. Children were prominent in Dickens' fiction, as they are in these road-kid stories. Dickens' child characters were frequently orphans, or otherwise separated from their true families, similar to the lost souls of the hobo runaways. The terrors of child abuse, and the contrast between kindness and cruelty, which children in their helplessness appreciate most acutely, are strong themes in common, resulting in extremes of sentiment.

In the *Adventure* readers poll, "Children of the Road" was voted fifteenth best story of 1921. The top vote-getters were better-known *Adventure* regulars like Gordon Young, J. Allan Dunn, Arthur O. Friel, Hugh Pendexter,

Talbot Mundy, and H. Bedford-Jones. Still, fifteenth reflects strong popularity, considering that there were twenty-seven issues of *Adventure* in 1921, averaging about ten pieces of fiction in each. In the 1922 article, Terence wrote "We think more [of *The Gay-Cat*] than of any of our books that preceded it." That probably would have been the feeling at the end of their careers, as well.

While thinking of the Frisco Kid's future, the Caseys opened up a new fictional front: modern Spain. After devoting time to studying the country, they sold a two-part serial, *The Last Conquistador*, to *The Popular Magazine* (Second August, First September, 1916). *The Popular* would turn out to be one of their two best markets, alongside *Adventure*.

In 1917, there were two stories in *Adventure* that were unaffiliated with any series: "The Reprisal," March, a World War story; and "That Heathen Chinee, O'Looney," June, a western. Both were bylined under Patrick's name alone; and this was after "Patrick and Terence" had been established. By this time, however, they've so muddied the water on questions of authorship, it would only be a guess as to whether these were actually joint works, or whether they represented Patrick working alone.

Their next story in *The Popular* was a four-part serial, *The Wolf-Cub* (July 7 to August 20, 1917). Its hero was Jacinto Quesada, a modern-day Robin Hood. It was reprinted as a hardbound in 1918 by Little, Brown & Company, Boston. It was generally well-reviewed. The *Oakland Tribune* noted: "if one of the authors has not been in Spain, he has done a fine bit of work for one governed only by geography and a little history." One negative review (*The Living Age*, March 16, 1918) sniffed out the Caseys' past:

> If there are readers, as presumably there are, so obsessed with a craving for stories of adventure that they do not care how crude they are, nor how wooden the characters who figure in them, they should be well content with *The Wolf-Cub* . . . To older readers who may stumble upon them, they will recall the traditional "dime novel" of their youth. . . . There is plenty of action, a great deal of stilted language, and romance of a certain rough sort in the story.

The *San Francisco Examiner* (March 3, 1918) published a short feature on former *Examiner* office boys who had made good. The impetus for the article was *The Wolf-Cub*, "one of the sensations of the recent book output." Photos of the brothers were included.

The Caseys had just finished writing *The Wolf-Cub* when the United States entered the World War, making the story their "last novel for a while." On May 4, 1917 they enlisted in the Naval Reserve as second-class seamen, a pair of Bob Storms. Patrick was initially stationed at Cape May, New Jersey; Terence in San Francisco. A Patrick Casey letter in the September 18, 1917 *Camp-Fire* discussed the brothers' future in the Motor-Boat Auxiliary:

> We are to be members of a crew of fourteen, handling a 110-foot boat, fitted out with three motors, an anti-aircraft gun, a three-pounder, etc., and capable of making some thirty-odd knots an hour. We are to engage in patrol work, mine-laying and submarine chasing. We look for a grand adventure. Also, we hope to aid a mite.

They both served into early 1919. Terence ended the war as a second-class seaman. Fittingly for Patrick, once a pretend Ensign—or half a pretend Ensign—he finished the war as an actual Ensign, ending his service as executive officer on a sub-chaser.

On May 26, 1917, the Caseys were honored by fellow members of the Newspaper Men's Club, with sixteen other San Francisco newsmen who had joined the service. This raises the question of how employed the brothers were outside of their writing career. Patrick quit his job with the *Examiner* after the first sale to *Top-Notch*. But, at some point, the brothers must have realized that publishing stories, as satisfying as it might have been, wasn't going to pay the bills, especially when the payment was split two ways. Their membership in the Newspaper Men's Club suggests they were both in the field in 1917. Information on their lives is spotty, particularly after the war. In 1920, the brothers were self-employed as writers. They were living at the family home at 155 Rivoli Street, San Francisco, in the neighborhood now known as the Haight-Ashbury, some distance from the Mission District where they'd spent their youth. They shared the home with their mother, and sister Gertrude. Their father had died in 1917. The overall evidence indicates, however, that Patrick became a career newsman; in fact, he was at the *Examiner* at the time of his death in 1941. His brief *New York Times* obituary states that he "worked for several local newspapers as reporter, drama critic, and editorial writer." Terence's life yields less information. When older brother John J. Casey died in 1930, his *San Francisco Chronicle* obituary labeled Patrick a "local newspaper man," and Terence a "short story writer." However, the only independent byline that could be discovered for Terence was the 1922 article. His 1945 death was noted in the *Examiner*, but there were no amplifying details.

John J. "Jack" Casey, incidentally, became better known than his two writing brothers, but it was for his soldiering and not his artwork. In 1909, he went to Paris to study painting. He was still in France, exhibiting his work, when the World War erupted in July 1914. On the day that Germany declared war on France, he joined the Foreign Legion, eventually becoming secretary of the American Division. In the second year of the war, he declined the offer of a commission as Captain in the British Army. He was wounded once, twice, or several times, according to varying accounts. He was cited multiple times for bravery, and received the French Medal of Honor. For surviving so many battles that had taken the lives of his brothers-in-arms, he became known as "Casey, the man with the charmed life." After three-and-a-half years, he was one of four surviving members of a unit called the "Suicide Club." With most of his comrades gone, in 1918 he transferred to the American Army.

In 1916, he married the Baroness Maria Berthe d'Aumont (1883-1927). After the war, he brought her back to New York. In 1924, the couple returned to Paris for several years, while Casey did illustrations for French magazines. He painted one American magazine cover, as current records show, the February 1928 issue of *The Danger Trail*. Patrick Casey had a prior story in *The Danger Trail* (June 1926), so perhaps there's a connection.

At the time of his death (April 26, 1930), John J. Casey was known as a portrait painter. He was stricken ill at the easel, in his Greenwich Village studio, and died of pneumonia.

The younger Caseys kept writing during their two years in the service, and their stories continued to appear in the pulps. All were shorter works. There were two stories set in Panama in *The Popular Magazine* (September 20, 1917; January 7, 1918). Another story for *The Popular*, "Halt for the Guardia Civil" (October 20, 1917), continued the adventures of the wolf-cub, Jacinto Quesada. "The Phoney Man" appeared in early 1918. They also appeared in *All-Story Weekly*, *People's Favorite Magazine*, and *Short Stories*. A proud moment came when "Tropics," their second story for *Adventure*, was reprinted in a textbook, *Today's Short Stories Analyzed* (1918), as an example of superior style.

The slow period continued through 1919 and into 1920. There were shorts in *The Parisienne* (August 1919), *Romance* (November 1919), a revisit to *Top-Notch* (November 1, 1919), and "The Playboy of a Back Street" in *Romance* (February 1920). Later in the year, Jacinto Quesada made it into *The Saturday Evening Post* (September 18, 1920) with a short, "The Wedding of Quesada."

Most of 1920 had probably been taken up with the writing of the next *Adventure* serial, the five-part *Toyama* (September 18 to November 18, 1920). It involved a treasure, and a Japanese secret society, which gave the story its title. *Toyama* is the first major Casey work that appears to originate from Patrick alone. The byline is his—which, of course, would be inadequate proof—but Patrick's letter for *The Camp-Fire*, accompanying the first installment, omits any reference to Terence:

Toyama was built practically out of a sentence. That sentence was the opening one. For years it had been running through my mind. It struck me as quite novel. To begin a story with it, particularly an adventure-mystery story, would be to begin where most stories of this type end—with the finding of the treasure. In *Toyama* the finding of the treasure is accomplished in the first sentence and whatever of adventure and mystery may be in the story hinges on the reason for that treasure and its eventual disposition.

The opening sentence, incidentally, was: "We stood over the treasure chest, Morley, his wife and I." Patrick wove in some of his Navy experience:

> In conveying the party of Americans south on board a former submarine-chaser, I but used a type of craft with which I became familiar during two years' naval service in the recent war. Even the transformation of the war-craft into more or less of a pleasure ship was living within the law of probabilities. To-day you may buy one of them for something like twenty-thousand dollars.

Patrick added another anecdote to show how one of *Toyama's* plot points had originated:

> There was that incident of the little Japanese girl, once she had landed from the foul schooner, removing her sandals and short white socks, and dabbling her feet in the tepid water. Her actions then—her giggles, the play of sunlight on cheeks and throat, the very picture of her silken kimono and glossy hair—were such as I had observed, years before, at a swimming-pool back of my rooms in Nuuanu Avenue of Honolulu.

Given the record of fabrication, we wouldn't assume that Patrick had actually been to Hawaii. We have no corroborating evidence. It's entirely plausible he visited there with the Navy.

Terence wasn't out of the picture—not yet, anyway. The brothers placed a pair of stories in *The Popular* in 1921 (January 7, May 20). Then, "Children of the Road" hit the July 18, 1921 *Adventure*. Thereafter, the record of their collaboration is thin, which bolsters the argument that they had *not* been blackballed by Hoffman; the collaboration may have been dissolving anyway. Terence's 1922 article may have resulted from there being no secret worth protecting any longer. It mentioned: "recently Patrick was in New York visiting with our elder brother, Jack Casey." We suspect that Patrick elected to relocate to New York at this time; that he'd decided—or was persuaded—that the fiction career needed to give way to steadier or more lucrative employment. He probably entered the newspaper field in earnest in New York. Over two years passed before the next Casey story reached print, a four-part serial bylined by Patrick for *Sea Stories*, titled *Sea Plunder* (November 5 to December 20, 1923). The setting was Hawaii. The story was issued in hardback by Small, Maynard & Company in 1925. It was Patrick's fourth book, and his first without Terence sharing the credit. The only other known Casey book was a 1927 Street & Smith reprint of "Bob Storm of the Navy" by Ensign Lee Tempest, U.S.N., which the brothers probably had nothing to do with. The Caseys collaborated on two stories for the Fiction House pulp *Illustrated Novelets* (March, May 1924). The May issue mentioned the Caseys in its monthly column of author profiles:

> So far as we know, these two good-looking chaps . . . are the only successful brothers team collaborating in story writing. Just how much each brother contributes to each story is a mystery to us, but we hope to be able to tell you some day. Still another brother, Jack Casey, is a first-line artist. We are planning one of these days to publish a short novel by Patrick and Terence Casey with illustrations by Brother Jack! This would establish a magazine record for a gifted family.

The promised combo apparently never came to pass. The only other known time the Casey name appeared in a Fiction House pulp was a novelette by Patrick in the November 1926 *Action Stories*. It was not illustrated by Jack. In fact, the only other known Patrick and Terence collaboration was a story in the March 20, 1927 issue of *The Popular*. *Illustrated Novelets* was celebrating a team that had all but split up.

In 1925, Patrick was living in New York, married to a New York woman, Rhoda, four years his junior. The couple moved to Paris, where Patrick served on the editorial staff of the Paris edition of the *New York Herald Tribune*. Since Jack Casey had returned to Paris in 1924, if Patrick had followed his older brother to New York, he now followed him to Paris. The Paris stay appears to have been measured in months, not years.

Patrick was undoubtedly back living in San Francisco in 1926. The evidence is nine stories he produced with a new collaborator, fellow San Franciscan John L. Considine. They appeared in pulps dated from August 1926 to August 1927. Six stories were in *The Popular*, two were in *Complete Stories*, and one was in *Short Stories*. Most were westerns; one was set in the Peruvian Andes.

Considine, although a peripheral figure in the Casey saga, is quite interesting in his own right, and had multiple connections to the pulps, making him worthy of a protracted sidebar.

John Lyons Considine was born on September 25, 1872 in Gold Hill, Nevada. His parents, Joseph and Susan (Lyons) Considine, had been born in Ireland. They married in Pennsylvania in 1870 and settled in Nevada. Joseph was a miner. John had a sister, Mary E., born about 1890. He apparently never married and lived with his sister.

He was educated in public and private schools. His early working life included five years engaged in railway mail service, and a stint as a tax agent for the state of Nevada. But most of his life was spent as a newspaperman. His first known newspaper job was as secretary for the Virginia City *Evening Report* for several months in 1891, during an ill-fated revival of the journal. It was revived again in 1897, and Considine served as editor and manager for four years. He quit in 1901 and, for two years, edited the rival *Virginia Evening Chronicle*. In the early 1900s, he was prominent in Nevada political circles. This may have led to him becoming warden of the state penitentiary at Carson City, a job he held at least into 1906. In 1908, he was heavily involved in Nevada Democratic politics.

Considine's first known published fiction was a short-short, "The Green That Walked," in the February 1910 issue of *The Black Cat*.

In 1910, he was living in Reno City, editing the *Reno Weekly*. By 1912, he was in California for good. He was the initial managing editor of the weekly *San Diego Examiner*, which launched in June 1912, a position which lasted into 1916. Also, in 1912, he was a publicity writer for Woodrow Wilson's first presidential campaign.

From November 1917 through January 1920, Considine was a Federal internal revenue officer, in charge of a district comprising ten Southern California counties including Los Angeles. When Prohibition went into effect on January 16, 1920, Considine was immediately promoted—or retitled—to Federal Prohibition director for Southern California. In July 1920, his jurisdiction expanded to all of California, Oregon, Washington, Nevada, and Arizona. Of more importance to our story, his headquarters moved to San Francisco where he would remain for the rest of his life. He quit the Federal government in March 1921, declaring: "Trying to enforce a new and not overly popular law with thirty men to cover the entire Pacific Coast is not the best job in the world." He intended to enter the insurance business, but that probably didn't get very far. In 1921, he became editor of *The Leader*, a weekly San Francisco Irish newspaper, a job that lasted thirty years, until his death, at which time he was considered a leading authority on Irish history.

In 1922, Considine found the pulps. In the February 4 issue of *Western Story Magazine*, he placed an article, "The First Train Robbery." It was the first of fourteen articles on the history of the American west for the magazine that appeared in a six-month span. It appears to have been his primary income during that time.

He had an oddball accomplishment in 1922. In March, under the name John Lyons, he won the *San Francisco Examiner's* Victor Herbert Lyric Contest with the song "San Francisco of My Heart," beating out a thousand other entries. Not bad for a relative newcomer, but San Francisco has always been a love-at-first-sight city. Victor Herbert, famed composer of *Babes in Toyland*, provided the music to Considine's words, e.g.: "California's brightest gem, First among Pacific's daughters / Proudest in the diadem, That crowns the world of western waters." Legendary *Chronicle* columnist Herb Caen mentioned "San Francisco of My Heart" in a 1969 column, as part of the endless debate over San Francisco's "official" song. He described the lyrics as "perfectly awful," and that's about the last time the song was heard from.

The steady stream of articles for *Western Story* ended abruptly. Within a few months, he started appearing in, presumably, higher-paying markets. He supplied articles to *Adventure*, most if not all on western history. Most were two-page fillers, but some could be longer. An eight-page piece for the December 20, 1924 issue rated the inclusion of his name on the cover's author list. He eventually supplied twenty-eight articles to *Adventure* from 1922-33. He also started placing articles in *Sunset: The Pacific Monthly*, a magazine published in San Francisco. He also wrote features for a variety of California newspapers.

Considine had strong points in common with Patrick Casey. They both lived in San Francisco, both had Irish parents, both wrote for magazines, both had worked in the newspaper business, and both, clearly, enjoyed research. So, however their paths crossed, it's easy to see why they might have struck up an acquaintance and a partnership. Casey's influence helped Considine cross the divide from fact to fiction. During the period of their collaboration, his nonfiction output diminished to a trickle.

The partnership lasted a year. Considine continued as a magazine writer, although he immediately reverted to short historical pieces. Casey's career as a freelancer came to a halt with the end of the Considine collaborations. He wouldn't appear in the pulps again for nearly ten years.

Considine's career in the pulps was only warming up. He appeared in the September 19, 1931 issue of Street & Smith's *Wild West Weekly* with a short story, "The Sheriff of Hangtown," published under the byline of Kent Bennett. He would ultimately place thirty-three stories in *Wild West Weekly* from 1931-37, all under the Kent Bennett name. The first half-dozen were written solo; after that, the majority were co-authored with Street & Smith assistant editors, Francis L. Stebbins and Hazlett Kessler. Since Considine had no real track record with fiction, it may be that he provided research or plot ideas, while the editors, seasoned storytellers, shaped the material to the magazine's standard.

Considine's public service endured one final chapter. In April 1933, he became Prohibition administrator for the district of Northern California and Nevada. With Californians going to the ballot box on June 26 to weigh in on Prohibition, Considine advocated "speedy repeal." This put him in conflict with A.V. Dalrymple, the national Prohibition chief, who opposed repeal. In August, citing "intolerable differences of opinion," Considine resigned his post.

Patrick Casey reemerged from the shadows in late 1936 with a five-part serial in *Mystery Adventures* (December 1936 to May 1937), *The Island of Lost Ones*, set in a French prison colony. He also had an 83-page western, *The Mystery of the Salted Mill*, in the February 1937 issue. The December 1936 issue was the first after Harold Hersey had taken over the magazine from another publisher. The changeover had been announced in the writers' magazines, and it's likely that Casey had dusted off a couple of unpublished manuscripts from the vault and sent them to Hersey. The stories may have been rejects from *Adventure* or *The Popular Magazine*. They are his last known fiction publications. Considine showed up with a short in the February issue, so it's plausible that Considine, being still active in the freelance market, had tipped Casey off to the opportunity.

At any rate, after the quantity of material published in *Wild West Weekly*, Considine's pulp career tailed off. From 1937-46, he had a scattering of shorts and articles in *Ten Detective Aces*, *Star Western*, *Five-Novels*, *Big-Book Western*, etc.

Considine died on February 8, 1951 in a San Francisco hotel. He was found drowned in his bath. He had been recovering from a recent abdominal operation and it was suspected he fainted. He was survived by his sister, Mary.

There are a few details remaining to wrap up what is known of the Caseys. In 1929, Terence traveled to Tahiti. The immigration documents reveal that his address was in Sausalito, a quaint bayside town north of the Golden Gate in Marin County. Patrick relocated to Sausalito, as well, date unknown. Before the Golden Gate Bridge opened in 1937, his commute would have included a ferry ride to San Francisco. If nothing else, the fact that the brothers moved to the same destination suggests that the demise of their writing partnership hadn't mirrored a rift in the family.

In 1939, Patrick was president of the San Francisco-Oakland chapter of the American Newspaper Guild.

His marriage to Rhoda ended, but dates and details are unknown. On April 25, 1941, he was found dead in his home, a heart attack victim. He was survived by another wife, Elsie Treacy Casey (1890-1965). She was the daughter of a San Francisco politician, Timothy E. Treacy, who became a California State Senator. She married Patrick no sooner than 1932.

Terence died on July 30, 1945, cause unknown. He was survived by two sisters, Margaret and May, also of Marin County. The brothers were buried in Holy Cross Cemetery in Colma, south of San Francisco, the southern horizon that Aloysius Columbkill O'Callahan had never ventured beyond.

The Playboy of a Back Street

THE DAY WAS ALMOST AT ITS NOON and even under the shade-trees that line the narrow walks it was very sultry on Seven Pines Street. Bartholomew, the letter-man, had left his leather pack under the lamp-post at the corner. He had left his coat there, too. A fistful of letters in one hand, he went from cottage to cottage. But he paused often along the garden fences to tear off roses which he tossed at the sparrows in the gutters, and honeysuckles which he put between his teeth and sucked at for the drops of sweet juice secreted therein.

Slowly he moved under the trees, sauntering through Seven Pines Street like Pan but in a gray uniform, but still recalcitrant; the noontide quiet of the back street, the dewy odors from the old-fashioned gardens and the shade under the trees making, for the nonce, a vagabond out of one of Uncle Sam's steadiest men.

A chap of eighteen watched the letter-man from an open attic window up the street. He was in his shirt-sleeves. As he leaned far out of the attic window to watch, the morning's sun flashed brightly on his hair. His hair was red and was brushed flat and back from his high forehead in a pushback. His hair was very red.

He saw the letter-man pause at a picket fence. The letter-man was talking through the pickets of that fence to a little, old lady. From the red-headed chap's attic window up the street, the little old lady hardly could be seen; there was a regular tangle of blue-and-pink sweet peas along the fence in front of her; but what could be seen of her showed her to be really quite a delicious old lady. Her face was soft and pink like the pink sweet peas, and her dress was clean and blue like the blue ones. She had very silvery, very scanty hair—you could see the pink scalp through it. But about her there still tarried the prettiness of a never-so-far-away youth.

"That Bartholomew O'Brien," said the boy, "is the slowest letter-man in San Francisco! When a man is under orders"—he liked to say that phrase, as always he thought of himself as being under orders—"when a man is under orders, he should only spare a moment to pass the time of day with persons. But there goes Bartholomew now—gassing for all he is worth with old Mrs. Mulrenin!"

There was in the boy's voice a certain note of exasperation. He was expecting that morning a letter from the publishers of dime novels, Clarke & Maxson of New York.

For two years he had been writing dime novels and half-dime, or nickel, weeklies. Blindly, two years before, despite his extreme youth and meager schooling, and out of the sheer force of his boy's dreams, he had written an adventure story, juvenile and sensational and crude, but withal interesting and even, at times, stirring. *Bob Breakaway and the African Witch-Doctors, or The Black Tigress of Timbuktu*, it was called, and it had been accepted by Clarke & Maxson as a nickel novel.

At that, the boy had felt as if his young muscles had gripped the world. He could earn money. By his boy's dreams he could earn money. It was not drudgery. To him in his youth it was a glamorous way of earning money. In that glamorous way he would continue to earn money. He became a dime novelist.

Abruptly the boy jerked his coat from the back of a chair. Bartholomew, the letter-man, had left the little old lady and was continuing his vagabondage through the block. The little old lady was looking over the pink-and-blue hedge after the letter-man. Her eyes were on the fistful of letters he carried. He had left none with her. In her eyes, as she looked after the letter-man, was a baffled and rather wistful look.

The boy shrugged into his coat as he ran. The cottage, so cool and still, rang with the clatter he made as he dashed first down the narrow attic stairs and then down the great staircase in the hall. His thin, pale face was alive with expectancy. Through the fanlight over the double front-doors, he could see the letter-man coming up the shell-lined walk. There was in the letter-man's hand a letter—a pink letter—which he knew from its color was meant only for him. He burst open one of the double doors.

Bartholomew, the letter-man, backed down a step in consternation.

"Is it knockin' me down you would be?" he cried sharply. "The divil take you! The whole house is shakin' with you and you all scarlet and pantin', you larrikins, and all to get a letter o' writin' such as I do be bringin' you 'most each day."

He shook his slouch-hatted head, the while he looked almost pityingly at the boy.

"Ah, 'tis using your strength workin' with men you should be," he said; "not breakin' the house down like tinkers do be fightin' together. Most people don't be takin' on so over what letters I'm after bringin' them. So 'tis small wonder they do be callin' you the Lord Duke Mulcahy. And no compliment it is to yourself, sure, with the whole street fixin' it on you—"

"Oh, come on, Bartholomew," said the boy; "it's the letter I want, not your gab."

He reached for the pink envelope.

"Whisht now! Is it robbin' the mails you'd be and San Quentin to end your days in; and that too good for you, too! Wait a minute; wait a minute, me bucko!"

"But I want my letter. Will you hurry, Batholomew? The pink one—"

"Aw, the pink wan, the pink wan, is it?" mimicked the letter-man. "Hands off, then, till I reach it to you. 'Tis no veneration for the mails you have at all, boy, at all."

There was in Bartholomew's eyes a certain twinkle of mischievousness.

"Here is your pink wan, Mister Lord Duke Mulcahy," he said.

He handed over to the red-headed chap the pink envelope.

Hastily the boy tore open one end of the envelope. But ere he could pull out the sheets of the enclosed letter—also pink in color—the voice of the letter-man halted him.

"Mark you that," Bartholomew was saying; " 'Tis so uppish and tony you be, and so lackin' in the common decencies toward a letter-man, that 'tis callin' you the Lord Duke Mulcahy to your face, I am! Not goin' behind your back to be sayin' of it, take heed, like the people o' the street do be after doin'—Mister Lord Duke Mulcahy!"

The red-headed chap looked down at the envelope in his hand and his face went as pink as that envelope. To call a man that name of scorn—the Lord Duke Mulcahy—is to say, in an Irish way, that he is "stuck up," that he is too "tony," that he puts on too much "side"!

"I suppose," said he, at last looking up, "that this is what comes of your gassing with old Mrs. Mulrenin. She tells everybody what an idle no-account I am. At least, she thinks I am all that, and she will have her way! It was she who first gave me that name of the Lord Duke Mulcahy. Just because I used to pluck her sweet peas for my buttonhole. I can't make her like me."

The letter-man shook his slouch-hatted head in dissent.

"Well," said the boy, "if she's not talking about me or against me, then she's everlastingly talking of the secret of the street. It must hurt her with all her gift of gab to have to keep that secret away from the ears of—"

"Whisht! Will you whisht now!" Bartholomew held up the hand containing the few remaining letters. He held up that hand warningly. " 'Tis of that neither you nor any one else of the street should speak, take care!"

And he glanced askance at the cottage opposite across the narrow street.

"And 'tis nothin' like what you say that poor, old Mrs. Mulrenin was after sayin' at all. No, truly. Only askin' for a letter, she was. But she do be askin' that of me, come this time every mornin'—the same way you do be watchin' me from the attic window every mornin', though I never let on.

"But 'tis botherin' me to pass her picket fence and no letters," he continued. "Smilin' she is and she waitin' for me, and her heart sobbin' with longin'. 'And is it a letter you have for me, Mister Bartholomew?' she says. ' 'Twas expectin' a letter from my son Denny in Paris, I be. He do be prosperin', I hear, though I can't see what keeps him away with no word for me.'

"And I answers, as always: 'Ah, artists is queer folks, Mrs. Mulrenin, ma'am. They do be always together away from other folks. That Paris is full of the likes of them, I hear. I was readin' in the paper this day week, and it seems they do have a saloon there and the pictures them artists draw is hung all over the wall back o' the bar.'

" 'People say it do be a wicked place, Paris,' says she, blushin'. 'I have heard it be like them Philippines, where they don't wear no clothes at all. But that, I don't believe at all, Mister Bartholomew; for how could my son Denny carry his money—and him, too, always a good, quiet lad, always drawin', sir, since he was so high—and 'tis plenty of money he has, I hear. And the priest do be tellin' me there is many and many of churches in Paris. And the pictures is hung there Mister Bartholomew; not in saloons, take heed!'

"And then she goes on, real proud: 'Ah, it do be a fine thing to have a son with pictures in all them churches, and him traveled a whole long ways. A fine thing and a queer thing, sure, to have a son an artist, and no one else on the block can say the like o' that. And 'tis not me would be wantin' him different—and him so far away!'

" 'But ah,' says she, and her old eyes yearnin'; 'isn't that a letter there for me from my son Denny in Paris? I think I see his writin'—he was always a scholar. 'Tis not foolin' me you be, Mr. Bartholomew, and it all the time hidden there in your hand, is it?' "

Slowly, at the memory, the letter-man shook his slouch-hatted head.

"And I goes away, lad, and me heart sick with pity for her."

"I suppose she's lonesome there all alone," said the boy thoughtfully. "And the poor thing, she doesn't seem to be able to rent her front cottage, and she living in the rear one."

" 'Tis a pity, truly," said Bartholomew. "But she do be always quarrelin', poor soul, with her tenants when she has them, and the neighbor children—"

"Hush!" said the boy. "Then she is 'away from herself,' as she herself says. It is not her fault."

"Ah, sure, it is not her fault, poor woman!" assented Bartholomew bitterly. "No, faith, 'tis not her fault at all that she is out of her mind at times. Nor is it the fault of the little children who make fun of her. But oh! If I could be a letter-man and walk down one of them grand marble streets in Paris, and should see her son Denny come gallivanting along, I'd tell him whose fault it was, and him listenin' "—his voice rose with indignation—"and himself with the pockets full of money!"

Once more the red-headed chap looked down at his letter.

"Perhaps," said he, "perhaps it's not so much money as great dreams he has, and a very high attic to dream in. Perhaps, it is no one's fault at all—only a pity."

"Perhaps, surely," said the letter-man.

He moved slowly away, shaking his slouch-hatted head over that tragedy of the back street.

The red-headed chap went indoors then. As he climbed the broad stairs within the cool and silent cottage, he pulled out of the pink envelope the pink typewritten sheets of the letter enclosed. He paused on the landing at the turn of the staircase and bent his head to read that letter.

> Dear O'Callahan (the letter read): "The Other Woman, or What Was She To Him?"—your fourteenth novel in the Lola Dean Lively Library— just to hand. We have read it and find that it is a classy love yarn.
>
> But for the love of Mike, O'Callahan, serve up a black-haired, dark-eyed heroine in your next novel. The heroines in your last fourteen novels have all been golden-haired, blue-eyed girls. No change; no let up. I can see them—a regular gallery of tall, golden-haired girls. They haunt me like a nightmare. Tell me: Are you in love with a golden-haired fairy yourself, or is your wife a peroxide blond?
>
> Either way, get an idea about a dark-haired girl and then let us have a swell love story of eighty thousand words. We will pay our usual rate for it—one hundred dollars—if it proves available.
>
> Sincerely yours,
> CLARKE & MAXSON,
> by S.L. Clarke.

O'Callahan made the turn in the staircase. As he did, he gathered together the typewritten sheets of the letter and slid them into the pink envelope. He stowed that envelope in the inside pocket of his green-colored coat.

"This change sure does upset my plans!" he said. "I never like in books, heroines dark-eyed and black-haired. Heroines are always best when they are tall, with proud, white throats and rose-flushed cheeks and hair like golden grain and eyes blue as flowers. That is the only kind—the most beautiful kind!"

The truth was—as Clarke had said—that that was the only kind of heroine O'Callahan wrote of. Never was he known to write a nickel weekly, or Lola Dean Lively dime novel, about a dark-complexioned heroine. Always he made his heroines blue-eyed and golden-haired.

The trouble with O'Callahan was that from making up stories, move by move, about his dime-novel heroes and heroines—about "Bob Breakaway" and the lovely ladies of the Lola Dean Lively Library—he had taken an easy step; a very natural step when you have youth and dreams. He made up stories about himself in which he figured as the hero. About himself he built stories in which he acted so like his own dime-novel heroes by rescuing a dream-girl from all manner of enemies and perils.

That dream-girl was a golden-haired, blue-eyed angel. She it was that he attempted to describe in his novels. She was his ideal. For, as the hero of his fancies, the poor, lonely, dreaming boy-man imagined himself in love with the golden-haired, blue-eyed and beautiful angel who played opposite him as the heroine of his dreams.

Only one reason there was for this love. That was that invariably in dime novels heroes love heroines. But to Aloysius Columbkill O'Callahan there could be no better, nor no stronger reason, than that such was so in dime novels.

Therefore, of her each day he day-dreamed. One day, a red automobile would shoot by him on the street, and she—he imagined her inside of it, of course—would drop a note to him ere she was whisked on into the distance. Another day, from the most drab of stores, she would make a sign. Still another day, as he walked along, she would appear in the dark doorway of a house and look an appeal for aid.

Always he answered her appeals for help with great daring and easy nonchalance. Always he went about her rescue in the most ingenious ways, in a thousand disguises. Always he burst out of the particular disguise "at the psychological moment," and covered her captors with "ready death-dealing automatic."

It was all in his brains. He it was who twisted and snarled the plots out of which he rescued his dream-girl. He it was, by the same token, who could name his own reward. In any manner he pleased, he could exact that reward.

It was all a sweet dream. But only, in each sweet dream, did he lead her gently by the hand from each den of deviltry. Back to her parents he brought her. Then gallantly he removed his hat from his red head and bowed, and said good-by.

She was tall and golden-haired and very proud. Always, for each rescue, she rewarded him with a proud smile. That was all the reward he ever took. And remember it was all in his brains. But so young he was, and so fresh in the world, that he never dared dream beyond that; he really was unable to dream beyond that smile. Aware he was of certain truths of life; but from her, he felt in his dreams, that proud smile was enough.

So, for a little, as he thought piquantly of his dream-girl, Aloysius Columbkill O'Callahan stood in the open window that looked down upon the quiet back street. But he did not look down at that street. His mind was keyed to the story-imagining point. And so, for a time, his mind went blissfully on and he lived in one of his day-dreams.

There was the splendid rescue; then that reward—one proud smile. He came out of the day-dream. He looked about the room. He looked about the room in a quick, shy way. His thin, pale face flushed scarlet as a girl's. It was as if he had surprized himself in some very intimate, piquant thought.

"Gee," he said, "I hate to leave her out of my stories!"

The better to think over the change of orders he had received that morning, O'Callahan left the cool and silent cottage to take a walk. As he closed the double front-doors behind him, he became aware, of a sudden, that the little back street was no longer quiet. Before the picket fence of old Mrs. Mulrenin's garden was gathered a crowd of the neighbor children; they were on their way home from school for the nooning; and from that crowd came a shrill clamor of sparrow-like voices.

Straightway O'Callahan marveled at seeing the shrilling crowd. What were they piping about? Who was that in the center of the crowd? He looked over the heads of the children and uttered, at the look, a little sound of surprize in his throat. In the center of that shrilling crowd was old Mrs. Mulrenin.

A ridiculous back-street quarrel, it seemed to be!

O'Callahan saw it was more than that. He saw that old Mrs. Mulrenin's eyes were oddly bright. That made the matter a tragedy. Old Mrs. Mulrenin was out of her mind!

"The poor, little, old lady!" he said. "Sick with loneliness and longing, she is away from herself!"

And she it was who first had dubbed him with that name of scorn—the Lord Duke Mulcahy!

He did not think of that. His whole being twinged with a great, a shaking pity. He ran down the street toward her, reached the nearest of the children and, with quick hands on small shoulders, pulled them back and aside. Then, wrathful and very pale, he was beside the little old lady and facing her shrilling tormentors.

"Shame on you!" he cried. "Why don't you leave poor, old Mrs. Mulrenin alone, you little pests! Can't you see she is away from herself!"

Uncertain whether to run or not, the children stood shocked and still and dismayed. But thus only for a moment. Then their thin backs stiffened. Indignant as outraged angels, they faced him, and the whole street shrilled with their sparrow-like cries:

"You Mister Buttinsky! You Lord Duke Mulcahy! Shame on you! And shame on you, Missus Mulrenin! Why did you tell Rosemary Brown the secret what her father done? Oh, for shame!"

There was in their sparrow-like voices a terrible strength of scorn.

Consternation sloughed over O'Callahan. So that was the reason for the whole hub-bub? He turned upon old Mrs. Mulrenin with something of the indignation of the children in his attitude.

But the little old lady no longer stood erect and defiant as she had before her wee tormentors. Woman that she was, with the coming of a man to take her part, she had weakened. She sat on the curbing, bent over the gutter, her arms in her blue-skirted lap, her head on her arms. A crumpled-up, tiny figure, she was shaking with great, tearful sobs.

O'Callahan bent over her and, for all his sudden indignation, his voice was quite gentle:

"Is it true, Mrs. Mulrenin? Did you tell Rosemary Brown the secret of the street—that her father stole money and wore stripes in prison?"

The crumpled-up, tiny figure on the curbing did not answer him. Only between great tearful sobs, she mumbled:

"Oh, Denny! Denny! You will not be leavin' me all alone and them treatin' your old mother so!"

O'Callahan looked up. In his eyes was a great, a shaking pity. The little old lady was wandering in her mind.

He looked up into the dark eyes of little Rosemary Brown. She was standing apart from the others, her arms clinging to one of the pickets of the fence, as if she were weak and lost. Dumbly her dark eyes were asking him a tragic question.

He had said "that her father stole money and wore stripes in prison!"

That tragic question fled from the girl's eyes. It was true, then, what old Mrs. Mulrenin had told her! Her head lowered on her clinging arms and her whole slim, young body shook. Just as old Mrs. Mulrenin was shaking with great sobs, just so did she shake with great sobs, heart-breaking sobs.

The Lord Duke Mulcahy turned away. In his attitude was the expression of a penitent.

"So the secret of Seven Pines Street is out at last!" he thought. "And it's been kept so long by the people of the street, by even the children of the street!"

Coming along the walk on his way home to lunch, O'Callahan saw, as he turned away, the tall, somber, black-bearded man who was Peter Brown—Rosemary's father. He watched the man aghast.

The man stopped and looked with grave eyes from the little old lady, bent over the gutter, to his little daughter, sobbing against the picket fence. He seemed at once to comprehend everything that had happened. He went to his daughter and put his arm about her, and whispered reassuringly to her. Then he led her, still shaking with sobs, up the street and across into the cottage opposite O'Callahan's.

O'Callahan looked after him, a growing respect in his soul.

"He acted just like a strong man should act in a great crisis," thought that dreamer of great crises. "Now, I suppose, it's up to me to do something for poor old Mrs. Mulrenin. I can't let her remain here sobbing in the gutter—a spectacle for the whole street!"

So he went to her.

"And 'tis not me would be wantin' him different, and him so far away," she was saying. "But isn't that a letter there for me from my son Denny in Paris?"

He touched her very silvery, very scanty hair.

"That's all right, Mrs. Mulrenin," he said softly. "It's all right, Mrs. Mulrenin; it's all right now."

From across the street a neighbor, Mrs. Schultz, came running to help him, a shawl about her head.

"Ain't it derrible!" she exclaimed. "Dot child, she take on derrible bad 'bout her fadder, now!"

The red-headed chap put a finger to his lips and looked down meaningly at the crumpled-up, tiny figure on the curbing. Then together he and the German woman helped old Mrs. Mulrenin to her feet and half-helped, half-carried her through her bright, little garden and around to the shadowy bedroom in her rear cottage. Upon the bed beneath the many-patched, though neat quilts, they laid her, weak and wandering in her mind. O'Callahan fetched water for her to drink and with which to bathe her forehead, the while the German woman bustled about in the numerous duties so native to a woman's hand in the emergency of sickness.

Later O'Callahan came out into the street again and sent after a doctor one of the awed, small boys who was on his way back to school. After a time the doctor came panting around the corner and then the door of the lonely, little, rear cottage closed after him.

"Well," thought O'Callahan, "the doctor will give poor old Mrs. Mulrenin something that will make her sleep, and so she will forget, for a while at least, all about that letter that never seems to come."

He stood behind the blue-and-pink hedge of sweet peas and looked thoughtfully up and down the back street.

Now that the back street was once more quiet, the afternoon seemed empty and the little street useless in its fragrant charm, and oddly deserted. Only Bartholomew, like Midas growing donkey ears in Arcady, turned clown and vagabond, and lingered in the back street.

Bartholomew always finished his morning rounds in Seven Pines Street and, contrariwise, always began in Seven Pines Street his rounds of the afternoon. Packless and coatless, he was sauntering through Seven Pines Street, a fistful of letters in his hand.

O'Callahan watched that letter-man as he moved so slowly from cottage to cottage, and as he lingered so lackadaisically at garden wall or picket fence.

"If he only has a letter for poor old Mrs. Mulrenin!" he thought.

He peeped over the hedge of pink-and-blue sweet peas.

"Have you a letter for poor, old Mrs. Mulrenin," he asked, "from her son Denny in Paris?"

Bartholomew, the letter-man, backed away a step in consternation.

"The divil take you, you Lord Duke Mulcahy!" he cried sharply. " 'Tis a ghost I was after thinkin' you was, what with me hearin' that poor old Mrs. Mulrenin was sick, and the secret of the street out, and all and all! And ah, 'tis not blamin' poor old Mrs. Mulrenin for lettin' the cat out o' the bag, I am—and she out of her head at the time. No, faith, 'tis only pity I have for poor old Mrs. Mulrenin, and me carrying no letter for her at all, boy, at all."

Slowly he shook his slouch-hatted head, the while he glanced at the Brown cottage farther up across the narrow street.

"And 'tis myself do pity Peter Brown, the silent father, and that little dark mother of Rosemary Brown!" he said. " 'Tis always afraid that little dark mother was of me and my friendly ways that might be after lettin' the cat out o' the bag to Rosemary. Haven't I seen her, times without number, watchin' me through the blinds, and me only talkin' a bit to the neighbors?"

O'Callahan nodded his red head.

"I know. She kept Rosemary out of school for a couple of years in order that the child should not grow up too fast. And Rosemary, though sixteen or so, still dresses in short skirts like her classmates of fourteen. But you can't blame the mother, Bartholomew. She was always afraid that some one would tell Rosemary, and ever more afraid as Rosemary grew older and more observant."

"Ah, sure, lad, 'tis a great fear she had always! And now that the child Rosemary is sobbin' her heart out because her father was foolish once. Oh, I do pity that little dark mother, lad, and that Peter Brown, too, with all his regrets!"

Thoughtfully O'Callahan looked down at the blue-and-pink sweet peas before him.

"Perhaps," said he, "perhaps there is something that I can do there. Perhaps I can do something to right the wrong that has been done Rosemary and her father."

"Perhaps, surely," said the letter-man.

He moved slowly away, shaking his slouch-hatted head over that new tragedy of the back street.

O'Callahan stood, then, behind the pink-and-blue hedge of sweet peas and for a very short time, in the peace of the little garden, studied over the whole matter. The secret of Seven Pines Street had been common talk of the neighbors and the neighbor children, but talk that never passed while the girl Rosemary had been within hearing. Even he who was scorned, and so was without the pale of intimacies of the block—the Lord Duke Mulcahy—even he had known all there was to be known about that secret.

He knew that the man, Peter Brown, was an Italian and that Peter Brown was not that man's real name. Pietro Ginocchio he had been christened in Italy, and he had come to the United States when he was twenty. A brother, some years older, had preceded him to the new world. When this brother became a clerk in the office of S.V. & E.T. Weir, building contractors of San Francisco, he changed his name from Giorgio Ginocchio to that of George W. Brown. When he installed Pietro as a file-clerk in the contracting office, where he was then cashier, he said to Pietro—

"You will have to go to night-school and you will have to call yourself Peter Brown."

All of which Peter Brown did. But as he was not so brilliant, and not nearly so ambitious as that brother, he went up more slowly in the firm. He became a cashier and married, however, at the time that his brother was made vice-president of the firm.

Then when Rosemary was a baby, he was accused of the embezzlement of forty-five thousand dollars; his own books convicted him; and he was sent to San Quentin for five years. He had ruined himself and almost ruined his brother, it seemed; for shortly after that, his brother had left the firm for which he had worked so long and so untiringly, and had started out for himself in a new firm—that of George Washington Brown, building contractor. When Peter Brown returned to his little family in Seven Pines Street—a saddened and somber man—this faithful brother it was who had given him a bookkeeping job in his own and now prosperous firm.

Aloysius Columbkill O'Callahan had the brains of a dime novelist—quick, flamboyant and ruthless.

"I've got it!" he exclaimed to the hedge of sweet peas. "I'll make up a story about Peter Brown that will deceive his little daughter Rosemary into believing her father once more her hero!"

Bold feather of a lad that he was, O'Callahan crossed the narrow, cobbled street and made, under the trees, toward the cottage opposite his own. Opening the garden gate, he swung up the shell-lined walk between daisy-dappled lawns. In the deep high doorway of the cottage, he pulled on the old-fashioned bell.

Right then, as he pulled on the bell and far in the depths of the cottage heard it jangle madly, O'Callahan, who was only a poor, dreaming boy after all, sensed something of the real spirit of adventure. Now never when he made up day-dreams, and had to ring a bell in a dark doorway in response to a call from her, the golden girl, did he feel like this. Always, then, the getting into the house had been so tame. The hard thing to do was to make something interesting happen once the door was opened. Now the very jangle of the bell woke a note that thrilled him with its promise of adventure.

"This is like an adventure," he told himself. "Anything can happen now."

The echoes within the cottage died slowly and there followed a period of profound silence. Then came slow footfalls. The door opened a bit, and the black-bearded and somber man who was Peter Brown, looked gravely out at him.

O'Callahan caught his breath.

"I heard how old Mrs. Mulrenin made Rosemary cry—I mean, I know what happened—I know what Rosemary was told—" In helpless confusion, he stopped; then quite desperately, he said: "I'm only the boy across the street. But can I come in, sir? Can I come in and talk?"

At the inarticulateness of the red-headed chap, the man smiled slightly.

"Oh, so you're the boy who lives across the street, the one that is always typewriting. Yes, sure, come in." And he held the door open.

Before O'Callahan really comprehended that he had succeeded in his first step, he was standing, quite abashed, in the parlor. All the blinds were closed in the parlor and a warm, drowsy dusk hung over the just-so place.

"My little girl," said Peter Brown, "is up-stairs crying. She is too broken up to return to school this afternoon. I, myself, do not feel fit to return to the office. I have always dreaded this moment and so has my wife. We knew it would prove a terrible shock to Rosemary, though we never thought that she would take it quite so badly. But you—if you have come to express your sympathy, I thank you very much."

He spoke in an odd, precise way, slurring the "s" in some words and making it crisp in others. He said the last almost as if it were a question, and looked inquiringly at the boy.

"Yes, I do sympathize with you and your wife," said O'Callahan hastily. "And I'm sure all the neighbors do. But there is no use being angry at poor old Mrs. Mulrenin. She is not a responsible sort of a person. She was out of her head at the time and she is out of her head even yet."

"Ah, no," agreed the man in his precise way; "there is no use, as you say, in being angry at poor old Mrs. Mulrenin. So frail she is and so old, and I know she never meant harm. Only she was bitter at this world which seems, at times, so terrible!"

O'Callahan's thin pale face glowed at being so readily understood.

"That's just it, sir. She was expecting a letter, and it never came, and she was sick at everything. But the doctor is with her now and there is nothing more that we can do for her. And I thought—I thought, perhaps, we could do something to make Rosemary take it all easier—to make it so she wouldn't feel so bad about you."

Peter Brown looked with a sudden respect at the almost inarticulate boy. He said eagerly:

"Yes, yes; I do not want my daughter to think so hard of me. She cries and cries and it hurts me here." He pressed his chest in a passionate gesture. "But what can I do? She won't let me explain. She won't let her mother explain. Her mother is with her now, but she only buries her head in the pillow and cries so it almost breaks my heart. And I stand by—I got to stand by like a log of wood. Oh," he added thickly, "it is all one dreadful, miserable, damn business! It is my own fault!"

He dropped upon the horsehair lounge and buried his head in his hands. There could be no doubt of his anguish of soul.

"Let me help you, sir," said O'Callahan breathlessly. "Let me fix it up for you. I'll fix it all up for you so everything will be just as it formerly was."

Peter Brown lifted his dark Latin eyes in wonder and evident doubt.

"But what can you do?"

It was a grave, a great question.

"Leave it all to me, sir! Let me do everything and I promise I'll fix it all up for you! You see, sir—you see, I make up stories—that's why I'm always typewriting—so I'll make up a story about you. I'll make up a story that will show you in a good light before Rosemary's eyes. I'll make Rosemary stop crying!"

Peter Brown got up. The way in which he got up showed to what race he had been born.

"If you could!" he exclaimed fervidly. "Ah, if you only could!"

• • •

The cottages in Seven Pines Street mostly have attics. The bedroom of Rosemary Brown was a room in such an attic. It sloped cozily down on either hand, and there was a little dormer window in front that looked down upon the back street and across, over the trees, at the window of O'Callahan's workroom. Upon the bed in that room, little Rosemary Brown lay, her dark curls tumbled about her face and her face buried in a pillow she had wet with her tears.

Slowly her father mounted the stairs to the attic and entered the rear-room next to hers. She raised her curls from the damp pillow, at the sound. He scraped a chair over to a window in the side wall of the rear-room, and sat down. The girl sat up in the bed, dewy-eyed and wondering.

Then more footsteps sounded on the attic stairs; a knock came on the door of the room in which her father was sitting.

"Come in," said her father.

On his face, if she could have seen it, was a puzzled and rather expectant look.

"You are Mr. Brown, aren't you?" said a new voice. "The lady downstairs, Rosemary's mother, told me I could find you up here. I'm O'Callahan, the boy across the street—Aloysius Columbkill O'Callahan, sir. I suppose I've bothered you working nights over my typewriter."

And he laughed a short nervous laugh.

The girl's face, where it had been pressed against the pillow, was very red; now, at O'Callahan's words, an even warmer red swept beneath her olive skin. She went softly to the door between her bedroom and the rear-room, and leaned her pretty head against the jamb of that closed door and listened.

"I ran over to see you about a letter, Mr. Brown. Bartholomew O'Brien— that's the letter-man—delivered it to me. My number was on the letter, but it wasn't for me at all; so I thought it might be intended for you, Mr. Brown."

"What name is it addressed to?" asked Peter Brown in a rather halting way.

"It's for a fellow named Pietro Ginocchio—"

"Ginocchio? Why that's my name!"

There was no doubting the sincerity of the astonishment expressed in the voice of the man.

"But you are Peter Brown."

"Oh, I changed my name many years ago. That is my right—my Italian name."

"But this is a terrible letter, mister—mister—"

"Brown."

"A terrible letter, Mr. Brown. I opened it in mistake, as I said. I'd been expecting a letter from Clarke & Maxson of New York, so I didn't look at the name; just tore it open. Only when I started to read the letter, I saw that it wasn't for me; but what I had read, scared me. You see, it is the confession of a fellow who says he sent you to prison for a crime that he himself committed. He says you were not at all to blame—"

"*Dio mio*, no!"

"Sure—take it easy—I mean, be calm, Mr. Brown! Here's the letter. I'll read it to you. You're too excited to read."

From the inside pocket of his green-colored coat, the red-headed chap pulled out a letter. But he did not extract the contents of that letter from the envelope. He did not even look at the envelope. He looked with bright, lively eyes at the man. And he spoke, not as a boy speaks to another person in conversation, but loudly and affectedly as a boy "speaks a piece":

"Listen, Mr. Brown. The letter says:

"Pietro Ginocchio:

"Any hour, any moment, now, I may die. I sit here in my room afraid to move, to turn my back to window or door. I am afraid to go out in the crowded streets. They are waiting for me—to kill me who was a *traditore* to them!

"Because I fear death and eternal damnation in punishment for the great wrong I did you, Pietro, I write this letter to you. I want to clear my soul before I die. I want to tell the truth.

"Remember, Pietro, how we were boys together in Italia? How we used to climb the mountain called Il Figlio and look down upon the village with its *salitas* of stairs and its tiny, red-roofed church, all clinging like a clump of shrubbery to the mountain-side? How we used, then, to lie a-sprawl and dream of America and of making our fortunes there? Remember, Pietro, how we used to swear we would always be friends and, in that new land, fight each other's enemies back to back? Ah, me! How I forgot those oaths when the time came for me to show myself your true friend!

"I started to America first, Pietro. The old folks—*Dio* reward them—had saved up my fare, and had sent me with their blessings to Genoa to take the big ship that was to bring me to the land of gold. But I did not go to America from Genoa, Pietro. For there in the *osteria*, or inn where I ate and slept, I gambled away my money at dice. I had no fare, no money at all. I was what we call in America, 'broke.'

"In the *osteria*, however, I met another young fellow who also was on his uppers. His name was Benedetto Zappettini, and he was from our *provenza*. He was a sly one. He said:

" 'You don't need money if you are a sly one like me. Come along; be *comerata* with me.'

"So I went with him to Naples, and all the way we begged our bread along the road. I was ashamed; but my friend Benedetto said:

" 'Oh, that will be all right. In Naples we will find friends, Then
we will not need to beg. What we want, we can take!' And he boasted
to me that he was a thief. He was a Camorrist, and he wanted me to
join the Camorra—"

"Camorra!"

"*Sh!* Keep quiet!" commanded the Lord Duke Mulcahy.

He turned from the man and began pacing excitedly up and down the
room. His voice thrilled. He even gesticulated with the envelope that was in
his hand. He was living over again a particularly high-colored nickel novel
he once had written called, *Bob Breakaway and the Neapolitan Flower-Girl,
or Thwarting Benedetto Zappettini, Czar of the Camorra!*

"Yes; the Camorra! The Mafia! The dreaded Black Hand! Ah, I
was a fool—Pietro—always a fool! My friend, Benedetto Zappettini,
gave me wine until I was drunk and drugged, and then he led me to the
Black Hand rendezvous. It was deep down in one of the catacombs of
ancient Rome—I mean, Naples, of course! The Camorrists were all in
black dominoes, and had blue skulls for heads. They made me swear
bloody oaths on a human skull. If ever I turned *traditore* to them, they
swore I was to die.

"But before I was admitted as a full-fledged member, they said I
was to kill a certain man, a Calabrese, whom they wanted put out of
the way. You know, it is a rule of the Camorra that a man must kill
one enemy of the Camorra ere he can join the Camorra. But I did not
want to join the Camorra, nor did I in the least want to kill a man.
So instead of doing what they commanded, I ran away on a ship to
America. In New York, I changed my name and remained in hiding.
Then I went out to San Francisco, hoping that far out there I should
not meet any one that knew me for a *traditore* to the Camorra. But in
the Peacock Alley of the St. Francis Hotel, one New Year's night, I
met Giovanni Zappettini!"

O'Callahan had forgotten, in his excitement, the name he first had
mentioned, but dime novelist that he was, he did not hesitate for another.

" 'Ah,' said Zappettini, 'it is you—*traditore!*'

"I said: 'What are you going to do with me, Angelo Zappettini?
Give me up to the hated Camorra?'

" 'No,' said he; 'I am your friend. Give me five thousand dollars—
and the Camorra will never know about you from me!'

"Now, I had got a job in a large company and, as I was both
faithful and industrious, I had worked myself up to a high position. I
had money saved from my big salary, so I gave him the five thousand

dollars. But one night he came again and demanded more money.

" 'Else,' said he, 'I shall tell the Camorra where is the *traditore!*'

"I gave him more money. But he came again, and again, and again. He bled me, Pietro, until I had no more money—until I could borrow no more.

" 'Take it from the firm, *traditore!*' he whispered to me—that dastardly villain, Cesare Zappettini whispered to me. 'Fix the books! The firm will never discover you! Steal it—or I shall tell the Camorra and they will stick a knife into you!'

"What could I do, Pietro? I was half-mad with fear. I tell you, Pietro, I was half-mad with fear. I stole from the firm—forty-five thousand dollars!

"Then, remember, Pietro, it was that night when you and I were working on the books. There was to be a directors' meeting, and you were to report the financial condition of the firm for the past six months. In that six months, I had stolen the forty-five thousand dollars from the firm. I felt weak with fear that you would discover the way I had juggled the funds.

"When I came back from my late supper, you still were working under the green-shaded lights. You lifted your head. Your face was white as the paper of the books before you.

" 'Look!' you said. 'There is money missing—forty-five thousands of dollars! It is in your accounts the deficit is! The thief made it appear as if it were you who stole!'

"Then, Pietro, did I forget our youth on Il Figlio and our oaths to be forever friends. I knew then you knew! I went blind with rage—the terrible rage of the exposed criminal. I grasped you by the throat!

" 'Yes—I am the thief!' I screamed. 'I stole the money! And you know I did! But you, you sneaky one—you shall never tell!' And I banged your head against the edge of the desk before you.

"Five times I slammed your head against the edge of that desk, and when I got back my reason, I saw you limp on the floor and bleeding from the head. Then I felt pity for you and lifted you up, and bathed your head. You opened your eyes.

" 'Speak to me, Pietro!' I cried in my anguish of fear.

"You could not speak. And your eyes were dull. Your mind was a blank. You were like a baby. You did not even know your own name. Your brain was paralyzed by the banging I had given you. The doctors call it asphasia.

"As I saw your helplessness, Pietro, the devil himself whispered an idea in my bead. So I said:

" 'Your name is Peter Brown. Say that! Say, "my name is Peter Brown." '

"After a time, like a child learning to speak, but quicker and clearer—more like a man picking up a tune he had heard long before—you said—'My name is Peter Brown.'

"Then I tried my devil's plan. With my heart in my mouth, I said:

" 'You are the thief! Say that! "I am the thief!" ' "

"You said: 'I am the thief!'

"Then I fixed up the books. I made them show glaringly that you had taken the money and that you had tried to cover up the theft. In the morning I had you arrested. You said—

" 'I am the thief!' "

The red-headed chap seemed carried away by his flamboyant imagination. Excitedly he shoved his flushed, thin face into the face of the man. He did not declaim cratorically. He shouted:

"Don't you see! This fellow sent you to prison for a crime you did not commit. He was the thief, the criminal. He shouldered his crime on you. You served the term as convict; you wore stripes for him. You never knew the difference. It's a clear case of asphasia. He struck your head against the edge of the desk—once, twice, five times. Your head bled; your brain was stunned; part of it—memory of that night—was put out of business forever. You recovered your tongue and memory of the things that happened before that night, but you never could remember what occurred on that particular night. You never knew!"

There was a sound like the sound of a quick sob from Rosemary's bedroom.

Peter Brown up-rose from his chair. His voice was no longer precise. It was labored as with a great agitation:

"But who was he—this other man?"

"He was George W. Brown, your brother!"

There was that in O'Callahan's revelation which wrought a strange change in Peter Brown. He seemed staggered by the shock of the revelation. He stood, swaying slightly back and forth on the balls of his feet. The shock passed; the meaning of that revelation seeped slowly into his brain, and slowly his dark face filled with blood. His face filled with blood until it was the color of brick.

He leaped forward. He got the startled boy by the shoulders. With his hands crushing the boy's shoulders, he shoved his brick-red face into the startled face of the boy. In his eyes, so close to the boy's, there glowed some tremendous, inward excitement.

"*E vero, vero!*" he cried passionately. Then he sputtered into English: "You are right, right! You are a devil, boy! You know all I know. It was much as you say. We were alone that night. I discovered his thefts. But he did not hit me. He pleaded. The thefts were not the worse things he had done. He had done other things—stolen contracts, forged. He begged me to save him. I could only be held for embezzlement; his forgeries would not be discovered;

he would have time to make good the forged notes. He wept. He had wanted to become rich—to become rich quick, that was all. There was no Camorra, no Zappettini—nothing. Only that damned want to be rich.

"I took the blame. I saved him. He supported my wife and child, as he had promised he would. He got me a short term, a parole. When I got out, he gave me a good job in his firm and he gave me this house—bought it for me. For now he is rich, this money-crazed brother of mine. He has his own business, and he has a young wife and many homes and automobiles, and he goes back on visits to Italy like a gentleman, while I—I—"

"Then it was your brother, George W. Brown?"

Peter Brown was aghast.

"Why—why—I thought you knew that! Have I told you—"

But O'Callahan was not heeding him. The girl Rosemary had entered the room, was running across the room toward her father. And her eyes, as she lifted up her arms to him, were great with a glorious proud tenderness.

"Daddy!" she sobbed. "Poor daddy! Poor, poor daddy!"

Aloysius Columbkill O'Callahan bent over and began an industrious search of the floor. He had lost that envelope which had started the whole gentle little drama. At last he found it in a corner where a gesture, in his excitement, had flung it. It was a pink envelope—the very envelope he had received that morning from Clarke & Maxson of New York. Hastily he shoved it into the inside pocket of his green-colored coat and looked up.

"My little Rosemary!" Peter Brown was breathing softly into the dark, rich hair of the girl. "But it's true, my little baby; quite, quite true!" And he kissed her.

O'Callahan looked down on that father and daughter almost as if he owned them. It was as if they were but characters in a dime novel, and he had made them to live and to speak. Surely enough, he had made them to be happy. He had directed their lives toward his dime-novel end where, always and inevitably, right was rewarded. He threw back his red, flamboyant head proudly.

But no one noticed him. So very quietly he turned and left the room, closing the door after him. He went down the dark and narrow attic stairway.

Now as he went down those dark and narrow stairs, he felt vaguely disappointed. Perhaps it was because Peter Brown had not called him back to thank him, or even to say good-by. All he knew was that in each of his day-dreams there had always been, after the splendid rescue, that reward—one proud smile. Here there was not a smile—not even a golden girl!

Then, back up the dark and narrow attic stairway, he heard a door open. "Wait a minute, Mr. Mulcahy!" he heard Rosemary call. And he heard her running down the stairs.

With her dark curls tossing about her round, olive-complexioned face, she ran down to him where he waited at the top of the large staircase in the hall. And he noticed now, as she stood flushed after the run beside him, that her face was very pretty, her skin delicate as rose-petals and her nose saucily up-tilted. He felt of a sudden as if he would like to touch that saucily up-tilted nose!

"Daddy," said she, "sent me down to thank you for him and to let you out. And I want to thank you for me!"

He did not know what to say. He gulped:

"Oh, you needn't thank me. I'm glad just because your daddy and you are happy once more. You're happy, aren't you?"

She nodded. But she did not smile. She was suddenly serious.

"You kiss me, too!" she said desperately.

And she thrust her pretty, round face up to his.

The Lord Duke Mulcahy snapped his face back from hers in shocked astonishment.

"Why?" he asked.

He could not understand this sudden surge of youthful daring on her part.

But reason quickly returned to his red head. He had seen her father kiss her, perhaps that was why she expected him to kiss her, too. Perhaps, for him to kiss her, would make her happy. And he had started out to make her happy at all costs. He stooped a little to perform the delicate task.

Then, even as he bent his head, he had one of his splendid inspirations. That splendid inspiration caused him to close his eyes. No longer did he see before him that little olive-skinned, tilted-nose baby. Before him rose a tall, blue-eyed, golden-haired and proud beauty—his golden girl! She it was he had made happy. Now, as a magnificent, unthinkably sublime reward, she had asked him to kiss her!

There on the half-dark stairs, with his eyes closed, the Lord Duke Mulcahy kissed his golden girl!

It was a quick, bird-like peck; but it so surprized the two experimenters that they jumped apart at the little sound. Then the red-headed chap turned and ran down the stairs. And little Rosemary Brown looked after him, a proud proprietary air in her attitude and in her eyes, great with recent weeping, a dewy, a tremulous happiness. He—the Lord Duke Mulcahy of the back street—had kissed her!

When Aloysius Columbkill O'Callahan entered once again his attic workroom, he was in his shirt-sleeves, his coat over one arm. He made at once for the typewriter near the open window.

"I'm under orders," he said. "I'll have to begin work on that Lola Dean Lively story. I think I'll use the same plot, but just change my heroine from a golden-haired girl to—"

He broke off. He looked, above the trees, at the little dormer window in the cottage across the street.

"Gee!" he said. "I could make my new heroine look like little Rosemary over there!"

For a while, after that, he stood in the open attic window and looked down upon the quiet back street. But down the back street, behind the picket fence, there was no little old lady with face soft and pink like the pink sweet peas and dress clean and blue like the blue ones. He shook his red head sadly.

"Poor, old Mrs. Mulrenin," he thought, "always waiting for that letter that never seems to come."

And then, as sadly he shook his head, he saw the doctor come out from behind the picket fence. And the doctor, too, was shaking his head sadly!

"Can it be"—he asked himself tremblingly—"can it be that poor old Mrs. Mulrenin will soon be done, with all waiting?"

He trembled all over. He trembled with another of his splendid inspirations!

That day, to Peter Brown and to little Rosemary, he had brought a tender and tremulous happiness. Could he not bring, to that lonely figure in this other tragedy of the back street, a happiness as tender and tremulous—and this, in the ebbing of her life?

With a sort of reverence, he sat down to the typewriter. Then, more slowly than ever he had written on that typewriter before, he wrote:

PARIS, FRANCE, AUGUST 1, 19—.

DEAR MOTHER:

The typewriter groaned its protest at the unusual slowness and at the unusual words. They were not words of rascality and beauty and bravery. They were simple, homely words; words of solicitude, words of love. For the letter O'Callahan made up then was the letter home of a son who, though far away among strangers, did not forget his lonely old mother.

At last, he pulled the crowded sheet from the typewriter. There remained hardly room enough to sign a name. But with a hand that shook a little—for O'Callahan always felt what he wrote—he signed:

"YOUR LOVING SON—DENNY!"

He tossed his red, flamboyant head proudly—that gentle, little back-street god!

Ah, then, in truth, was he the Lord Duke Mulcahy!

The Gay-Cat

By Patrick Casey

IT WAS A NIGHT OF FOG. Slowly over the sleek, wet ties the two hoboes shuffled. They were a man and a boy. The boy did not walk an even stride with the man. He followed, like a shrunken shadow, a step behind. It was significant. Both were tattered, blackened by grime and chilled with the fog. They were hunched of shoulder, heavy-legged. They were alike save for that interval of a step. That marked a difference. It was a difference old as the world. It began when first a slave stumbled after the dominator through the bleak dusk of the primeval. It showed that the one served the other.

The face of the boy burned with the chill of the fog. They had ridden the brakes from Ogden in cramped proximity to the roadbed and the clacking wheels. Flying pebbles had cut their skin with nasty scratches. Dust and cinders had eaten like acid into the cuts. The damp of the fog loosened those gatherings. Like salt in the wind it made the cuts sting.

The boy rubbed his face with a threadbare sleeve, stiff as sandpaper with dirt. He whimpered. The man went on. He heard the boy. He did not turn his head. The boy, had he done so, would have backed away in fear. He rubbed his face again. Again he whimpered. It was not to arouse sympathy. It was the outpouring of a soul's misery. It was like an animal's. Misery was inside of him. Like an animal he whimpered to rid himself of that misery. All the while, at that interval of a stop, hunched of shoulder, shuffling legged, he slouched on after the other through the fog.

Neither the man nor the boy caught the moan of the dog that followed them. It was like an echo of the boy's. It came from behind them, at each whimper of the boy, like sympathy. It echoed, as they reached the hangout, the last whimper of the boy.

The hangout was down from the railroad embankment in a field of rusted car-wheels. The wheels were in immovable twos, a three-inch axle slung between. At the end of the stretch of wheels was the hangout, barricaded on one side by a corrugated iron windshield, roughly thrown up, and on the other by a derelict gondola freight car.

The man and the boy halted at the end of the car-wheels. The hoboes in the hangout had finished eating. They lay on stray ties or on the scattered straw and excelsior with faces to the fire. The light of the fire disclosed the man, and behind him the boy.

"If it ain't Frisco Red!" exclaimed one prone figure.

A number of the hoboes sat up and greeted the man.

No one spoke to the boy. He made at once for the fire. A stew was cooking there in a smoke-blackened oil can. He sniffed the stew like an animal as he drew near. He peered into the blackened can. There was enough left. It was a mulligan. Everything was in that stew—meat, potatoes, onions, bread—an appetizing hodge-podge. They could eat their fill. What remained of the stew, now that the hoboes had eaten, was any one's that would come and take.

The man had appropriated a tie near the fire. On it on his stomach he basked, his face to the blaze. It was a large face. The red stubble of a week's growth thickened the outline and made it appear more bloated. His nose was fatly bulbous. He had borrowed the makings from one of the hoboes. He puffed deeply. At long intervals, in thick complacent streams, he exhaled the smoke.

The boy hunted around for the tin plates. With excelsior he cleaned two. He fished out, on a stick, potatoes and onions and meat and bread, and heaped them in a smelly steaming mess upon the plates. To Frisco Red he brought one of the plates. The stew steamed fragrantly about the red shaggy head as with grimy fingers the burly hobo dug for the first mouthfuls among the potatoes and shreds of meat.

"That's some kid yuh got, Red," said one hobo. He watched the boy as the youngster carried his own smoking dish to the outer rim of the crowd and sat down with it on his knees. "Say, how much yuh want fer that kid?"

The boy ate ravenously. He did not lift his head. He ate as though he had not heard the offer of purchase. He ate inelegantly, quickly, greedily, with a thorough and wholesome enjoyment of the coarse food. It was his first meal in twelve hours.

"You wanter buy that kid?" Red said. He looked at the boy. The other hobo was watching the boy. "Wal, that kid ain't for sale. He's a valyable road-kid, that's what, and he ain't for sale. There ain't a kid like him this side of the Hump—nor t'other side, either. He's valyable, I tell yuh. You should have seen him batter the back doors up in Ogden. Handouts every time. Handouts for me. That kid don't want no handouts. He gets setdowns. Yes, siree, bo; every time. Setdowns in the kitchen.

"And State Street, Chicago, bo. He sure mooched that stem. Dimes every time. No nickels. Dimes, buddy, and most like a quarter or a half. The women fall for that kid. Them high-waisted farmers' wives most of all—'He's so wis'ful kinder,' one says to me—him bein' that white and thin and scrawny, though yuh see how he sure digs into that stew. But he handles 'em cute, that kid. He's too valyable. He don't need to batter no back doors. He can beg coin. He don't have to throw his feet. He can beg coin enough to keep me in booze regularlike. He's a valyable prushun, that kid. Yuh can't buy him."

He fell to again on the food. He thrust a dripping meat-coated bone into his mouth. He sucked at the brown cells greedily with a clucking of licking lips. He gnawed the bone. He looked around like a huge mastiff, bone in mouth, greasy fingers upholding the ends, to view his property. The boy was bowed-head over his food.

"No, bo." He removed the bone and shook his great shaggy head. "I don't sell that kid, not for no money! I've had him for three years, that kid. He was twelve. He's kept me in grub and rum money for all that time. Three years I've spent a-trainin' of him to be a blowed-in-the-glass stiff. I'll make him that, like you and me, blowed-in-the-glass stiffs. He's not what yuh call attached to me. I'm a wicious man when drunk. But he knows enough, that kid. He knows enough to do what I say and hand me the coin.

"I learned him that, yuh see. One time it was comin' over the Hump under the headlight. It was cold under them snowsheds and black. That light overhead was without any heat. Its beam 'ud make yuh shiver. It was cold. The kid he was whimperin' like a sick dorg. You know the way. It got my goat—that and the cold and that light in all the dark. I told him I'd shove him off. I did bend him over the irons. I guess he never forgot that. Did yuh, Kid?"

"No, Red," said the boy without raising his eyes from the plate.

The man looked triumphantly around at his listeners, smudgy faces trembling red in the light of the fire.

"Three years ago that was. Three years I've spent a-trainin' of him to be a blowed-in-the-glass stiff. But he's still enough of a kid to be worth coin to me. Not fur five bones would I sell him. He's too valyable. No," he added, more to himself than to the tramps, "I won't sell him."

The boy was thin-wristed and slim. His face was pinched and very pale where it was not streaked with dirty scratches. His eyes were the blue of the gipsying Celt. They were pitifully deep-sunken.

He was a road-kid who begged at back doors and along public streets for the hobo who had appropriated him. There are many such road-kids. Their youth assures success at begging. Therefore they are of value. The hobo with a road-kid lives a life of ease. The kid is his drudge, his slave. It was that way with Frisco Red and the Kid. The Kid's appearance gave him power to attract sympathy. The burly hobo exploited that power. In return there were lessons in the tricks of the hobo trade. Also there were lessons in brutality. By sundry cuffs and kicks, the man made the boy's life almost unendurable. At regular intervals, there were thorough beatings.

Frisco Red had appropriated the Kid to his own use. Had he not, another hobo would have done so. Three times they had tried to steal the Kid. The boy had clung to him. Kicking, biting, screaming, the boy had clung to the red-headed, unlovely hobo. It was not attachment. He was afraid of the others. He was afraid of the road alone.

The Kid threw the bones and few left-over scraps of his meal upon the ground. He went over to Red to borrow from that borrower the makings of an after-dinner cigarette. He came back deftly rolling it.

In a sort of piteous delight, as it nuzzled the bones the boy had thrown away, the dog was making soft noises. It had been haunting the shadows since it had followed the two along the tracks and into the jungle. The Kid had turned his back. Thereat the smell of meat had lured it in.

The Kid ran toward the dog.

"Hello, pup," he said. "How are you, old hobo?"

The dog was a yellow dog. He was a mongrel. There was some strain of terrier in him that made him small. He backed away, growling. He would not trust the Kid. He was starving. Yet, as the Kid approached to pet and make friends with him, he left the meat and, growling, backed away.

"Aw, bo," the Kid pleaded; "let me pat you, will yer? What yer 'fraid of? I ain't no gay-cat that 'ud kick you after makin' friends. I'm a blowed-in-the-glass stiff, I am. Come on, old-timer. Let me pat yer. Aw, will yer?"

He leaned forward. His breath came in gasps. His hands went out. The partially rolled cigarette dropped from his fingers. The fingers moved in soft caresses. They were wasted on the air. But they were pitifully significant; they were significant of how the Kid would treat that dog.

On his pale dirty face was a peculiar expression. Rapture was in the deep-sunk eyes. In his eyes was the look some unmarried women have when they see a child.

"Tryin' to scare me, huh?" Step by step he advanced on the slowly backing dog, his body crouched, his hands patting the air with infinite tenderness. "You old gay-cat, you can't scare me. I'm a-goin' to make chums with you. You see. Aw, yer old gay-cat, what you 'fraid of?"

The dog turned tail. With the indescribable hunched back of a cur, yellow tail snuggling between his legs, the dog bolted in fear of him into the shadows.

The boy sat down on a tie. He fingered his ears.

"Aw," he said, "I wouldn't 'a' hurt him."

The dog was starving. From a different angle he stole into camp. He breathed with fear. The meat drew him on.

The boy did not look up. He did not know that the dog had come back. He had lost all faith in that dog. The dog would not trust him. The dog was not a blown-in-the-glass stiff. He was a cur. He was a gay-cat!

"Not a real gay-cat," qualified the Kid. "No, not a real gay-cat. It's mean treatment that's a-done it. He's horstile to everybody, even boes like me. He's a stiff, all right. But he's 'fraid like a gay-cat. That's all."

A gay-cat is the scorn of hoboes. He is a fake hobo. He lacks altogether the qualities of a blown-in-the-glass stiff. He will "peach" on his mates. He will turn against a friend when that friend is down to tomato cans. Anything and everything vile and despicable is worthy of a gay-cat. To call a man that is to brand him with the most loathed name a hobo knows. It is the quintessence of contempt.

The dog made the final whimpering plunge. Down on forepaws he went and burrowed his slant muzzle in the straw for the meat. He made soft sounds of self-pity and of joy. The while teeth and forepaws struggled over the bones, the tragic curl of tail, so used to snuggling his back in fright, wagged forlornly in a daze of happiness.

Neither the forlorn tail nor the squeals of joy did the boy see or hear. His elbows were on his rocking knees. His fingers rubbed slowly up and down, with the gentle unconscious motion, under the lobes of his ears. It was not often he thought of home. But now, while his boy's soul was possessed by an utterness of despair, he visualized the little cottage clearly. Whenever he thought of it, it was the same—always as it had been in the morning when the air was sweet and the marguerites near the picket fence had no dust on their whiteness.

It was up in Grass Valley. Before the damp had got him, his father had been a workman in the mines. His mother always gave setdowns to hoboes. Year after year, she did that. All the hoboes knew the white-faced little woman. "The lady in the shawl," they called her. Always she asked them, in return for her kindness, to look for her baby who was out there among all those lost boys and men.

For him every night she kept a lamp lighted—an oil lamp in the window. That was his room. A hundred road-kids had slept for a night within the pink-papered little cubby. They had told him.

But the Kid did not go back. He felt he never could go back. He knew when the train shrilled high up on the side of the valley and the sounds dropped down, he would go as he had gone before. He never could stay on. An urge was in him. That urge had drawn him out of the arms of his graying mother when he was twelve and after a circus train that had dipped into the little valley to extract its tribute of quarters and the irretrievable tribute of boys. That miserable urge kept him moving—moving to find peace. It was the *Wanderlust*. The *Wanderlust* held him in a crueller and more irrevocable slavery than did Frisco Red. For it, he endured Frisco Red. But the urge for always moving on was his real master. The accursed *Wanderlust*!

The dog sought beneath his feet for more scraps. But the Kid did not know. He remembered one morning when the train whistles came clear across the valley and there was no dust on the white marguerites. He had played that morning with a black-and-tan puppy beneath the smelly bushes near the picket fence. The puppy was the gift of a miner. The boy called it Prince. All the time it had struggled in his arms in an ecstasy of affection to lick his face. The round bundle of fat had made him laugh. He remembered he had rolled, shrieking with laughter, over on his back and the puppy had licked his face. He remembered exactly how it had licked his face.

He thought he imagined that wet kiss on his downheld cheek. It was as wet as real. A cold breath fanned the scratched cheek. The Kid's lack of movement had won the dog over. The mongrel that had fled from him was making friends. But it did cringe in a terribly abject way when the Kid leaped to his feet at the kiss.

"Yer not a gay-cat, are you?" he said exultantly. "You came back like a regular stiff. Now yer did!"

He reached down and quickly lifted up the dog, the while the frightened mongrel struggled and tried to bite. He sat down and began to pet to reassure the dog. Against his pinched white face he rubbed the cold muzzle. The dog whined piteously. Then the dog squatted down and, cocking its head to the movements of the petting hands, tried to lick them. The little brute whimpered softly. The whimpers came every now and then as if in an excess of gratitude. He climbed up on the boy. Just as the other dog had done he tried to lick the boy's face.

"Like Prince," the Kid glowed. "He tries to lick my face just like Prince." He put his cheek, in the restfulness of whole-souled affection, against the cold muzzle.

"What yuh got there, Kid?" asked a hobo, sprawling near.

"A dog. Can't yer see?"

Frisco Red looked around at the proud rejoinder. "A dorg? Wot yuh doin' with a dorg, Kid?"

"Aw, playin'. Jes' playin', Red. But ain't he some dog, though?"

The better to show off the mongrel, the Kid put him down upon his feet. Frisco Red returned, without another word or a second look at the dog, to his conversation with Pittsburgh Shorty and Cheyenne Joe. Dogs did not interest him at all, and his road-kid but little.

Some time later, Frisco Red spoke a short word. The Kid went out into the darkness to gather a few staggering armsful of wood. It was to keep the fire blazing through the night. He paid with toil for what he and his master had eaten; also for what the dog had eaten. That was a last thought. It made the boy stoop with a certain thrill of pleasure to the task. He ripped off planking from the floor of the derelict flat car. He trotted back and forth with the weighty armsful. All the while at his heels the dog sniffed.

The hoboes drew nearer the fire and curled up preparatory to going to sleep. The Kid drew up his tie. It was not so near the fire as theirs. He knew his place. He took off coat and vest. He placed the folded vest under him for a pillow. Loosely over him he cast the dirt-stiffened coat.

The dog wriggled and squirmed, pulled with his teeth and tossed with his head, until he had worked under the coat. Snuggling close for warmth, he lay on the Kid's chest. So they slept, the Kid and the dog. The lean, hairy body was held tightly in the boy's arms. Against his neck lay the warm-breathing muzzle. The Kid waked from time to time with the cold of the night. The dog whimpered each time and ran a wet tongue along the Kid's neck. Then the Kid smiled and hugged the dog the tighter.

The Kid awoke in the brisk of dawn. "Get out, you old Gay-cat," he mumbled to the hairy bundle of warmth on his chest. He called the dog a "gay-cat" and smiled—gay-cat, which means all that is despicable and loathed! It was a species of mock contempt. So a man calls his wife "old woman." It was to hide, in masculine fashion, the thrill in his voice of love.

The camp was heaving awake, like so many maggots in the dew. The hoboes crawled out of their floppings like dead souls awakened by some inexorable law in which they had no wish or say. They stood up and stretched grotesquely and shivered in the damp. Frisco Red stood up, raw of beard, ashen of face and seedy. He kicked into cowering life one who was old and who overslept.

"Get up, bo," he said, the before-breakfast husk in his voice. "Got to throw your feet if yuh want scoffin's."

He turned a gray face to the Kid.

"Kid," he said, "you'll have to batter for handouts this mornin'. I'll get my own scoffin's. Gee, I feel like I used to when I'd downed three cups. But you batter for handouts, Kid. The women are horstile to me. I look rough and raw. But you're sure to get 'em snivelin' over yuh, a pretty kid like you. We got to walk to the water tank this mornin' and we need handouts."

The boy started to leave the hangout. The Gay-cat stalked into life at his heels.

"Say, Kid," said Frisco Red, "can't have that dorg 'round. Lose him in the first back yard. Hear me, Kid?"

The boy turned back beseechingly.

"Aw, Red, can't I keep him? Can't I keep him, Red?"

"The first back yard, Kid. Get me? I don't want no pet dorgs for mine. How yuh goin' to batter back doors with him all the time snoopin' 'round at yer heels?"

"Aw, say now, Red, he ain't hurtin' yer none. He's only a dog—a hobo dog, Red. He won't a-hurt me beggin'."

Frisco Red looked into the deep-sunk eyes of the Kid.

"The first back yard," he said with monotonous insistence.

With shoulders hunched and head drooped miserably forward, the Kid led the way. There was the field of rusty brown car-wheels, two by two, forever two by two. Then it was up the rough embankment of gravel where the tracks shot on either way into the lift of distance. Beyond that, after they had mounted it, could be seen a gray flat of marshy land that lay far to a blue

suggestion of hills. Hunched of shoulder, shuffling-stepped, the black hulks
of the hoboes, at regular intervals along the embankment, punctuated the sky
like perverted question marks.

The Kid led the way. The dog ran by his side. His head drooped in
sympathy. Every now and then the Kid spoke.

"Aw, Red shouldn't be so mean," he would say. "What's eatin' Red? He
acts awful mean."

A side-tracked train of disreputably old boxcars bulked ahead. A man was
climbing down the ladder of the first bunk car as, with the dog at his heels,
the boy shuffled by. The dog barked at him as he leaped to the ground.

"That your dog, Kid?" he greeted.

The Kid halted. The other hoboes slumped spinelessly by toward town.

"You've said somethin', bo," he answered quite manfully. "Say, yer
couldn't stack us up to some eats, could yer, boss? Jes' the dog and me."

The look of the drooping dog and the pale, thin-wristed and wistful Kid
had its effect. It was a picture so boyish and forlorn. The Kid ate with the
foreman of the block-signal installation crew. And the Gay-cat ate also, out
of a tin plate of his own. The boss liked dogs. He placed, so he could watch
him, the dog and his tin plate upon the oilcloth-covered table.

Smoking a cigarette he had borrowed from the construction boss, the Kid
went back to the hangout. There, in that deserted field of rusted car-wheels
he tossed sticks for the Gay-cat to fetch. It was a trick the dog had learned
from some one in the past. Proudly he showed it off. All the time the Kid
swore in fond raillery at the dog. When the little brute drew near, he loved
him with petting and as often with gentle cuffs. It was a strengthening of
comradeship.

Frisco Red slouched into the jungle. He looked at the quieted dog. Then
he looked at the Kid. The Kid cowered. He put out his hand. In it was the
handout he had obtained for Red from the foreman.

Frisco Red squatted down on a tie and munched the cold meat and bread.
To the constant clicking of his jaws the burly hobo watched steadily the boy
and the dog. When the last mouthful was finished he wiped his fingers on
his stubbly lips. He drew from his overalls pocket the inevitable little white
muslin bag and sheaf of brown papers. These he fortunately had forgotten,
the night before, to return to their owner. He lighted the cigarette. He drew
deeply a few times. Then, half-consumed, he flipped the cigarette away. He
got up in his track-worn shoes.

"Goin' to keep the dorg, Kid?"

"Aw, Red," said the Kid with dry lips. "Aw, let me keep him, Red."

"I told yuh to lose him, didn't I? The first back yard it was, wasn't it?"

"I only went as far as the construction train, Red. Let me keep him, will
yer, Red? I didn't pass no back yards; honest, I didn't. Aw, Red!"

Frisco Red reached for the cowering Kid. He grasped him by the nape of the neck. He threw him on his face. He kicked him. He kicked more than once. He kicked viciously.

"The first back yard. Yuh was to ditch him. Yuh didn't."

The Kid sobbed from the straw and excelsior: "Don't, Red! Aw, Red!"

The dog snapped at that swinging foot. A well-directed kick caught him in the soft hanging part of the neck beneath the bristling ears. Over and over into the crackling litter the dog sprawled.

At last the Kid crawled out of it. He lay on his face behind a tie. By a roundabout path far from that booted foot the dog slunk to him. The dog licked his neck and exposed ear.

Frisco Red walked at a sharp stride toward the embankment. At the foot of the embankment, he slowed up. He came back.

"Kid," he said, "you ditch the dorg."

The huddle behind the tie did not answer. Only in a tumult of sobbing it shook all over.

Frisco Red drew out papers and tobacco. Rolling a cigarette he moved away.

Two hours later, one of a reeling lot of hoboes, he reappeared. All were more or less drunk with cheap whiskey. In Sacramento, in an alley behind the Capitol Bar, they had "rolled" a drunken rancher for his pocketbook.

The Gay-cat crouched in fear, at sight of Red, behind the Kid's legs. He whimpered softly in tense nervousness. Frisco Red stood absurdly hesitant on legs askew. He paid no attention to the Kid. He did not see the dog.

There was a consultation among the unsteady men. Then the grotesque squad moved forward. They moved forward in what appeared an exaggeration of their peculiar hobo shuffle. Dully, with heads lolling on necks, they followed the tracks away from town; the while, as occasional accompaniment, they bawled obscene songs or the hymns learned in some slum mission where he that would sing might eat.

The endless punctuation of ties led on and on until even the marshes rose and became level with the tracks and were prairie land. Here, behind a barbed-wire fence and beneath soughing eucalyptus trees, a weather-worn farmhouse stood. About the foundations of the farmhouse was a flurry of chickens. But there was no other sign of life.

Along the line of wire fence, the water tank upreared on its stilts. Frisco Red and the litter of tramps lay down upon their backs and drowsed in the shade of it. A little apart sat the Kid, the dog between his knees.

It was stinging noontide. The sunlight pelted down upon the drab eucalypti and the drabber men. Everything was silent and dead with heat as high noon of an Indian summer Sunday.

"I'm hungry," said one youngish hobo some time later. "I'd like ter throw my feet at thet house. I'd batter it myself only—only it's horstile."

All knew it was hostile. On the water tank was plainly written that it was hostile. Beside the monikers, or road names, of a hundred hoboes were scratched such messages as: "Beware of dog." "Farmer has gun." "Farmhouse horstile." The messages were of a nature to cause the boldest of the hoboes to hesitate ere begging at that particular farmer's door.

Frisco Red got up. He drank for long minutes the drippings of the water tank. Then he went over to the trough that was an adjunct of the tank. He dowsed his head at the uncovered end. He came back. The hair, red and sodden, was dripping into his eyes. "Gee, that stuff had a kick to it!" he said. "I'm burnin' up. Burnin' up and hungry."

The dog escaped, at sight of Red, from between the Kid's knees. Backing away into the sunlight, he barked once in fear of the dripping red hair of the man. Frisco Red stared at the dog. A stupid expression of surprise marked itself on his hair-streaked face.

"You here?" he asked the air. "Where's the dorg?"

He looked around, his head moving stiffly on his neck. The Kid shrank into the sunlight. Circuitously he made toward the burly hobo.

"Aw, let me keep him, Red," he whined.

That dull apathetic surprise in his eyes, the hobo looked at the boy. He looked at him for a long time. Slowly, as he looked, his eyes narrowed into a certain squint of craftiness.

"The whole push is hungry, Kid," he said. "I'm hungry."

"Yes, Red," said the Kid submissively. His body fell into the conventional hobo slouch. Shoulders hunched, head lowered toward the ruts in the road, he followed in the shade of the trees the line of the fence. He turned back a short space on and whistled for the dog. The Gay-cat trotted out with spirit at that call and commenced the inevitable dogging of his steps.

"Kid!" called Frisco Red, "better leave the dorg behind. You can't batter that horstile house with him along."

The Kid kept steadily on. He was suspicious.

"Aw, let him come along, Red," he flung over his shoulder.

"Send the dorg back, Kid," said Frisco Red. "Better send him back."

The Kid gave in to that monotonous repetition of command. He shooed the dog back toward the water tank. Dejectedly, tail snuggling between his legs, the dog walked slowly into the shadows of the tank and stretched out, with only now and then a questioning look after the Kid.

The Kid climbed over the one-hinged, wire-secured gate. He approached the front door of the sundozing farmhouse. He knocked and repeated the knock. The door was opened by an asthmatic and worn old woman.

"Such as I have I'll be givin' you with the help of God," she said in a remote way. She invited him into the stifling shadows of the kitchen.

When he came out he carried what the gasping old woman had given him for the other tramps—eight egg sandwiches. He himself in the shadowy kitchen had eaten his fill. An anxious frown knuckled his forehead as he came back. His eye was agile for sight of the dog. He handed the sandwiches to Red and the others.

"The little Gay-cat, where is he gone to?" he asked, his breath coming short and hard as though he were the gasping woman. "My dog? He was here a little while ago."

A great to-do of struggle in the trough made him look past the munching Red. The trough was partitioned into halves. One half was open. The other was covered by a stout board. Under the board Frisco Red had shoved the dog. He had slammed the board tight. There was no chance at all for the dog to climb out. Paddling desperately in the water, with that board but a few inches above its head—scant inches of air and life—the dog was struggling for life. It sobbed passionately. As the Kid looked toward the trough the sobbings rose into a long, echoing whine.

The Kid's pale dirty face was much paler than usual and by contrast much dirtier. "Aw, Red!" he sobbed.

He ran toward the trough! His dog! Quite unconsciously, as he ran, he pulled up his sleeve for the plunge. The whine died away in a choked sob.

"That's all right, old feller. I'll—I'll—"

Frisco Red sidled out of the shadows between him and the trough.

"I ditched the dorg, Kid," he said hoarsely. "Now you leave him there. You're not goin' agin me in this. Myself, I'm horstile to him from first sight. The first back yard it was, Kid. The first back yard and yuh didn't."

The burly hobo spread his legs. In the old known gesture, he reached out his hand for the Kid's collar. The Kid tried to slip past him for the trough, but Red got his grip. By the collar, as the Kid squirmed, the hobo swung him around into his arms.

"The first back yard, Kid!" he muttered.

A certain pride was in his voice. It broke in a scream of pain. Red dropped his hold of the Kid. Frantically he pushed him away. All the while, as he did, he screamed as with pain unendurable.

The Kid had bitten his arm. The Kid had clawed with long fingernails across his temples. The blood was burning into his eyes. The hobo backed away. He screamed with pain. He screamed with fury. He pulled from beneath his overalls apron his miserable weapon. Brushing the blood from his eyes Frisco Red groped forward for the Kid.

Quivering, ghastly white, his eyes aglare with an intensity of outraged feelings, the Kid crouched. To his ears came the shrill wails of his dog. Frisco Red groped toward him. In the hobo's hand was the razor doubled up against the crotch of thumb and forefinger in the regulation hobo manner. It was a glistening, terrible thing. But the Kid did not shrink away. The wail

of his dog shrilled on his ears. He was in a madness of revolt. He had bitten
Frisco Red's arm. He had scratched Frisco Red's temples. He had aroused
in Frisco Red an anger that lusted for blood. The Kid did not shrink away.
It would do no good. He had drawn blood. In blood he would have to pay.
Always that has been primitive law.

The half-blinded hobo came on. The Kid sprang in. As he sprang, he
caught that razor-wielding wrist. He turned that wrist. He was half-crazed
with a madness of revolt and with fear of that vicious weapon. With strength
born of his desperation he turned and turned Red's wrist.

Frisco Red was blinded by blood trickles. To the core of his being he was
shocked by the Kid's frenzy of fighting. It was a thing utterly unlooked for.
It was an appalling thing to him. It overwhelmed him. The razor fell from
his wrenched wrist.

It fell into the gray-yellow dust. In a trice it was stamped out of sight. It was
stamped under the feet of the Kid. Upon the blood-blinded and bewildered
hobo, at his bloated stubbly face, the Kid leaped. He shrilled curses. He beat
upon that face. He scratched. It was a frenzy of fighting.

It was the fight of a wolf and a wounded moose. With the tireless pursuits of
his slavery the Kid was strong and healthy. It was a wiry strength, an emaciated
healthiness, like that of a lean-flanked wolf. His tissues were not wasted by
cheap whiskey. He had all that makes for the courage to fight fairly; but his
education had run in different channels. He had seen men fight, kicking and
clawing and shrieking like depraved souls. Always they had been in liquor.
Always the fight had been vicious. It was only for him, in the madness of
revolt, to fight as he had been taught. He could not take any chances.

The Kid was on the hobo's neck. Like a wolf dragging down a moose
he hung to that neck. Beating and scratching, shrilling curses the while, he
worked around. He never released his hold on that neck. He jumped upon
the hobo's back.

It was the dreaded "strong-arm" that is the road-kid's standby. Thus
upon a man's back, forearms entwined about his neck, a puny boy can exert
enough leverage to curl that man, gasping, upon his back. It was that way
with the Kid. His thin bony wrists were knotted about the hobo's throat. He
pulled back on them. Frisco Red, as he cursed, swallowed hard for breath.
He struggled to heave the Kid off. The Kid pressed his right knee against the
joints of the man's backbone at the small of the back. Red shrieked terribly.
His back gave. It gave like a fish spine. Drawing for breath, on his back in
the dust, he collapsed.

The Kid was on his feet. He was sobbing. The madness of revolt was still
on him. He must knock out Frisco Red. It was the law of the road. Ere he
could save his dog he must prove his right thereto—his right to run his own
game. The Kid had learned from Frisco Red to be cruel and brutal. Cruelty

and brutality are the gods of the pagan road. Frisco Red was supine—flat on his back in the dust. With his foot the Kid applied two finishing blows. They were cruelly placed. They were brutally given.

It had all occurred in a shock of time. The Kid looked down at the still heap on the ground. Then the Kid looked full at the many eyes in the shadow. He had beaten Frisco Red. Viciously, in brutal fashion, he had beaten his master. That brutality was the fault of his education. But that brutality was effective with the many eyes in the shadow. He was free to run his own game, to work his own will, to do as he pleased.

The wail of the dog shrilled on his ear. He stepped over the body of Frisco Red. Precipitantly, breathing hard from the fight, he ran to the trough.

"Come out, old-timer," he called. "You're in a deuce of a fix, aren't you?"

His voice was, for all its gasping, strangely pliant and tender. He jerked up the board cover. By one of the frantic forepaws, he lifted out the drowning Gay-cat. He hugged the whimpering, wet, shaking form to him. He laughed once, hysterically.

"You little drownded rat," he whispered. "You should have seen how I beat up Frisco Red."

The dog whimpered and snuggled close.

Hugging the dog in his left arm, the Kid came back. He felt around with his right hand until he found the razor. That he examined with great pride. He doubled it up against the crotch of thumb and forefinger and, like a regular blown-in-the-glass stiff, slashed about with it in the air. Then very carefully he tucked it away in an overalls pocket.

Silently he joined the hoboes asprawl beneath the tank. They had no word for him; but they made space for him—for him and for his dog. It is the way of the road. As soon as a road-kid is strong enough to beat his master the domination of that hobo ends. Age makes no difference. It is the primeval law of strength. The kid becomes a masterless road-kid, a younger hobo. The Kid had beaten Frisco Red. Impossible it was for him longer to serve that hobo. He was free. He was free to wander wherever the *Wanderlust* called. He and his dog were free. That thought made freedom sweet. He was for at once being off along gipsying roads where Red would be forgotten and the dog could chase sparrows through the fallen leaves.

"Give me a smoke," he said to the hoboes.

In his voice was the note of equality. In the silence of equality they gave it him. The Kid rolled the brown-paper tube. The Southbound whistled far up the track. He lighted the cigarette. The rumble of the approaching train shook through the ground. The Kid got afoot. Walking to the trough, the Gay-cat at his heels, he filled his cap with water. He dowsed it on Frisco Red.

"Get up, bo," he said, the gruffness of manhood in his voice. "Can't yer hear the train?"

Frisco Red opened his eyes. The Kid turned and walked away. Dazedly Red rolled over and felt in the dust for the razor. But the Kid did not notice the futile search. The hoboes had spread out. The train was slowing at the tank. The Kid lifted the dog in his arms.

At ten o'clock that night at a way-station the Kid was ditched. The bark of the startled dog at sight of a brakeman was the cause. The Kid with the dog had been riding all alone on the bumpers between two freight cars. The others were not discovered. The Kid stood on the tracks, the dog in his arms, as the train foreshortened into the night.

"Good-by, Frisco Red," said the Kid soberly. Then his head lowered to the dog's drooping ear and he whispered:

"It was for you I done it, Gay-cat, old-timer. Honest, it was for you I done it."

"Always movin', always movin' on," the Kid would say to the dog. "Gay-cat, when we gets tired of bein' boes we'll go back to the valley and surprise my ma. But I guess"—with a wistful smile—"you and me'll never get tired of bein' hoboes. We're blowed-in-the-glass stiffs, we are, and it's in our blood."

The Kid was, when he said that, an older boy by a full year. Also his love for the Gay-cat had made him thoughtful. Sometimes on dewy mornings he saw, more clearly than the road he walked, the cottage up in Grass Valley. The marguerites near the picket fence were white and fresh. It was sweet where he was born. Sometimes he wished he could go back. But there was that itch in his boy's soul that kept him wandering—wandering to find peace.

And the dog understood. It was wonderful. The dog understood why he could not go back. The dog, too, was cursed with the *Wanderlust*. The dog whimpered in sympathy up into his face. Then onward into the dawn the dog led the way.

They came back over the Hump for the fall and winter in California. The freight from Ogden was headed for Sacramento, the great dumping-off place of the wintering hobo. It was here near Sacramento, just a year gone, that the Kid had found the Gay-cat and that he had beaten Frisco Red. It was near Sacramento, up in Grass Valley, where were his mother, graying in her shawl, and the cottage with the picket fence and marguerites. Perhaps that was why, while the Kid still wandered, he wandered close.

They rolled in that train of flat cars through the Sacramento Valley, golden with autumn, until Sacramento neared. The train slowed down. The Kid swung off. He feared the railroad police in the terminal yards. The train clacked onward in a cloud of hot dust as he stood to one side, the dog in his left arm. He set the dog afoot, and the dog led the way up the levee for a look at the river where so often they had gone swimming.

In a flushed sky slowly the sun sank. It dropped behind the black feathers of tule on the other levee. The levee dimmed and grew remote. A sternwheeler from San Francisco coughed upstream. Its whistle sounded, through the screen of dusk, weary and lonesome. The swell from its paddles broke in tiny ripples at their feet as the steamboat rounded a bend in the river and was gone with the day.

Thoughtfully the Kid and the Gay-cat turned their backs on the darkened river. They walked down the slope. The Gay-cat barked. He dashed, with a sudden show of spirit, across the tracks and into a little faded road hidden in the mystery of twilight.

The Kid followed his brave lead. The lane was pungent with fruity odors. It wound between green curtains of hop vines, softly stirring in the breezes of the evening. A strange peace was on the Kid. Something about the lane, lost in the thick of twilight, the smells and random breezes filled his soul with a gipsy content. That gipsy content it was that made his wanderings with the Gay-cat sweet. And so they came to a white wooden gate beyond which, on the black flat of a patch, melons lay cut and tempting, splotches of gold and green.

"Cantaloupes," said the Kid. "Cantaloupes would go good now. Wet and cool after that ride, huh—Gay-cat?"

The Kid clambered over the creaking gate. The dog bellied under the gate. They were inside when, in the gray house that squatted down in the field, a door was flung open and voices came from the lighted doorway in the uncouth vocables of the Japanese tongue. The Kid crouched. The dog barked sharply. The Kid pulled the dog off his feet and quieted him.

The door slammed shut. The house slept grayly. Sniffing the air for danger, the Gay-cat trotted out on the black loam of the patch.

"Come here, Gay-cat," the Kid whispered. "Keep close to me and don't think you own this here patch. Them Japs don't invite boes in here to mooch melons. They sleep in the fields sometimes with guns."

The Kid made short dashes between the muskmelons to see how ready for eating each was. Some were green. Others were overripe. One, cut from the trailing vine and leaves, was a golden temptation. He lifted that. It was quite heavy.

The dog scuffled ahead. The Kid, ready for retreat, called softly. The dog answered in a yelp of fright. Abruptly the dog came back. He came back as if shoved by some invisible hand on his quarters.

To see what was the matter the Kid moved forward. The dog was whimpering nervously at his heels when he came full upon the Japanese laborer asleep on a mat among the vines and leaves, his brown, shiny, stupid face upturned. The Kid stepped back in fright just as the dog had done. His heel caught in a melon vine. The vine tripped him. His arms flung behind to ease the fall. The muskmelon bounded from his flinging arms and rolled against the laborer.

The laborer leaped afoot. His arms were upraised before his face in an almost articulate gesture of bewilderment. The Kid leaped afoot. Thereat the laborer, seeing what had awakened him, screamed shrilly in Japanese. He gave chase. He showed in his hands a long-handled shovel.

"Gay-cat!" yelled the Kid. "Oh, Gay-cat! Come here!"

But the dog did not run for the gate at the heels of the Kid. He dashed, barking and snapping, toward the oncoming laborer. The laborer cried out. He cried out in what appeared to be genuine fear of the dog. Full on the head of the rushing, snapping dog he brought down the sharp metal edge of the shovel.

The defiant barking of the dog rose into a shrill yelp of pain that was almost a scream. A second yelp followed on the heels of the first. Then another, and another. The yelps were continual and hurried.

The Kid ran back. Unconscious of all personal danger he ran back to the yelping dog. He had no eyes for the Japanese laborer. He saw only his dog, bleeding from a red gash in the head and staggering, as he yelped, on bending legs. He scooped the bleeding Gay-cat up into his arms. White and cold and blind with grief, he rushed past the bewildered laborer. He floundered through the soft field to the gate. He sobbed love words. The yelps of the little Gay-cat dropped to whimpers, slow and dull as moans.

The Kid walked in a miserable dream. He was stupefied by his despair. On the outskirts of Sacramento he stumbled into a drugstore. At sight of his anguish-filled eyes and the bleeding dog the druggist was won over to mercy. With a gauze bandage he bound up the gash in the Gay-cat's head between the drooping ears.

The pain of the dog was somewhat soothed. The Kid staggered on through the railroad yards, through the city and along the road to where, in a grass-disheveled field, a haystack bulked. The wretched search was ended. In the hay he would find some soft nest wherein to lay the wounded Gay-cat.

All that night in the haystack the Kid watched and worried over the whimpering dog. He was a boy alone in a waste where sympathy was not. Yet out of those barrens of brutality had come to him a great love. And that love was stricken, sick with pain. Through that long night, as the dog whimpered continually in dull agony and the moonlight silvered down, the Kid accused himself:

"It's all my fault that you're half dead, Gay-cat, all my fault. Cantaloupes! I couldn't do my own moochin' for cantaloupes! And look at the other risks I let yer take. I let yer ride where you could be killed. You could fall off the rods. You could slide from the roof. A piece of coal thrown from the cab could mash yer. You, the only one that loved me, and I let yer hobo with me like that for all these months and days and days."

The dog licked his face. That only made him the more miserable. He wanted to ask forgiveness of the dog. And the dog reached up and licked his face. It was terrible, such love. He would prove himself worthy of that love!

"Hoboin' is no place for to keep a dog!" he told the dawn. "Jes' supposin' he was killed!"

His white face was set with lines deeper than ever had been the dirt scratches. He lifted up the bandaged head of the whimpering little brute.

"Gay-cat, we'll square it!" he said fiercely. "It'll be hard for you. It will be hard for me. But it's got to be done. This night has give me a lesson. Right now it's got to be done. This mornin' I gets a job, see? I gets a job. We'll square it, Gay-cat, old-timer. You and me, we'll square it."

That was an appalling step, but after the tragic happening of the night it had to come. The Kid took that step without quiver of lip. He would prove himself worthy of the dog's love. He would cease to be a hobo. He would fight the lust for moving on. He would settle down in one place. In one place—that was the appalling thing.

The Kid slid down out of the stack in the early morning to beg food for the hungry dog. He had little choice. There was the camp beyond the fence of the field where ate the workmen who were macadamizing, for the county, the road into town. There was the shanty of a farmhouse. The Kid looked at the house.

The house was two-storied, clapboarded and drab. It stood sullenly alone in the grass-disheveled field. On the second floor were two windows, opaque with dirt. Yet some one lived in that house. As the Kid looked a wisp of smoke lifted out of its roof. It was a pathetic wisp of smoke, like the draggled exhalation of an old hobo's last cigarette. All that night no lights had showed in the house. The wisp of smoke was the only sign of a life within.

The Kid decided. The miserable aspect of the house made that decision. Its occupant or occupants would be as miserable. Were the Kid to approach that house it would be discovered that he was living in the haystack and he would be routed out. There was no better nest, no softer flopping for the wounded Gay-cat than that hollow in the hay.

The Kid begged food from the camp cook. He fed in pinches most of the bread and meat to the dog. In a battered tomato can, sunk in the hay, he left a supply of water. He pressed the warm muzzle of the dog to his cheek. Then he went into Sacramento to make, along K Street, his last clean-up of dimes.

With a load of groceries and a singing heart he reappeared at noon. He had landed a job. A man from whom he had begged a nickel had offered him work. It was in a cracker factory, piling empty boxes at the bottom of an endless hoist. It was treadmill work, but it was an anchor to hold him fast.

The while he fed the dog the Kid talked happily, but there was no hiding the sacrifice. It was a sacrifice. Day in, day out for a full year the dog never had been out of eyesight of the Kid. And now the Kid was going to leave him for the greater part of the day. It was a terrible sacrifice. But they were squaring it. That meant sacrifice.

As the Kid left in the damp earliness of morning the dog whimpered miserably. The Kid, as he tore himself away, muffled his ears with his hands. He worked manfully; but his thoughts were not with the empty cracker boxes. They were out in the sun-scorched haystack with the dog. He knew it was lonely for the dog. His own life, while he was away, seemed desolate. Through the dragging hours he heard, as he bent over the boxes, the whimpers of the lonesome Gay-cat. He even remembered how the love-mad dog had licked his hands, his face, and forlornly wagged its tail when he had hurried back at noon to the farm.

They lay, that night of the first day's work, side by side in the haystack. Over their heads the stars breathed.

"I know it's lonely, Gay-cat," said the Kid. "It's lonely for me as well as for you. But yer got to bear it. I got to bear it, Gay-cat. I hates the smell of crackers. The piles of boxes jes' bear me down. And I hates to think of you so lonesome. Perhaps if we went home, Gay-cat, if we went up the valley to my ma it might be easier. She could take care of you and love you for me. It would not be so lonesome for you while I was away at work, and we would love her so much we could square it. There would be no longin' to be hoboin' it again. We'd never want to leave her no more."

The dog lifted up his bandaged head and licked the Kid's face for all the world as though he understood and sympathized.

The Kid fell into a period of uneasy slumber. Rose, against the lids of his eyes, a bush of white marguerites, clean of dust and sparkling with dew. Behind it shaped the cottage and on the doorsill a pale little shawled woman. He could see the dimmed plaid of the shawl about her thin shoulders. Her pale face was that near and distinct he could see the blackness of her once brown eyes. She looked over the marguerites along the road. She called. She called his name. Then she faded from sight. The white marguerites faded.

The Kid looked up at the breathing stars. The air was thick with odors. It seemed to quiver with his name. That call of his mother seemed, in all reality, to be quivering through the heavy air. He sat up in the crackling hay. The dog stirred. The Kid sat thoughtfully still. Deep in his brains that call stirred poignant memories.

"She must be a-callin' me up there in the valley," he said, "a-callin' me all these years."

The dog grew strong enough to play feebly about the top of the haystack. Forever he was sliding down the slopes of the hay to the ground. Often, at noon or night, the Kid found the dog nesting in some nook at the base of the stack. Because of that the Kid grew afraid. He was afraid lest, in this way, their presence would become known to the inmate or inmates of the house and the Gay-cat mistreated while he was away.

But there was another thing that worried the Kid. The Gay-cat was growing indifferent to the Kid's leavetakings. True, he still tried in forlorn attempts to follow the Kid, but why did he not whimper at the partings? The Kid brooded over the case. The dog's indifference was quite natural. The dog was growing used to being left alone. The Kid should have foreseen it. Yet to see it now pained the Kid.

One still noon as he hurried, in a cloud of self-raised dust, up the road and under the fence, no Gay-cat ran from the haystack to jump on him and lick his hands. The Kid went to the stack. He whistled. No wise old head shoved above the ragged edge of the hay. No four-legged streak of yellow flashed out from some nook in its base. The farm was steeped in noontide sun. There was not so much as a rustle from the hay. The Kid was alone.

"Where is he?" he asked himself. "The little Gay-cat! He's a-foolin' me to make me skeered."

Under the gray of dust his face was white. He searched the field. He looked along the road. There was no sign of the Gay-cat. He whistled. He called. He was in a panic of dread. Despite his fear of the occupants of the house he called and called in loud shouts. Nor dog nor answer of any kind came to him.

That which was broad noon closed like night, black and elemental, about the Kid. He stood in the dead field stooped to an unutterable despair. From his heart, weakening him like the loss of blood, something was running out. And he could not cry. For all his loss and his despair he could not cry.

Some time later, with hard eyes, he advanced on that old derelict of a farmhouse.

"Maybe," he choked—"maybe he's in there."

The door, lacking knob and lower panel, opened to his touch. He reeled into shadows. The place was thick with dust and dirt. A musty smell hung heavy in the air. There was no living thing on that whole lower floor, excepting some horseflies that thrummed back and forth through the dusty dark.

Up one wall from the entrance tottered a rickety staircase, thick with dust and sanded white near the wall with fallen plaster. The Kid went up. At the top he moved across a creaking flooring in a room where the sun fought through a dirt-coated window to light a bed and a bureau.

Upon the bureau were a tin plate of food, a cup and a prayer-book. A woman lay upon the bed. She was fully dressed in the workworn clothes of a woman that struggled on her feet until the last insufferable pang. Her hair fell disheveled and white about her unbonneted head. She lay, eyes closed, on the edge of the bed. One hand hung limply over the side of the bed, and snuggling and licking that hand was the Gay-cat.

The dog, at the creaking sounds of the flooring, turned from licking the hand. He saw the Kid. He did not leap up and upon the Kid. He turned back to licking that hand.

The old woman did not move. The Kid leaned over her. Her eyes opened, but she did not see him. She was looking up at that window as though to pierce its dirt-thick panes and see into the day.

"Ralphie," said she. "Oh, darlin'!"

Her voice was plaintive with longing. With sudden strength she lifted herself up from the pillow. On her old worn face was the radiance of love.

It faded suddenly as it came. Her strength ebbed. She fell back upon the bed. The dog at her side whimpered.

"Mamma!" cried the Kid. "Oh, ma; don't you know me? It's Ralphie that's askin' you—Ralphie."

She saw with eyes undimmed by sickness, by years and by worry. She saw with a brain unclouded by sorrow. Her love saw. And in an indescribable voice she cried out:

"My boy! Ralphie!" It's prayin'—prayin' on my worn old knees that brought you. Four years and me prayin' all alone. Oh, my boy!"

There was everything in her voice. Sorrow suffered, and age, and joy transcendent.

Until she could stand no longer the loneliness and the longing she had lived in the little cottage up in Grass Valley, where the marguerites were fresh and white. She had fed hoboes, and as she rocked in her misery before the fire they had given her advice. They had told her to go to Sacramento. That city was the clearing-house of all the hoboes. Soon or later he would come there, they had said.

For a small sum she sold the place in the valley. She came down to the city. She was pitifully wrought up for the meeting; but he did not come. She waited and slowly spent her money. She became penniless and then, with lack of nutritious food, sick. Sick of workworn body and sick of living, all alone she crept to the ramshackle farmhouse to die.

So she cried and yearned and faded. He did not come. Only came a little yellow dog to lick her hands. It was the Gay-cat. He came every day. She told the dog of her lost boy, and he seemed to understand. In pity he licked her hands. She called that dog Prince.

And now her boy had come!

The Kid put his tousled boy's head on the pillow beside her. She touched and kissed his hair. The Kid wept as she crooned over him.

"It was the Gay-cat," he gulped to himself. "It was the Gay-cat that done it. The little old hobo Gay-cat brought me here to her."

The Kid went to work in the sunny, pungent hopfields behind the levee below town. He had lost, on account of his absence, the job in the cracker factory.

Bare of foot and happy he picked hops. At noon, his old mother brought him his lunch. She sat in the shadow of the vines and watched the boy—her boy—eat. She picked a few hops for his basket. She picked, as much as he would let her. Then she went softly into the peace of the afternoon.

The Gay-cat was growing stronger and friskier. Of afternoons she left the Gay-cat with the Kid. The Kid would weigh in his hops at four o'clock. Then it was over the levee with the dog, to take in the mellowness, a swim in the river.

Thus each day the road called. The sunset lured. The tracks had in them some magnetic pull.

The day was mellow and golden. Again were they fresh and tingling from the swim. The dog was wet and draggle-haired. He was eager. He leaped upon the ties. The Kid fell into the slouching stride, shoulders hunched, head lowered. The dog whined with happiness. Down the tracks he followed the Kid. He was eager. Down the tracks he followed the Kid toward the glow of sunset.

The Kid drew up. Pale with the effort of it he drew up. He turned slowly around. The Gay-cat whimpered. He kept on. The Kid stood still. He watched. His face was drawn. He whistled. The dog looked back. The dog barked once shortly. The lust surged up in the Kid. The world reeled—the world of glistening tracks and glowing, beckoning sunset. He bit his lip. That held him from taking the first step—that first step that would give momentum and send him onward all his days!

The Gay-cat went on. His head was lowered to the ties. His tail was a-droop. There was in that drooping tail something that appalled the Kid. He stood aghast. After a time he called:

"Gay-cat! It's for her!"

The dog halted. All that time he had been going on. He sat up. Over a wet, hairy shoulder he sent back one look of utter misery. He dropped down. Alone and drooped to the long walk the dog swung on into the sunset.

Flat on his face on the grassy bank the Kid threw himself. He raged against fate. He cried hotly. He was to cry for love and longing of that dog later in his mother's arms. But just then, as he cried, in his voice was all the contempt of those that resist temptation for those that fall:

"The Gay-cat!"

For the first time he said the word as a blown-in-the-glass stiff should say that word.

Stories of Life, Love and

15¢

Adventure

JULY
1916

"BEYOND
THE RIM"
*A Complete Novel
of the South Seas
by J. Allan Dunn*

"TO CRACK
A SAFE"
*A Tale of
California
by Patrick
Terence Casey*

Stories by
H. S. Fullerton
F. W. Wallace
Robt. V. Carr
Henry Oyen
Thos. Addison
H. Liebe
Geo. L. Catton
W. C. Tuttle
D. L. MacKaye
and Others

TO CRACK A SAFE
by Terence and Patrick Casey

UNDER A CROWD OF STARS IN THE WIDE AND SILENT NIGHT, the Kid came along the road where the road dipped down into a little valley. He was hungry. That day, for many weary miles, he had walked without a setdown, without a handout, without a chow of any kind. His peaked, pale face was turned not to the crowd of stars, but to the ruts in the road.

He wore a coat that was many sizes too large for him. It had been made for a man. About his slight boy's form, that coat hung so loosely that he looked in the shadowy night like a shriveled-up old man.

But the coat did not hang loosely on the left side. On the left side the coat bulged out oddly. It was as if he had shoved a considerable bundle beneath that coat on the left side. And it was a bundle that moved restlessly at times. At these times, about the bundle, the Kid tightened the clasp of one long-sleeved arm. At the last time, he said:

"Don't git res'less, old feller. There's no use yer sniffin' like yer never et fer a week, and whimperin', and wishin' yer had some eats. It's no use, old-timer. You jes' gotta make up yer mind you git no supper tonight—not even a handout. Tonight, Gay-cat, you and me eats wind-puddin', and you jes' make up yer mind to that fac' and be satisfied."

There was a little yellow dog beneath the boy's coat. As the boy spoke, the dog stuck his sharp yellow nose out of the top of the coat. In his throat he whimpered hungrily, piteously.

"Aw, say now, Gay-cat! Be a sport and quit yer grumblin', will yer? I never et, either, did I? And yer don't hear me complainin'. I'm tryin' to be a good hobo, I am, and eat my wind-puddin' when I'se got ter, see? And it'll soon be dawn, bo. You stay in there, Gay-cat, and jes' wait. It'll soon be dawn and we can strike a farmhouse fer some eats."

But the dog only shoved his yellow and wise old head altogether out of the top of the coat. Nervously he cocked his ragged ears. Of a sudden, he squirmed quickly out over the hugging arm and, dropping to the road, stood tense and excited, barking toward the shadowy slope to one side.

"Sh, Gay-cat!"

The dog quieted with a growl. The Kid listened fearfully. He heard a cavernous yawn as if from some one who slept by the road—some one who had been awakened rudely by the dog's barking.

From out of the echoing night, in a man's gruff voice, came a low guarded call:

"Ho, bo! Ho, bo!"

It was the tramp call. It told what the speaker was and asked if the Kid were a brother.

"Hello, bo," the Kid answered, no longer fearful. "What yer got there?"

"Floppin's fur the night," answered the gruff voice.

"Floppin's, huh? Then I guess we'll pound our ear, too, Gay-cat and me." The Kid left the road, the dog tagging wearily at his heels. "I was jes' snoopin' by when my dog smelled yer sleepin' here."

"Yuh got a dorg? I oughta knowed it was him barkin' what woke me up."

"Sure," the Kid answered proudly. "And he's some dog, too. He smelled yer sleepin', old-timer. He can smell a hobo a mile!"

Making blindly across the slope, the Kid stumbled on to the edge of a gully. The gully was deep between two little knolls of the slope and was soft with a thick tangle of dry grass. Below in the hollow he could see the dark, outstretched figure of a big, heavy man.

The man lay, in a position of complete ease, on his broad back, his arms flung up above his head. His face was in shadow.

The dog sniffed at his legs.

"Them's nuthin' to eat, Gay-cat, old hobo," said the Kid. And he tried to chuckle.

"Gay-cat's some hungry, bo," he explained. "We'se both hungry, Gay-cat and me. We ain't et since mornin'. It's been one horstile town after t'other, bo. Them hayseed bulls has been as thick as the fleas on Gay-cat hisself this day. We'se had tough hobo luck, that's what, old-timer. Every Johnny Tinplate has made us beat it out o' them towns without us even moochin' a measly handout. Say, yer don't happen to have a handout on yer, do yer, pal?"

"What d'yuh think I am, kid," growled the man, "a walkin' free-lunch counter? I ain't et myself tonight. I'm only waitin' fur dawn to breeze down into thet town in the walley and show good kale fur a meal—I'm thet empty inside!"

He grunted sourly, and continued:

"Hobo luck, nuthin'! Yuh hoboin' shif'less, thet's what. What you need, kid, is to have a couple o' dollars in yer jeans. Git some coin, and then when yuh hit a horstile burg yuh can drill right by them hayseed coppers and buy a square, and them coppers can't say a word. Take thet from me, kid, and yuh won't be shooed out o' no towns no more. Git a road stake."

The Kid sat down beside the supine man, the dog in his lap.

"Mebbe yer is right, old-timer; but that don't buy me nuthin' now. I feel all holler inside. But mebbe a smoke 'ud fix me up, though. Yer hasn't the makin's on yer, has yer?"

"Nope. But d'yuh chaw terbacker? A good chaw o' terbacker 'ud be jest the thing to wet up yer mouth, kid."

"Do I chaw terbacker? Aw, say, bo!"

The man did not move from that position on the flat of his back. Only he fumbled in his trouser pocket and drew out a ragged oblong of chewing tobacco. He held up one end in his hand, while the Kid leaned over and from the other end bit off a mouthful.

While the Kid leaned over, the man said less gruffly—

"Say, yuh haven't met up along the road with a stiff name o' Swaggerin' Bob?"

"Swaggerin' Bob? No, I ain't never met that bo."

"Bo!" the man snorted. "Bob ain't no bo. He's none o' yer bindle stiffs, or back-door moochers. He's a sorter strong-arm stiff and horstile to everybody. Him, he'd be crackin' a safe!"

"Gee!" breathed the Kid. "What a proud and reckless feller!"

Savagely the man rolled his head in the grass.

" 'Tain't no use talkin'! Yuh ain't seen my friend so I won't cough on him no more. Me, I guess I'll pound my ear."

In a short time, with the easy adaptability of the true blown-in-the-glass stiff, he was snoring in loud sleep.

It was coming on dawn. The crowd of stars was fading from the sky. Over in the east the sky was tinged with the first color of gray chill dawn.

The Kid drew his huge coat close about himself and his hungry snuggling dog and lay back, in the soft nest of grass, looking up at the brightening sky. He chewed. He chewed manfully. But his stomach still gnawed with a cramping pain. He could not sleep.

A particularly loud snore caused the dog to turn, with cocked ragged ears, to watch the sleeping man alongside. The Kid sat up. The dog fell in a little ball upon the dew-wet grass of the hollow. He gave a startled yelp. Then he unwound and stretched his crooked little legs.

But neither that yelp nor the keenness of dawn disturbed the loud sleep of the man. He still lay in that position of blissful unconsciousness, his arms flung up above his head, his face to the pinking sky.

The Kid could see his face. His was not a hobo's face. There was no stubble of a week's growth smutting his face, nor was his face thin and pale in that unhealthy way peculiar to so many hoboes. His was a broad red face. Down that face from the corner of the left eye, across the mouth, to the cleft in the too-strong chin was a great quarter-inch scar. Against the red health of his face, that scar was a streak of hideous white.

"Gee," said the Kid to himself, "that's some scar he got on his face, that stiff. Must 'a' got it in some drunken fight in the jungles. Fer fancy work with his razor, the bloke what done that sure was a blowed-in-the-glass stiff. I never see'd a hobo carved jes' like that. Bet he got his road name from that white scar—some moniker like 'Scar-face' or 'Split-cheek' or 'White-scar'!

"And jes' look how Whitey-scar pounds his ear, though! Jes' like a baby, easy-like and without worryin' none where he's gonna mooch the next meal. He's a big fat stiff, too, is Whitey-scar. Ought to be up early huntin' fer scoffin's, 'stead of floppin' like he never slept fer a week."

With sudden thought, the Kid looked down more closely at the man.

"I wonder, now," he said, "I wonder is he a blowed-in-the-glass stiff! Ain't he sleepin' like he had money in his jeans hisself and can buy his scoffin's any old time? And didn't he tell me to git a road stake—to work fer some money? I'll bet he's a guy what works but is temp'rary-like out of a job. He's a fake hobo, that's what—jes' a Gay-cat!"

The boy's voice, as he spoke, lowered to a whisper, as if he feared that the sleeping man might hear. He leaned forward, his mouth half open, his breath sounding in little eager gasps. A thought had leaped full-fledged and with brutal startlingness to his brain. That thought was that he should "roll" the sleeping man. He should go through his clothes and rob him!

It is not a brave thing to rob a sleeping man. It is a coward's trick. Also, it is a true hobo's trick. It is a true hobo's trick because all hoboes are criminals and cowards. They are criminals at heart, but without the courage. Only what they surely can get away with, that only will they do.

The Kid was a true hobo. He had an education only in the ways of hoboes. Nearly all that he knew had been taught him by the roads he tramped, the hoboes he met. Hobo ideals were his ideals; and hobo ideals are strange ideals.

The Kid got to his knees beside the sleeping man. He watched the man's closed eyes. He watched the man's closed eyes with an intense fixed stare. The least flutter of an eyelid would spring him to his feet.

He pulled up the long sleeve of his right arm. He felt along the man's belt. The man's money might be in that belt. It was a likely place. But there were no pockets in that belt, no bulges.

The money might be in the man's shirt-front. The Kid knew that some hoboes carried their stakes in the knot of a bandanna around their necks and over their chests. He leaped closer. His eyes were on the man's eyelids. His eyes never left those eyelids. His lowered head was close to the man's red and scarred face. His breath on that face might awaken the man. He held his breath.

Light as a walking fly, the fingers of his right hand moved from the belt to the brown vest over the man's chest. Through that vest his fingers felt a hard bulge. He breathed once. Here was money hidden.

His eyes on the man's eyelids, his breath held, he felt that hard bulge. Then he got to his feet. Slowly and deliberately he got to his feet. He backed away. His face was death-white with an absolute bloodlessness. There was no need to hold his breath. He had no breath.

Beneath the man's vest, his sensitive fingers had felt the shape of a revolver. It was not a large revolver; its barrel had been sawed down. It was in some sort of cloth sling beneath the vest. On either side of the cloth sling, the vest was padded deeply. That was to round off the bulge of the revolver. It was to lessen, if not wholly conceal, the outlines of that revolver.

The Kid backed up the slope of the gully.

"A yegger!" he breathed in a cold whisper of fear. "A strong-armer! Now I know, I don't monkey with Mr. Whitey-scar. Lucky I found out what he was. I don't want to make no road stake by rollin' him. Him! He might 'a' croaked me with that stick-up gun!"

On top of the knoll to one side of the gully, the Kid whistled for the Gay-cat. As quickly and suddenly as a rabbit, the dog bounded up out of the hollow. He looked open-mouthed and eager up at the Kid, then down at the big blissful head of the sleeping man.

"No, Gay-cat," said the Kid, interpreting that look. "We is gonna leave Mr. Whitey-scar. He ain't like us, Gay-cat. He don't have to wake up early and throw his feet fer scoffin's. He ain't no beggar. He can sleep late, he can, and git money fer his chow out of any old safe he meets, with that stick-up gun he has and a little soup!"

The Kid looked back down the hollow. Across the sleeping man's red face, he saw that long ugly white scar. Into his eyes, as he looked, crept a peculiar expression. Hobo ideals were the Kid's ideals. Like all hoboes, he thought real criminals fine men. He stood in awe of criminals. Admiration and awe—that was the expression in his eyes.

"Gee!" he whispered. "A proud and reckless stiff, jes' like his friend, Swaggerin' Bob!"

Then he turned and, the dog running by his side, fled toward the road.

The Kid fled along the road where the road dipped down between hop-fields that were a thousand leafy trellises, curtaining off the peeping sun. In the flat of the valley near the river was the town.

As he approached the town, he saw standing to one side of the road a little one-storied structure with a corrugated-iron roof. So tiny was that structure that it looked like a tool-house. The Kid saw that it was more than a tool-house. In the exact center of its front door was a square aperture barred with vertical black rods of iron.

"The town lock-up!" breathed the Kid. "Come here, Gay-cat!"

His tail snuggling his back in sudden fright, the dog crept to the boy's side. So the two, boy and dog, slunk by that tiny structure. The boy was a hobo, an outcast. He had all a hobo's fear of the lawful instruments, both animate and inanimate, of that society from which, as a hobo, he was cast out.

The town beyond was a town of four buildings. There were a general merchandise store, a nickelodeon, a saloon and, a little apart from these, a yellow-painted shack that looked like a railroad station. All were labeled with the same name, "J. Curtis Haines." But the yellow-painted shack had the glory of the additional words, "Ranch Office."

The yellow-painted shack stood back from the road in a field overgrown with tall grass and rank weeds and thistles. In the clear gravel sweep before its door, five buckboards were drawn up in line. Through the open door, as he passed by, the Kid saw two clerks working behind a counter. In the rear in a swivel-chair before a huge safe was a tall gray-mustached man who was talking vehemently to the five field bosses who had driven up in the buckboards for the morning orders.

But the Kid did not halt here to ask J. Curtis Haines for a job in his hop-fields. Beyond the bridge over the shallow river and up on the side of the valley, he saw a low whitewashed farmhouse. Toward that he made to ask for a handout.

The windows of the farmhouse were open. He could see a Chinese smiling philosophically over a broad cook-stove, crowded with tall pots. But there were no sounds of eating from the open windows of the farmhouse or from the hundred brown-canvas tents of the hop-harvesters across the road.

The Kid understood thereat. It was harvest-time; the hops were being hurriedly picked; and the men had eaten before dawn and at dawn had gone down into the fields.

As the Kid debated with himself whether to ask the Chinese for a late breakfast, he saw a man with a pail in his hands come out of the kiln or oast-house a little up the road, a slim, tall, youngish-looking man with a blue army shirt that draggled its ends outside his trousers.

"I'll strike him fer a meal," he decided. "I'd ruther strike him than a Chinaman, 'cause he's a hop-glomer and sorter like a hobo."

He started up the dusty road, the Gay-cat tagging after him. He approached the man with the draggling blue shirt.

The man wore no hat. His face was brown and pleasing; his eyes of a twinkling gray; and his hair black, with those little tight curls that the Greeks so loved to carve on the artistic heads of their statues. He set down the empty pail and, hands on slim hips, looked at the approaching boy and dog.

"A hobo kid!" he ejaculated. "And by the Lord Jimmy, a hobo dog! Say, kid, what manner of name do you call that strange admixture of dog you've got there—The Survival of the Unfittest?"

He looked down at the dog with the trace of a smile. The Gay-cat was sniffing his legs and cocking his round yellow head at the draggling shirt-tails.

But the Kid did not feel so familiar as that dog. He had judged the slim young man, when he had seen him far off, to be a hop-picker and therefore, by reason of his roving life from one harvest to another, more or less of a hobo. Now he felt, of a sudden, that if the man were a hop-picker, he was no ordinary hop-picker. There was something about the man's words, about the manner with which he threw back his curly head, about that odd twinkle in his gray eyes that made the Kid feel suddenly inferior, suddenly shy. Hunger was gnawing at his stomach; it was no time for bashfulness; yet the Kid felt too abashed to make his request for food.

"No," he gulped; "he's the Gay-cat, my dog. That's all. Jes' Gay-cat."

"Just Gay-cat?" There seemed displeasure in the curly-haired fellow's voice, a royal displeasure. "Well, that's sure a queer name for such a remarkable yellow dog. Really, kid, I don't think it very fine of you to give the little pup that name. It's a no-account name. It means he's not a good rodeo, but only a fake hobo. You can't be a real blown-in-the-glass stiff yourself to give your dog such a shiftless sort of name!"

The Kid was surprised and a great deal touched in his pride.

"Me not a blowed-in-the-glass stiff? Aw, bo! Aw, say now, bo!"

The tall slim young fellow smiled down at the Kid's rueful face. He smiled down at the Kid's rueful face until the Kid smiled back wanly. Thus heartened, the Kid said:

"Yer couldn't set us up to some chow, now could yer—jes' the dog and me? Me and Gay-cat, we ain't et in a long time, bo—since yisterday mornin'. I feel all holler inside. And Gay-cat, he's sniffin' and whimperin' awful. Yer couldn't stack us up to some eats, could yer, boss?"

"Can I? Kid, you've come to the right man this time! Even old Curt Haines with all his rocks couldn't do more for you than give you a feed; and he wouldn't do as much, take it from me, until you had worked and earned your chow. But come on, kid. I'll introduce you to Jim, our Chinee cookey."

He paused suddenly in striding away as if he were struck by a new idea.

"But what name will I give as yours to his Yellow Highness of the Pots and Pans?" he asked whimsically. "What's your moniker, son?"

"Kid."

"Only Kid? Huh, that's no name, that's no hobo moniker! Why don't you get a real name like 'Salt Lake Kid,' or 'Orleans Kid,' or 'Chi Kid'? Those would be monikers, now! But no self-respecting blown-in-the-glass stiff would want to be called just plain Kid. It's no moniker at all. Why don't you take a moniker? Tell me: where did you come from anyway?"

"I used," the boy faltered, "I used to beg fer Frisco Red—"

"Frisco, huh? You come from Frisco?"

"No-o, I—"

The Kid hesitated and looked away. There was something in the man's question that brought up a picture before the Kid's eyes. He saw the cottage up in Grass Valley and his pale little, shawled mother sitting by the window near the bush of white marguerites. She was waiting for his return, he knew, as she had waited for three weary years.

He became aware that the blue-shirted young fellow was speaking.

"I haven't forgotten the last time I was on Howard Street, or warming the benches in Portsmouth Square down in Chinatown. That's a good old town, Frisco. And there's a name for you, Kid. You take it. You're Frisco Kid from now on—get me?"

Grandly as any Edward or George ever bestowed the garter, just that grandly did the blue-shirted one give the Kid that name. And the Kid received that name humbly, thankfully—with that exaltation a broker or brewer must feel when he is given the privilege to call himself "Sir." Proudly he felt himself to be, then and forever, the Frisco Kid!

"Come on," said the slim young fellow. "Now for putting your legs under for a square."

With long strides he walked down the dusty road toward the farmhouse, his shirt-tails flapping over his trousers. His black curly head was thrown back and he whistled a few variegated notes. It was Musetta's song from "La Bohème."

The Kid as he followed with the dog, listened to those whistled notes, the notes of a tune he never had heard before; and as he listened he became possessed of a great idea. That idea rose in him like a yeast of admiration. It filled him, at last, to overflowing. He could hold it no longer.

"Say, bo," he called. "I betcha I know what your moniker is! I betcha I know who you are!"

Smiling a little at the naive tone of the boy, the man half turned his head.

"Who am I, Frisco Kid?"

"Yer—yer Swaggerin' Bob!"

The man stopped. He stopped suddenly. He whirled around. A tall upstanding figure, he stood cold and still, his arms stiffly at his sides. There was something ominous in that position of his arms. The Kid did not know why that position of his arms was ominous. But he knew that the man's gray eyes were no longer twinkling. They were dark with the shock of a complete surprise and with, perhaps, a certain terror.

The man's arms were stiffly at his sides for a reason. Under the flapping shirt-tails beneath the man's belt there was a revolver. At the least strengthening of his alarm, he would reach for that revolver. But a swinging arm is never ready to reach for a gun. The man's arms were stiffly at his sides. One lift of his rigid right hand, and the revolver in his belt would be lifted. It would be the matter of an eye-wink.

Thus unconsciously prepared, slowly the man asked a question.

"Why do you say that, Kid?"

But at the change in the man the Kid had lost heart in his idea. He said lamely:

"Aw, yer fixed my name over to Frisco Kid, so I thought I'd fix yer name over. Swaggerin' Bob, he's a proud and reckless feller—and yer sorter proud and reckless, so I thought yer might be him. And if yer isn't him—if yer isn't him—aw, Swaggerin' Bob's a kinder proud and reckless name what 'ud seem to fit yer, somehow."

The man laughed oddly. He laughed as if a choking gag had been pulled from his mouth. Very plainly, he was relieved. But he was not altogether relieved.

"Who told you of Swaggering Bob?" he persisted.

"Aw, a friend of his."

"A friend of his?"

"Yes; Whitey-scar. A bo what we shared floppin's with last night. A big, fat stiff what carries a stick-up gun, and is horstile to everybody."

"Whitey-scar? Never met that stiff. Nor do I know your friend, Swaggering Bob, Frisco Kid. But if he's as proud and reckless as you say, he'd be worth knowing, I think. He's my kind, your stiff Swaggering Bob is. A fellow might find work for a stiff like him, now."

He looked down at the Kid very seriously.

"As for my name, Frisco Kid," he said slowly, "my name at present is 'Slim,' 'Atlanta Slim.' Don't you forget that—understand!"

"No, Slim."

But the Kid would rather have called the tall, slim young fellow, "Swaggering Bob." He felt strangely disappointed.

That disappointment gave a certain quirk of seriousness to his thoughts. As Slim opened the creaking-hinged gate to the farmhouse, the Kid said—

"I knows I ain't proud and reckless like Swaggerin' Bob, Slim; but if yer got work to do—if yer got work to do, Slim, and is needin' help, mebbe yer could give me a job—huh, Slim?"

"A job? And you a true blown-in-the-glass stiff! What does a hobo like you want a job for, Frisco Kid?"

The Kid raised his deep-sunk eyes to Slim. In his deep-sunk eyes, as he looked up at Slim, there was a kind of desperation.

"I knows we'se hoboes," he said. "We'se proud as Sam Hill 'cause we'se blowed-in-the-glass stiffs. But sometimes Gay-cat and me, we don't eat. It ain't our fault, Slim; we knows how to panhandle all right; but it's 'cause the whole country is horstile, and we has no money to buy eats. Once, 'way back in York State, a Galway named Father John Bresnahan, he tole us we oughta put by some money fer a rainy day. But Gay-cat and me, we don't think nuthin' o' that till yesterday. Then all day long them hayseed bulls chase us out o' them towns, and us hungry, too. And last night when we flopped, Whitey-scar, he tole us we oughta git a road stake. 'Then,' he says, 'yer can buy yer eats any old time and them constibools can't say a word.' So I wanta job where I can earn that road stake and—"

Slim put his arms around the boy's frail shoulder. His arm around the boy's frail shoulder, he looked down at the Kid.

"We'll go in and chow first, my Frisco Kid," he said gently, "and then we'll talk about earning that road stake. I'm not sure, but perhaps I have got a job for you—a job like you never thought to work at in all your life. And there's a road stake at the end of it, Frisco Kid—a road stake that's big and beautiful with gold!"

They entered the kitchen of the farmhouse. Said Slim with a wave of the hand to the old Chinese:

"Jim, I have here a kid who has not eaten, he says, since the revolution in China. Now I want you to throw a dozen flapjacks into that pale, frail body of his. Also, Jim, a few eggs and ham, some mush, and a baker's dozen of those hot biscuits of yours—"

The Chinese interrupted with a string of frightful oaths.

"You get no more b'eakfast out of me!" he exclaimed. "That clock, it at seven. You chowed at five. Now you want chow again. What you t'ink— make fall-guy out of me? You get every blame' down-on-luck guy on roads and shove him in fo' chow off me. I don' stand it no more!"

"You poor slangy Chinaman!" said Slim grandly. "You've been so many years shooting grub into a lot of roughnecks and bindle stiffs, you've lost all your manners and your fine Chinese sense of decency. I ask you for one meal for one starving kid all alone in a world of chill dawns and long brown roads and hungry sunsets. And you tell me that you have given too many meals to his kind. You balk at too much charity.

"Ah, Jim," sadly, "there is not too much charity in this world. There is not enough. If there was, this motherless little kid would not be a wanderer of long hard roads with only a mournful-eared cur dog for a companion. Nor would I be skulking here in the daylight as a hop-picker, when I'm not a hop-picker at all, only a man who—"

"Allight, allight, Slim," broke in the Chinese, smiling broadly as a mule and showing himself by his quick assent to be another slave of the artful Slim. "I set him up fo' you. I don't care. This nine-tenth guy I feed fo' you in t'ree days; but I don't care, Slim—so long you cut out hot-air talk!"

Slim thought that a good joke. He laughed uproariously. And he continued to laugh while the Chinese brought out plates of food for the boy and plates of food for his dog.

After a bit, he stopped laughing. He watched the Kid eat. At last, he seemed to grow weary of watching the Kid clear the plates of flapjacks, and mush, and ham and eggs, and coffee and biscuits. He stood at an uncurtained window, his back to the Kid, and stared moodily into the white morning.

"I'll do it," he muttered with a shake of his curly head. "I'll declare Frisco Kid in on the job."

The Kid scraped back his chair. He got up, wiping his mouth on his long sleeve.

Slim turned around. His face was gray, his voice very gentle.

"You had enough, Frisco Kid?"

"Sure, Slim; I'm stuffed like a turkey. But yer don't happen to have the makin's on yer, do yer, Slim? A smoke 'ud top off the meal jes' swell-like!"

The tall slim young fellow passed him the papers and tobacco. Gravely and very deftly, the Kid rolled a cigarette. The tall slim young fellow smiled a little as he watched him.

"Now, my Frisco Kid," he said quietly, "now we'll see about that road-stake job of yours."

Smoking the cigarette contentedly, the Kid walked with Slim back to the kiln. On the ground floor of the huge double-towered kiln was a door like a barn door. That Slim shoved aside. They entered a half-dark place.

By the morning sunlight streaming in over his shoulder, the Kid saw that he was in a large earth-floored room. Over against one wall was a pile of cordwood as high as a table. Against the other wall, set in bricks, were two furnaces for drying the hops spread over the grating-floored loft above. A wood-fire crackled in the furnaces, reddening the iron fronts and spitting out live cinders upon the floor through air-vents near the bottoms. The place was hot and stuffy; yet as the Kid entered after Slim, a voice called sharply from within:

"Close thet door! Do youse wanta let in th' cold?"

Hastily the Kid shoved to the large rusty-wheeled door behind him—so hastily that as the Gay-cat squeezed through his tragic curl of tail was almost pinched off.

"Have a swig, Slim?" said the voice. It came from the top of the cordwood pile, where shadows bulked. "I got a pail o' beer here. Got ut down at th'

Portugee's when youse went out with t'other pail an' didn't show back. Say, wot happened to youse? An' Slim, who's thet kid youse got there?"

"Just a hobo kid off the road, 'Yorky.' Bummed me for a meal—that's why I forgot all about getting that beer. But where's the beer you spoke of, Yorky?"

"Over here."

The owner of the voice sat up on top of the cordwood and showed his face. The room was shadowy dark save for the red glow cast by the furnace heads and the live coals upon the earth floor; yet even in that red furnace-light, the man's face was white, unhealthily, morbidly white.

The Kid stood near the door, the Gay-cat squatting on his haunches at his feet. Slim left the Kid. He drew close to the pile of cordwood. He looked down at the shadows in the gloom. He looked down narrowly.

Then he turned his back and walked to the opposite side of the room. Suddenly he kicked open one of the furnace doors. The room leaped vividly all at once with bright light.

Slim whirled around. He backed against the wall beside the open furnace door. He crouched against that wall. At his sides his arms were ominously stiff.

"Who the hell's the other guy here?" he cried sharply. "The new gun— what's he doing here? What's he doing so still and quiet? Yorky—why are you so tight-faced? You —— mugged gun, is this a plant to double-cross me!"

There was anger, a hot anger, in Slim's voice. In his gray eyes was more than anger. In his gray eyes was desperation. He waited. Hunched back against the wall, his arms stiffly at his sides, he waited like one trapped, at bay.

The two men on the cordwood pile were silent. It was as if they had been shocked, by his sudden fierce outburst, into that silence. Then the nearest on the cordwood pile laughed nervously. He was Yorky. He said hastily:

"Oh, there's nuthin' fer youse to git so horstile about, Slim. I'm all right. And this other gun is all right. Youse'll be glad ter meet him, Slim. Stand up, blokey, an' let Slim look youse over!"

Very soberly the other man sat up on top of the cordwood pile and, crawling over Yorky, got to his feet on the earth floor. He stepped forward a bit and faced the firelight and Slim for inspection.

He was a big heavy man with a broad red face and a great ugly white scar that ran down one cheek from the corner of the left eye, across the mouth, to the cleft in the uncompromising jaw.

"Whitey-scar!" breathed the Kid.

The man with the ugly scar faced Slim in an attitude of ease and indifference. But it was an attitude that only affected at ease and indifference. His arms were folded across his chest. The Kid knew, as he watched him, that under those folded arms was a sawed-down revolver concealed.

"I'm all right, buddy," said that man to Slim. "I'm a good gun. I'm no fingers or elbow or stool. I'm one o' the good people."

The man spoke English; yet undoubtedly he is not intelligible to you who read. You understand English to be sure, but you understand the English of the upperworld only. He spoke in the bastard English of the underworld.

The underworld has a language of its own. It is a secret language. It is a language designedly invented to keep those not of the underworld from understanding what those of the underworld mean when they speak that secret language.

A "gun" in that secret language means a criminal. "Fingers" are policemen; detectives, "elbows." "Stools" are stool-pigeons who go down into the underworld as men of that underworld and who then report the doings of the underworld to the police. They are spies of the law who, by the upperworld and the underworld, are despised and hated as betrayers of men.

The "good people" are the pick of the pickpockets, of the second-story men, of the safe-crackers. That is their own name for themselves. By "good" is meant that they make crime pay. They are the brainy, clever, daring and dangerous criminals.

The scarred man was one of the good people, self-avowed. He was one of the brainy, clever, daring and dangerous criminals.

Slim looked him over closely.

"Scar-face Mike Hagan!" he exclaimed suddenly. "Why you mugged gun, anybody's blind that wouldn't know you! I'd know your beauty mark a block. But I heard you tried to yegg a peter in Toledo and was nabbed. I heard you were in stir for ten years. And here you are—Scar-face Mike, the best peterman in the Middle West! When did you get out, Mike? I won't ask how!"

"Me?" said the other. "Oh, I got out three months ago. And I'll tell yuh this, Atlanta Slim, as they call yuh 'round here: no screw or warden shook my fin when I made my gitaway from thet stir. They could only hold me on the inside fur six months.

"And I'll tell yuh sumthin' else, Atlanta Slim. I never heard yer moniker afore; I have no quarrel with yer moniker—Atlanta Slim bein' as good as most; but I knows a name what 'ud fit yuh better'n thet. It's the name of a high-class yegg, a peterman so well knowed he don't need no white scar like me so guns will know him. But I won't say yer old moniker, Slim, boy, fur there's a man badly wanted by the Burns men fur a couple o' bank safes drilled, and by the Govamint elbows, too, fur a bunch o' post-offices what found their peters were cigar-boxes when Slim boy put the soup to 'em!"

"You may be right, Scar-face," Slim half-admitted cautiously. "But what have you been doing since you got out?"

The man's red face went a darker hue with sudden passion. Against that dark hue, the terrible scar was death-white, ghastly.

"I've been down and out—down and out since I made my gitaway from stir! I've bin no better'n a hobo. I've bin on my hunkers, I tell yuh. I've bin wanderin' here and there, on the rods and blinds and in John O'Briens. Yes; and I've had to walk—walk the roads like a dirty bindle stiff!"

He raised his clenched hands in impotent rage.

"Oh, it's bin a hard long three months fur me—a starvin' dirty three months! No money, no drinks, no decent chow. I've bin bummin' my eats—panhandlin' like a bo fur nickels and dimes. I ain't poured one skee into me. Five-cent grease joints fur coffee and—thet's bin my limit. Park benches and city lots and haystacks fur months. Oh, I've bin on my hunkers, down and out, I tell yuh—me, Scar-face Mike Hagan thet slept in the swellest hotels in Philly and York and Chi, and at Augustin' and Del Monte when I pulled down a good clean swag! Black luck—"

"You've lost your nerve, Scar-face," Slim said quietly, as if sounding out the man.

"Me, a yegg with science, lost my nerve? What about St. Joe and Chi, Slim. Yes, and thet little burg out in lower Illinois—Simpson? Three times I tried it and three times sumthin' went wrong. But Simpson—thet was the place. I'd joined out with a feller name o' Blondy, a bo what I had picked up in a boxcar goin' West. He said he did peterwork; knew most o' the swell mobs in Louie and York and Chi, too. He said the post-office in thet little one-horse town o' Simpson was good pickin's.

"We broke in one night. The place was full o' post-office elbows. That guy Blondy had coughed on me. He had got me trapped. He was a stool, —— him! But I went through the winder backward, and before I went I got *him!* I broke his head with one swack o' my gun—and he won't ferget me soon!"

As if to include every one present in what he was about to say, he turned to the listening man on the cordwood pile.

"Guns," he said, "ef ever yuh meets a lanky yaller-haired bo named o' Blondy, what says he does peterwork and knows all the good people—croak him! He's a Govamint elbow, workin' as a tramp. I hit him a good one, but I ain't satisfied none. I'm sure horstile, I tell yuh. I'd like to cook—to kill that stool!"

Slim was thoughtful.

"Never met your friend Blondy," he said seriously. "But I do know the road is thick with stools these days. A yegg's got to have nerve with all these spies pretending they're guns and leading on the real yeggs to break in peters, and then nabbing them or giving them away to the fingers. A yegg never knows, nowadays, which one of the guns who cracks a safe with him is going to betray him. Sometimes he is betrayed and is sent up for twenty or thirty years. And sometimes, Mike, he never knows who it was betrayed him!"

Slim fell thoughtfully silent. He turned away from Scar-face and looked through the open furnace door into the crackling flames. Behind him in the gloom Scar-face stood, a heavy and somber look on his face.

"Black luck!" he muttered gruffly. "Black luck I've had ever since I made my gitaway from stir. I've bin on my hunkers with black luck."

Slim whirled on him sharply.

"It's time for your luck to change! Your luck's going to change, Scar-face Mike—'cause you're going to do a safe-cracking job with the guy called 'Atlanta Slim'!"

Scar-face Mike Hagan drew back. Startled by the suddenness of Slim's action, the suddenness of Slim's words, he drew back as a man instinctively draws back when menaced by a clenched fist. Then the meaning of Slim's words leaped into his brain. His close-set eyes brightened. His scar-cleft mouth opened like the mouth of an eager dog.

"Work to do!" he cried. "Yuh got a safe to crack! And yuh'll let me in on the deal! Slim boy, to hear yuh say thet is better'n a swig of whisky to me—me thet's bin thirstin' fur a safe to crack, like it was a woman!"

Swiftly he stepped forward. He held out his huge hand. Slim shook his hand on the partnership.

A change swept over the man's broad red face. The eager look dropped from his face like shed skin. His broad red face became engraved, of a sudden, with lines of caution. With furtive eyes, he looked past Slim at Yorky and the Kid.

With the hand that gripped Slim's hand, he made a peculiar signal. It was a signal as peculiar to the underworld as is the language of the underworld. It was a crook's signal with a certain secret meaning.

With his index finger, as his hand gripped Slim's hand, Scar-face Mike Hagan tapped the back of Slim's hand twice. That meant—

"I want to talk with you alone."

Slim's black eyebrows drew together. He was surprised at the request and a little puzzled. He swept the red-lighted shadows of the room with his gray eyes. Suddenly his brow smoothed. He laughed shortly.

"Oh, Yorky's all right, Scar-face. Don't be leery about shooting your mouth off before him. Why Yorky's a peterman as good as the best, though you can see he's still a bit pale from a recent rest-cure at Sing Sing. We're all one mob here, Scar-face."

"But the kid there?" objected Scar-face. He scowled at the little fellow, pressed back in the gloom against the door.

"Yes, him," said Yorky. "Youse is shootin' off yer mouth consid'able afore him, Slim. Me, I don't trust no kids at all. As soon as a bull gives him th' third degree, a kid will toin stool an' peach on us guns an' th' whole works, an' send us up. I'm scared o' kids, Slim. I done time enough in stir an'

I knows wot ut's like. I bin in stir too much fer one man."

Slim lifted his hand for silence. He turned around and stepped nearer the Kid. Putting his hand under the Kid's chin, he tilted up the peaked pale face. Thoughtfully he looked into the deep-sunk eyes of the Kid.

"Frisco Kid," he said. "Frisco Kid that I've fed and named and taken for my chum and buddy—you wouldn't give me away to the bulls? And these guns who are my mob, you wouldn't act as stool against either of them—would you, Kid?"

"No, Slim," said the Kid in a desperate whisper.

Slim put his arms around the boy's frail shoulder. His arm around the boy's frail shoulder, he turned and faced the others proudly.

"Behold!" said he with a return of his grand manner. "Behold, you low-browed guns! Let me introduce to you the Frisco Kid. A walker of roads and a beggar at back doors and a talker of the hobo tongue, he was, until Slim saw him and thought him cute and pitied him, he looked so homeless and forlorn, the —— little ——"

Slim never finished. A look almost like that of bodily anguish swept his face. His arm tightened about the boy's frail shoulder.

"Guns," he began again. "Guns, I'm not kidding you. I'm telling you something. I'm telling you that this is my last job. After this job, I quit gun work for good. I'll be no thieving hiding-out yegg any longer. In this job, I'll make my stake—that fortune I hoped to earn as a merchant prince when I was a dreaming boy.

"How do I know? I've got a hunch. I've adopted Frisco Kid and that measly cur dog he calls the Gay-cat for mascots. With the Kid and his dog for mascots, I can't fail in this last job. One look at him and I knew he brought my luck. One look at him and I said, 'I'll take him with me to Europe on this haul, and show him all the old churches and the pleasant, sweet old lanes and all the pictures in the great picture galleries!' That's my dream, guns!" His face was frank and enthusiastic and boyish. "Frisco Kid's one of our mob from now on. I've adopted him for my buddy!"

"Slim, d'yuh mean to say yuh declarin' thet kid in on the mob?" asked Scar-face gruffly. "D'yuh mean he's to share on this haul with the best o' us?"

Slim shook his curly head.

"No," he said. "You, Scar-face, and Yorky and I will split the haul even between us. We'll share thirds. But the Kid wants to earn a road stake. Now you guns have nothing to do with that. The Kid's my buddy. I'll give him half of my share. Whether we go to Europe or not afterward, I'll give him half of my share. That will be his road stake."

The two men woke the room with gruff mumbles of dissent. Slim's promise seemed so preposterously prodigal!

Slim regarded them not. He had another one of his ideas. As usual, it controlled him seriously and utterly. He turned once more to the Kid. Once more he put an arm around the Kid's frail shoulder.

"But my Frisco Kid," he said softly, "I haven't taken you into consideration at all. Do you want to be the buddy of a fellow like me? Do you want to stick with me through this job and go with me where I go afterward and share with me my good fortune?—Slim and the Kid, buddies together! Do you, Frisco Kid?"

The boy in the over-large coat looked up into the gray, thoughtful eyes of the man. His own eyes were serious, very serious.

"Sure, I do, Slim," he said, "if Gay-cat is buddies too!" He nodded his head. To himself he added, "Sure, I do, Swaggerin' Bob!"

From far off, a rumble of sound shook through the ground and slid through the interstices of the rough-board structure. The men listened. That rumble of sound thrummed heavily in their ears. They listened with pale, strained faces.

"What's thet?" asked Scar-face. "Thet don't sound like no train!"

His only immediate answer was the steady increase of that sound. It was the distance-dulled sound of mules' hoof-beats on the dust-carpeted road, the creaking of heavy wheels on axles, the cracking of long mule-skinners' whips—all the blended noises of an oncoming procession of wagons.

"Thet?" said Yorky of a sudden. "Why thet is only a bunch o' skinners comin' up with hops from Ranch Number Four."

The face of Scar-face broadened with comprehension and a vast relief. Ranch Number Four was just across the river and had no kiln of its own for drying and purifying the hops.

But Slim's eyebrows remained drawn together. It was as if he did not accept Yorky's explanation. He puzzled. He seemed, at last, to come to some conclusion of his own. He smiled. There was in his smile something of superiority and something that was sardonic.

"Listen, guns," he said. "Listen close, especially you, Mike. I'm giving you the plans!"

His back to the still open furnace he faced them in the red glow.

"It's like this: Down in the flat of the valley across the bridge, there is a little yellow shack like a railroad depot. That's the ranch office of old Curt Haines who is the whole gee in these parts. In that ranch office is the safe we're going to crack. Guns, in that safe is $30,000 in gold!"

Outside, the rumble of the teams had grown louder and nearer, as if they were toiling up the road between the farmhouse and the kiln. That rumble now thrummed through the red-lighted room like a formidable blast of wind. Scar-face raised his gruff voice:

"Thirty thousand dollars in gold! Why the harvest ain't hardly started yet! Slim, how comes all thet money 'round a hop-ranch at the beginnin' o' the season?"

"True words, them!" put in Yorky. "Scar-face is right, Slim, though I hadn't knowed enough ter ast about ut afore!"

Slim smiled in that superior sardonic fashion.

"Frisco Kid," he said quietly. "Open that door!"

With implicit obedience to Slim's command and a valiant surge of strength, the Kid shoved open the great rusty-wheeled door at his back. The white fingers of the day came in and poked into the eyes of the men. As if from the mouth of a tunnel, they looked out into the sparkling morning sunlight.

Drawn up before the door of the kiln was a two-horsed farm-wagon and behind that, down the dust-carpeted road, strung farm-wagon after two-horsed farm-wagon. Each wagon was crowded with men. They were brown men. They were brown men, long and starveling of limb, with heads wrapped in red and yellow and white turbans.

Yorky cried out. He cried out in a great voice—

"Th' ragheads!"

"Now do you understand?" said Slim. "It's the ragheads, all right—a whole army of Hindoo laborers. Old man Haines has imported them to finish harvesting his crops!"

"But th' whites? Youse mean, Slim, thet Haines is goin' ter toin out all th' whites?"

"Sure, Yorky—turn out all the whites! Whites are not like these niggers. Whites don't do whatever they're told to do and for whatever money Haines sees fit to give them. Whites quit when they —— please."

Scar-face stepped closer to Slim.

"Thet thirty thousand dollars in gold is fur payin' the whites off—huh, Slim boy?"

"There's a gun with brains!" said Slim admiringly. "That's it, Mike! But that thirty thousand dollars is not only for this ranch—those hop-picking bums get only a buck and a quarter a day, above their chow. This money is also for Ranch Number Four across the river, and for all the Haines ranches that border this river right down the valley—Ranches Three, Two and One.

"At each ranch to-day, while the whites work all unaware in the hop-valleys, there is arriving quietly just such a train of niggers as that outside. Tomorrow morning the field bosses of each ranch will drive over to that yellow shack down in town, receive a pile of twenties and fives, and at noon pay off and discharge all the whites!"

"But them whites will raise ructions, Slim," objected Yorky. "They'll raise ol' Cain if they're put out fer a parcel o' ragheads. I knows I would."

Even as Yorky spoke, Slim's face lighted up. Once again he was possessed by a new and brilliant idea.

"Guns, I've got it!" he fairly shouted. "We won't wait for the whites to learn the truth tomorrow. We'll whisper about the ragheads in their ears today. That'll get them. They're just big kids, roughnecks. They'll want revenge. It'll be just as Yorky says. They won't think of the money due them—what's a measly half-month's pay to a bunch of hop-picking hoboes when they're ousted by these niggers!

"They're roughnecks, I tell you, boys; natural Reds. They'll see red now. It'll be worse than a strike, worse than any lockout. All they'll want is revenge—revenge on Haines, revenge for his selfishness, arrogance and wealth!"

Slim stepped, in his vehemence, closer to Scar-face.

"We'll help them get that revenge! We'll distribute a little of our nitro among them. *We'll* start the fireworks! We'll start the fireworks so quick the most cool-headed pickers can't turn back. There'll be ructions tonight, Yorky! Under cover of it all, tonight, we'll crack that safe!"

"Tonight?" Scar-face seemed taken aback. "Slim boy, yuh don't mean to knock off thet peter tonight!"

"Sure, tonight! Tomorrow the men are fired and paid off. Where's the gold in that peter, then? Tonight's the only time!"

"Yes; I guess so," said Scar-face surlily. "But I didn't expect to be rushed so. I was figurin' on a couple o' nights to—well, say, to prepare sorter."

He seemed inwardly perturbed by the fact that the safe was to be broken open in so short a time. Slim regarded him curiously.

"Scar-face Mike Hagan," he said, "do you want to come in on this peter job?"

The man's surly mood sloughed from him. Against the quick reddening of his broad heavy face, his white scar grew whiter and uglier.

"Do I, Slim boy!" he shouted. He leaped forward. He shoved his red face close to Slim's. "Am I bughouse! Thirty thousand dollars in gold, and me with my black luck! Do I? Sure I wanter git in on this job!"

He shoved his huge hand forward. On the compact, there with the white fingers of the day sparkling upon him, he shook Slim's hand.

That night a high fog slid over the mountain-tops to the west and sheeted, as with a monstrous gray blanket, the whole valley with its green treasure of hops. The new moon that had elbowed up, round and yellow, among the crowd of stars, was blotted out. The night fell cold and thick and black.

On the edge of the dark tent-colony on the side of valley, two men and a boy and a dog lay on blankets inside of a tepee tent. There was no light in that tent; it was as dark as the tents about and the night above; yet neither men nor boys nor dogs slept. In subdued and guarded voices, the two men were talking together.

"Thet's good work, Slim," one was saying. "But ef they boins th' hops on this side o' th' river, how are we a-goin' ter git down to the shack? Me, I don't trust them hop-pickin' bums."

"Do you think they're crazy? Their tents are up here. Well, do you think they'll burn the hops on this side of the river and take chances of the fire cleaning out their tents? Not them, Yorky! They'll burn the hops on the other side of the river, but on this side they'll only tear down the vines and trample upon the pods. There'll be no flames licking across the road when we go down!"

"But th' town? Youse gave 'em some o' th' soup, Slim. Wot ef they shoots sky-high thet little shack an' thet peter with all th' gold?"

Slim rolled over to face Yorky in the dark.

"I left that all to Scar-face," he said. "Mike was afraid of just what you suggest—that they might fire the office and the safe by mistake. He said he'd stay behind until the soup was planted under every building but that shack. I was against Scar-face staying behind. I don't know whether he'll be back in time. If the mob gets separated like this, we may not be able to pull off the job!"

There was that in Slim's voice which disturbed Yorky.

"Ain't there sumthin' else, Slim?"

Slim sat up restlessly.

"Well, I'll tell you, Yorky—there is! I'm running this mob; not Scar-face. But what I say doesn't go at all with Scar-face. You saw him when I said we'd crack that safe tonight—it was the same about him staying behind in that town! I was opposed to him staying. But he has stayed, hasn't he?"

"Aw, wot's eatin' youse, Slim!"

"Just this: Scar-face Mike Hagan has something up his sleeve. What it is, I don't know. But I tell you, Yorky, I'm afraid of Scar-face!"

"Youse mean, Slim—"

"That Scar-face Mike Hagan is a stool!"

There was a strained and breathless stillness. Then Yorky laughed nervously.

"Aw, youse is too imagin'ry a guy, Slim," he faltered. "Scar-face, he's a gun—a mugged gun, too. Youse is allus imaginin' things, Slim."

Slim drew a deep breath.

"I hope you're right, Yorky!" he exclaimed earnestly. "That's sure a hard name for such a mugged gun as Scar-face. But I'm afraid of him, I tell you. I'm taking no chances. I've fixed his gun!"

"His gun! Why, Slim, I allus thought he packed his gun on him."

"He did, Yorky, till we went down into that town in our shirt-sleeves so we'd look like the hop-glomers. He left his vest behind. That vest was all padded in front, and between the pads was his gun in a cloth sling. I drew out all the shells."

"But wot ef he gives us away afore we cracks thet peter, Slim?"

Slim's voice showed irritation.

"You don't get him at all, Yorky. He's playing a deep game, that Scar-face. And —— it! What stool is going to come out and betray us before we do the job, when by staying under cover, he can crack the peter with us and then escape while we get nabbed? We get nabbed red-handed, and then we never know it was he gave us away to the fingers. We never try to fix him for it."

"Thet may be his game, all right, Slim. But wot ef he's jerry thet we'se wise ter his game—thet we knows he's a stool? Wot ef he don't come back, Slim?"

"Oh, he'll come back, never fear. Why, he's leery that we may back out of this job altogether. That's why he's helping out now with these hop-glomers—firing the town and the crop across the river. He'll come back just to sic us on to that peter. I know his kind. He's after the rewards offered for me, Yorky. He may have followed me clean West!

"I tell you, Yorky, this helping out in the destruction is all a cloak—a mere blind to hide his hand, to give us nerve. He wants us to go on under cover of the destruction; he wants us to crack that safe. When we're right on the job, when he's sure he's got the goods on us, then, Yorky—then he'll nab us!"

There in the blackness a cold damp beaded Yorky's pasty, white face. He wet his lips.

"Slim"—he gulped—"Slim, I'm scared. I'm losin' my noive. I done time enough in stir. I bin in stir too much fer one man. Wot d'ye say, Slim? Can't we—can't we pass up this job?"

Slim laughed shortly.

"Not Slim, Yorky! This is my last job. There's that thirty thousand dollars in gold! There's the pictures in the big picture galleries and the Kid and the dog and I—"

He broke off huskily. With sudden desperation, he bit out:

"I'll tell you what we'll do! We'll watch him. He'll be easy. He's not even heeled. We'll make him pack the soup. We'll make him do the drilling—get the gold for us. We'll watch him. If he tries any funny work, we'll—"

A sudden blast of sound drowned Slim's threat. It was a tremendous blast of sound as of dynamite shot off under pressure. It rocked through the ground. From wall to wall of the valley, it boomed.

A bright red light flooded the tent. That bright red light showed out the big, heavy form of Scar-face, crawling on hands and knees under the flap at the rear of the tent.

"Down, guns!" He threw himself, panting, on the blankets. "Thet's the nickelodeon—the start o' the fireworks. Git down, will yuh! Yuh can see right through the tent, yuh simps!"

Within the confines of the tent, the men lay flat on the blankets and close together, like little children huddling from some terror.

Scar-face was breathing heavily, quickly. With each of his breaths came a resounding boom from the flat of the valley below. Those booms came continually. The men counted like a death-watch. They counted ten.

Scar-face laughed harshly:

"The drunken fools! They've gone crazy! They're runnin' amuck with them nitro' sticks! The whisky did the work."

"Whisky!" Slim sat up. "Scar-face, you don't mean—"

"Sure I do! The skee got 'em! I knowed it would. As soon as I broke in thet saloon door, yuh oughta see them stiffs make fur them bottles! Thet was my cue. I faded. I ran some up this walley, I tell yuh. But the skee did the work. They're wild as fire!"

Slim shoved an oilcloth-wrapped bundle toward Scar-face.

"Here's the kit. Everything's in it—the bottle of soup, the rods and the electric flash. Grab your coat and vest, Mike. We gotta act. That whisky may prove too strong. If we don't act quickly now, there may be no shack, no golden peter for us to crack. Come on, guns!"

A rolled-up blanket under his arm, Slim crawled silently out under the flap at the rear of the tent. As similarly burdened and as silently, the others followed. The Kid, the dog under his arm, was the last to belly out. He blinked in the red leaping glare that fired earth and sky.

Below in the valley where the huddle of shanties of Haines Depot had stood, were many immense black holes. About those holes was strewn shapeless far-flung wreckage in which fires burned fitfully. But that red glare came from farther away. That red glare came from the hop-fields beyond the river. Running along and dancing upon and leaping up from the thousand high wires to which the hops had been strung, were a thousand-thousand flames.

It was as if the whole world were afire. The heat of those flames had dissipated that gray blanket of fog. They had reddened the moon. The very river was a river of blood.

"They've fired the hops!" breathed Slim. "The drunken glomers!"

"But the office is safe and all the gold!" shouted Scar-face. "Yuh can see the yaller paint on its sides. And the winder, guns! The shock o' them blasts has shattered the winder fur us. It'll be a cinch to git into thet office!"

On the outskirts of the flames, men were rushing about and reeling drunkenly. They looked like little black cinders spit from those flames.

"Go on!" cried out Slim, brandishing his clenched hand in the air. "Wreck things and burn things, you drunken overgrown kids!" He swung on the others. "Come on! We're men. We've got work to do!"

Amid all that glare and hullabaloo and havoc, the little yellow shack seemed quietly asleep. The men threw down their blankets in the field of grass and weeds and thistles and clustered together, stooping, furtive shadows.

Scar-face eyed the Kid.

"Come here, Kid," he said suddenly. "You go and hammer on thet door, while us three go through thet winder!"

"No, you don't, Scar-face!" said Slim quietly. "The Kid stays out of the whole thing. He's not to get nabbed if we are. He stays out here and plays the lookout—"

"Lookout? We don't need no lookout!"

The words were significant.

"—— youse, Scar-face!" cried Yorky. "Slim's runnin' this mob! Wot he says goes!"

Scar-face grunted surlily:

"What's the plan, then?"

"This," said Slim. "Scar-face and you, Yorky, go 'round to that front door. Bang against that door. While the racket is on, I'll go through that window!"

He turned to the Kid.

"Frisco Kid, you wait in this field near the road. Lie down in the weeds so you can't be seen—so any shots will go over your head. If any one comes, yell to me!"

The Kid, the dog under his arm, walked back toward the road.

Scar-face and Yorky were upon the front porch of the shack. They hurled their combined weight against the door. The door shook and groaned, but held firmly.

"Clear out of here!" yelled a voice from within the shack. "Clear out or we'll drill you, you drunken bums!"

The two men simulated the drunken hop-pickers they were supposed to be. They shouted and cheered and jeered.

"Thet youse, Curt Haines!" Yorky jeered. "Guardin' th' money ter pay us off termorrow—huh?"

From within the shack a shot cracked out. It shattered through an upper panel of the door. That panel was above the men's heads. But they scattered to either side. Yorky ran far back on the gravel sweep.

Slim dashed forward at that shot. He dashed through the field toward the window. The window was four feet above the field. He took that window feet first. Feet first he crashed through sash and fragments of glass.

Yorky, out on the gravel sweep before the shack, saw him disappear. He ran back toward the porch, calling in subdued but excited tones:

"Scar-face! Slim's got in!"

A cry shrilled out from the shack. It was a cry of surprise, a cry of warning.

It broke off in a dull sound. A pistol cracked. Then the hand that pumped that pistol seemed to be held in a terrific struggle. Furniture was scraped about, was overthrown, was rended apart with groaning noises.

The men on the porch forgot to assail the door. They listened. They sweated.

Again the pistol cracked. A resounding thump came from one wall of the shack. It was as though some heavy weight had been hurled against that wall. The shack shook to its very mudsills. There came a scream—a man's scream—a scream as of pain unendurable. It was hideous.

"Slim!" yelled Yorky. "They've broke Slim!"

With one savage kick, he splintered the door into halves. He went through, revolver in hand. After him followed Scar-face.

Outside in the weeds, the Kid waited. The dog was under his left arm. His heart pounded against that dog. Then he heard a panting voice, Slim's voice:

"Come—on in. I—fixed—those two guys. Flash the—light."

Behind the shattered window, a single shaft of white light bored through the blackness within the shack. It came from the flash-lamp in the hands of Scar-face. It was turned full upon Slim.

Slim had been through a hideous fight. His blue army shirt had been torn completely off his back. One torn sleeve draggled from his left wrist. From the waist up his body glistened white in that light, save where it was dirtied by powder smoke and streaked with bloody welts and scratches. His head was bleeding. As the Kid glimpsed him, he tore off the sleeve from his wrist. He wrapped the sleeve about his bleeding head.

"Gee!" muttered the Kid to the dog. "What a proud and reckless feller—that Slim!"

Yorky straightened up behind the window.

"Where's ol' Curt Haines? Didn't I hear he allus guarded his coin hisself afore pay-day? Slim, he didn't slip youse?"

"No, Yorky; he wasn't in here at all. There were only the two guards."

"Thet's all right," said Scar-face suddenly. "Now where's the peter?"

Slim took the electric torch from his hand and flashed it toward the rear of the office. There stood the huge safe. Stumbling over the broken furniture and the unconscious forms on the floor, the men followed Slim toward that safe. Slim knelt down and by the single shaft of light examined closely the door of that safe.

"Let's get to work. We can shoot it in no time. Here, Scar-face. You do the drilling."

"Me?" Scar-face was startled.

But he knelt down beside Slim. Followed the sounds of low directions, low orders; then the grind of drill on steel.

The Kid stood up stiffly in the thicket of weeds near the road. Like a little nervous bird, he cocked his head now to the right, now to the left.

The red glare was dying out of the sky. The fire in the hop-fields far away was lessening for lack of fuel. The wreckage of Haines Depot was only scattered and smoking heaps. Overhead where the blanket of fog had been, was now a slowly thickening blanket of smoke. The night was even blacker than before.

From the little yellow shack came a sudden outburst of voices:

"Hurry up, Scar-face! Rush it, man! Don't take all night on a tin can like that!"

"Shet up, will yuh! Yuh git me all rattled. Where's thet rod?"

The Kid could see neither Slim nor Scar-face. The sill of the window obstructed his vision. But he could see the shadowy form of Yorky bent over the kneeling men with tense watchfulness.

Suddenly Yorky straightened up. He said disgustedly:

"Yer too slow, Scar-face! Me, I thought youse was a yegg!"

"I can't work faster, I tell yuh! These drills are sumthin' fierce. Give me anuther iron!"

"That iron is all right, Scar-face!" cried Slim sharply. "—— you, you're stalling!"

Yorky broke in nervously:

"Aw, let's hurry, Slim! Slim, youse open ut!"

"Out of my way!" from Slim.

There came the slight scuffling of feet. Then again the chill grind of steel on steel.

The Kid listened excitedly. To the dog under his arm he breathed in excited little gasps:

"Slim's crackin' her now! Scar-face is too slow. It'll be a cinch fer Slim!"

Suddenly Slim said:

"Where's the soup?"

Just then, the dog that had hung drooping and forgotten under the Kid's left arm came to sudden life. He broke out barking. It was startlingly abrupt. The Kid had heard no one approaching. It was so startlingly abrupt that the Kid dropped the dog in his first panic of fear. The dog ran toward the road. He barked loudly. He barked excitedly.

"Gay-cat! Gay-cat!" cried the Kid. He ran through the weeds after the dog. "Yer'll give us away! Yer'll give Slim away!"

From the shack came oaths and the quick scraping of feet. Said Slim sharply:

"Douse the light! That dog heard something. Yorky, you see who's coming!"

The little shack went black. Some one said:

"I'll go, Slim."

Then the big heavy form of Scar-face appeared through the shattered door. He stepped to the edge of the porch. He peered down the road toward the bridge. Then he stepped back to the door, and listened.

"I'll shoot it anyway!" Slim was saying. "It's all ready but for the blankets. It's my last job. I'll shoot it anyway. Flash on the light, Scar-face!"

"Scar-face took th' torch. He went out—"

"Scar-face? Scar-face took the torch?" Slim's voice shook. "Yorky! He took that torch to signal them! My God!"

A chair crashed over. Yorky screamed out. He screamed out horridly:

"I'll cook—I'll kill thet stool!"

Scar-face at the door raised one hand above his head. In that hand the electric flash-lamp flared. It flared once. A single shaft of white light cleft the blackness. In that black night it was a stark signal.

Yorky leaped through the door. Scar-face jumped from the porch. He dashed straight into the field of weeds. A revolver glinted in Yorky's hand. He raised it, pointed it at the fleeing stool.

The night was loud with a fearful sound. That sound was the pounding of many racing feet. It came from the road. It was near.

With a crash, the revolver dropped from Yorky's hand. He stood swaying on bending knees. He tried to cry out, but he could not cry out. Words struggled in his throat. At last, in a terrible whisper:

"We're trapped, Slim! They're comin'. It's a plant. They've got us! And—I couldn't git thet stool! I lost my noive. I couldn't shoot! I bin too much in stir. And now—they've got me agin! They've got me agin!"

The last was a shriek. With that shriek, Yorky plunged from the porch into the field of weeds.

The Kid reached the road. He was chasing the barking dog. Coming toward him along the road were the black crowded shapes of men. They carried rifles. Their heads were wrapped in turbans. The Kid leaped back into the field. He ran toward the shack.

"Slim!" he shouted. "They's comin'! The ragheads is comin'!"

A tremendous blast of sound answered him from the shack. It was Slim's last job. In face of everything, Slim had cracked the safe!

Slim was at the door. He walked out into the arms of the ragheads. They closed about him like rats about a bit of food.

A big, heavy form bulked up in the weeds before the racing Kid. It was Scar-face Mike Hagan. As the Kid ran by toward Slim, Scar-face reached out and got the Kid by his overlarge coat. He pulled the Kid back and threw him flat in the weeds.

"They's got Slim!" sobbed the Kid. "The ragheads has got Slim. Slim, he's my buddy. Lemme go to Slim!"

Scar-face put a big hand on each of the boy's frail shoulders. By each of the boy's frail shoulders he held the boy down as in a crushing, terrible machine.

"They've got Slim all right," he said. "But yuh can't go to Slim. They'd nab yuh, too. They'd put yuh in a black hole on bread and water. They'd put yuh there fur life! But I held yuh back. I held yuh back 'cause I didn't want yuh nabbed. I saved yuh!"

But there was in the Kid's soul no answering thrill of gratefulness. His frail shoulders ached under Scar-face's hands. He felt only fear of Scar-face.

"Kid," said Scar-face, "now I'll show yuh how to earn some money. I'll show yuh how to earn thet road stake yuh want so bad!"

He shoved his scarred face closer to the Kid.

"Yuh'll come with me. When Slim's trial comes off, yuh'll git on the witness-stand and tell all yuh knows about Slim. I can't come out in the open and tell on Slim myself. And I knows a lot about Slim; I've follered him fur months! Yes, Kid; I've tracked Slim boy right acrost from thet peter job in the First National in Hartford!

"I don't care about Haines. There'll be only a measly handout o' a reward fur Slim in this case. I knowed thet. Thet's why I didn't bother none to save Haines' crop er town. He never knowed all what was comin'—Haines. I jest threw a note, tied to a stick o' wood, through thet winder where ol' Haines was settin' there in the dark, a-guardin' his money. Thet was the time Slim boy thought I was breakin' in the saloon. But thet note, it said only thet some one was goin' to crack his safe, and to watch out and nab him when I flashed the light!"

The Kid listened and, as he listened, he forgot the ache in his crushed shoulders. He lay flat in the weeds and saw only that white-scarred face above him. He was shocked by what that white-scarred face now meant to him. At last, he understood who Scar-face was.

Scar-face Mike Hagan was not one of the good people. He was a professional stool-pigeon. He faked that he was a yegg and betrayed men to get the reward on their heads. And he was telling the Kid to be a stool, also—a stool on Slim!

"Yuh tell all yuh knows about Slim, Kid," he was saying, "all what I said up there in the kiln about them bank safes drilled and post-office peters cracked. Them's the rewards we're after, Kid! And it's all straight goods, too. I knows, I tell yuh. I ain't follered Slim fur months, clear acrost the States, fur nuthin'. I knows a heap about Slim boy!

"But I can't come out in the open and tell all what I knows. I wish I could tell on Slim myself! I ain't skeered o' these yeggs; it's not thet, Kid; they'll go up, sure! It's the other yeggs. I got to work under cover o' bein' a yegg, and I got a lot more work to do. I can't git mixed up in this at all. My life ain't worth a beer ef the other yeggs knows I'm a stool!

"They'd never touch you, though. You're a kid—only a kid. Slim wouldn't let 'em touch yuh. And, Kid, there's a heap o' kale offered fur Slim boy! You and I'll divide the money. But yuh won't have to wait fur yer half, Kid. See—here's a hundred dollars!"

He held up a roll of bills before the boy's eyes.

"A hundred dollars!" he repeated hoarsely. "Yer road stake, Kid! Jest promise me yuh'll tell on Slim!"

From the gravel sweep before the shack came gruff commands in a voice that sounded like the voice of Haines. Then came sounds of marching feet, of men passing back along the road. The ragheads were taking Slim right by that tangle of thistles where the Kid lay.

The Kid lifted up his voice. It was his answer to Scar-face. He lifted up his voice so that the man passing on the road might hear.

"Slim! Slim!" he yelled. "Scar-face is the one that done yer! Scar-face! He's the stool!"

Scar-face leaped afoot. He made a sudden vicious movement toward his vest. He tore out his revolver. The Kid tried to squirm away through the weeds. Scar-face held him flat with one foot on his chest. He pressed the trigger. There was a soundless eternity. He pressed that trigger until his finger was white.

With an oath, he threw the harmless revolver away. He removed his foot from the Kid's chest. He kicked the boy. He kicked the boy until the boy could no longer feel those brutal kicks.

Then he spit into his hand. He spit many times into his hand. He rubbed that moistened hand on the cheek where was that scar. He rubbed and rubbed at that scar. When he drew his hand away from that flaming red cheek, there was no longer a hideous white streak of scar. He had rubbed off the paint of that faked-up mark.

He looked down at the bruised, unconscious form of the boy.

"Now try to cough on Scar-face to Slim!" he said. And he turned and strode away through the weeds.

It was gray empty dawn when the Kid awoke to the world's sorrow. A warm tongue was moist on his cheek. A whimper sounded in his ears, fear-filled and forlorn. It was the Gay-cat. The dog was whimpering miserably at his lack of life. The dog was licking his face frenziedly. He scooped up the dog into his arms.

"We'se lost Slim, Gay-cat," he said sorrowfully. "But that's no fault of your'n, old hobo. Didn't yer hear them ragheads first? Yer smelled them a mile! Yer sure some watchdog, Gay-cat!"

After a time, the Kid got painfully to his feet. Along the road, away from the wrecked town, he walked, limping at every step like a little broken old man.

Ahead near the blackened hop-fields stood the little tool-house of a jail—too tiny and too useless, perhaps, to be burned or dynamited. But in this dawn a certain use had been found for that little tool-house of a jail. On either side of that barred door, two ragheads squatted, their rifles across their knees.

The Kid forgot his painful bruises. His heart leaped with a great gladness. He ran toward the little jail.

"Slim!" he called. "Slim, it's me!"

The two Hindoos watched him wonderingly. He got on tiptoes and looked through the barred opening in the door.

Within, in that dark and foul-smelling hole, there was the sound of a man stirring. Then there was the sound of Slim's glorious voice—

"Is that you, Frisco Kid?"

"Sure, it's Frisco Kid, Slim. And Slim—Gay-cat's here, too!"

Slim appeared behind the bars. The Kid saw the manacles on his wrists. He went serious. What a fall had come to his proud and reckless Slim! He went terribly serious.

"He wanted me to tell on yer!" he gulped. "He said he'd give me half the reward—"

"Half the reward?"

"Yes, Slim, fer a road stake. All of a hundred dollars!"

"A hundred dollars? A hundred dollars for me, Atlanta Slim! Oh, the dirty, thieving—"

Slim broke off. He said quietly:

"That would be a lot of money to you, Frisco Kid. A hundred dollars would be some road stake, now. But you wouldn't—huh, Kid?"

"Aw, Slim! Aw, say now, Slim!"

Slim breathed hard. His voice when he next spoke was labored:

"My little buddy! I was going to take you with me and show you all the beautiful pictures in the great picture-galleries. I can't do that now; but I can do something else. They haven't frisked me yet, Kid. That's how I happen to have that road stake I promised you!"

He fumbled with one manacled hand in his trousers pocket.

"It's not much—only an ace spot. But it's from Slim who loved you and your little yellow dog. I may never see you again; but this may help you over the road that is hard and long and lonely. Take it, my Frisco Kid. Good-by!"

Slim reached his hands out from the dark. There was something in one of those manacled hands. It was a dollar bill.

The Kid could not see that bill. His eyes were blinded with tears. He felt that bill in his hand. With his hand, the bill between, he held on to Slim's hand.

"Good-by, Slim! And Gay-cat—he says good-by too, Slim!"

Blind with tears, hugging the dog and that bill convulsively, the Kid turned away and stumbled up the road—the road down which he had come the dawn before.

Slim peered through the grating after him. Softly he said:

"Yorky ran away! Scar-face turned Judas! But he came back to me—the little hobo kid and his little yellow dog!"

Up on the side of the valley the Kid looked back. There was in his deep-sunk and dewy eyes a wonderful light of triumph.

"No, I couldn't tell on Slim," he said. "Not fer no money. Slim, he was good to me!"

Adventure

JULY 1917
Vol.14 - No.3

According To His Caste
A Complete Novelette
by Patrick & Terence Casey

I

NO TROUSERS TO HIS BACK

ONE MORNING IN INDIAN SUMMER, a morning of pelting sunlight and of hot little gusts that drove brown and crimson leaves whirling down the road and that drove down the road, also, a golden chaff of dust, the Frisco Kid shuffled along, his hands slouched in his pockets, the yellow dog, Gay-cat, running at his side. And the Kid's thoughts were all wistful thoughts of winding rivers, of cool pools, and of swimming.

The Frisco Kid, small for his fifteen years, scrawny of neck, was a boy hobo, a road-kid. He had been railroading for two nights on the "rods" of freights. He had been hiking the whole long, hot Indian Summer dawning.

The countryside, brown and baked with Autumn, seemed a countryside that raised nothing but whirling leaves and dust. The dust was fine, powdery. It sifted through the ragged clothing of the boy. It lay upon his face like a brown flour. It choked his nostrils and sanded his throat. He longed for a "wash-up."

And then, beside the road he followed, he caught the flash of water between willow-trees.

To that side of the road lay a broad field, yellow with mustard weeds; and, squatting in the field, among the weeds, was a gable-roofed dusty-red building which, from the runway of planks leading up to the wide door in front, had every appearance of a barn. Behind the barn, to one side of it, a line of washing was hung out to dry: a man's undershirt, limp and khaki-colored, three pairs of black socks, two white outer shirts, and a pair of short, faded-green breeches which may have been used as swimming—or running—trunks.

Beyond the line of washing drooped the row of willows from between which the water glinted as from a mirror that catches the sun.

"There's swimmin' over there, Gay-cat!" said the Frisco Kid, his deep-sunk eyes eager. "Swimmin', old hobo, and a chanst to wash our clo'es. But farmers is grouchy sometimes," he admonished, "awful grouchy to hoboes. And the river is on his land," with some faint knowledge of riparian rights. "I wonder, now, is that farmer near his old barn?"

He looked closely at the dusty-red barn. The barn lacked windows in front; it seemed to sleep in the middle of the field. The line of washing was the only flaunt of life. As the Kid looked, it swayed and napped in the little gusts of wind.

The Gay-cat had caught the flash of water. His yellow head came up. He did not hesitate there beside the ramshackle fence. He wriggled through and trotted out, smart and boldly, into the tall mustard weeds. A few yards and he looked back, his black-tipped nose uptilted in surprise over the Kid not following him, and his stump of a tail wagging his fierce impatience.

The Frisco Kid took heart. Another look at the sleeping barn, the flapping line of washing, the impatient yellow cur, and he was out in the field, running through the wild mustard, racing along, his little body bent low, his course set directly for the glint of water.

They came, panting, into the cool shade of the belt of willows that followed the near bank of the stream. Here the Kid stood erect, done with his fear of the farm people. They could not see him, now, from the barn.

The stream was but a little stream. It was low and shrunk with the drought of Autumn, and either side of its bed was hot sandy beach. There were places where the water rippled over pebbly bars as over glistening white washboards; but there were places, too, that were deep—slow green pools, overhung with willows and cotton-woods, and cool with shadow.

The Frisco Kid did not shout, "Beat yer in, Gay-cat!" and, running down the bank, shedding his clothing piece by piece as he ran, plunge right in. That would be a boy's way. That would be the way of a boy who had been ardently wishing for a green-shadowed river in which to swim—the way of a glad, glad boy who had chanced at last upon his wish. And the Kid was more than a boy, more even than a road-kid. He was a full-fledged "blown-in-the-glass stiff."

Now, the great army of hoboes that railroad and foot it about this country, form a complete order of society, a markedly defined caste. It is a low and pariah caste, forsooth; yet it is nevertheless a large caste of beggars, vagabonds and outcasts. And like every other caste, this large caste allows of being divided into several smaller, distinct and inner castes, for hoboes believe in the complete equality of men in all things no more than does any one else.

Wherefore, there is within the great hobo caste, a meager class of Brahmins, an aristocracy which dominates the riffraff and arrogates to itself a feeling of superiority over the rank and file. The men of this high inner caste call themselves "blown-in-the-glass stiffs."

They are the real McCoy. They are those who are "comets," "tramps royal," "good moochers." A comet is a hobo who can railroad with ease and nonchalance over the whole country in a few weeks. He never pays a fare. He rides only the fastest trams. A tramp royal is one who hoboes across continents rather than countries, a paradoxical globe-trotter who neither pays toll nor works, yet never misses a meal or a decent bed. And a good moocher is he who can "panhandle" the "main stem" of a town or "buzz" a mansion with equal facility, and withal beg so winningly as to amass a small fortune in a surprisingly short while.

These men are, therefore, the most efficient men in the hobo caste. They consider themselves the true hoboes. They look with contempt upon less efficient hoboes. They abhor "bindle stiffs" who never ride trains. They abominate "tomato-can bums" who never wash. They are proud, consciously proud of their position in the hobo caste; that makes them content to be hoboes; and they are fiercely jealous of their position. They shun contemptuously lower orders of tramps as a Brahmin shuns a Sudra. They associate with the blown-in-the-glass stiffs.

The efficient men in every caste, up and down the whole tremendous edifice of civilization, keep themselves most clean. That is part and parcel of, and a bit of the reason for, their efficiency. It is the major reason for the blown-in-the-glass stiff's efficiency. What with railroading on rods and trucks and tops, it is impossible to keep clean for even a short length of time. Yet it is necessary that they keep clean, that they have a "front," as their argot has it.

With their bodies scrupulously washed, their hair cropped, their faces shaved, their clothing so well-brushed and free from travel-grime as to look almost respectable, they can "brace" the finest mansion or "drill down" the "main drag" of the town without chancing being pulled as a vag.

The Frisco Kid was something of the comet, a bit of the tramp royal, and a deal of the good moocher. He was, in a word, a blown-in-the-glass stiff. He was a boy, too, and like a boy, he desired to rush pell-mell down to the stream, undressing as he ran, and plunge straightway into the water and splash and play about.

But pride of caste held a check-rein on his impulses. He was a blown-in-the-glass stiff, one of an efficient few in a shiftless and lackadaisical caste. And his front, his clothing, was in a horrible condition. It was not fit for any blown-in-the-glass stiff. It unfitted him for the business of being a blown-in-the-glass stiff. Wherefore, ere ever he could think of swimming, as a true blown-in-the-glass stiff, he must wash his clothes.

The Frisco Kid went to the water's edge and slowly, thoughtfully, methodically, he undressed. The Gay-cat was already frolicking in the stream, barking to him to come on. The Kid paid him no heed. With slowness, with thought and with method, he dipped his damp and dusty blue shirt into the water, wrung it out, and dipped and wrung it out again.

The Frisco Kid did not wear much clothing in the hot months: a blue shirt, a pair of blue jeans, a ragged over-large coat, a cap, and track-worn shoes.

The coat he did not attempt to wash. He removed the precious matches he always carried for his cigarets. He beat out a great cloud of dust by swinging the coat against a boulder left high and dry on the beach. Then he draped the coat over the boulder beside the matches and his misshapen shoes.

But the blue jeans were stiff with oil and dust. They needed a thorough washing. The oily jeans he dipped in the water, wrung out, pounded, dipped, wrung out, and pounded again and yet again. Then, his arms tired and his washing accomplished, he left the shirt and blue jeans to soak out in a shallow pool, where they were anchored to the bottom by a rock as large as his two fists.

He now joined the dripping, frolicking Gay-cat in a swim. The swim would constitute a wash-up, cleansing away all the thousand fine grains of dust which fretted his skin.

The Frisco Kid was brown, brown almost to the color of chocolate, with much swimming in the sun and in lazy, winding, green-bordered tiny streams such as this. His brown slim young body rose upon a convenient rock above a pool just made for diving, flashed down, and came up again. The hair dripping into his eyes, his mouth spouting water and great shouts of happiness, he chased the barking blissful Gay-cat, splashed him; and was chased in turn by the happy-go-lucky mongrel.

It was a golden hour, an hour of care-free hearts, an hour of morning sun and sweet clean water, an hour of madcap pranks, laughter, shouts, frenzied barking, of an altogether abandoned joy in nakedness and freedom—a happy pagan hour in a pagan day.

But soon the shadows huddled close about the boles of the willows and cottonwoods, and the little stream became like a mold of silver under the stark sun, straight overhead. It was noon.

The Kid left off shouting and racing about. He thought of lifting his clothes from their anchorage in the shallow pool and spreading them out upon the sandy beach to dry. He thought of spreading himself out upon the sandy beach to bake. It was very warm now, and, in a little, his clothes would be fit to wear and then, in the cool of the afternoon, he could "batter" the back doors for lunch. He felt hungry.

He waded over to the side of the stream where was the shallow pool. The blue shirt was dragging at the anchor rock, the current pulling at it as a wind pulls at a flag. The Kid lifted the shirt. His brown face, shiny from the swim, was suddenly pale. The blue jeans had been torn away from under the rock by the steady pull of the current. They had floated down-stream. They were gone.

The Gay-cat was playing with the pasty body of a dead bullfrog on the opposite bank. The Kid called to him:

"Come here, Gay-cat. I've—I've lost my pants. They's floated away. We gotta hunt 'em up quick, old-timer."

He wrung out the shirt and spread it upon the beach to dry, the while his eyes darted about in search of the only trousers to his back. He was very methodical, very quiet, like one a little stunned.

He ran along the bank, looking for a blue soggy mass that should be floating down with the current. He stood for moments beside a pebbly bar over which the water trickled so thinly that surely the jeans must be caught and held fast there. But no jeans floated with the current, no blue jeans lay in the slack water or along the sandy banks.

Thus, he had run a little distance downstream, around several bends, when there uprose before him, overhanging the stream, the back porch of a white two-storied house. Full in the sun on the back porch, his chair tilted on two legs against the wall, a man slept, a ratty little man, hardly bigger than the Kid, his bare head close-clipped and shaped like an upended egg.

The Frisco Kid stopped shortly. He motioned the Gay-cat to draw near. Then dog and naked boy watched that man sleep on the porch.

Finally the dog looked up at the boy, an intelligible question in his animal eyes.

"No, Gay-cat," counseled the Kid, his face turning ruddy-brown with a sudden sense of his nakedness. "We can't go no farther, you and me. That's the farmer what owns that barn and this river. This is his old farmhouse. And he looks kinder horstile, don't yer think, old hobo? We'd better go back."

The Kid made back, examining closely the bars, raking the bottoms of pools with a stick, poking under bushes and about the water-whelmed roots of willows and cottonwoods, searching everywhere it was possible for the jeans to lie concealed. He grew ever more hurried and anxious. He rushed from one side of the stream to the other at the merest whim; rushed back again; and all for nothing.

His breath came short after all his anxious dashes, and he felt weak in the knees. He was sick with disappointment and despair. He would have cried only—only the Gay-cat would have seen.

At last, dull with despair, he went to the bank and struggled into his shirt, though it was still wet. He replaced the precious matches, and put on cap and coat, for somehow he felt a sensation of cold and loneliness. And then, his shoes in his hand, he turned from the stream and, without another look, in his bare feet climbed the bank.

The Gay-cat followed at his heels, head down, tail drooped, a silent dog with all light-heartedness gone out of him. The Gay-cat had accompanied the Kid on all the futile hunts for the missing blue jeans. There had been said no word, but the Gay-cat knew the Kid was heartsick and miserable, and that misery of the Kid had communicated itself to the dog.

The Frisco Kid halted among the willows at the top of the bank. Before him lay the field of mustard weeds, and beyond that the wandering road, and still beyond that the world, big and empty, inhospitable and pitiless.

The Kid had no home to go to, no lunch awaiting him in a kindly mother's kitchen. Yet that is the normal condition of all hoboes. And the Kid was a hobo. That was his normal condition. Now, however, something else had been added to the particular sum of his hardships, something wrong, abnormal and staggering. He had no trousers to his back.

The Frisco Kid was in a pitiable fix. With the jeans covering his nakedness, he might have gone forth at once and begged a handout at a farmhouse door. But he was in his shirt-tails and coat-tails. All on a sudden he had become unfitted for the business of being a hobo, of being a blown-in-the-glass stiff. What could he do, a half-grown boy, a hobo and a vagabond, naked in the stark day, with an empty road of long silent miles ahead and the big soundless world to either hand, unfriendly and pitiless?

II

A KNIGHT OF THE SQUARE CIRCLE

THE FRISCO KID STOOD AMONG THE WILLOWS, hesitant, fearful of venturing forth. All at once, he turned as if to run back down the bank. A great clatter from the barn had frightened him. But it was only the line of washing, swaying and flapping in a sudden hot gust.

The Frisco Kid looked at that line of washing, then at the barn, a dusty-red bulk. As in front, so in back, there were no windows. The barn slept quietly among the mustard weeds.

"Keep quiet, Gay-cat," breathed the Kid, "keep awful quiet, 'cause we'se gonna mooch." And he stepped, on bare tiptoes, out into the mustard weeds.

The dog followed with a certain caution that seemed to have come abruptly at the Kid's words. It was almost as if he imitated the Kid, move for move. He followed behind, and lifted each leg carefully, and put each leg down with the same silence and precision. Often he paused, even as the Kid paused, one foreleg raised and bent above the paw, poised for the next forward step, while, with sharp nose, he sniffed the air and looked, now to the right, now to the left. There was something about him that seemed almost wolfish then, as if the ferine strain sleeping within him had awakened and gripped him, and now dominated him utterly.

The Frisco Kid advanced between the wild mustard with body bent and head lowered, looking now to the right, now to the left. When but a few yards from the barn, he broke into a quick run. He ran along the line of washing, the shirts and yellow undergarment flapping in his face.

Standing on tiptoes beneath where the faded-green trunks hung, he reached up to the line, pulled out two clothes-pins, and then bundling the trunks into a tight round ball, scuttled forward and flattened himself against the rear wall of the barn. Now was he safe to get into the stolen trunks.

The Kid felt no compunction at stealing the trunks. He was a hobo. The ethics of the great hobo caste were his ethics. A hobo considers it no sin to commit a petty theft. And it was a petty theft to steal the trunks. For all that they were made of some good jersey, soft and agreeable to the touch, their faded color told a story of many washings. They were old. And the Kid needed them sadly. His, then, was a necessary theft and hence, according to hobo ethics, a permissible, even an advisable theft.

The dog humped himself on his haunches and watched the Frisco Kid as he slipped into the trunks. They fitted him after a fashion. They may have been the swimming-trunks of the farmer's son. An elastic cord ran around the top of them and, while the Kid's lean stomach did not distend that cord, at least the cord circled his waist snugly enough to hold up the trunks.

The Kid's face glowed a happy red beneath its coat of tan, as he put on his track-worn shoes.

"I've got it, old hobo!" he nodded brightly to the dog. "Now we can go down the stream and that little hayseed on the porch can't say a word agin us. We'll bring back these trunks, mebbe, after we find my pants."

The Kid came back to the stream. The faded-green trunks were almost hidden by the ends of his man-size coat, and his brown legs beneath looked very stark and spindly. His feet slapped in their sockless shoes. Yet the Kid no longer felt naked. He started down the bank of the stream at a fast clip, the dog following close behind, his sharp-nosed yellow head raised pertly in a renewal of interest.

But no little ratty man with close-clipped egg-shaped head now slept upon the back porch of the two-storied white house. The porch lay empty and deserted in the sunshine.

With an accession of boldness, the Frisco Kid and the dog strode along the bank toward the porch and under it where it overhung the stream. And there, in the shadows, wrapped about one of the stilts which upheld the porch over the stream, the Kid came, quite unexpectedly, upon his blue jeans.

Making up the bank and further under the concealment of the porch, the Kid doffed the faded-green trunks and cast them upon the sand at his feet. He was in haste to get back into his jeans. But the jeans were very wet. He wrung them out and beat them against the foundation timbers of the porch.

"They's gotta do, Gay-cat," he said to the dog. "We hasn't no time to lose. Don't yer hear them sounds of eatin' upstairs?"

From overhead came the clatter of knives and forks against plates and of spoons in cups.

"That little hayseed didn't look a bit jake, old-timer; he sure looked horstile. But let's get up there and mebbe we can get a setdown. I'se awful hungry, old hobo. I guess it's that swim and all the runnin' about, that's done it. We'll try to mooch a poke-out, anyways. Say, Gay-cat, where is yer?"

The Kid looked about for the dog. The dog had disappeared into the dark under the house. Also had disappeared—though the Kid did not notice this—the faded-green trunks at his feet. But now, as the Kid looked round, the dog scurried out to him, his stump of a tail wagging energetically as if in happiness and triumph over some achievement done.

The Kid and the dog stepped out from under the porch. Come of the hunger pangs that were gnawing his stomach, the Kid had wholly forgotten now about the faded-green trunks, which he had meant truly to return to the wash-line. Quickly, by means of one of the stilts, he clambered up into the porch. He was going to batter the back door.

The dog sat up on his yellow haunches upon the sand below and lifted his nose and animal eyes in a pitiable expression of helplessness. He could not climb up into the porch. It seemed as if, in a moment, he would yowl.

"Aw, come on," urged the Kid. "And don't yer make no noise, old Gay-cat. Do yer wanta queer me? Jes' you make around this house, old-timer, and see if yer can't come up the front way."

The dog got upon all-fours and strode, with many a backward glance, toward the front of the house.

The Kid went around the sun-bathed porch. Where the sounds of dining emanated through a screen door, he paused to knock. He could not see through the close screening of the door, but he knew, from the sounds of dining, that some one was within in the shade of the room. And hurriedly, lying fluently like a true blown-in-the-glass stiff, he said:

"Aw, yer couldn't stack us up to some eats, now, could yer, boss? Me and my dog, we's come a awful long ways, this mornin'. We're makin' down to Midvale Junction to my brother there. Mebbe yer knows him—a one-armed guy what lowers the gates acrost the road. My mother's sick in a hospital up Frisco way, and I'm a-goin' down to live with my brother. We's come a awful long ways, this mornin', the dog and me. Yer couldn't stack us up to a lump of somethin', could yer?"

A heavy voice stopped the Kid.

"Cut it, bo, an' beat it quick. We don't fall fer that line of yer's one bit. What'd yuh do—crisscross with that bum that was here last night, an' come back to work us agin? Beat it now, or we'll git a dick after yuh. G'wan!"

"Aw, boss; aw, say now, boss," pleaded the Kid incoherently, his sunburnt nose pressed so hard against the wire screen that it was almost white. "Couldn't yer give us jes' a little scoffs—a poke-out, a ball-lump, jes' a sand'ich even, jes' for the dog and me?"

He waited. There was a whispered consultation going on within. And he could make out, now, three men seated about a linen-covered table that steamed with hot food. They did not have the appearance of farmers or farm laborers. Two of them wore sweaters that looked very out of place in the warm Indian Summer noon. The other ate with his coat on. He was a stout, florid-complexioned man, with a white vest and a red necktie from which a diamond, big as a pea, sparkled. The Kid knew him, right off, for the "main gee" of the three.

"Oh, don't tell me what the Gouger'd do," this fellow was saying to the other two, with a show of anger. "Gouger Meehan's too superstitious. I'm afraid he's losin' his nerve. An' I'm bossin' him anyways—I'm bossin' this whole shebang! I tell yuh, I won't have these boes buzzin' us fer meals no more!"

He turned toward the screen door and the Frisco Kid beyond it. A sneer bent his large mouth.

"Yuh got yer orders, bo," he said. "Beat it!"

The Frisco Kid turned away. As he did, he almost stumbled over the dog who had come around the porch from the front of the house and was then hugging his knees.

" 'Tain't no use, old hobo," he said to the dog, a melancholy wistfulness in his voice. "We don't eat here, we don't even get a hand-out. This is sure a horstile place."

The Frisco Kid looked up quickly. A man was watching him.

The man had just come around the porch from the front of the house. He was a little man, hardly taller than the boy, about five-feet-four, with close-clipped egg-shaped head, a battered face blue-black from much shaving, and uncommonly broad shoulders. He was the little ratty man the Kid had seen asleep on the porch when he had been searching for his jeans. He smiled now with open friendliness at the boy, his face screwing up into a network of wrinkles.

"What's thet yuh say about this place bein' horstile?" he asked.

"Aw, I didn't mean no harm, boss," said the Kid, quite taken aback, scraping the flooring with one sockless shoe. "I only wanted some eats." His face glowed. "Aw, yer couldn't stack us up to some chow, now, could yer, old-timer?"

"Me?" said the little man, and he laughed. "Why don't yuh ast me somethin' hard? I guess I sure kin! Say, kid, yuh never heard of Gouger Meehan turnin' down a stiff, did yuh? Don't know when I may have ter hit the rods an' back doors myself. Come on; I'll fix yuh up."

He made to go by the Kid toward the screen door. But the look in the Kid's deep-sunken eyes stopped him. It was a look of stupefaction, as if the Kid were dazed by some great intelligence.

"What's eatin' yuh, bo?" he asked with his frank, wrinkled smile.

The Kid stuttered quite helplessly.

"Aw, bo; aw, say now, bo! Ye ain't stringin' me none, now, is yer? Yer really mean yer is Gouger Meehan, the fighter?"

The little man laughed outright and slapped his knee with one knotted hand.

"Thet's me, pal—Gouger Meehan, the best 133-pound boy on the coast. Yuh ain't leery, are yuh? I won't eat yuh. But I will give yuh somethin' ter eat."

He turned toward the screen door.

"No, yuh don't, Gouger!" broke in a new and heavy voice.

The screen door was open and the stout, red-faced man in the white vest, who ate with his coat on, was filling the oblong of it, the pea-sized diamond in his red necktie flashing violently in the sunlight.

His full lips slapped together.

"Yuh don't set up no more of these boes, Gouger! Oh, I know all about yuh bein' afraid to turn down a bo fer fear it'll bring yuh bad luck; but I'm gittin' sick an' tired of yer superstitions. I'll have no more stiffs eatin' here."

"Shucks, yuh wouldn't turn this kid away, would yuh, Briggs? Looket his neck! Why, he looks like he hasn't et in a week."

The large mouth of the stout red-faced man curved again in a sneer.

"Aw, yuh don't come over me any with that soft stuff, Meehan. I know what yer afraid of. An' I'm gittin' sick an' tired of yer good-luck bosh. Yer losin' yer nerve, Gouger. Yuh wouldn't train in any place but this joint, with that barn of a gym 'most a city block away. 'Cause why? 'Cause yuh happened to win a couple of fights in this neck o' the woods when yuh trained here afore. An' now yuh wanta set up every bo fer a square at the same table with me. 'Cause why again? Jes' 'cause yuh think it'll bring yuh luck. I'll stand it no more!"

The Frisco Kid looked from the prizefighter to the stout red-faced man in a great wonder. It was as if he could not understand the domineering tones of the stout man when speaking to the prize-fighter, the almost pleading tones of that celebrity of the square circle.

"Gee," he whispered in a hot breath of amazement, "I'd eat him up if I was the Gouger! The Gouger can lick any one, one hand!"

As if actuated, telepathically, by the Kid's idea of him, the Gouger's face had set, of a sudden, into firm wrinkles of determination. His voice dropped its pleading tones and he said quietly, without any bluster:

"Thet's enough, Briggs. Yuh listen ter me. Yer my manager, but yer gonna quit me ef I lose this fight. Aw, I know. Every one'll put the skids under me ef I go down fur the count. I'll be jes' a punk pug, down an' out. But it won't be the first time. Thet's why I wanta feed this kid. I know what it is. An' I'm gonna feed him, right now. Yuh kin chase yerself off, ef yuh don't like it. Now git outta my way."

The manager changed face with a suddenness that seemed hypocritical. He laughed perfunctorily.

"Oh, don't get sore, Gouger. Have it yer own way—have everything yer own way. But I wanta tell yuh one thing. Yuh ain't goin' to lose this fight; but win or lose, I won't throw the skids under yuh. Yuh know me, Gouger. I'll stand by yuh."

"That's us," spoke up the two sweater-garbed men at his back. "We'll stick by yer, Gouger."

"We'll see," said the prize-fighter almost morosely.

He turned to the Kid.

"Come on, old-timer," he said, his battered face once again wrinkling into a contagious smile. "An' bring the hound-dawg along, too."

III
THE GOUGER OBEYS A "HUNCH"

THE FRISCO KID PAUSED BETWEEN TWO MOUTHFULS as with a sudden fear.

"He won't quit yer, will he?" he asked. "That big feller, I mean. He's your manager, huh? He won't leave yer 'cause of me, now?"

The prize-fighter laughed.

"Don't yuh worry none, son," he said. "He'll throw the skids under me soon 'nuff. Yuh jes' go ahead an' eat."

He sat back and looked up at the ceiling.

"I've got a hunch—got it the moment I lamped yuh, kid. Yuh stick around here awhile. Terday is my last day of trainin'. Termorrer I dry out ter make the weight. Gotta fight at two-thirty termorrer. Yuh stick around till after the fight."

The Kid looked at the prize-fighter, his gipsy-blue eyes shining with thankfulness and awe.

"Gee," he said, "I'll be awful glad to stick around, Gouger. And Gay-cat—can Gay-cat stick around, too?"

The Gouger looked blank for the moment.

"I mean him, my old pup," said the Kid, and he motioned to the dog, erect on his haunches on the chair alongside of him, his forepaws upon the table and his jaws snapping into a juicy cut of steak that was smeared with fried onions.

The Gouger smiled, his battle-hacked face a network of wrinkles, and then nodded quickly.

"Cert," he said. "I made a dead fall ter thet yeller hound-dawg the moment I lamped him. I've got a hunch, kid, I tell yuh; an' my hunches are usually pretty good. Yuh stick around awhile, you an' the hound-dawg, an' after you've finished chowin', it'll be about time ter go up ter the gym an' do a spell of indoor work. Yuh come along an' tote the dawg. An' don't yuh take no orders from nobody but me."

The Kid could not speak. Like all hoboes, he always had thought prize-fighters great men. Now, having met one of their number in Gouger Meehan, and having plumbed to a warm spot in the Gouger's heart, he was sure that prize-fighters were great men. He could only look his thankfulness and awe.

After a little, he fell again to eating. He finished the bounteous helping of buttered potatoes, juicy steak and fried, pungent onions.

The pugilist ceased drumming with his knotty fingers on the edge of the table to order, from the kitchen, a second helping for the Kid and for his dog. As the Kid attacked the second helping with undiminished gusto, the ring-man no longer drummed on the table. He watched the Kid, his gray eyes thoughtful, almost somber, beneath their projecting frontal bone.

After a little more, the Frisco Kid looked up, and his eyes, the blue of the gipsying Celt, were spread wide in their deep-sunk pits.

"Gee!" he breathed as if to himself, looking full at the Gouger. "It must be swell to be a fighter like him and lick everybody, one hand!"

The pugilist started, as if rudely awakened from deep thought. He tilted his head to one side.

"What's thet yer spieling, pal?" he asked. "Yuh know," he added," a little shamefacedly, "I can't hear so well. Sometimes, when the wind's away from me, I can't hear the tap of the gong at the end of a round. It's these things—cauliflower ears." He touched his ears.

The Frisco Kid looked at his ears, then almost unconsciously felt of his own. He could feel the curves and indentations in his ears; but the prize-fighter's ears he could see, had no such curves and indentations. They were red and bloated from helix to lobe, and, where once had been the great cave of the ear, was now only a hole of pinhead size.

"I'm gittin' old," said the pugilist soberly, with a tinge of gloom. "Thet's why I clip my hair so clost—so the gray hairs won't show. Yes, I'm gittin' old," and he shook his oddly-shaped head. "I'm not the Gouger enny more. I don't bore in like I used ter. I guess I've taken too many beatin's about the head ter care much about doin' it now. Thet's why I can't hear—too many beatin's on the head."

He leaned toward the Kid.

"But this other guy, Slugger Sweigert, he's young. He's a back-blocker, a Cockney from Australia. An' he don't know nuthin' about the game; he's a tin-eared boob. But he's never bin beaten about the head like me—he's only had about ten fights—an' he's fresh an' young.

"Gee, thet's why I gotta train so hard," he said with a kind of sigh of regret. "I hate it—the road-work, an' sparrin', an' gittin' down ter weight. But I have ter go through with it ter stand a chance in this fight. Ef I lose this fight, I'll be a back-number, a has-been. There'll be no more long goes fur me, no more big money; only the four-round glove-fests with a bunch of hams. But yuh'll help me win this fight, huh, kid?" he ended almost pleadingly. "Yuh'll lemme try out my hunch, an' stick around awhile, you an' yer dawg, eh, kid?"

The Frisco Kid, feeling suddenly weighed down by this new if vague responsibility, could only nod in dumb assent. The dog beside him on a chair, sat up and licked his chops to signify that he had had a sufficiency. In significance of the same, the Kid shoved back his chair and asked for a smoke.

The Gouger shook his close-clipped, egg-shaped head.

"I'm in trainin'," he said meaningly. "I can't smoke while I'm on this gag. But I'll buy yuh a cigar round in front. Kin you smoke a cigar, kid?"

"Can I smoke a seegar? Aw, say now, Gouger!"

The Kid and the dog followed the prize-fighter out of the dining-room and round the porch to the front of the roadhouse. The Gouger's manager and two sparring mates, known as Bud and Steve, were not in front. According to the tavern-keeper, they had gone on ahead to the gymnasium.

At the information, the prize-fighter pulled out a heavy gold watch from a little pocket in the front of his trousers.

"Whew!" he whistled, as he scanned the face of it. "One-forty-five. It's time we oughter be strollin' up the road ter the gym." He turned to the Kid. "Yuh passed it in comin' down, didn't yuh—a big red dusty-lookin' barn?"

The Kid nodded remotely, his mind and fingers busy over the business of removing the label from a stout black cigar. Then, out upon the road and on toward the gymnasium he followed the Gouger, exhaling great puffs of white smoke into the hazy Indian Summer air, the Gay-cat trotting, round-bellied and contented, beside him.

The wide door of the red dusty barn was open and a number of men were standing about in the sunshine. They made room for the Gouger to enter, eyeing him with singular admiration and venturing a word of greeting, even though their acquaintance might be of the slightest. They were fight-fans.

They filed somewhat sheepishly into the big, ill-ventilated gymnasium and took seats along the walls, sitting alert and stiffly postured.

The Gouger left the Kid sitting on a chair near the punching-bag frame, his legs dangling above the floor and the dog sitting up in his lap with ears cocked and black-spotted nose sniffing.

There was a smell of sweat in the air. The Gouger opened a trolley-weighted door in one wall and went into the little room beyond—the rub-down room.

After a short wait, he came out, girt in a gymnasium suit which was different from fighting-trunks in that it had an upper, like a swimming-suit, covering his chest. For a run of minutes, he caused the punching-bag to beat a tattoo against its frame.

The Kid and the dog watched him in an immeasurable admiration.

"Gee, Gay-cat," the Kid breathed to the dog, "what an arm that Gouger has! Jes' see how he makes that bag dance. And he can keep it up! I wouldn't wanta be hit like that for anything—not us, huh, Gay-cat?"

The yellow dog watched the thudding bag as if it were some disturbing fly, buzzing above his head.

The pugilist swung hard on the punching-bag and then turned away to lift the pulling-machines on the wall. That was to strengthen his back muscles. He skipped rope like a tomboy, to limber his legs and quicken his footwork. A fast game of handball, with the Gouger opposing his two sparring mates, sped through an interval of ten minutes.

Then, when the Gouger and the two sparring partners were freely oozing moisture, the gloves were donned for sparring. The crowd of fight-fans stood up, thereat, and formed about the Gouger and his particular opponent an eager hollow square.

The Frisco Kid stood up upon his chair in order to see over the heads of the men. The Gay-cat, disturbed from his lap, bounded down upon the flooring and crept between the legs of the fight-fans. But the Kid called softly to him and when he at last drew near, lifted him up beside him upon the top of the punching-bag stand.

"Now yer can see, old hobo," the Kid whispered into one twitching ear. "You stay right there, and yer'll see the Gouger lick those two guys, one hand."

The men, in sparring, used gloves an ounce or two heavier than the regulation boxing-gloves. The extra weight of padding protected the sparring partners from receiving damage at the hands of the Gouger; the constant pistoning of those heavy gloves strengthened the Gouger's arms; and when the time came, the following day, to put on the fighting-gloves, the regulation five-ounce calfskins would feel very light to the Gouger after the daily weight of the large gymnasium gloves. For rounds, he would be able to lay about him with those light fighting-gloves, ere awakening the fatigue poisons in the muscles of his arms.

The Gouger took on one sparring partner, the red-headed freckled fellow called Bud. They fiddled about and, for two short rounds, tapped each other quickly but lightly. Then the Gouger boxed the second sparring mate for three rounds.

The Frisco Kid breathed a deep sigh of relief when the second set-to was over.

"Gee, I was kinder leery of that feller," he said as he lowered the dog to the floor, referring to the second sparring partner called Steve. "That feller looks sorter fierce, he's got so much black hair on him. But the Gouger fixed him all right. I'll bet Steve's glad it's all over!"

However, despite the Kid's anxiety and tension, the mains had proved very tame. The Gouger had not wanted to extend himself on the day preceding the fight, and both sparring mates had been fearful of inflicting any material damage. Were they to lay open his lip, or bruise him about the deep-set eyes, Slugger Sweigert would surely remark it, ere the fight began the following day, and he would then attempt to aggravate with further blows that cut lip or bruised eye. Truly, a little thing; yet a blinded eye or streaming lip have been known so to bother a man as to lose the contest for him.

The sparring terminated the day's work. The fight-fans crowded out of the barn, discussing among themselves the Gouger's appearance and his chances of winning or losing the following day. As the Gouger swung open the trolley-weighted door of the rub-down room, he beckoned the Kid to follow him.

He was waiting for the Kid, as the boy entered, the dog squeezing in after him. And a far-away look was in his gray eyes—his seconds, had that look made itself visible during a fight, would have called it "the rattle" and shaken their heads.

"Say," he said to the Kid, "once I thought Hackett's gym was a palace, when I used to read about it in the fight-news back East. A palace!" He grunted. "Huh! Looket it, will yuh!"

He pointed about him at a sun-riven chink in the roughly-shingled, slanting, raftered roof; at the paneless window in the side wall, patched up with photographs of men, stripped and in fighting pose; at the antiquated stove, thrumming with heat and sputtering grime; at the rough rub-down tables.

"It's yer own fault, Gouger," spoke up Manager Briggs.

The manager was standing to one side, behind the scales. His red face glossily moist in the sweaty closeness of the little room, he was looking over the arm of the scales, at the Gouger and the Kid, with a surly eye.

"Yep, it's yer own fault," he continued, his mouth bent sourly. "When yuh fust came West, yuh conditioned here. Yuh beat 'Spider' Feeley then, an' ever since yuh've trained here at Hackett's. They won't fix the place up fer yuh an' they don't have to. They know yuh'll come back. 'Cause why? 'Cause yuh believe yuh'll win, if yuh train here. Yer too superstitious a guy, Gouger."

The pugilist laughed easily.

"Oh, I'm used ter it. I guess I've trained in this camp fur every go I've fought in this neck o' the woods, sence I knocked out Spider Feeley in the fifteenth round, ten years ago. An' I oughta be used ter—"

"Come, Gouger," snapped the manager. "Git outta yer duds an' see what yuh weigh today."

Meehan pulled off his gymnasium suit. He was black-haired and hence, by nature, given to browning under the sun; yet because in doing road-work he was always bundled up sudorifically, in order to induce sweating off the pounds of extra weight, he was not tanned. He stood forth then, upon the scales, as white of skin as a babe. He tipped the iron bar at the 135-pound notch.

"Yuh'll have to dry out that extra two pounds between now an' tomorrer, or we'll forfeit our deposit," said Manager Briggs, sharp as ever. "Cut down on the liquids, Gouger—water, soup, an' so forth. The weight's a hundred an' thirty-three pounds, one-half hour afore ringside, remember. A couple of shots of water, after weighin' in, will make up the pounds yuh lose today."

The Gouger, stark naked, disappeared into the darkness and slipperiness of the shower-room, as the little boxed-off portion of the rub-down quarters was dignified. Came, then, the splash and spray of water on his body. It sounded more like the drip of running oil than of a pure fluid. It sounded thus because of the thick sweat which coated his body.

The Gouger took especial pains to allow the jet to stream on his lean stomach. His stomach was the keystone of the arch of his strength, that he had to render callous to blows, smashes and lifting punches.

Emerging from the shower-room, dripping wet, the Gouger stretched himself contentedly, at full length on his back, on a narrow rub-down table. He enjoyed the soothing, oily lotions rubbed into his body by the lightning-like strokes and pats of his sparring mates. He drew a deep breath of happiness as, his muscles limbering under the process, he felt fresh and vigorous once more.

And then, as if to shatter his happiness, Manager Briggs said:

"Better tell this kid to git a move on, Gouger. This is all fer today. We can't have him hangin' round no longer. Better tell him to move on."

The Gouger threw off the stroking hands of his sparring mates and sat up. His gray eyes flashed in anger like cold stars.

"Yuh heard me once, Briggs. I mean what I say. I've made a dead fall ter thet kid an' he's not goin' ter skid till he wants ter. The kid's goin' ter stick around. He's my mascot fur luck—him an' his hound-dawg. An' he's goin' ter be at the ringside termorrer. Ef he can't swing a towel, he kin pack one of the buckets ennyways."

"You cop!" grunted the manager sulkily. "Yuh're sure a bug fer luck."

The Gouger paid him no heed. His gray eyes were on the Kid and there seemed, now, a warm light in them.

"Kid," he said, "yuh'd like ter see the fight termorrer, now wouldn't yuh? Stick around, you an' the dawg, as mascots ter bring me luck. An' mebbe, ef I come out on top, there'll be a slice of the purse fur yuh, an' you an' the hound-dawg kin take a ride on the cushions fur a change, an' see how it is ter put yer legs under fur three squares a day."

The Kid looked at the white body of the man. He nodded. But he did not look up.

Soon he came out, with the Gouger and the dog, into the road. There was a great red blush upon the western sky where had sunk, behind the trees, the Indian Summer sun. A golden haze was falling upon the road like the chaff from unseen fairy mills, and long shadows were walking out from trees and bushes. Everything seemed very quiet in the peace that comes with sunset.

The three walked along the golden road toward the tavern. And the Kid was very thoughtful. Suddenly, with his deep-sunken blue eyes, the Kid looked up into the gray deep-set eyes of the prize-fighter.

"I don't know, Gouger," he said hesitantly. "I jes' met up with a guy, name of Slim, and he wanted to crack open a safe, and he wanted me to join out with him to bring him luck. And I didn't bring him no luck at all. He put the soup to the peter, all right; but they got Slim. I don't seem to bring no luck to no one."

There showed, in the Frisco Kid's deep-sunk eyes then, the struggle that was being waged within him between desire and doubt. The pugilist stopped abruptly.

"But mine's a straight game, pal," he said argumentatively, seriously. "Of course I've fixed everythin' it's possible ter fix in order ter win, but the fight itself is on the dead level. It's a straight game, I tell yuh. An' mebbe yer luck has changed, Kid. I tole yuh my hunches are usually pretty good. I don't see why I'd git sech a hunch, ef it wasn't so. No," he ended, "don't yuh worry none, son, but stick around till after the fight. Bring me luck, kid, 'cause yer my mascot."

The Frisco Kid looked at the ring-man and his blue eyes livened. The words of the pugilist had put an abrupt quietus to all his fears. He was alive now with desire, with admiration and with awe.

"Sure I will, Gouger," he said happily. "I'll be awful glad to stick around and see yer fight. I'm a blowed-in-the-glass stiff, I am, and I'll never slope— I'll never run out on yer. I'll help yer to a win, Gouger—all we's able, me and—"

A sudden thought that was almost a fear struck the Kid.

"Gouger," he began hesitantly, as if begging some great favor, "can—can Gay-cat see yer fight, too?"

The Gouger looked down at the yellow dog trotting between them and nodded quickly, his face a smiling fret of wrinkles.

"Gee," muttered the Frisco Kid, "won't I have it on the comets, the tramp royals even, when I hit that next jungle and tell the boes that I helped Gouger Meehan to win! They'll never believe we was mascots, Gay-cat and me!"

IV

"MEBBE I KNOWS WHERE THEY IS!"

THE THREE ROPES, STRETCHED AT INTERVALS of a foot and a half above one another from the iron poles at the four corners of the ring, were the bars of his cage, as it were, and like an animal, Slugger Sweigert strode angrily along, with his right hand loosely encircling the topmost cord and sliding up and down over the braids of the strands.

The Slugger was a chunkily-built, leathery-skinned little chap, not more than twenty-one years of age and not over five feet and a quarter in height. He was rangy of shoulder. He had the shoulders of a middleweight, a man fighting at twenty-five pounds more weight and usually half a foot taller. His legs were hairy and stocky, almost heavy. While he had not been in the game long enough to have cauliflower ears, his nose was cracked, smashed to his face, and one cheek bone was more prominent than the other.

Beneath him, in the wooden bowl-shaped open-air arena, the house was seated and packed. A few stragglers were tripping down the aisles, but otherwise every one that held a ticket entitling him to a seat was squatting attentively and impatiently waiting. The hot sun of a California Indian Summer was streaming disturbingly down.

Slugger Sweigert stalked the ring. Twenty-four feet—twenty-four feet—twenty-four feet—twenty-four . . .

That was the tenth time he had measured the square of it with his footsteps. He strode past his corner. Here were his manager, seconds, folding-stool, buckets and bottles, towels, sponges, fans—all that sort of thing. And all waiting—waiting for fifteen minutes!

He kicked a piece of rosin from under his feet and glanced truculently up the center aisle toward the rude shed that served as the fighter's weighing-in and dressing quarters.

"Don't git hangry, Slugger," his manager called to him in the peculiar nasal Australian accent. "Kype cool, blokey!"

Up in the dressing quarters, as he leisurely drew off his trousers, the Gouger smiled expansively, so that his puffed lips tightened to a normal size. Well he realized what was occurring outside. Those savage glances of the Slugger hurled at this rough outbuilding above his head, he could almost feel. And he smiled again, grimly.

"I can't go no faster, I tell yuh. I know, but I can't help it," he lied deliberately to the nervous, bespectacled youth who was trying to hurry him into the ring. "I've gotta take my time," he pursued. "Everythin' must be jes' so when I climb through the ropes. Aw, the crowd be ——! I'm the one thet's fightin', not them. He is, is he?" he sneered. "Well, thet tea-guzzler won't be near so sore er anxious when I git through with him. Sure, I'll do my best," he ended, "but yuh kin see fur yerself, I can't go no faster!"

The young promoter, who was staging a prize-ring encounter for the first time in his brief career, slammed the misfit door, in leaving, with a bang. Despite all his youth and inexperience, he could not help but see that the Gouger was doing his best to drag and delay the affair.

Surely enough, back in the dressing quarters, Gouger Meehan had paused in removing his trousers to screw up his face into another smile, and wink knowingly at the Frisco Kid who stood, wide of eye, to one side, the yellow dog squatting attentively at his feet. He knew this Queens-burry game, did the Gouger. He had not been in it eleven long years for nothing. He had not worked slowly up from the bottom without also learning from the bottom up. And he was but using now one of the tricks of the game to his own advantage.

To get his man unreasonably angry; to have him fight fast and furious, extravagantly expending his strength, in resentment from the opening tap of the gong; to cause him to fight a strength-destroying, self-defeating fight—that was the Gouger's purpose in allowing an interval of time to snail by between the appearance of the Slugger in the ring, and his own appearance. He had his fight to win and, though the crowd ranted and the promoter threatened, he would fight his fight in his own way, the way surest of success.

"Shoot me anuther glass of water, Bud," he said to the red-headed, freckle-faced sparring mate who was acting now as one of his seconds. "I wanta take on a few more pounds over thet 133-notch I jes' made, an' water's the quickest way ter turn the trick. My insides is all dry; they'll jes' soak it in."

As he drained the glass, he fidgeted a bit nervously with the towel across his naked thighs.

"Say," he burst out of a sudden, "when are yuh guys ever goin' ter bring my fightin'-trunks?"

"We forgot 'em, Gouger, 'nd Steve's gone back fer 'em. He'll be here enny minute. Briggs went with him in his machine, 'nd they oughta make it in no time. It's only a single mile down the road. I could run it 'nd back in less'n a quarter-hour."

"Well, I won't fight without 'em. I've worn them old green trunks in every fight I've had since I knocked out Spider Feeley in the fifteenth round, back in—"

The misfit of a door complained on its rusty hinges and Steve, the dark-haired second, entered, closely followed by Briggs. Steve was chewing gum, his jaws clicking and snapping very fast as if with some excitement. Briggs's florid face was redder than usual, feverishly, hectically red, and glossy with sweat. He dabbed his brow nervously with a blue silk handkerchief.

"We can't find 'em," he said. "We looked all over yer bloomin' room an' in that barn of a gym, but we couldn't—"

The Gouger's black brows drew down over his eyes, and he swore.

"Hang it, they were strung out ter dry. I washed 'em myself, yisterday mornin'. Bud here wanted ter do it fur me, but I was leery he'd tear 'em. I think an awful lot of them trunks. I've worn 'em in every fight since I knocked out Spider Feeley in the—"

"I know," said Briggs. "An' I saw 'em myself hangin' out to dry behind the gym—let's see—yes, yesterday mornin'."

"So'd I," corroborated Steve. "But they're simply not there. Yer undershirt was there, Gouger, the yeller one an' the socks an' other shirts, but the trunks was plumb gone. The clothes-pins was still on the line. I'll bet some tramp copped 'em."

As though born of the suggestion, Manager Briggs swung round on the Frisco Kid.

"That kid there. Mebbe he took 'em."

The Frisco Kid looked frightened. He was thinking of the faded-green trunks he had robbed from the line of washing behind the gymnasium, the day before, and trying to recollect where he had left them. He remembered having taken them off beneath the porch of the roadhouse; he remembered throwing them on the sand at his feet; but what he could not remember was having seen the trunks on the sand, once he had got into his jeans.

The manager noted the frightened look in the boy's eyes. His own eyes narrowed to black pin-points of suspicion. And he reached over and pulled the Kid by one arm to him.

The dog, at the Kid's feet, watched the man, ears flattened back and the hair along the ridge of his spine rising on end, as the manager, in an effort to see if the trunks were on the boy beneath the blue jeans, felt of the Kid's waist.

"Lay off that stuff!" objected the Gouger sharply. "Whadda yuh think the kid is, Briggs—a yegg thet yuh gotter frisk like a dick? Thet kid didn't take 'em. Ef any one took 'em, I'll bet it's one of the Slugger's Cockneys. Slugger Sweigert knows I'll win ef I wear them trunks. I've worn 'em in every fight since I knocked out—"

"Mebbe," gulped the Kid, "mebbe I knows where they is. Mebbe I can find 'em for yer."

The manager grabbed the Kid by the shoulders.

"Yuh took 'em! Yuh took 'em, yuh little yegg!" he bit out, and he shook the Kid.

The dog's nostrils quivered and a low growl welled up through his throat ominously.

"Lay off thet stuff, Briggs!" exclaimed the Gouger, leaping to his feet and coming between the manager and the boy. "He says he knows where they are. Thet's all we wanta know."

He turned to the frightened boy and, one black-taped hand holding the towel about his middle, he put the other on the boy's shoulder.

"Kid," he said, a great anxiety shaking his voice, "yuh'll tell us where yuh last saw them trunks, won't yuh?"

The Frisco Kid looked up at the pugilist, then lowered his eyes guiltily and slowly nodded his head. He would have liked to have told all—how he had lost his jeans, while in swimming, and had taken the faded-green trunks from the line to cover his nakedness. But he was not sure he could find the trunks now. And should he not find the trunks, the Gouger might lose the fight and blame it all on him. No, he decided, he could not tell all.

He looked up into the gray anxious eyes of the pugilist again, and a woebegone expression was in his own eyes.

"I don't know, Gouger, I don't know jes' where they is. But mebbe—mebbe I can find 'em for yer. I saw 'em last under the porch down—down at Hackett's."

Bruskly the manager interposed.

"You come with me," he said. "I'll drive yuh down an' see if yuh can find 'em. Curse all yer good-luck bosh, anyway, Gouger. Here's more stallin' over a pair o' old trunks. Yuh wait here for us, but you'd better be gittin' inter some others in case we don't find these."

Dragging the Frisco Kid by one arm after him, the dog following and making little threatening growls in his throat, the manager slammed out of the dressing-quarters.

V

THE BELL CLANGS

BY THE TIME THE MANAGER BROUGHT the low-hung racing-motor to a halt before Hackett's roadhouse, the Frisco Kid and the dog in his lap were coated thickly with brown dust.

Briggs sprang out. He jerked the Kid off the seat to the ground with such suddenness that the Gay-cat rolled out of the Kid's lap and landed on his back in the dust of the road.

"Now yuh git 'em!" he commanded savagely.

The Frisco Kid followed the line of the house toward the porch over the stream in the rear. He was filled with hideous doubts. The dog slunk at his heels.

Coming down upon the bank of the stream, he turned and made beneath the porch. A little puddle of water lay black in the sand of the bank. There was where he had wrung out the jeans upon finding them. But no faded-green fighting-trunks were near.

Where they had gone to he could not remember. He thought he might have thrown them out into the stream and that they might be caught about one of the stilts upholding the porch, even as his jeans once had been caught. He sloshed in his sockless shoes through the water and searched about the piles beneath the porch. They were not there.

He searched along the bank again. He was in a panic. He ran into the dark up the bank beneath the porch. He lighted the precious matches he always carried for his cigarets. They were nowhere to be found.

He came out at last, a harassed look in his deep-sunk eyes, his tan face pale and slick with dust and the sweat of anguished dread. The manager was awaiting him on the bank just beyond the porch. The Kid shook his head as a sign of his defeat. He could say no word.

Briggs sprang at the Kid as if to strike him down. But on the instant, as the dog growled deep and menacingly in his throat, he thought better of it. He turned away, his thick lower lip between his white, clenched teeth.

"Curse the Gouger an' his good-luck bosh!" he muttered. "We'll have to go back without his trunks. That's all there is to it."

He spun round once again on the Frisco Kid, his heels digging savagely into the sand.

"I'd leave yuh behind, yuh little yegg, only—only I'm afraid the Gouger'd throw the skids under this fight. It's bad enough to lose his old trunks. Now I can't take any chances on him throwin' this fight jes' because o' the loss of a thievin' kid mascot. Come along, yuh yegg!" And he flung toward the car.

The Frisco Kid followed, very subdued, and the Gay-cat sniffed almost guiltily at his heels. All the way to the arena, the manager cursed the Gouger and the Gouger's superstitions. The Kid sensed that the manager feared that the Gouger might not fight, had he not the faded-green trunks to wear.

But when they reached the bowl-shaped open-air arena, they found that the Gouger was already in the ring. Come of their impatience, the waiting crowd had created so much disturbance and the young promoter had become so insistent that the Gouger had thought it wisest to don a new pair of fighting-trunks and appear before them.

Three-quarters of an hour after Slugger Sweigert had crouched through the ropes, Gouger Meehan had emerged from his dressing quarters. He had not run down the aisle as the Slugger had done, a distance of two hundred feet. He had ridden on the swarthy back of Steve, while Bud, the other second, had brought up the rear with buckets, sponges, towels and a folding-stool.

When, finally, they had reached the roped enclosure, Bud had opened the folding stool in the Gouger's corner and, instantly, the Gouger had sat down on it. He was crowding all the knowledge gained through his eleven ring years—as much of it at least, as he possibly could—into this one fight. And to begin with, he was conserving his strength.

Now, as Manager Briggs, followed by the Kid and his trailing dog, came down the slope of the aisle toward the elevated ring, the Gouger sat and watched his opponent. The Slugger was standing up in his corner with a frown on his face, his hands on the angle of the topmost rope and his feet crunching under him lumps of rosin, preparatory to rubbing the granules upon the soles of his shoes. The Gouger felt like advising, "Have yer beef-chewin' seconds do it!" but instead he only smiled grimly. Here was another way in which the Slugger was uselessly expending his strength.

As Slugger Sweigert seated himself, scraped his shoes in the granulated rosin and glowered across the ring, Manager Briggs pulled his bulk through the ropes behind the Gouger.

"I guess they jes' died of old age, Gouger. We couldn't find 'em, anywheres," he said with a forced and anxious attempt at jocundity.

A shadow crossed the Gouger's face and he made to speak; but at that moment the Slugger bellowed across the diagonal of the ring, his voice quavering with poorly suppressed anger—

"Yuh bloody, stinkin' bloater, Hi'll teach yuh not to kype me w'ytin'!"

The Gouger smiled wryly.

"Jes' in the mood I want him," he murmured. "He's a nice-mannered Cockney, he is." His battered face darkened. "I guess I won't need them trunks after all, Briggs," he said, looking up at the manager. "I'll make thet tea-drinkin' tin-eared boob eat them names!"

Briggs breathed an audible sigh of relief.

"That's the stuff, Gouger!" he said with what seemed hypocritical encouragement. "Give 'im the boots with both hands fer them names, an' you'll win!"

Bud, the Gouger's red-headed second, was in Slugger Sweigert's corner, examining the surgical bandages on the latter's hands. Sweigert's manager was doing the same in the Gouger's angle of the ring. It was merely a precautionary move against either man carrying anything stouter than knuckles beneath the bandages and black tape.

While it was in progress, the Gouger twisted his oddly-shaped head around. He saw the Frisco Kid standing below him with the yellow dog in his arms, and both boy and dog looking very bewildered in all the crowd. And his gray eyes lighted and his face screwed up into a myriad of wrinkles.

"Thet's the idea, kid," he said encouragingly. "You stay right there. Ef there's a bottle er a sponge er a fan needed, yuh sling it up. An' wish me luck, kid—wish me luck all the time, every round!"

A tall, stout, white-haired old man whose deep chest concealed a voice of megaphone volume—the official announcer—swung through the ropes with a set of boxing-gloves in his hands.

"Hurry up, boys," he urged, throwing a pair in either direction.

How light the five-ounce calfskins felt to the Gouger after the daily weight of the large gymnasium gloves! While Steve was lacing them on his hands, he looked over the second's shoulder at the ring-men who were flocking through the ropes from all sides.

Most of them he knew; not a few, he had defeated once and several times; and, as an honest opinion, he would say that Slugger Sweigert was the toughest nut of the lot. Beat him, and his fears of being forced down among the second-raters could be laid away in lavender for some time.

"Ben Furley, the California Cyclone, challenges the winner!" bawled the announcer from the center of the ring. "Loco Rafferty challenges the winner. The Saginaw Slasher, Jack Oleson, challenges the winner for a thousand dollars a side. Clyde Dean, Red Jim Brady, Mickey Maharg challenge the winner. Say, how many more of you, anyhow?" He swung upon them.

There still remained a half-dozen to be introduced. There were always more youngsters, longing for the first-rate pugilist's insecure seat in the Hall of Fame, arduously bending every effort toward that goal, the apex of their dreams. And then, when the aged announcer was hoarse from hurling defies, a newsman at the ringside, with a telegrapher and a direct wire to his office at his side, looked up and said:

"Jerry, just got a telegram at the office from Hugh Belcher, challenging the winner. He's willing to bet five thousand dollars on the side."

The announcer nodded his white head, moved largely to the center of the ring, lifted his hand for silence, got it, and cried:

"Hughie Belcher of Pontypool—the Welsh Ter-rr-ror—challenges the winner for five thousand dollars a side!"

Another prize-fighter elbowed toward him to be introduced and to submit his challenge, but the announcer coldly ignored him.

"Come on, you fellers," he called testily to the two principals.

Slugger Sweigert tossed his robe aside and sprang forward. The Gouger rose leisurely, tucked his old dressing-gown closer about him, stepped easily to the center. Sweigert had crouched into fighting pose. His manager came up and threw the robe about him.

Erect, wrapped snugly in his gown, the Gouger waited for the signal from the newspaper photographers that they were ready to snap. Then, and not before, did he throw off his dressing-gown and, planting himself firmly up on his feet, crouch and extend his arms in fighting posture. The four cameras snapped in unison, and the next instant he was erect again and in his dressing-gown.

"Give us another," cried a precautious newspaper photographer, and it was done.

But through it all the Gouger, unlike his more youthful opponent, was ever calm, ever careful of himself, of uselessly expending his golden strength.

They were introduced to the spectators, a pure matter of formality, as both were better known than the governor of the state.

"The Glory of Rushcutter's Bay, the Australian Avalanche, Slugger Sweigert!" roared the announcer.

And then—

"The Old Master, the Pride of Garry Owen, the best 133-pound boy on the Coast, Gouger Meehan!"

The crowd had shouted and stamped and clapped for the Slugger. They thundered at this last:

"Good boy, old Gouger!" "Show him you're not an old 'un yet!" and such dubious encouragements swelled up from the bowl-shaped arena.

Silencing the crowd after a time, the announcer brought forth a short pock-fretted man, a former lightweight fighter, whom he introduced as "the Greatest Exponent of Fair Play in the West, Thady Burke, who will referee this contest!"

The referee went into one angle of the ring, the men back to their respective corners. The folding-stools, buckets, and other paraphernalia had been removed and the pugilists stood, now, in the diametric angles of the ropes, white-bodied and naked save for the trunks about their middles, their eyes conning each other, their gloved hands at their sides. Everything was ready and waiting for the signal to lay on.

The white-haired announcer moved grandly across the roped arena, his right hand raised.

"Gentlemen!" he boomed. "This—will be a twenty-round contest—br-rr-eak—at the order of the referee"—his body half through the ropes, he flourished his hand—"let 'er go!"

The bell clanged. The three men within the ring acted as on one impulse.

The pugilists strode quickly to the center, closely followed by the referee, barely touched each other's right glove in a species of handclasp, half circled. For a moment more they fiddled about each other. Then, like some bird of prey, the Slugger darted in and jabbed the Gouger upon the bulb of the nose with his right glove. The fight was on.

VI
THE FIGHT

THE FRISCO KID'S EYES WERE SPREAD in their deep-sunk sockets, and his neck-apple felt thick and round in his throat. He watched the Gouger, the Gay-cat held awkwardly before him and very tight in his arms. He saw the Gouger shake his egg-shaped head and, by way of retorting to that jab, hook the other man before he could step away, at the same time blocking a right cross to the heart.

With a rush bespeaking anger, Slugger Sweigert came on. He jabbed, he swung, he crossed, he hooked—he blocked never. He had little need to. The Gouger was doing a sufficiency of that for both of them.

Meehan was covering his stomach, barricading his face, or tapping the Slugger on the biceps, as this arm or that shot forward for a blow. Blocking always, and all blows almost. Ducking, backing, stepping this way and that, but seldom countering. The Gouger's defense was masterly, if not impregnable. It bore mute testimony to his clear head and eleven years in the square circle.

There was the difference. Had the Slugger but a tithe of the Gouger's wisdom and ring generalship, he would not be fighting as he was fighting. But the Gouger had seen to that. He had his man angry, revengeful, irrational.

Anything for a win! That was the Gouger's code. Anything, even if it be a trifle shady—anything for a win! His dilatory tactics had been one of the things which made for a win. His present system of engaging was another. He had his man fighting a whirlwind, strength-destroying, self-defeating battle, that was a third. And there were more to come.

"Last ten seconds!" shouted Steve from the corner of the ring, at the end of the second round, making ready to throw in the folding-stool and buckets.

At that, the Gouger worked, backing and filling, toward his corner. At that, Slugger Sweigert pressed him hard and harder. At the bell, the next moment, the Gouger sat plump down upon the stool in his corner.

He looked up and smiled tauntingly at the sweating Slugger. His back against the iron pole, his arms raised on the angle of the topmost rope, his legs spread wide on the lowest, he was being invigoratingly sponged and fanned, what time the Slugger still was striding across the canvas floor to his corner.

The Gouger turned his oddly-shaped head and smiled significantly at the awestruck Kid.

"Did yuh wish me luck them rounds, Kid?"

"Sure," muttered the boy stoutly. "Sure I did, Gouger. And the Gay-cat—he wished yer luck, too, Gouger."

The bell brought the men together for round number three, but not in the center of the enclosure. The Gouger had taken but five slow steps from his corner in the while that the Slugger had rushed, like a gust of wind, toward him.

They met, and the Slugger backed the Gouger as far as the angle of his corner would permit. There the Slugger lived up to his name. He slugged away at the blocking Gouger until the latter, somehow and cleverly, worked out of the corner.

The Slugger was after him then, like a wildcat. Clear across the diagonal of the ring, into his own corner, the Slugger hammered the Gouger until the angle of the ropes once more intervened in the backward rush.

The Gouger could not block the multiple blows which were showering, fast and stronger than hail upon him. A crack of the Slugger's glove caught him on the point of the jaw below the ear. He felt a severe pang shoot through his head, seeming to lift the roof off his head. A fur of blackness closed over his eyes. As he tottered, something crashed into his stomach like the head of a battering ram. He doubled up and there, upon the wet and rosined canvas floor of the Slugger's corner, he went down, inert.

"Three! Four!" the official timekeeper was shrieking from the ringside, as the Gouger aroused to a semi-consciousness. In lower tones, immediately above him, the pock-fretted referee was doing the same, his pudgy right hand falling with each count.

Afar, beyond the diametric corner of the ring, the Frisco Kid clutched the dog to his chest and watched through the intolerable seconds, his blue eyes whelmed with an anguish of fear for the Gouger.

"He's got the Gouger!" he muttered, his lips beating dryly together. "The Slugger's got the Gouger, Gay-cat, and—and it's all 'cause the Gouger didn't wear them lucky trunks!"

"Five! Six!"

The Gouger strove to rise.

"Stay down! Git a rest! Take yer time! Gather!" in his seconds' voices, shrill with an intensity of excitement.

"Seven! Eight!"

The Gouger got to his knees, his gloved hands still upon the canvas flooring, but the glassy look quickly fleeing his eyes, as some of his senses came back to him.

"He ain't out yet!" exclaimed the Frisco Kid. "The Gouger ain't out yet. Yer'll beat 'im, Gouger! Get up, get—"

The Kid stopped shortly, as if the words had been sucked down his throat. A sudden and unaccountable action upon the part of the Gouger had stopped him.

The Gouger had turned the backs of his gloves upon the wet and rosined canvas floor of the Slugger's corner and now, his senses gathering, amid all the excitement within and without the square circle, beneath the very eyes of the Slugger's seconds and manager, he was rubbing the backs of those gloves, slowly, surreptitiously, over the rosin on the floor.

"Nine!"

The Gouger was up. He was crouching low, gloves over ears and head, elbows protecting his stomach, and lurching toward the Slugger for a clinch. Just then the bell rang.

The Gouger did not appear to hear the bell. But that came, undoubtedly, of his cauliflower ears. He tried for a blow at the Slugger's face. The Slugger stopped the blow with his forearm and shoved him toward his corner.

He understood then. The crowd was on its feet, hissing, catcalling, attempting by boos and scurrility to show that he had outraged their sense and tenets of fair play. He paid them no heed, for all the truth as if he did not hear them. He staggered into his corner.

His wits were still a bit wool-gathering. Those cracks on jaw and stomach had been no love-taps. But still, withal, he had retained a certain canniness, a trick of reasoning resultant from his many long years of fighting. As his seconds sweated as never before, with soaking sponges and fans and revivers, he warned them sharply:

"Git away from my gloves. Don't rub 'em er drop enny more water on 'em. I'm goin' ter try the Kid McCoy trick. I rubbed them gloves in the rosin when I was down. I wanta tear the skin off his beak with the rosin on them gloves. He almost got me in thet last frame, but I'm gonna git him now fur callin' me names!"

The fourth round opened with the Gouger striving hard to tear the skin of Sweigert's face and body with the rosin on his gloves, brittle as glass crumbs. But the rosined gloves appeared to have little effect upon the weather-toughened skin of the Slugger. He suffered only a scratch or two about the broken nose. And the rosin quickly wore off the Gouger's gloves.

Now, perhaps it was that the Slugger had tired himself—fought himself out, as sporting parlance has it—in trying to do for the Gouger in the prior round. He did not open up in this fourth inning, sufficiently to inflict a staggering blow on the Gouger, let alone knock him down again. And by the time the round was ended, the Gouger had won a long way back to himself.

The intervening one-minute rest-period capped his recovery. Once more, when the fifth round opened, was he clear-headed and calculating. He remembered then, as in a vivid flash, all he had to forfeit by a loss, and he thanked his good-luck stars that the bell had terminated the third round when it had. Over and over again, he thanked his good-luck stars.

"It's the kid what's done it," rang through his superstitious head. "It's the kid an' his hound-dawg wishin' me luck!"

No more than he had opened up in the fourth and fifth rounds did the Slugger open up in the sixth frame. He must have tired himself considerably in trying to do for the Gouger in that third round. It might be that he had injured one of his hands in delivering that battering-ram blow into the Gouger's stomach. But, in either case, the fact remained that the Slugger seemed unable to follow up that knock-down of the third round. This fact was not without a certain effect upon the Gouger.

As he had not opened up since the starting gong of all had clanged, the Gouger opened up now. He set the pace. He jabbed his man, tilting his head backward like a reed before the wind. He jabbed him again, yet again; then, having him as he wanted him, he cut loose on the body and, by punch upon shattering punch, backed the Slugger, at a fast clatter, full across the ring into the ropes.

Here was exhibited why the Gouger had refused to fight, should his three-rope proviso not be complied with. Two ropes, and the retreating man would back through them and be upheld, from falling into the ringside, by the aroused and standing spectators beneath.

The Gouger could not punch him then. He would have to play the cavalier—a bit of clap-trap—and extending one of his gloved hands (with which he was supposed, according to the rules, only to fight) gallantly draw his opponent back into the ring. And that would be more than a useless outlay of strength. It would be to put himself in wraps, stave off the finish of the fight, and probably save the other man from a knockout, then and there.

True, shouts of approval at the gallantry of such conduct would be excited from the crowd; bits of clap-trap always excite shouts of approval from crowds; but that did not win him his fight. The same crowd would shout more loudly, were the Slugger to come back, immediately after, and knock him—the cavalier—out.

But with the three ropes, there was the game! The other man could not slip through them. They formed a veritable net behind him—top rope back of the shoulders, middle at the base of the spine, and the lowest rope behind the crotch of the knees. Everything for a win!

The Gouger had his man so, cringing, doubled up, one arm before the face, the other wrapped about the stomach.

The Gouger stood off, his left glove on the Slugger's shoulder. He drew back his right arm, measured, and let fly. The Slugger's midriff caved in and he dropped instantly, like an ox felled in the shambles. Three seconds later, against the frantic advice of his manager and seconds, he was up again, staggering.

The spectators were on their feet, waving hats, canes, gloves, and shouting distractedly from throats sanded with excitement.

"Git him, Gouger! He's groggy!"

"Biff 'im on th' kisser!"

"Now's yer time!"

"Give 'im the half-scissors hook, the Gouger's famous half-scissors hook!"

"Don't take all day! He's all in!"

"Stall, blokey, stall through th' round. Hi've bet on yuh to st'y tin rounds with 'im!"

"Hang a haymaker on him, old boy!"

"Give him th' one-two!"

"Take it easy, Gouger! Keep yer head!" called Manager Briggs across the ring, his voice thick and shaky, the blood pouring into his face with overwrought emotion. "Follow up careful. Place yer blows, man, place yer blows!"

The Frisco Kid's chin was pressed against the ropes along the edge of the ring which bound down the canvas cover on the flooring.

"Yer got him, Gouger!" he half sobbed with joy and intense excitement.

"Yer can lick him, one hand! Put him out! Put him out!"

The Kid felt the canvas-covered flooring vibrate, as the Gouger rushed in to finish his man.

The Slugger jabbed at the Gouger's face in a desperate but feeble effort to keep him off. He could not keep him off. The Gouger closed with him and pummeled him about the reddened region of the stomach with hook after half-scissors hook. It was the Gouger's famous right-hand punch to the stomach. The Gouger was trying for the solar plexus and a knockout.

He was trying arduously for a knockout, the while he could feel himself tiring. His feet were sore from gripping the flooring, his legs weary, and he could feel the muscles standing out on his arms and he could feel those arms, heavy as bars of lead. Although he realized that the sound undoubtedly saved the Slugger from a knockout yet it was with a grunt of distinct relief that he caught, of a sudden on the wind, the terminating sound of the bell.

He was worn out. He had tried supremely.

He stretched himself in his corner with a heavy sigh, closed his eyes, and sought comfort in relaxation. He must needs get as much out of this one-minute rest-period as he possibly could. The next round would find him bang up against his hardest task. He must knock out his man in that next round, or the pace would kill him and the Slugger, strong with the resilience of youth, would get the credit of it.

He caught a squeaky voice from near at hand:

"Didn't I tell yuh? He's old, the Gouger is. He'll have to give way to the young feller. We all do, we old 'uns."

Vaguely the remarks incensed the Gouger. He was too weary to open his eyes and see who had uttered them. He listened.

"Nuthin' of the kind," objected an impudent voice. "This old boy's gonna win. Anyway, that's the way my money's bet."

"Yuh lookit here, young feller. If the Gouger wasn't old, wouldn't he have settled the Slugger's hash in that last inning? He had Sweigert dazed, dead to rights. There was a time when I saw him knock out a man with two blows when he had him so—"

"Who was that?"

"Jim Bristoe, Nigger Jim, that was. But he's too old now, the Gouger, and the other feller's too young and good. Did yuh see him take all the Gouger had, with only one flip-flop?"

"You're right there, pap."

"I tell yuh, I know a thing or two about this game, my boy. The Slugger will come back the next round, sure as yuh live, and as strong as a bull. Yuh jes' watch. The Gouger's all in. That last frame was too much for him. He put in his best licks then. He can't do it again."

"Aw, the Gouger'll come back all right, all right."

"My boy, I know a thing or two about this game. I was followin' the game afore yuh was born. The old-timers can't come back. They never have in the past. It takes youth to come back. That's one of the things I know."

The Gouger troubled now to open his eyes, shift on his stool and gaze out between the ropes. He saw, below him and but two rows away, a weazened old man in a frock coat and a pink-complexioned unbearded youth. And the odd part of it all was that the old man, paradoxically, was upholding the power of youth over age and the young one, just the reverse.

But was it true? Had the old man spoken wisdom, the youth, youth's customary folly? The Gouger had to admit to himself, now that it was pointed out, that he should have done better in that last round—that he should have knocked his man cold when he had him in such a bad way. Truly enough, when he had had Nigger Jim groggy, in that fight years before, he had knocked him out with two clean blows. The recollection stirred up within him something that was like anger and yet was akin to apprehension.

"Say, whadda yuh think I am!" he rasped out at Bud. "A sponge, thet yuh've thrown all thet water over me? Cut it out, will yuh!"

Then he saw the Frisco Kid, standing so frail and nervously attentive in his over-large coat below him, the alert yellow dog hugged in his arms, and his sun-tanned face white in the draw of the excitement he was going through. The Gouger's battle-hacked face wreathed into the wrinkles of a pathetic smile.

"Kid," he said huskily, "yuh'll wish me luck the next round, huh? Wish me luck, Kid, like yuh never did afore!"

The Kid looked up, his eyes great in their deep-sunken pits.

"Aw, say, Gouger," he gulped. "Aw, say now, Gouger. I'm a-wishin' yer luck like everythin' all the time!"

The Gouger turned away, his gray eyes filmy.

"What round's comin' up?" he asked.

"The seventh," returned Bud, wiping the water off his heaving chest.

The seventh! He used to have some luck in the seventh. It was in the seventh round of that fight, in Butte, Montana, that he had knocked out Jim Bristoe, Nigger Jim. It was enough. He would win in that next round. It was the seventh—his lucky round!

He felt fresher at the thought, albeit his arms did ache a little. He wished, all at once and quite unaccountably, that he had, about his waist, that old pair of faded-green trunks. Then the bell.

He would finish it speedily. With the one-minute rest, he should now be in condition to trim the Slugger in no time. The Slugger had called him names!

He strode forward. The Slugger was awaiting him in the center. He strode forward and, almost without bothering to put up his props or feint, he caught the Slugger a right-hander on the side of the head.

The Slugger had called him names! He followed it up quickly. He lifted the Slugger with a smash in the stomach. He was maliciously angry. He would pay the Slugger back for those names. At the same time, he would do what he had failed to do in the previous round. It would be the Jim Bristoe fight over again. With two clean blows, he would put the Slugger out. It was his lucky round.

Again he lifted the Slugger with a half-scissors hook. The Slugger came on, his gloved hands flailing the blocking left forearm of the Gouger. The Gouger worked fast and hard. Again he clipped the Slugger a revengeful right-hander on the side of the head.

The Slugger shook his head. He came on. God, he was smiling!

"That th' best yuh got, yuh bleedin', glass-armed bloater!"

The Slugger feinted, as he cursed, and as if in contempt pushed his left glove slap into the Gouger's face. For the instant the Gouger could not see. He was momentarily rattled. He attempted to cover up.

The Slugger's right glove coiled round his back to his kidney. The Gouger felt the blow jar through his digestive organs, thud against his navel, run agonizingly up his spine. He snapped erect. He hugged his left glove to his side in a try to shield the exposed kidney with the crook of his projecting elbow.

The Slugger shifted with a swiftness amazing and, with a squash that sounded sickening, his left glove coiled round the Gouger's back to his other kidney.

The impact of the blow hit the base of the Gouger's brain with the force of a bludgeon. His head reeled and he rocked upon his feet. Desperately he lurched forward, head bent, arms up weakly in fighting fashion. The life was gone from his arms. He tried to get close to the Slugger. He rested his chin on the sweat and blood of the Slugger's shoulder, and—he could not help it—his eyes closed.

He felt done for. Yet he did not want to show it. He smote the Slugger in the stomach with his left hand. There seemed little force to the blow. His extensor muscles ached and feared to act, his arms were numb and heavy as though water-logged. But he continued to piston his heavy arms into the Slugger's stomach, the while, using another trick of the ring in an attempt to conceal his feebleness, his breath drawing cavernously through his lungs, he talked wearily and disjointedly to the Slugger.

"Yuh would—call—me names, huh? I've got yuh—now—yuh tin-eared boob! How'd the canvas feel—thet last round? Sorter soft, what? Well—here's where—yuh hit it again—*ugh!*"

The Slugger's right glove ripped up under his chin, uppercutting him, lifting him upon his toes, shaking every brain-cell in his head, shocking painfully, like overcharged wires, every nerve that ran through his body from those brain-cells. The white form of the Gouger, so piteously like a babe's, doubled up momentarily like a ten-penny nail that had been hit glancingly by a sledge-hammer.

The Slugger drew away. As he felt the Slugger draw away, the Gouger straightened and his eyes opened hurriedly in a terrible dismay. He stumbled after the Slugger. And there was in his stark gray eyes now little sign of knowledge, in the flail-like arms he held out gropingly, hardly a vestige of strength.

The Slugger continued to keep away. He kept just so far away. He smashed fist after fist into the Gouger's stomach. He pounded the Gouger again and yet again, into the ropes, out of the ropes and, reeling and groggy, across the ring.

Back, back went the Gouger, his head rolling on a neck that seemed too weak to uphold it, his feet not lifting up and down, but apparently unable to leave the canvas flooring—dragging like the feet of a fly caught on gummed paper.

The Slugger was after him.

With squashy sounds, the Slugger thudded his wet gloves against the Gouger's stomach that was red as an angry crater, into the Gouger's blood-smeared face that showed no human intelligence. Step by step, blow upon blow, he forced the Gouger into the ropes, out of the ropes, and around and around the ring. The Gouger was like a man sick with liquor; too drunk to defend himself, seeking only rest, the Slugger like some pitiless white machine that forced him relentlessly, that crooked and sped its arms mercilessly. It was abominable!

"Put him out!"

"Lean on 'im, Slugger! This ain't no vycytion!"

"What kind of a manager are yuh, Briggs! Throw in th' sponge, yuh slave-driver!"

"Come on, Slugger!"

"Haven't yuh enny punch, yuh zob?"

"Drop, Gouger, old boy! You've had enough!"

The Slugger pulled back his left, calculated rapidly, let go. He caught the Gouger flush upon the nib of the jaw. For an agonizing trice, the Gouger shivered on his toes, then slapped down upon his face.

"One! Two!" shrieked the official timekeeper at slow second intervals, his blazing eye on his stop-watch, his hand knotted with excitement about the lever of the bell.

The pock-fretted referee above the Gouger tolled off the unendurable seconds with the fall of his pudgy hand.

But the Gouger did not move. Feverishly Bud and Steve, his seconds, dipped their sponges into the buckets and spattered water on him. The Gouger did not move.

"Three! Four!"

The Slugger walked around warily, watching the white form upon the wet and rosined canvas like a spider that is not sure its victim is dead, but only simulating death. Manager Briggs clung to the lowest rope of the angle of the ring, his face no longer red, his mouth stiffly open. Steve chewed feverishly, audibly. The Frisco Kid clutched the dog frantically tight in his arms. The crowd stood on its seats.

"Five!"

A tremor, as of pain, shook through the white form of the Gouger.

"Six!"

His arms bent under him and he humped up on those bent arms, his chin still digging into the canvas.

"Seven!"

He swung dizzily on all-fours, his eyes stark and staring, his head lolling like the head of an animal mortally wounded.

"Eight!"

The referee, with his free left hand, held back the Slugger.

"Nine!" shrilled the timekeeper. His eye was on the stop-watch. He jerked the lever. The bell clanged. The round was ended.

VII
According To His Caste

The round had ended not an ace too soon. The Gouger never could have arisen at the unuttered count of ten. The bell had given him a new lease on life, a longer tenure of fighting. Now, of a certainty, it was up to the Gouger either to recover a deal of his strength and faculties, in the allotted one-minute interval of rest, or return for the next round groggy and weak and already beaten.

He tottered into his corner on the arms of his two seconds and dropped like a dead weight upon the folding stool. The Slugger turned away, a broad smile expanding his mouth and, as he pranced into his corner, debonairly greeted some friend at the ringside.

The radical contrast in the aspect of the two pugilists, at the end of that seventh round, was not without visible effect upon the Frisco Kid. He looked up at the trembling white body of the Gouger, slumped upon stool and ropes above him, and his deep-sunk eyes seemed stunned as by some terrible knowledge.

"He's done for, the Gouger!" he muttered sorrowfully into the ear of the dog in his arms. "He can't win. And it's all my fault, Gay-cat. I lost them green trunks on him, and he can't win without them lucky trunks. It's all my fault. I's a blowed-in-the-glass stiff no more, Gay-cat. I've fallen down on the Gouger like a measly termater-can bum!"

There was a vast soberness in the Kid's words. He felt he was no longer an aristocrat of the road, a blown-in-the-glass stiff. It is an unwritten law of the high inner caste of blown-in-the-glass stiffs to help a friend when that friend is down and out, when that friend is a down-pin. And the Frisco Kid felt he had not lived up to the law. He had lost the Gouger's lucky green trunks. He felt he had lost for the Gouger, thereby, this fight. He was no longer a blown-in-the-glass stiff. He was a bum, a tomato-can bum, one of a low, vile and faithless caste.

"Yuh'll have to stall, Gouger!" Manager Briggs was saying, above him, to the slowly reviving pugilist. "Yuh'll have to stall. I've got money on yuh to last ten rounds with the Slugger. Yuh sure can last that long, Gouger. It's only three frames more. Stall through, old man, an' win that money fer me!"

There was something in the advice which encouraged and yet hurt the Frisco Kid.

"I wonder, now," he muttered, "I wonder jes' how long the Gouger can stall. I hate to think of the Gouger havin' to stall, but mebbe if he could only stall long enough, mebbe then we'd have time, Gay-cat and me, to run back and find them lucky trunks for him!"

He looked up, a great hope dawning in his deep-sunk eyes.

"I'll bet if he had them lucky trunks—I'll bet then the Gouger wouldn't have to stall no more. He'd lick that other guy, one hand! And then we'd be blowed-in-the-glass stiffs again, Gay-cat and me. We'd 'a' helped the Gouger to a win!"

His eyes dropped hopefully and with grave question to the yellow dog in his arms. The Gay-cat whimpered softly; but whether from pity for the Gouger or with pain at being held so tightly in the boy's arms, the Kid did not know. He took it to mean assent. And a tremendous idea that partook of the nature of an inspiration bourgeoned, on the sudden, in his brain.

"Gay-cat!" he whispered excitedly. "Does *you* know where them lucky trunks is! Did *you* hide 'em, old hobo!"

He lifted up the dog. He could feel the dog's stump of a tail beating against his chest now, as if in a frantic effort to make answer. It was as if the dog were attempting to convey, in this manner, some message to him, his tail beating out, like a telegraph instrument, the dots and dashes of the words he could not express.

Yes, the dog understood. It was wonderful. But the dog understood how direfully necessary it was to find those lucky green fighting-trunks. The dog was a blown-in-the-glass stiff, too! He would help the Gouger to a win! He would aid the Kid in finding those lucky trunks!

The Frisco Kid plucked at the sleeve of the manager, who was hanging on to the ropes above him and attempting to whisper, in his heavy voice, words of advice into the Gouger's ear.

The Kid wet his lips in nervous preparation. He purposed making a great request of Briggs; he wanted to ask the manager to drive him back to Hackett's, once again, in his racing-car.

Briggs swung his big slick face around. He saw the Frisco Kid. And his large mouth bent in a snarl, and he prodded the Kid away with one foot.

"G'wan, yuh little yegg!" he snapped. "The Gouger don't know yuh no more. Beat it!"

The Frisco Kid turned, then, to make up the center aisle of the arena and, alone and unaided, back to Hackett's, a mile distant. As he did, to the stretched-out white body above him, he breathed:

"We's gonna find them lucky trunks for yer, Gouger. Jes' you stall. And don't think we're quittin' yer cold, like termater-can bums. We're blowed-in-the-glass stiffs we are, Gay-cat and me, and we stick by our friends. We'll be back with them trunks in no time. And then yer won't have to stall, Gouger! Then yer can lick him, one hand!"

VIII
THE INEVITABLE VICTOR

AT A KILLING PACE, THE FRISCO KID STARTED along the brown road. Hackett's was a goodly mile away. Where the road wound about great fields, he cut across through the mustard and tule and disheveled stalks of corn. He ran at top pitch. He climbed fences; he sloshed through the sogginess of truck gardens; he paused never.

And the Gay-cat ran before him. He wriggled beneath the fences; he led the way through the weeds and corn; and he stopped, now and anon, to look back and beckon the Kid on. Indeed, he seemed to enjoy the run as though it were altogether fine fun.

"Gay-cat," purled the Kid very soberly, slowing for the while to a jog trot, "we's not off, free-like, on a tramp, now. And yer gotta help find 'em, old hobo. We're blowed-in-the-glass stiffs, we are, and the Gouger's our friend. He was good to us, Gay-cat. We can't go back on him now, and him needin' us so bad-like. We're blowed-in-the-glass stiffs, old-timer, and we stick by our friends!"

Boy and dog ran on, very fast. They passed, after a time, the red dusty barn of a gymnasium which squatted in the field of mustard weeds. Around the bend of the road they came to the white two-storied building that was Hackett's roadhouse and, following the line of the house, they emerged at last upon the sandy bank of the stream.

The dog ran before the boy, under the porch, his tragic stump of a tail stiffly erect. The Kid's face was very serious as, once again, he felt to searching the sand of the bank beneath the porch. The dog watched him impatiently for a brief moment, then turned and darted up the bank into the darkness under the house.

A short sharp little bark surprised the Frisco Kid. It came from the dark beneath the house. The Kid vaulted, at that bark, into a quick excitement.

"It's Gay-cat. And I'll bet he's found somethin'! Gay-cat, Gay-cat!" he called. "Where is yer?"

The dog bounded against the Kid's legs, tossing something in his jaw from side to side and growling playfully. What it was, the Kid could not discern in the semi-darkness; but, his brown face almost white with some violent emotion, he grabbed at the dog. The Gay-cat darted out from beneath the porch into the sunlight of the bank.

The Frisco Kid came out, his face very pale, his hands patting the air to reassure the dog. The Gay-cat approached and laid the something in his jaws upon the sand of the bank at the Kid's feet. He cocked his yellow head triumphantly. At the Kid's feet lay a pair of old faded-green fighting-trunks!

Slowly the Frisco Kid picked them up. All color seemed to have been sucked from his face; his face, now, was ghastly with pallor. He examined the trunks with a pitiful anxiety. The trunks were soiled from being buried in the ground, and they were terribly torn where the teeth of the dog had ripped and slashed in worrying and playing with them.

The Kid shook his head ruefully.

"I don't know that the Gouger can wear 'em," he muttered, "but we'll bring 'em back to him, anyways. We's blowed-in-the-glass stiffs, Gay-cat, and we gotta do our best! And mebbe—mebbe, if he'd only tie them round him—mebbe then he could win, one hand!"

The Frisco Kid started back along the brown road toward the open-air arena. The soiled and hopelessly torn trunks were wrapped in a tight bundle under his left arm. And he felt very weary. But that which was under his left arm sped him on in a hot, panicky run.

Running as if fresh, his short, numbly-tired legs lifting and pounding without sensation, as if they were parts of a machine that had been wound up and could not run down, clambering over and under fences, sloshing between cabbages and tomatoes, clattering over leaves, stones, roots, along the straight lengths of dusty road, through the weeds and corn of the fields where the road curved in and out, doggedly back the way he had come, the Kid made, for minutes, for blocks, on, on, on!

The yellow dog loped beside him with hung head. Quickly there spread upon the western sky a great red blush where had sunk, behind the trees, the Indian Summer sun. A golden haze was falling upon the road like the chaff from unseen fairy mills, and long shadows were walking out from trees and bushes.

The sunset saddened the Frisco Kid. He felt heavy with a vast dread, heartsick, weary beyond telling. Yet he had something under his left arm which must be brought, forthwith, to the Gouger. He was a blown-in-the-glass stiff. He must help the Gouger to a win. It was the law of his hobo caste.

A bit more, and the Frisco Kid panted up a rise from the top of which he could look down into the bowl of the open-air arena. There were a number of persons on the rise and they all were standing, as if suddenly they had been jacked afoot by some crucial happening within that arena. Breathing hard, his head throbbing and aching from the blood that was being pounded up there by his incessantly working feet, the Frisco Kid paused to look down.

Afar off, he could see the black crowd within the arena and, raised aloft in their center, two white midgets performing upon a platform. He could make out the Slugger standing close to the cringing white body of the Gouger, his arms flying in and out like the eccentric rods of an engine, his gloved fists speeding punch upon merciless punch into the Gouger's stomach. And it seemed to the Kid that all the while he had been running, all that while, machine-like, the Slugger had been standing close to the Gouger, repeatedly smashing punch upon unendurable punch into the Gouger's stomach.

The Gouger went down upon his knees. The Slugger walked around, very warily, a little way from the kneeling Gouger.

Then the Kid saw the Gouger up upon his quaking legs, his arms, thin with distance, held out gropingly like the feelers of a bug. He saw the Slugger leap forward, crash one fist into the Gouger's stomach. The Gouger's midriff caved in. The Slugger stepped back. The Gouger went down.

Once again the Gouger was down. But he was not still. His oddly-shaped head twisted under him; his white legs lifted; he somersaulted, heels over head! For an intolerable breath, he lay still. Then heels over head, again he rolled!

It was as if the organs, cramped and knotted in his battered stomach, were doubling him up with agony, rolling him over and over. It was as if he were some reptilian creature, dead to all appearances, yet showing, spasmodically, quiverings of dying life. It was hideous!

The Frisco Kid waited, unable to move, his breath coming wheezingly, his eyes spread with horror and with pity.

The Gouger's legs lifted a third time. They hung in the air, hung white and waveringly in the air, then fell back heavily. His arms went wide. And flat upon his face on the white flooring, the Gouger spilled out.

He tried to rise. His outspread arms flapped like the fins of a landed fish. But he could not rise. From without the corner of the roped enclosure, his seconds doused water on him. But he could not rise. Spread-eagled and white-bodied, he quivered upon the rosin-prickly canvas, while over him the pudgy hand of the referee tolled off the unhurried moments of grace.

His white legs knotted up in a convulsion, then shot out straight. The agony was over for the Gouger. He was unconscious—at last, out!

The referee raised aloft the gloved right hand of the Slugger. The Slugger had won. Youth—youth resilient, with unused cells of strength ever awaiting the call of trial and stress—youth the inevitable, had won.

But the Frisco Kid did not realize that. He wanted to get away from the persons on the hill and the view of that terrible arena. He went on down the hill, impelled toward the arena by he knew not what, his tired legs dragging, his head hung penitently, the dog sniffing up at him as if dumbly sympathizing with him in his anguish.

"It's all our fault, Gay-cat," he said to the yellow dog at his feet. "We lost the trunks on the Gouger, and he couldn't win without them lucky trunks. I's awful sorry, Gay-cat. The Gouger, he won't ride on the cushions hisself no more, but batter the back doors and be a ornery hobo jes' like you and me. Gee, old-timer, we gotta see the Gouger once more. We's blowed-in-the-glass stiffs, we are, and we can't go back on him now."

IX

"It's Money, Money, Money, Everywhere"

—*Old Song*

The only sound, in the Gouger's dressing-quarters, was the fleshy slap of the seconds' hands as they massaged his aching limbs. They wiped his body dry of the water they had doused on him to bring him to consciousness;

they rubbed him to a glow; they slapped shut the steaming pores of his skin with lotions of alcohol; they bathed the bruises on face and body with an antiseptic wash composed of a solution of carbolic acid and hot water. They said no word. Only Steve chewed his gum very rapidly, the click and snap of his incessantly working jaws sounding, now and then, audibly.

At times, bursts of unrestrained laughter would come through the interstices between the unplaned planks of one wall where, beyond, were the dressing-quarters of the Slugger. At these times, Steve and Bud would look at each other in a kind of fright, and then askance down at the Gouger. But for all that he was conscious, the Gouger lay stiff and unmoving, his eyes closed.

The misfit of a door complained on its hinges and, out of the pressing, passing crowd, Manager Briggs hustled in. The Gouger opened his eyes to look at him. He looked at the manager then as a dog might look at its master, dumbly pleading to be petted, yet fearful that instead of patting it might feel the weight of the hand of the master. The Gouger was the first to speak.

"Well," he said feebly, yet with a sort of peevish challenge in his voice, "I lasted the ten rounds fur yuh, Briggs."

"Thet yuh did, ol' boy," spoke up Bud quickly, as if welcoming the chance to speak and encourage. "Youse is all right, Gouger."

"Thirteen's an unlucky number ennyways," from Steve, as he bathed the bruise on the right cheek of the Gouger with the solution of carbolic acid. "He got yeh fer fair in thet thirteenth round. Yeh couldn't last anudder."

Briggs had failed to answer. But at these words of Steve, his large mouth bent in his habitual sneer.

"Couldn't last another? Well, if yuh'd only have lasted two more frames— through the fifteenth—I'd have doubled on muh money."

"Aw, Briggs, I did the best I could," pleaded the Gouger. "Didn't I bring home the ten-round money fur yuh?"

"I know, I know," snapped Briggs savagely. "Yuh did the best yuh could—I ain't sayin' no to that. But yer best wasn't good enough. Yer old, Gouger. Yuh can't go it no more. The pace got yuh as much as any of them blows of the Slugger."

Briggs shaped his remarks without a care for the feelings of the Gouger. He was without tact, worse than blunt, brutally unfeeling, barbarous.

"Looket," he expounded, "looket how the Slugger opened up, fightin' all the time, every minute, an' you coverin' up, backin' an' fillin'—an' yet the Slugger finished strong an' beat yuh to a pulp! Yer old, Gouger. The Slugger had yuh right from that fust flip-flop in the third round. Oh, yuh know the game, all right. The Slugger's a tin-eared boob, as yuh say. You got the science, all the tricks. But it won't do yuh no good. All the Kid McCoy tricks in the world won't do yuh no good. Yer old."

A bitter light filled the two caverns that were the Gouger's deep-set eyes. He looked up at the unplaned ceiling. Very quietly, he asked—

"How much yuh win, Briggs?"

Briggs started and his left hand went toward the inside pocket of his coat. But instantly he thought better of the move. His hand dropped away and, his eyes drawn tight, he stared down at the Gouger as though attempting to ferret out what underlay the query.

The Gouger was looking up at the ceiling. Briggs opened his mouth to speak. At that moment, from the dressing quarters of the Slugger beyond, went up a discord of laughter. Briggs waited as if for a quietude in which he might be heard.

But ere the sounds of laughter had died away, the Gouger turned his head and gazed full at the manager.

"I'm askin' yuh, Briggs," he said almost testily. "Was it so much yuh've gotta hedge about it?"

"Oh, no!" returned Briggs hastily. "Yuh've got it sized wrong. It ain't so much I feel like boastin' about it, I'll tell yer."

"How much was it, Briggs?" and the Gouger exchanged a swift meaning glance with his two seconds.

Briggs did not miss the glance. He became almost apologetic.

"Aw, whadda yuh think? I'm not holdin' nuthin' back on yuh. I'll tell yuh how much I won. Only I gotta explain it." He hesitated. "Yuh see, I bet five hundred—no, yuh see, I bet a thousand dollars, on the short end of the bet, that yuh'd last fifteen rounds—"

"But the ten-round money, Briggs?" The Gouger sat up, never removing his eyes from the flush-faced manager. "What I'm askin' is what did yuh win on the ten rounds?"

Briggs's eyes fled, in a kind of consternation, from the Gouger to his seconds. Bud was watching him closely, the bottle of carbolic acid poised in his hand. Steve had left off chewing.

"Aw, jes' five thousand dollars," he snarled like a cornered lynx.

The Gouger nodded thoughtfully, as if making some notation in his mind.

"All right," he said. "Yuh won five thousand dollars on me."

"But that fifteen-round bet," Briggs hastened to add. "I bet a thousand dollars on yuh to last—"

"How much? One thousand bones? Aw, come off yer perch!"

"Well, it was somethin' like seven-hundred an' fifty, anyways," persisted Briggs, coloring cholerically.

"I thought yuh said it was five hundred."

"Five hundred?" repeated Briggs, as if shockingly surprised. He flourished one diamond-glinting hand. "Well, have it yer own way," he said with seeming magnanimity. "It was seven hundred an' fifty—but that's all right. Call it five hundred. I'm no piker."

"Well," said the Gouger slowly, "yuh won five thousand dollars when I lasted out the ten frames. Outer thet five thousand, yuh had ter pay back five hundred sinkers 'cause I failed ter last fifteen rounds. Thet makes four thousand five hundred dollars yuh won. Ain't I right—eh, Briggs?"

Briggs did not answer. He kept looking at the Gouger very studiously.

"Say," he blurted out at last, "what yuh drivin' at, Gouger?"

"Jes' this."

The Gouger lifted himself on his hands until he sat on the end of the rub-down table, his legs dangling over the edge. He draped a towel across his middle.

"I didn't pike my bets, Briggs. I had a hunch I was goin' ter win." He looked around as if, on the sudden, he missed something. "I thought," he went on, "thet hobo kid an' his yeller hound-dawg was a-gonna bring me luck. I bet every cent I had. Even what I hadn't at the time—the loser's end of the purse. An' I didn't bet on lastin' ten er fifteen round; I didn't pike—I better win. I lost. I'm broke."

Briggs's large mouth had curved into his habitual sneer at the mention of the Frisco Kid. At the Gouger's frank admission that he had no money, the sneer deepened witheringly.

"Oh," was all he said, "I got yuh. Yuh're broke."

His words showed little interest in the Gouger's unhappy state. They committed him neither to sympathy nor to charity. They were chosen with thought prepense. He realized that the Gouger had some idea in the back of his head; he felt that that idea had somehow to do with the money he had won on the fight; and he hoped, by his non-committal answer, to stave off any attempt at a loan upon the part of the Gouger.

"Yep, I'm broke," repeated the Gouger, nothing daunted, knowing his man. "Yuh hear, Briggs? I'm broke."

The words were forced from Briggs's mouth. He could not again reiterate what the Gouger had said. There was no other way.

"Well," he said with very ill grace, "whadda yuh want me to do?"

"Jes' this. Give me two hundred an' fifty dollars ter git along on. No, I'm not askin' yuh ter lend it ter me. I say give it ter me. You won yer money on me. I'm askin' yuh ter share with me in yer winnin's, ter give me a bit of 'em."

"But I didn't win the money on yuh. You didn't cop the fight. I won my money by placin' it—placin' it wise."

"Yuh turn me down then, huh?"

Briggs fidgeted with the pockets of his white vest.

"No, no, Gouger—not that. But I got a lot of expenses. I bet five hundred dollars on yuh to win—"

The Gouger was angry.

"Yuh didn't!" he snapped. "Yuh're a ——— liar! Yuh never even hoped ter see me win. Aw, I know yuh, Briggs!"

The Gouger got to his feet. Briggs backed away, one hand out conciliatingly.

"Sit down, Gouger, sit down! Don't git sore, old man. Lemme explain it."

"Explain what? Ain't yer turnin' me down?"

Despite the vehement resentment in his words, the Gouger was very weak. His hammered stomach felt squeamish. As he stood up, his head reeled. He held with one hand to the edge of the rub-down table. His head continued to reel. He sank back upon the table.

"I bet five hundred dollars on yuh to win," insisted Briggs, "so that leaves me only four thousand dollars ahead of the game. An' then there's other incidentals. I gotta pay Hackett's all of a hundred dollars fer yer room an' board, an' the use of the gym."

The Gouger removed his hand from his head. His head had cleared, albeit he still felt dismayingly weak. He looked at the manager with a wan smile that had in it something of bitterness but a great deal more of scorn.

"Briggs," he said slowly, "I got yuh. Yuh turn me down. I knew yuh would. I knew yuh'd throw the skids under me, ef I lost this fight. I tole yuh so. But I didn't expect yuh'd do it so rotten. Yuh turn me down cold!"

The Gouger grasped the sides of the table with hands streaked by red welts where the tape had been wound. He grasped the sides of the table tightly, until the red welts turned white.

Briggs waited as a man waits during an earthquake, mute under the shock, hoping for it to pass, knowing naught else to do.

The Gouger spoke. And there was no longer any whine in his voice. There was only in his voice a great and just acidity.

"I'm all in. I've fought the fight of my life. An' yuh turn me down on a measly couple of hundred. All right, Briggs. But lemme tell yuh. Ef I only could stand on my pins, without my head goin' round an' my stomach comin' up—ef I only could stand, I'd git thet money!" menacingly. "I wouldn't ast fur it. Naw! I'd take it away from yuh—yuh big, bloated toad!"

Briggs backed toward the misfit door at this threatening turn to the conversation. The Gouger looked away from him, at his two seconds. As if with some malicious meaning, he said:

"Yep! Ef I was as fit as yuh two fellers, I'd git my money! I'd git my money, er I'd git him!"

Briggs's hand was on the knob of the door. The Gouger swung his eyes on him suddenly. He snapped:

"Briggs, ain't yuh gonna pay these boys fur trainin' me? Ain't yuh gonna pay them the hundred apiece yuh promised!"

"No!" bawled the manager, and he slammed the door behind him.

The two seconds started for the door after the manager. Steve had recommenced chewing, chewing very fast.

"Thet's it!" the Gouger spurred them on. "After him! Git yer money! Git him!"

The men slammed out.

X

"FOR NONE CAN TELL TO WHAT RED HELL HIS SIGHTLESS SOUL MAY STRAY"
—Ballad of Reading Gaol

THE GOUGER WAS ALONE. There was the sound of running footfalls fainting away along the wooden flooring of the entrance; there was the bang of a closing door in the direction of the Slugger's room; and then, in the rude shed of a dressing quarter, there was no longer any sound.

He sat on the edge of the rub-down table, a towel draped across his thighs. He could feel the air breathing sharply through the interstices between the unplaned planks of the walls; yet there was in him not sufficient strength of desire to cause him to draw on his clothes. Only necessity and then bitterness, a kind of rancor, had upheld him in the wordy duel with Briggs.

Now his stomach was turned upside down; black spots chased themselves across the retinas of his eyes; and his brain gyrated in his head, at times, like shaken kernels in a nut. His strength was sapped, his vitality low.

It is a law of nature that the thoughts engendered when the vitality of the body is low are invariably morose thoughts. The Gouger was thinking morosely.

He had been turned down cold. At this extremity, when he needed help most, Briggs had thrown the skids under him. He had refused him even a loan. And his seconds were gone. Whether they got the money from Briggs or not, he knew they would not return. Everybody had deserted him. Yes, everybody—even that hobo kid and his yellow hound-dog.

And he was old. The crowd so had said. Briggs so had said. That was the sorry part of this game of his. He had given the best years of his life, every hour, every minute of those years, to this game. The game had unfitted him for any other pursuit of bread and butter. Now it had spit him, old in vigor though young in years, out into the unknown to shift for himself. What could he do?

Only healthy bodies under a high pressure of vitality aspire to Olympus. Men in the Gouger's state, with viscera gone, nerves frayed, vitality ebbed and the supreme effort of their lives foiled, tread mentally a Cimmerian gloom, an Abaddonian blackness, and lift their hands to Heaven and question the why of it all.

Thus the Gouger. His body ached and was weary and cried for rest; and now his continuous tenor of morose thinking had led him into a slough of morbidity. He lacked education; he was without a philosophy; there was nothing in the back of his head to temporize the aloes and vinegar of his downfall. He was walking innumerable *cul-de-sacs*, short-sightedly stubbing his brains against the wall of the future. He was treading a Dædalian maze, in which there showed no light, in which he was lost—helplessly, hopelessly lost. He could see no end.

And the Gouger was brave. He was braver even than the run of men. He had fought all his life, arduously, against odds and handicaps, preterhumanly. Yet now he thought to quit. He thought to give up the fight—the fight against the future, the fight of life. He had lost hope, all heart in the future. The future and life itself held nothing for him. He thought to die.

Quickly in vivid flashes, through the morbidity of his brains, reeled a horrid procession of the different modes man takes to end that which God has given. He thought of Nigger Jim who, after losing the fight in Butte, had cut the last filament of life in his body by streaking a steel razor across the jugular of his neck.

But there was, in the idea, something instinctively abhorrent to the Gouger.

"Thet's all right fur niggers," he said, "though Jim was sure white—the whitest man I ever knowed. Pore Jim!"

He thought then of Spider Feeley who, marked through dissipation by a fatal disease, had killed himself, but the year before, with a steel-capped bullet spit from a shooting-iron in his own hand. The thought burst on him like a tremendous inspiration. He imagined himself doing the same. He could almost feel the fatness of the butt of the revolver, the chill of the muzzle rubbing against his temple, the tension of his finger pulling the trigger.

His head jerked away. His oddly-shaped head jerked away as if from the impact of a steel-capped bullet.

There was something terrifically dismaying to him even in the visualization of a bullet thudding against his head. He had been so brutally mauled, his brains had been so sickeningly upset by the many pitiless blows smashed against his vital organs and head, that he could not think, now, to withstand another blow. He dodged and shivered before the idea of a bullet hitting his head, breaking through his head, shattering and scattering his brains. He could not stand it. The shock as of a blow would be too great.

"No, no!" he cried in an unutterable dread. "I've bin beaten enough about the head—too much. I'm losin' my noive! I can't do it! I can't do it!"

In a species of desperate frenzy, he looked about him. There were other and easier ways of ending one's life than by shooting oneself with a pistol. There were ways by which one floated into death without effort, without shock, as on sable wings. And the Gouger was weary. He wanted to glide into sleep gently, and never wake up.

A peculiar and pungently tarry odor was breathing into the Gouger's nostrils. He perked his head suddenly like a pointer whiffing quail. It was the odor of the carbolic solution with which his bruises had been bathed. There was a small quantity in a graniteware dish on the floor. There was fully a pint of unadulterated carbolic acid in a large thirty-two-ounce bottle that stood in the medicine-chest hanging on one wall.

Here was the way! It was no easy way, no blissful method of euthanasia. The acid would scorch his throat like undiluted alcohol; it would burn the lining of his stomach; it would terrifically sear him. It might cause him to retch and vomit, and be knotted up in convulsions. But he felt that he was so weak he would quickly collapse, and he knew that it would kill him in the end as certainly as a pistol shot and with no shocking, shattering, rending blow. He had been too much beaten.

His head reeling and a great ringing in his ears, as if already he had swallowed the acid, he slipped down upon his feet. Then toward the bottle that was gruesomely labeled with a skull and cross-bones, and a large warning, "Poison," he staggered.

XI

"Me and Gay-cat and You!"

THE MISFIT OF A DOOR SWUNG INWARD and the Frisco Kid entered. He was very weary. He had been buffeted by the outpouring crowd like driftwood on a wave. He had been darting between and around the shrieking automobiles that were leaving the arena, freighted with human cargo. The lashes of his deep-sunk eyes were laden with dust, his mouth was open for breath, and his brown face was a dusty white from the exertions he had undergone.

The Gouger staggered back and slumped down upon the rub-down table and shivered as if the freezing draft of air that accompanied the Kid's entrance had chilled him awake out of a bad dream. He brushed one hand before his eyes. The Kid still was there. He kept looking at the Kid in mute and stupefied bewilderment.

The Frisco Kid was in the throes of remorse and penitence. He could say no word. He could only stare at the Gouger with anxious, pleading blue eyes.

And then, as if to relieve the intolerableness of the situation, the door behind the Kid opened a crack, a mere trifle, and in squeezed the yellow dog, Gay-cat.

The Gouger shrugged himself together. Then these figures before him were indeed real and not visitants from God as his superstitious mind had first told him. Slowly, at sight of the dog, a stiff smile worked itself up his face.

"Hullo," he said. "Where yuh bin, Kid? Where yuh bin, you an' yer dawg?"

The Frisco Kid, in his poignant consciousness of guilt, felt the Gouger's greeting as if it were an accusation.

"Aw, Gouger; aw, say now, Gouger. I didn't go back on yer. I didn't slope. I didn't quit yer like a termater-can bum. Gay-cat and me, we's blowed-in-the-glass stiffs, and we left yer 'cause we thought we knowed a way to help yer.

"We saw the knockout, Gay-cat and me, and we's awful sorry, Gouger. But mebbe if yer could 'a' stalled longer, mebbe then we'd 'a' been in time. We ran all the way, like everythin', Gouger. But we was too late. And I'm awful sorry, Gouger—Gay-cat is sorry, too. But—but here it is!"

The Kid drew from under his left arm and held out before the Gouger's startled eyes the remnant of a pair of faded-green fighting-trunks.

The Gouger had listened to the Kid's gasping utterance in a bewilderment that was not unmixed with guilty qualms lest the Kid had observed that which he had been just about to do. But now, as the Kid held up the dirty and hopelessly torn fighting-trunks and questioned and entreated him from gipsy-blue eyes, the Gouger understood all at once, and smiled sadly and indulgently.

"Yep, I think yuh is a bit too late, Kid. But where—where did yuh git 'em? Is thet why yuh left me?"

The Frisco Kid nodded hastily and almost happily at being so readily understood.

"I ran all the way back to Hackett's for 'em. I heard Briggs tellin' yer to stall in the seventh round, and I knew then yer couldn't win. But I thought if yer could only stall till I got back with the trunks, mebbe then yer could win, anyhow. I knew them trunks was som'eres about Hackett's, though I hadn't been able to find 'em that time Briggs went back with me. But Gay-cat here"—and he looked in a kind of pride and thankfulness down at the yellow dog at his feet—"he promised to help out, and I jes' knowed he'd find 'em."

The Gouger was arousing to a definable interest in what the Kid was saying.

"How'd yuh know thet, Kid? How'd yuh know them trunks 'ud be about Hackett's?"

The Frisco Kid hesitated. His face went red and white by turns. He felt inexpressibly guilty and contrite.

"Well, yer see, Gouger," he stumbled, suddenly determined to tell all, "yer see, I lost my pants yeste'day when I was in swimmin'. I was in swimmin' right behind the gym. And I see'd yer trunks hangin' on the line—though I never knowed they was yers—and I pulled 'em down and got into 'em. And then I found my pants under Hackett's porch, wrapped about a pile, and I took off the trunks to get into them pants. But I never knowed where the trunks had gone to when yer asked about 'em—sure I never, Gouger. Gay-cat here, he had buried 'em and he only brought 'em out when I went back the second time. It's all our fault, Gouger. We ran all the way back, but we was too late. And I guess yer sore at us, huh, Gouger? We's awful sorry. But mebbe if yer wear them trunks in yer next fight, mebbe then yer'll win, one hand!"

Slowly the Gouger shook his oddly-shaped head.

"There ain't gonna be enny next fight, Kid. Oh, I'm not sore at yuh, bo. Yuh're the only one what tried ter help me. Briggs turned me down cold, an' Bud an' Steve has run out on me. But yuh—yuh can't help me, Kid. I'm up aginst too tough a proposition. I'm old, Kid. I can't go the gait enny more. I'm through."

The fighting-trunks fell from the Kid's hand in the shock of a complete and ecstatic surprise. The dog at his feet pounced upon the fallen trunks as a cat might pounce upon a ball. But the Kid did not know that. His face was beaming with uncontainable joy.

"Then yer comin' along with us, with Gay-cat an' me! I knowed yer would, Gouger, I jes' knowed yer would! And we'll be blowed-in-the-glass stiffs, me and Gay-cat and you. We'll tramp along the roads and talk and whistle, and sleep under the trees and stars, and in haystacks sometimes, and ride the rods, and batter the screen doors and—and—oh, everythin'! We'll be buddies together, huh, Gouger?"

But the Gouger only shook his head.

"I'm too old, Kid. Yuh couldn't learn me ter be a stiff. I'd blow up on it, jes' like I done on this fight. I'm too old."

The Frisco Kid was astonished.

"You blow up? You too old? Aw, Gouger; aw, say now, Gouger! Yer'd be a blowed-in-the-glass in a week. I'll show yer all, Gouger. And a fighter like yer—why yer'll be king of the hoboes in no time!"

The Gouger could not refrain from smiling wanly at the Frisco Kid's confidence, his sublime hopes, and his glorified vision of the future. Yet, at the same time, it could not escape him how intrepidly brave was the Kid's outlook; and, as is always true of bravery, there was, in the Kid's suggestions, something so wholesomely infectious and tremendously stimulating that the Gouger felt himself lifted completely out of his morbidity.

He realized the change in him. He could feel that change refreshing him as a good night's sleep refreshes a wearied body. He felt renewed. He was no longer debilitated of body, depressed of spirit, desirous of dying. He wanted to live. He did not feel strongly the urge to live. It was merely that the hankering for death had lessened consciously its fell insistence. No longer did he want to die.

"Kid," he said very seriously, his soul on the ascendant, "yuh've learned me a mighty big lesson. Here yuh are, without a thing ahead er behind yuh, an' yet ye're willin' ter take a chance—ye're jes' foamin' over with pep an' gameness. Yuh make me feel measly, honest yuh do. Thet's why I've changed my mind. Thet's why I ain't gonna do what I was a-gonna do. I've changed my mind. I'm gonna be game, I am, an' see it through."

The Gouger had changed his mind! Bewilderment fled the Kid's face, and his heart plumbed to his track-worn shoes. The Gouger had told him that, should he lose this fight, he would probably have to go on the road himself. And the Kid had thought to accompany the Gouger. But now the Gouger had changed his mind. He would not go on the road; he would not be the Kid's buddy! The Frisco Kid's thin face became, on the instant, pathetically rueful.

The Gouger noted the change, but misjudged the reason for it.

"Aw, no!" he hastened to add. "Don't be skeered, Kid. I tell yuh, I won't drink the stuff!"

The Gouger looked up at the medicine-chest, above his head on the wall, and full at the gruesomely labeled bottle of carbolic acid. The Frisco Kid did not know what to think, then. His eyes, very wide, ran over the array of bottles in the chest in a puzzled endeavor to discover the particular one the Gouger meant.

"Which, Gouger? What is it?"

"Don't yuh know?" The Gouger's deep-set eyes searched the deep-sunk eyes of the Kid. "Didn't yuh see me reachin' fur it when yuh came in?"

"I didn't notice. Is it skee?"

"Skee?" gasped the Gouger, the force of his surprise allowing him nothing to say save a repetition of the Kid's word. His face was stupid with blankness. Then, in an eyewink, an indivisible trice, his face grew bright, his eyes all a-twitter, with the agitation of a sublime and fortunate thought.

"Thet's it, thet's it!" he said, very fast, as if unable to mouth the words quickly enough. "It's old man Red-Eye! I was goin' ter swaller it ter bluff out my defeat. I needed somethin', Kid. I felt awful rotten jes' afore yuh came in. Briggs turned me down, an' Bud an' Steve sloped on me. They all turned me down cold. Only you came back, kid—you an' yer hound-dawg!"

"Aw, Gouger; aw, say now, Gouger! We wouldn't run out on yer. Yer was good to us, Gouger, and we couldn't go back on yer nohow. We'se blowed-in-the-glass stiffs, Gay-cat and me, and we stick by our friends."

There was the sound of footsteps approaching along the wooden flooring of the entrance. As if fearing that some one might intrude, the Kid added hastily, yearningly:

"And yer is comin' with us now, sure, Gouger? Me, I allus wanted to go back into the great hobo country t'other side of the Hump, but I was kinder leery since I left Frisco Red. But now I won't be leery of crossin' the Sierras no more. Me and you, we'll ride together through the snowshed, Gouger, and yer can button old Gay-cat inside yer coat to keep yer warm. Gee, it'll be swell—me and Gay-cat and you!"

The Frisco Kid looked at the prizefighter and there was, in his gipsy-blue eyes, admiration and ardent longing. The Gouger was very thoughtful.

"I've half a mind," he began; but at that moment, when he was within an ace of making a decision, the misfit of a door swung inward and, in an utter and overpowering astonishment, the rest of his words were sucked down his throat.

Standing in the doorway was the squat, broad-shouldered form of Slugger Sweigert, his face beaming between criss-crossings of court-plaster, a soft black four-dented hat pushed back upon his head, a tight double-breasted suit accentuating the breadth of his chest, a gold-headed cane held lightly in one chamois-gloved hand, and a necktie showing a violent streak of red between the choking lapels of his blue coat.

XII
Into the Darkling Night

The slugger radiated good nature and action from his criss-crossed, beaming and battered countenance and violent red necktie down to the shimmering square toes of his patent leathers. He did not wait for the Gouger to recover from his astonishment. He could not contain himself. He plunged right in on that business which had brought him.

"Hit's a dirty stinkin' shyme, th' w'y Briggs polished yuh off," he said heatedly with nasal and aspirated accent. "Hi wuz in my dressin'-hapartment next door, y' know, so yuh cawn't bli' me fer hover-'earin' a bit. But wot Hi mean to s'y his that that wuzn't wot brung me 'ere. Hi sez t' myself, sez Hi, 'This chap's a bleedin' beggar, a blawsted down-pin, an' hit's a bloody shyme. 'E knows th' gyme, 'e does though really, y' know, 'e is a bit ole.

" 'Now, 'ere, Mr. Featherstonehaugh,' I sez t' my manager, sez I,' 'ere y' are goin' back t' Austrylia, next wyck. Hi need a manager, but no bally rotter, y' know. An' 'ere's this chap, Gouger, a down-pin, Lawd lumme, but a chap wot knows th' gyme. 'E won't fight henny more; 'e's a bit ole fer th' gyme; but Hi'm blessed, Mr. Featherstonehaugh,' Hi sez, sez Hi, 'Hi fawncy to 'ave 'im teach me th' gyme, be my manager—that sort of thing. 'E thinks Hi am a—haw, wot d' ye call it, suh?—'e thinks Hi've got a storage utensil hover my ears. Blimey, 'e's right. So wot s'y? Wot s'y to 'ave 'im teach me th' gyme, all 'e knows?'

" 'Yuh're balmy,' sez 'e, 'but go a'ead,' sez 'e. An' 'ere, like a silly ass, Hi am. But really, ole fellah, Hi want yuh t' come along with me. Eh? Wot s'y?"

As the Australian spoke, the Gouger recovered more and more from his astonishment. His puffed and broken lips drew into a whimsical smile. Yet there was in the smile something less superficial than any whimsy, something indescribably deeper—as if, indeed, the motive that actuated the man's oddly-accented words had touched soothingly the very wounds of his soul.

He knew now. This was not the Slugger who had called him names. This was the victor, the generous victor. Yet he feared that the Slugger was more than the generous victor. He feared the charitable victor. And he who had been within a wink of death, did not yet hold life so dear as to be bought at the price of dishonor. He dreaded lest the Slugger was proffering to him some form of charity.

"This ain't salve, is it, Slugger?" he asked probingly. "Yuh think I kin learn yuh somethin'—yuh think so, on the level?"

"Somethin'?" In unfeigned surprise, the Slugger exerted the superciliary muscles so that the court-plaster bunched on his lifted eyebrows. "Well, really, matey, yuh cawn teach me everythin' habout th' gyme! Lawd lumme, Hi felt wot yuh knew when Hi wuz sparrin' yuh. Oh, Hi could tell. Hi felt like a silly ass, blimey! Hi've bin only a twelve-month in this gyme, y' know, an' they tell me yuh've bin in hit fer eleven years. 'Ere, tyke this, come along with me, an' we'll call hit a tryde." He offered to the Gouger a sheaf of greenbacks.

The Gouger looked from the man to the money, from the money to the man; and, weak as he still was, he could not help it—at this unexpected and unstinted generosity, his eyes filled. He swallowed once or twice in an attempt to speak. But he could not speak. He put out his hand and grasped the unencumbered hand of the Slugger. Holding onto the Slugger's hand, dumbly thus he expressed his appreciation and his thanks.

The Frisco Kid watched in a fine admiration. He was markedly susceptible to sympathy and generosity, not alone because of his youth, but also because of his hard-earned knowledge of the inhospitality of the world.

"Gee!" he muttered. "The Slugger's a blowed-in-the-glass, too! They's both blowed-in-the-glass stiffs, the Gouger and the Slugger!"

" 'Ere, tyke it," repeated the Slugger, affecting impatience. "Don't myke a bloomin' scene, ole chap. This bit, why hit's only yer first wyck's wyges. Tyke hit, matey, an' come along."

The Gouger took the money without daring to utter a word, then turned away hastily and donned his undergarments, trousers, shirt, shoes and coat.

The Frisco Kid waited, the dog worrying the faded-green fighting-trunks at his feet. As the Gouger went out, followed by the Slugger, the Kid accepted the chance offered by their turned backs and picked up, from between the dog's paws, the pair of dirty and hopelessly torn fighting-trunks.

As the Frisco Kid emerged, with his dog, from the entrance to the arena, the Gouger seemed suddenly to awake to his presence. A sheepish expression laid itself on his battered countenance. He stepped down from the footboard of the Slugger's automobile and, approaching, tendered to the Kid one of the greenbacks the Slugger had just given him. It was as if he wished to propitiate the Kid for his change of heart, to atone somehow for the loss of himself as the Kid's buddy.

"Remember, I promised yuh a slice of the purse, Kid?" he said, with a sorry attempt at a smile. "Well, here it is."

"But yer didn't win. And I wasn't to share unless yer won. No, Gouger; I can't take it."

There was, in the Kid's deep-sunk eyes, a woeful wistfulness. The Gouger saw the look; he understood; and quickly he turned away, his hand crushing the greenback into a ball under the stress of some strong emotion. Finally he swung about again and laid one red-welted hand upon the Kid's frail shoulder.

"Kid," he said, "I'd like ter go along with yuh; I'd like ter go like everythin'. But I can't, kid. It 'ud be a dirty trick on the Slugger here. He believes in me. He believes I kin give him some pointers on the game. An' I gotta live up ter his opinion. I gotta show him all I knows. I gotta make him a champeen!

"Yuh see how it is, Kid. I've bin in this game fur eleven year—eleven hard, long, fightin' year. I know it from A to Israel. It's all I do know. An' I can't slope, I can't run out on the game. I gotta stick ter it, an' show the Slugger what I knows, an' pay back through him all thet the game learned me. If I threw the skids under the game an' sloped with yuh, I'd queer the Slugger, an', Kid, he's a friend of mine now. I don't wanta do thet. I wanta stick ter my friends like—whadda yuh call it?"

"A blowed-in-the-glass stiff, Gouger?" faltered the Kid.

"Thet's it—a blowed-in-the-glass stiff, Kid. A guy what sticks ter his friends; a guy what tries ter help his friends fur helpin' him; a guy what never quits his game. Thet's what I wanta be, kid—a blowed-in-the-glass stiff!"

"And yer is, Gouger! You and the Slugger, yer both blowed-in-the-glass stiffs!"

In the vocabulary of the Frisco Kid's hobo caste that was the finest compliment one could pay a man. The Kid, as he uttered it, held the remnant of fighting-trunks out to the Gouger.

"Yer don't need 'em now, Gouger," he said. "But if yer'll give 'em to the Slugger in his next fight—if the Slugger'll only wear 'em, Gouger, mebbe then he'll win for yer, one hand!"

The Gouger crushed the trunks in his hands as once before, under the stress of strong emotion, he had crushed the greenback. He started to say something; his throat-apple moved up and down convulsively; but he could not speak. He tore his eyes away from the Kid and leaped in a kind of flurry into the automobile.

The Slugger, waiting and ready, slowly released the clutch. The automobile rolled away.

The Frisco Kid looked after the dust-raising car; the wistfulness turned moist in his eyes. The car disappeared into the darkling night. And the Kid felt then, all at once, inexpressibly lonely.

"Gee," he gulped to the yellow mongrel at his feet, "I didn't want the money. I wanted Gouger—along—as buddies!"

Excerpt from The Camp-Fire

FROM PATRICK CASEY something about the story ("According To His Caste") by himself and his brother in this number:

In 1909 and 1910 I was employed on the San Francisco *Examiner* as an assistant to the late W.W. Naughton, then the dean and premier of newspaper fight critics in the United States. It was my business, with other things such as reporting "outlaw" baseball, to cover the vicinal training-camps while pugilists were conditioning, to jump into the ring after the contests and get the boxed interviews of principals and referee, and once back in the office, to take Mr. Naughton's dictation of the story of the fight directly upon the typewriter.

In this way, refreshing my memory from my newspaper clippings, I find that I witnessed some dozen championship or near-championship fights, and an innumerable number of preliminaries and four-round goes. In this way, I met ring-men off and on their guard.

I rode in a machine with Billy Papke and his brother, Ed, and listened to their vituperation of Ketchel. I was invited by Battling Nelson to dine with him. I came to know Willie Ritchie very well, ere he won to his short-lived championship.

And once I was "bidded" by Jack Johnson to ride in his racing-car, but thought more of my neck than of notoriety.

I was at the ringside of the Nelson-Hyland fight, the fourth Ketchel-Papke go, the Young Corbett-Johnny Frayne contest, the "Harlem Tommy" Murphy-Owen Moran set-to, and the nimble exhibition of the bantams, Frankie Neil and Monte Attell.

I saw, close up, Jack Johnson's "golden smile" when Ketchel was supposed to have knocked him down, just before Johnson himself leaped up and knocked out Ketchel, breaking off, with one punch, two teeth in the front of Ketchel's mouth. I saw Johnson lift, with extended arms, the over two hundred pounds of Al Kaufman, then step, smilingly, into the very corner out of which Kaufman had been so anxious to get. I could hear the click of the incessantly working jaws of Leach Cross' gum-chewing brothers, as they seconded the New York dentist in his encounter with "Fighting Dick."

I noticed the boil on Battling Nelson's wrist, the night before he lost his championship to Wolgast in the Richmond arena. I stood up in the drizzle, that held through that fight, and splashed through the mud of Richmond in a try to follow the victorious Wolgast and get an interview. I remarked red-headed, clean-fighting, tragically fated Tommy McCarthy in the preliminaries at Coffroth's arena, long before he was killed in the ring by hitting his head upon a poorly padded canvas floor. I remember, now, I once saw poor Tommy in the mortar-whitened jumpers of a bricklayer—he was truly proud of his trade—awaiting Coffroth's pleasure in an outer office. A clean fighter, a sound liver, a good boy, Tommy, who tried too ambitiously.

Another clean fighter I used to delight in watching was Lew Powell. Maybe because he was tinged a red like myself. But anyway I'll never forget his twenty-round go with Wolgast, when Wolgast looped over his kidney punch, snapping Powell erect, sapping his vitality almost with the one blow. Powell told me about the effect of those loop kidney blows, afterward. I have attempted to put over those effects in this story of a fight.

I have introduced other realities. The somersaulting of the *Gouger* in the end is one of these realities. I actually saw this occur. It was in the Powell-Johnny Frayne go. Powell knocked Frayne down, but not cold. Frayne's head bent under him; his legs lifted; he rolled over. He rolled over two, three, four times, very slowly. Then he lay still, unconscious. It was awful. It left a deep effect on my mind. And I remember it was a cause of wonder to me why none of the newspapers mentioned it, the following morning. Perhaps it was one of those shocking things of the ring which would not make good reading at the morning breakfast.

But we have made use of it. I actually saw Frayne roll over four times. We have had the *Gouger* roll over twice, with an attempt at a third roll. We do not feel that any reader would believe that a man, practically knocked out, could be able to somersault in agony four times. Yet I actually saw this occur. It is one of those instances where fact goes fiction one better.

In this story we have introduced some well-known figures and places of the ring-game out here. The large white-haired announcer, with a voice of megaphone proportion, is, to be sure, the late Billy Jordan whose "Let 'er go!" was quite famous. The wooden, bowl-shaped arena is, thinly disguised, Coffroth's arena at Colma. And Hackett's is an utterly changed Millet's, where Nelson and Ketchel trained on several occasions. Truly,

Millet's is a white two-storied road-house about a mile or more from Coffroth's arena along the Mission Road; but there is no stream anywhere near it and the gym is a barn, not a block away, but immediately behind. Our story necessitated the extra trimmings.

We have had the *Gouger* make use of Nelson's famous half-scissors hook. Nelson is very proud of that punch. Also, the *Gouger's* waiting tactics, ere entering the ring, are another leaf out of Nelson's book. I never shall forget how we waited in a drizzle for a full half-hour after Wolgast entered the Richmond arena ere Nelson appeared. And in that fight, as in our fight, Youth triumphed over Age: Nelson lost his championship to Wolgast. The *Gouger's* expression about thinking, once, that "Hackett's was a palace," is the identical expression I heard Dick Wheeler give vent to, what time he was a sparring mate of Nelson at Millet's. We inserted it into our story in an attempt to show the great illusion young fighters have before they come up against the dismal reality.

I was talking to Jim Griffin, the referee, some time ago and I mentioned the fact that we were writing a story of a prize fight in the course of which we introduced Kid McCoy's resin trick. He thereupon told me of some forgotten fight in which, he said, —— had rubbed mustard and vinegar, or some such preparation, upon his gloves in order to smart the eyes of his opponent, thereby blinding him temporarily and having him at his mercy. There are endless stories about ——.

The Phoney Man

A Complete Novelette by

Patrick and Terence Casey

I

The Frisco Kid Makes a Mistake and Has His Love Tested

IT WAS ONE OF THOSE LONG SLEEPY SUMMER AFTERNOONS when the cool of a bush or a tree is welcome, and not a thing stirs or makes a sound. The white road drowsed, drenched in sunlight, and the plucked and empty fields of the Mississippi Bottoms lay flat to either hand and very still.

Beside the white road, in the patch of shade of a cypress-tree, the Frisco Kid sprawled—a ragged, dusty little vagabond. At his feet, beyond the cypress patch of shade and altogether out in the sun-drenched road, the Gay-cat was outstretched, sunning himself and dozing. They were lazying away, thus, the long soundless Summer afternoon.

A gang of heavy horseflies thrummed the air above the blissful dog. They disturbed his peace of mind. Out of the dust he lifted his yellow head and viciously he snapped at them. Yet did the flies continue to pester him. He turned up his round little belly and pawed at them. Also, quite desperately, he snapped again. But they gyrated out of reach and thrummed only louder and shriller. It was all no use.

He lay on his back, his paws and jaws motionless, his brown canine eyes closed to mere slits; and thus he eyed and studied the thrumming horseflies, the while he puzzled within his sharp yellow head just what next to do.

And then, as he lay there in that absurdly attentive posture, he heard the sound. It was a loud sound in all that sweet hush of drowsing white road and Summer afternoon sunshine and hot, empty, Mississippi Bottoms cotton-fields.

Tap, tap, tap—an unusual staccato sound. The dog scrambled afoot. Ragged ears cocked forward, he stood, in the middle of the road, watching the approaching man.

The man came tap-tapping on a stick along the road—a seedy, stoop-shouldered, shriveled-up man who wore large silver-rimmed glasses before his dim eyes. Once he paused and turned around to look back the way he had come and to listen, head on one side.

Then on again he moved, slowly tapping up the road toward the shady cypress-tree where the Kid watched and the Gay-cat bristled. The Gay-cat was within an ace of barking, when the Kid said:

"What yer excited about, Gay-cat? It's only a old-timer stumpin' along on a stick. He's all dressed up like a jedge. He's a planter, mebbe, and most-like a mean and horstile one. Come here to me. He'll mash yer, Gay-cat, with that stick he's a-carryin'. You come here to me, old hobo."

The approaching man was dressed in a suit of a somewhat precise cut. It was of an old-fashioned swallow-tailed effect. It had once been black; it was now green and shiny. The coat bulged and flared at the hips as though it concealed bundles, while beneath the swallow-tails behind, little torn tags of lining hung down like the ragged underfeathers of a bird.

He wore a shapeless black hat with brim turned up in front. His black hair draggled low on his forehead and was matted and oily with sweat. His face was brown as a walnut. It was wrinkled as a walnut, too—a lean, shrewd, quizzical bird-like face. And the large silver-rimmed glasses, outstanding, peering, increased that resemblance he bore to a bird. They gave him a somewhat malignant look, a somewhat predatory look—a look like that of a huge bird of prey.

The man did not go tap-tapping past the cypress-tree. Blind and groping he seemed, yet he became aware of the Frisco Kid's presence as by some mysterious sixth sense—certainly not by sight or sound. He drew, on the sudden, to a full stop.

Then, very deliberately, he faced toward the Kid and, standing stoop-shouldered and all hunched over to one side, he peered through his glasses into the shade of the cypress.

Presently, in an odd singsongy whine, he said:

"Evenin', neighbor, evenin' to yo'. The ole man cayn't see so elegan'-like, but he cayn listen right pert. He hearn yo' speakin' when he wuz down the road a piece. Shaw! he cayn hear yo' breathin' now, en yo' sittin' thar tight as a possum. 'Lowin' yo'd fetch the ole man a s'prise, yeah?

"Most all the folks tries to fool ole Jerry," he whined on, "but nobody up en down this heah river cayn do hit, skasely. Ole Jerry Mears, he's too spry en foxy, sho'. But hain't yo' wantin' a elegan' steel razor, sharp as fo'ty-rod whisky, er a dad-fetchin' pair o' spectacles, er a nickel-plated scissors fo' the missus, er the jim-crackiest whittlin' knife fo' love o' money?"

He edged closer, his bushy brows lifting questioningly over the tarnished tops of his glasses and his free left hand feeling toward his hip.

"Hain't yo' wantin' enny o' the things I'm totin', neighbor? A watch now, a elegan' gole watch, Massachusetts-made en warranted to keep time tell the river flows this far back, en gran' en gaudy to behold?

"I's got silver watches, nickel watches, en watches made out o' that gun-metal stuff with streaks in hit. En joolery—man alive, I's got bracelets, di'mond earrings—seventy-five cents them—en rings with garnets in 'em, big as rubies en so elegan' the Queen o' Sheba hernsef would be powerful proud to weah them—yeah, to weah them, as the Good Book says, on her lily-white ban'."

"Hain't yo' jist feverishin' to see some o' the quality stuff I'm totin', neighbor?" he asked again, almost petulantly. "I's ben totin' these things a mighty long spell, neighbor, en skasely peddlin' enough to keep body en soul together.

"I'm a ole man, boss, though my hair hain't white as it oughter be, what with all the sorter hit done seen en passed through. En I's toted my pack a consid'able ways this evenin' in the hot sun, neighbor, en showed my elegan' things fo' a passel o' —— darkies to paw over en 'Yah-hay!' about, en me not able to see more'n a foot at a time befo' my—"

He stopped short. Edging wholly within the patch of shade, he peered over the tarnished tops of his spectacles with sudden suspicion.

"Dick," he said abruptly, "I's got gran' things fo' a colored man, elegan' things, jist the kind o' joolery en things a strappin' good-lookin' colored man like yo'-all wants to give yo' gal. I's traveled a powerful long ways jist fo' to show yo' em, Dick. Fo' they're cheap, Dick, cheaper'n—"

The Frisco Kid leaped up. His usually pale face was an angry red, and there was in his deep-sunk eyes an expression of commingled resentment and scorn.

"A phoney man!" he cried. "Lookit him, Gay-cat—a walkin', peddlin', buzzin' phoney man! And so blind, he don't know another hobo like hisself when he sees him! He's a-tryin' to shill off some phoney jul'ry on a blowed-in-the-glass stiff like the Frisco Kid! And worser'n that, old feller, he calls me 'Dick,' what ain't my moniker at all, but is a way a bo has when he spiels to a smoke!"

The blind man straightened put of his hunched-over, peering attitude. His face went darker than the brown of walnut. It was shocking, that vehement change which swept over him. Somehow he did not seem so old nor so decrepit as the peddler with the stoop and whine.

"Yo' is hoboes, huh?" he cried indignantly. "Yeah, ornery, low-down, ring-tail bums—that's what yo' is! Yo' didn't spill yo' wuz George. Yo' kep' close as possums. Yo' let me palaver en palaver, me 'lowin' I had fetched up neah a darky.

"Yo' on'y made game o' me! Dod-rot yo'!" he ended, his shriveled frame all a-tremble. "I'll show yo', no measly bar'l-house stiff cayn come enny sich game on ole Jerry Mears!" And he lifted up his heavy knobby stick.

The yellow dog growled rumblingly, threateningly. The Frisco Kid backed away. His eyes fearfully upon the upraised stick, his arms above his head to ward off the expected blow, he lifted his voice in remonstrance.

"Aw, bo! I didn't speak up at first 'cause I didn't know yer was a phoney man at all. I wasn't George, honest I wasn't. I didn't lamp yer peddlin' packs under yer coat, till yer showed 'em. And Gay-cat, he's a blowed-in-the-glass, too, and he most always k'n tell a blowed-in-the-glass stiff even when far off—but yer fooled even him, bo, yer fooled even Gay-cat. He wasn't wise yer was a phoney man at all."

Now there was that, in the Frisco Kid's mention of the Gay-cat, which caused a quick and drastic change in the attitude of the blind peddler. He lowered the stick abruptly. He leaned toward the Kid, and once more gazing over the tarnished tops of his spectacles, he asked cautiously:

"Blowed-in-the-bottle stiffs yo' be, yeah? Shore how menny is yo'?"

But there was bothering the Frisco Kid a kind of vexation. That he, a blown-in-the-glass stiff, had not recognized in this blind man, at the very outset, another hobo and a phoney man was a mistake which savored of a lack of road knowledge. And the Kid prided himself on his knowledge of the road.

Of course, the truth was that this Southland was new territory to him. Yet that would not fully account for his mistake. And the Frisco Kid felt it was incumbent upon him somehow to account for that mistake. Wherefore, taking no note of the peddler's question but thinking only of what he himself last had said, he added in shamefaced apology:

"Yer see, yer is all dressed up. Gee, I thought yer was a planter and mebbe a mean and horstile one. And I ain't never see'd a blind phoney man before, leastwise one what carried a stick and was all dressed swell-like, like a jedge."

"I do dress elegan'-like," said the peddler, the long bony fingers of his left hand smoothing the green shiningness of his coat. "Ethiops en sich trash alwuz treats a white man a heap better, I raiken, when he's got a fine front like a jedge.

"But that feller with yo', bo—that feller yo' calls Gay-cat—he hain't sayin' much, is he? Powerful quiet, mainly; hain't got no tongue, I s'pect; one o' them sign-makin' fellers, yeah?"

"Aw," said the Frisco Kid apologetically, "he's only a dog. Gay-cat. A hobo dog."

"A dorg! Dingnations, thet's funny! I nevah had no idee o' thet. I raikened he wuz yo' buddy. But a dorg now, en the ole phoney man thinkin' all the time he wuz a stiff—hain't that the beatenest thing, though! Lemme see the little feller—he's little, hain't he?"

Proudly, in answer, the Kid put the Gay-cat into the blind man's arms. The hair crested on the Gay-cat's neck and again he growled. But the peddler lifted him up, and held him close to his peering, straining eyes, and inspected him, with the nodding head of approbation.

"What a powerful cute little feller," he said. "I hain't nevah see a wiser-lookin' dorg. En sich a elegan' yaller color! Knows the roads, I cal'late, en when a team o' mules is comin', he does, huh? I 'low yo' is right fond o' him; had him a long time; reg'lar buddy to yo', yeah? I raiken, now, yo' nevah would part with him, huh?—not fo' love o' money!"

Hastily the Frisco Kid snatched the dog from the peddler's arms. Something in the man's oily tone, a sort of cunningness in his questions, impinged upon the Kid's heart a sudden fear for his dog. And fortunate it was for the peddler that the Frisco Kid acted so precipitately, for just then, as if to bite, the dog snapped at the man's wrist.

"Aw, bo," said the Kid incoherently. "Course, I wouldn't part with Gay-cat. Not for all the money ever made!"

The blind man listened closely, head on one side. The Kid swallowed and wet his lips.

"Yer see, bo," he tried to explain, "he's a blowed-in-the-glass stiff hisself, Gay-cat. And he's my buddy that's been with me a awful long time, now. I won't never give him away. No," he repeated, "not for all the money ever made!"

"Shucks!" said the peddler. "How yo' do take on, bo! How yo' do talk en sentimenter! Don't yo' s'pect ole Jerry's merely a-foolin' o' yo'? Dang it, bo! I wuz jist 'lowin' to fathom how fond yo' is o' him. I figgered yo' must think a mighty precious lot o' him, that he wuz jist ole pie to yo'—hem!—him bein' sich a pert little articule—yeah, en sich a elegan' yaller color! I cal'late, now, consid'able menny folks has wanted fo' to buy him o' yo', huh? Yeah, or to steal him?

"Yo'd raiken, now, a blind man like me 'ud want a dorg jist like him—a dorg to be a-leadin' o' me along the roads en up to farmhouses, en a dorg what 'ud bark consid'able when a span o' mules is comin', er a drove o' pigs, er—er a ottermobile behind, heh?

"But too menny dorgs has bit me in back yards, I cal'late, en lit out arter me along the roads. I'm all over bites, 'deed en 'deed I is, en I jist cayn't stand the pesky varmints. By Jefferson, I hates 'em! Yas, I does. All but thet dorg thar. He's a mighty smart little animule."

He cleared his throat.

"Neighbor," he said unctuously, "I raiken I sorter tuck to him right off—jist like I done tuck to yo'!"

II

"THE COMPINSASHUN O' THE LAWD"

THE FRISCO KID WAS ODDLY DISTURBED by the oily tone of the blind man, his fawning manner and flattering words. To change the subject, he asked, apropos of nothing—

"Where yer headin' for, this afternoon, bo?"

"Perkins Landin'."

"Perkins Landin'!—why that must be on the Mississippi. And here I've been aimin' to hit the river all along. I made up my mind, up Nebraska way, I'd strike for the Mississippi and then hobo south, mebbe walkin' the levees or floatin' down in a skiff or a raff.

"Hoboes north say it's lots of fun, and the eats is fattenin'—coon and watermelons and—and sech stuff. I guess I'll join out with yer for the walk to Perkins. I'm a-goin' to mooch the main drag there. That's the closest town, ain't it?"

The blind man nodded quite eagerly.

"Hit's the closest, all right—on'y 'bout fo'teen mile along. But the Landin', hit ain't on the river nohow. Some year ago, hit wuz on the river fo' faih, but one night in the Spring-risin', the river she jist raked up en cut a new channel through a big bend, en put Perkins a swingin' good piece in the back country. En thar Perkins be yit, waitin' fo' the ole Mississipp' to tuck another dern-fool, whoop-jamboree notion, en fetch back, en make hit a river-town once moah.

"But arter we gits to Perkins, hit's on'y a tolerable short walk to the river en Shanty-Boat Town, which is the real landin' nowadays. I got a shanty-boat thar. Yo' bundle along with me; we won't fetch up thar ternight; but toreckly we does, yo' cayn come aboard en float down the river on the boat with me en the Ole Woman, en the colored wench, Phœbe, en that blame' ornery little runt, Gamaliel.

"Thar's a sight o' room fo' the dorg en yo' on the boat, en plenty to eat— sugar-cane, corn pone, chickens, bacon, roast ears o' corn en all sich prime quality stuff. En thar hain't nothin' like floatin' down the ole Mississipp' in a shanty-boat. Thar hain't nothin' like the river nohow.

"Wunse yo' fish en swim en laze along hit, en float down quiet as cayn be through the nights, en the ole shanty-boat goin' lap-lap very soft-like, en the moon over the levee big en fat, en a banjo tinklin' way off among the nigger cabins en—en, bo, yo'll nevah want to leave the river ag'in, no moah!"

"Go with yer? Go with yer, a-floatin' down the river?" cried the Frisco Kid, his imagination aflame. "Sure as shootin', bo, I'll go with yer! And the Gay-cat, he'll go, too!"

The Frisco Kid led the way out into the hot white road. The peddler tapped after on his heavy stick, a shrewd smile on his lean brown bird-like face. Once he paused and sharply queried:

"Don't fo'git the dorg. Is the dorg a-comin'?"

"Aw, Gay-cat, he never gets left behind. Yer don't have to watch *him*. Why, bo, he's here right at my side—kinder skeered to come 'longside of yer, I think; kinder skeered of yer stick."

"Give me yo' han', bo," said the blind man, "en yo' cayn lead me. Hit's hard a-walkin' the road in the dark, en alwuza-listenin' fo' hawgs er mules a-comin'."

"That's so. I was wonderin' how yer tramped about, peddlin' phoney stuff, and you blind."

The Kid held out his hand. The man did not answer, but pawed about once or twice; then grasped the hand and closed his long bony fingers around it, tight as talons.

"Dingnations!" he said, startled. "What a small han' yo' got, bo! Why, yo' must be a little shaver, not much bigger'n that thar dorg o' yores, I cal'late, er thet ornery little runt, Gamaliel."

"Gay-May—" began the Kid at this second mention of the name. "Say, bo, that's a moniker jes' like Gay-cat's here, only longer. Who's him?"

As though suddenly he remembered something, the man paused and still holding tightly to the Kid's hand, turned around to look back the way he had come, and to listen, head on one side.

"Hear ennything?" he asked suspiciously. "Hear him a-comin'?"

"Who?"

"Gamaliel."

"Aw, say now, bo," remonstrated the Frisco Kid, "I wouldn't know him if I see'd him. Who is he, now? A dog like Gay-cat?"

"A dorg!" repeated the blind man. "Gamaliel, a dorg! Naw, he's a boy— jist a plain, no-'count river-rat. What in tarnashun caused yo' to 'spect he wuz a dorg? Gamaliel, a dorg!"

The blind man snorted. He said nothing more, however, but quite complacently put up his stick on the crook of his right arm and, by pressure on the Kid's hand, signified his desire to go on.

Thus, the Frisco Kid leading the way, the dog tagging at his heels, they went along the winding white road, now up over little hills, now down between bottoms of cotton-fields. And sometimes the fields were drab, thoroughly plucked and empty; and sometimes all mottled white and black, with the down of the bursted pods and the shapes of the pickers moving in and out, and bending down and up—and all lazily, for it was very warm.

There were rows of ramshackle negro cabins where pigs and starved hounds and half-naked piccaninnies waddled between sunflower stalks and through broken reed-overgrown fences and out, in a conglomerate scramble, into the road to meet them; and now and anon, on a rise of ground, a cool white house of many tall pillars and long small-paned windows that flashed, from far off, between interlacing roses and urns of orange marigolds and purple petunias.

The blind man snorted afresh. He turned, altogether suddenly, upon the Kid.

"Bo, hit's mighty sartain to ole Jerry Mears, now, that yo' be a sinful lad. Yo' hain't nevah read the Good Book, I raiken, er yo'd nevah have made sich a mistake. Gamaliel a dorg's name!" And he snorted once again.

"Accordin' to the Good Book," he whined on, "Gamaliel means the compinsashun o' the Lawd. That's what it means—the pay o' the good Lawd fo' what He done tuck away en destroyed. En thet little runt, how'd he come by that name? Why, he wuz jist cast up by a flood.

"One night hit wuz, fo' year agone—the same year o' the Spring-risin' thet fetched ole Perkins Landin' into the back country. The ole Mississipp', hit had done gone en tuck one o' hits reg'lar dern-fool whoop-jamboree notions—swapped 'round from a natchal color to most a yaller, en raired up, en cut loose fo' faih.

"Racin' like a ottermobile hit wuz—racin' like a road full o' yaller ottermobiles, sixty mile a hour, never-endin', hellbent fo' fury, en totin' all befo' hit—pigs, bridges, skiffs en raffs, horses, yaller pines, willers, mules, chickens, en hull houses sum'times.

"Arter a spell, the rain stopped—hit had ben rainin' blue murder like the sky wuz cracked. Logs en drift o' all kinds wuz still boomin' along, en I wuz layin' on en off, in a skiff, fetchin' it to shore to sell bimeby down the mills. I could see a consid'able sight better them days than now.

"Wal, one night, all of a sudden I see, down the river a stretch, a hull house snagged on Hawg-Back Towhead. I hitched my britches en lit out arter it same as if it wuz a bar'l o' fo'ty-rod."

The blind man paused and ran his tongue out over his puckered lips with a kind of relish. It was for all the truth as if he were inventing the story, bit by bit, and finding surprise and delight in the total of his invention.

"Thet house, hit wuz a ornery little two-story clapboard affaih that had skipped down from Gawd knows whah—mebbe from Illinois, mebbe up Mizzoura way, or mebbe ag'in from ole Kaintuck.

"The lower story wuz plumb under water, tangled fitten to hold tell the Judgment Day in the tops o' the cottonwoods of ole Hawg-Back Sandbar, en the hull shootin'-match wuz tilted over, same as if it had drank too much licker.

"I went a-scootin' down to hit, fo'ty mile a hour. When I fetched up aneah the house, the current wuz a-tearin' through the cottonwoods en 'round the sides o' the wrack so powerful strong en loud, I jist couldn't hear mysef think. I pulled 'round to the slant side en dumb, easy as pie, right out'n the skiff upon the sill o' a winder.

"Hit wuz darker'n a Ethiop's skin inside, en some quieter; en as I set on the sill, I could hear the water a-washin' 'bout—hit must 'a' covered the floor tolerable deep. En thar wuz a squashy thump, too, now en ag'in.

"Bimeby I got to see sort o' middlin' well, en I made out a bundle o' rags floatin' in the water on the floor, en thumpin' ag'in the wall kind o' squashy-like. It thumped the wall powerful heavy fo' a rag bundle, I jidged, en I begun to suspicion sum'thin'. I waded through the water, en catched hold, en—dingnations, hit wuz a woman en she wuz daid!

"Mebbe I warn't scared! I backed away, all over shakin' en cold, en then—kabump! my head hit agin sum'thin' that wuz hangin' from the ceilin', en I thought hit wuz sperits, en my hair stiffened en begun to climb, en I could hear the current tearin' 'round the house en the body thumpin' plain as day, en I didn't look round, not immedjit.

"En then I hearn a cry, kind o' small en feeble, same as a ghos' makes when a-rovin' in sorrer, en the starch went clean out'n me, en I drapped to my knees en wrastled in pray'r.

"But the good Lawd wuz with ole Jerry Mears, thet night, en He raised me up en He done showed me thar warn't nothin' to be frightened about, pertic'lar. Jist a little tad hit wuz, a-slung from the ceilin' in a sort o' swing so's the water wouldn't rise to hit tell the last.

"That drownded woman wuz the little feller's mammy. I went through the hull upper story, en everythin' wuz washin' about; but thar warn't no one else besides, no man, so I 'spected that baby had ben half a orphing.

"Wal, he wuz a full orphing sure enough now, I raikened, so I tuck him along en I says, 'This pore creetur, he be the compinsashun o' the good Lawd fo' all He done tuck away en destroyed.' En I felt right down sorry fo' the little tad, en I wuz jist all pie to him. En thet's why I calls him Gamaliel."

While the blind phoney man beguiled the time thus, the long afternoon drew into the lambency of sunset. The darkies moved away through the deepening purple of the cotton- and corn-fields, and only the great-bosomed "Yah-yah!" of some healthy happy black woman floated across the lonesome acres to the two upon the straggling road.

The fragrance of magnolia blossoms before a negro's cabin-door sharpened in the cool of the evening. The road became, all at once, very peaceful and very very lonesome.

"Hit's shore comin' dark; le's camp heah," suggested the blind man. "We cayn't fetch Perkins ternight, I cal'late; leastwise, not unless thar be a moon to walk by."

They turned off the road and sat down, in the twilight, between the roots of some live-oak trees.

"I's some corn-dodgers en bacon lef sence noon. We cayn eat thet snack fo' supper, share en share alike—yo', me en the dorg. Oh, the dorg'll git his share; I don't fo'git him, sho'. I's tuck to him consid'able. Indeedy, I never knowed mysef to tuck to a animule like that befo'.""

The Gay-cat backed away from the peddler's outreaching hands. But the peddler only laughed and, when the corn-dodgers and bacon were equally divided, flung hunks of meat and cake to the dog, and talked to him and tried, with a remarkable mildness and patience, to coax him near enough to pet him.

Said he—

"No, I hain't never knowed mysef to tuck to a animule like that befo'.""

Just then, the Frisco Kid sat up to listen, a hunk of corn-cake halfway to his lips. Some one was coming along the road, someone that whimpered and sobbed out shocking curses in a high piping treble. The dragging steps drew nearer, and the childish plaintive voice.

"Dod-rot thet ornery ole houn'!" said the child's voice fiercely. "The ole no-'count pirut, I 'spec' he'll be a-wallopin' me double, now. And I cayn't git outer tellin' him what the Ole Woman done said—'n' he'll whale me worser when he's hearn it.

"Oh, golly, I wisht I might nevah fin' him, but jist keep walkin' 'n' a-walkin' so far away he cayn't nevah fin' me to wallop me, no moah. The ole son-o'-a-steambo't-whistle, why in tarnashun cayn't he leave off a-wallopin' me!""

The face of the peddler lost its smile. It was shocking, that vehement change which swept over him. His hand tightened on the heavy knobby stick.

"Gamaliel!" was all he said.

But the youngster on the road heard him. His plaintive whimperings stopped abruptly. Very quietly he came in between the trees.

"I's heah, Jerry," he said with a sort of forced, oldish nonchalance. "Large as life, I be, 'n' chipper as a oriole. And I's brung some truck from the Ole Woman fo' yo', yo' raspy ole rapscallion!"

III
THE KID GAINS AN ADMIRER AND LOSES AN ADHERENT

HE WAS A TINY FELLOW, clad in the most unexpected costume imaginable. He wore a huge flapping straw hat, turned up in front and fastened with a safety-pin. A red bandanna was knotted about his thin neck; a cap-pistol protruded from the little leather holster at his belt; and below, on his short legs, were a pair of chaparejos—black, hairy, toy cowboy leggings.

"Yo' consarn'd little cuss," said the blind man. "None o' yo' sass, now. What did the Ole Woman say fo' yo' to tell me?"

From under the big rakish hat, the little sunburnt baby face looked up at the blind peddler. The eyes were blue, a clear sapphire blue, and oddly round, and very old with a depth of worldly wisdom strange in a child so small and young. The sweet pouting upper lip trembled.

"She says yo' warn't to come back to the bo't, nohow. She gimme a snack fo' yo', 'n' she say, 'Jerry, yo' ole rip, look betwixt the slabs o' corn pone fur the bacon.' Them's her very words, mainly. And she says thar's bin men a-ha'ntin' the bo't like ghos's. And—'n' she says yo' warn't to wallop me this time, no moah."

The peddler sat up.

"She hain't—she hain't nevah said that last, nohow! Dad fetch yo', what did she say?"

The little fellow began to cry all at once, his knuckles in his eyes.

"Wul—wul, hang it, she says yo' war to dust me good. The Ole Woman, rot her, she says yo' warn't to fohgit to tuck off my cowboy leggin's, so's to make it a good job."

The blind man rose up, reaching for the boy.

"Tuck off yo' leggin's—why did she say thet? Dog my cats, don't she know I cayn wallop yo' without tuckin' off them things? Why did she say thet?"

"I dunno, only mebbe so's yo'd hurt me worser."

"I'll show yo' if I cayn hurt yo' a-plenty; I'll give yo' a power o' med'cin; I'll show yo' how I cayn wallop yo'!"

He reached for the boy. The boy ducked away. But blindly, viciously, the stoop-shouldered man flung himself upon him. Then he arose to his knees and raised, above the boy, the heavy stick.

Now, the hair and leather of the leggings did not protect the seat of the boy's trousers and, when the stick fell under the man's full strength, it hurt and the boy screamed.

The Frisco Kid sprang up. White and hot—for he remembered a time when he himself had been cruelly beaten by the hobo that had taught him the life of the road—the Kid sprang up.

"Stop!" he cried, his voice choking. "Stop larrupin' that kid!"

The stick remained upraised.

"Me stop thrashin' my own kid?" the peddler snarled, turning a furious face upon him. "None o' yo' lip, yo' dod-rotted tramp! Yo' keep out'n this, er I'll tan yo'!"

"Come on, then!" cried the Frisco Kid, desperate and seething within with a hot anger. "I ain't been a hobo roughin' it for nothin'. You jes' try to larrup me—I'm some bigger'n that poor little kid!"

The phoney man jumped to his feet, his mouth snarling. He raised the stick. The Frisco Kid crouched for a rush. And then the snarl fled the man's face; the stick dropped to earth; he calmed suddenly. He even forced a smile.

"Bo," he said, "we hain't got no business, yo' en me, quarrelin' en raisin' jist ole Cain. Hit's plumb foolishness. En I won't wallop the little tad heah, not if yo' don't like hit. I wuz jist a-foolin' him, ennyways.

"I gen'ally hates to beat him, I do, though he does act low-down en ornery to me who's fed en clothed en kep' him, en treated him lovin' en elegan'—jist like ole pie. But I hain't hankerin' to quarrel with yo'. I's tuck to yo' consid'able, en them I's tuck to, I nevah sour on er quarrel with. Bo," he ended unctuously, "le's all be frien's."

"That's me," said the Kid; "I'm agreeable if yer is." Still he eyed the man coldly. "But I don't want no beatin' of kids around me. I seen too much of it."

The peddler turned away, anxious to hide his chagrin.

"I wonder what the Ole Woman meant 'bout his leggin's," he murmured. "She's a bothersome lot, the Ole Woman. Why in all dingnations don't she speak out plain? En, too, 'bout the bacon betwixt the corn pone."

He reached down suddenly and picked up, from where Gamaliel had dropped it, the paper bag of food. He opened the bag and, his dim eyes looking over the tarnished tops of his glasses, peered within. On the sudden he made to put a hand into the bag, then thought better of it and covertly glanced about him, his spectacles outstanding and peering in the twilight like the pop-eyes of some great bird.

The little boy had ceased crying and was watching the Frisco Kid, a sort of admiration in his moist blue eyes. The peddler turned his back on them and put his hand into the bag. There was the crinkle as of rumpled paper. Then Mears drew out a closed fist and surreptitiously transferred something from that closed fist into one of the pockets of his swallow-tail coat.

"By jingo!" he ejaculated softly, "thet Ole Woman, she's shore the smartes' one! I couldn't make hit out noway, head nor tail. But bacon 'twixt the corn pone! Hain't that the elegan'est dodge, though!"

He grew all at once serious.

"En so I cayn't go back to the boat, nohow. They's watchin' hit, huh? I 'spect we'll have to cler out'n heah, en drap down the river a piece befo' we cayn work hit strong ag'in."

He swung about with sudden thought. The little fellow, Gamaliel, had clasped, rather stealthily, the Frisco Kid's hand and the Frisco Kid had held on to his tiny hand tightly, warmly, a strange feeling in his heart of commiseration for the boy and of glad guardianship.

Now, however, as the peddler swung about so abruptly, the little fellow, as though gravely guilty, pulled his hand away and, in a kind of fear, retreated.

"Heah, yo' Gamaliel!" said the peddler. "Yo' hump along to the boat ternight, en tell the Ole Woman to cast off en drap down fi' mile to the big crossin' below Chel'sfo'd Township, and to tie up the boat in the crick thar. I'll bundle down thataway along the road in 'bout another day, I raiken, moah or less."

"All right, Jerry," agreed the boy, very subdued.

"Wal, yo' be up to snuff en foot it mighty tight. En yo' meet me, bright en early termorrer mawnin'—en no slouchin' if yo' know what's good fo' yo'—at the big slantin' bay-tree neah the canebrake a swingin' good piece this side o' Perkins Landin'.

"En yo' tell the Ole Woman to give yo' some moah stuff fo' me, en to be powerful cautious—to drap the boat down, night-time, en tie up whah the willers en rushes is bunchy, en—en not to mind 'bout yo' leggin' things whin I wallop yo'—I'll 'tend to that, by Zachariah! En now yo' git up en git."

Submissively, yet with an admiring look back at the Kid, the little fellow walked out into the road and headed along it, the great hairy chaps on his short legs moving slowly and heavily into the thickening night. The Frisco Kid knew how lonely, how hedged with strange menacing shadows was a road at night; how long a mile seemed when one walked solitary in darkness and in silence.

"Aw, bo!" he interposed. "Yer can't let him go alone all that way. It's dark along the road, and kinder scary and lonesome."

The blind man cackled.

"Oh, he's not afeard—Gamaliel. He's traveled alone heaps o' times, nights. En he knows the roads, he does—knows 'em like a spellin'-book er a singin' jawgraphy. He'll take shelter in some farmhouse er negro cabin if he gits tuckered out. Bo, yo' leave thet kid be!" The last was almost a threat.

"We'll sleep heah," continued the phoney man. "Thar'll be no moon ternight, er termorrer night, I cal'late; en the tuck is all out'n me; en I hain't carin' to fetch Perkins er even the next farmhouse, pertic'lar. So we'll doss heah. En termorrer we'll go on ag'in, en mebbe the next day we'll hit the shanty-boat en float down the river lazy-like, as I done said—yo', me en that thar cute little dorg."

The Frisco Kid was not so sure, now, that a shanty-boater's life on the Mississippi was the happiest of lives—at any rate a shanty-boat on which lived, also, Jerry Mears, the phoney man. But he curled up between the roots of the trees, the Gay-cat snug and warm under his coat.

He awoke before dawn. There was just the faintest paleness in the east. He sat up and stretched himself and looked at that pale patch in the sky which was spreading out and brightening up. Then he rubbed his eyes to get the sleepers out, and yawned loudly to awaken the others.

But there were no others. The Kid first missed the Gay-cat. The Gay-cat was not lying beside him, quiet and heavy-headed. But then the Gay-cat often had nightmares, and crawled away and burrowed under some leaves. The Kid looked around for the peddler. There was the flattened place in the fallen leaves where the peddler had stretched out; but no peddler.

The Frisco Kid remembered, then. In the deep of the night, as he lay asleep in the leaves, he had heard a little yelp and some one had leaned over him. Then it seemed only the disquieting dim part of a dream. He had turned over, no more than half awakened, and insensibly had slipped back into sleep.

But now he knew. The peddler had leaned over him in the night, snatched up the frightened dog, and gone quietly away into the night. He had stolen Gay-cat!

IV
"NOBODY AT ALL IN THE WORLD WOULD TUCK ON SO 'BOUT ME!"

THE FRISCO KID WAS AFOOT, SHAKEN AND DISTRAUGHT. There was a desperate drawn look to his peaked pale face, to his anguish-filled eyes.

He must find the little hobo dog, his only friend, his one buddy, the comrade that had made hoboing pleasant, the companion and bunkie in his wanderings and railroading, in his times of fortune and good setdowns, in rain and cold and slammed back doors and hunger. Without the Gay-cat, life was empty, unthinkable. He must get back his little yellow dog.

He started along the road at a run, his grimy hands clenched tightly. Then, realizing that perhaps the whole day and many long miles were ahead of him, he slackened to a walk; but still he walked with a certain killing eagerness that permitted of no rests nor idled moments near cool, boy-luring creeks or sun-brightening thickets.

He stopped at no farmhouse or cabin to beg breakfast—he had no stomach for breakfast. Only, every little while, he shook his clenched fist at the road ahead and, his pale face grimacing threateningly, he whispered—

"Yer measly old phoney man, I'll learn yer to steal my dog!"

Unsparingly he blamed himself for not having been more wary of the oily leering old peddler. The man had paid too much attention to the Gay-cat. He had "tuck" to him too much.

The Kid saw it all now. The blind man had told him stories of the river and of shanty-boating merely to beguile him until such time as he could steal, quite sneakily, his dog. And he wanted the dog, of course, to guide him along the road. With the Gay-cat leading him, mules and automobiles, farm-wagons and pigs would be no great danger.

The morning was still young and dewy when the Frisco Kid approached a huge bay-tree which was tilted over at a dizzy angle. Here the blind man had instructed Gamaliel to meet him that dawning.

There were crumbs of corn pone on the trampled grass where, in all probability, the blind man and Gamaliel and the stolen dog had broken their fast; but there was no sight of the trio. Everything was hushed and Sunday-like.

The Frisco Kid footed it on, fast and desperately. But never, through the morning, did he catch sight of the stoop-shouldered seedy man, the cowboy-attired Gamaliel, or his little mongrel dog.

It was coming noon when he paused at a negro cabin, not to beg a handout, but to ask whether the incongruous trio had passed that way. As he opened the rickety leather-hinged gate, he almost trod upon a little piccaninny lying in the weeds of the yard, naked save for a short dirty cotton shift, and blissfully sucking upon the rag stopper of a bottle of milk.

The urchin drew his mouth from the stopper with a kind of *plub*, gurgled and gooed, and playfully pawed up at him with pudgy little black hands and legs.

At the baby's feeble sounds, four or five great gaunt hounds, stretched out on the threshold of the tumble-down cabin, raised their lean heads, saw the Kid, yawned and got sleepily afoot. Then followed by a perfect mob of puppies and half-grown dogs, fifteen strong at the least, the hounds came out to nose him.

The Kid waded through them with difficulty. He made up to a youngish black mammy, with bandanna-wrapped head, who was sitting, fat and gross in a none-too-clean gown of calico, on a bench to one side of the cabin door, and contentedly smoking a cob pipe. She was a picture of complacent and utter indolence.

Said the Frisco Kid enviously—

"Yer got plenty dogs here."

The woman removed the pipe from her thick lips to laugh uproariously, as at some good joke.

"Houn's? Oh, Lawd A'mighty, yas! We got plenty houn's, honey—got 'nuff houn's foh a body to be satafied wid, toler'bly, Ah raiken. But most ebbery pusson has a passel ob houn's daown disaways."

The while the woman laughed and rolled out her words, there had arisen, within the cabin, the sounds of some one moving about. Then a kinky white-haired old grandfather or great-grandfather, with bushy snowy brows above spectacles that lacked lenses, came out to the threshold of the cabin, and stood there attentively listening, and shaking all the time in the sunlight with palsy. As the woman finished, he broke out volubly:

"But Lan' ob Canaan, didn't we done pu'chase de fines' dawg dis mawnin', Rosamun'! He wahn't no low-daown trash houn'. He wah a prime quality dawg, an' pow'ful fotchin'! A elegan' animule, de blin' man what done sold him to us himsef done said; a prime relegjus man, he wah—he could rattle off de Good Book better'n enny pahson Ah eber hearn—jis' lak nuff'n!"

The Frisco Kid started at the old man's apt description of Jerry Mears. He was on the right track then. He asked eagerly—

"Was it a yellow dog with nothin' much of a tail to speak of?"

The old man beamed and nodded so vehemently the glassless spectacles slid down his black nose and he shook all over and could not speak. Smiling broadly and greasily, the woman said:

"Dat's him, a li'l dawg wid a li'l tail an' my! de most oncommonest yaller culluh. He wah no slouch, dat dawg. Run to de gate, he would, an' scratch it wid his laigs, an' moan—Lawsy, it wah fitten to make a body's heart bust to hearn him tuk on.

"An' dat blin' man, he done gib him to us foh a cup ob coffee—said he had tukken his bre'kfus' undah de slant bay-tree, daown de road a spell. An' he gib me dis ring, too."

She held up one hand to exhibit, amid the folds of flesh of her second ringer, a cheap glassy gimcrack.

"An' he said dat de Queen ob Sheba would be pow'ful glad to weah it on her lily-white han'."

"An' dat she would, Rosamun'," said the old man, by this time recovered. "Dat she would, de Queen ob Sheba hernsef."

"Was there any one with him," asked the Kid—"any one besides the dog?"

"No, honey; he wah alone—a pow'ful smaht man what could fin' his way alone an' he blin' as a ole bat."

"An' den, two hour agone," broke in the old man, eager to talk, "a li'l chile come along, cryin' lak some one wah daid, an' he says it wah his yaller dawg what his pappy done sold. He said his pappy wah awful raspy wid him, times, an' de las' time his pappy had up an' sold de dawg jis' out'n plain ornery cussedness.

"He said he wanted dat li'l quality dawg back ag'in, not foh nuff'n but foh good money. An' he bo't him ob us foh a dollah. We wah plumb against sellin' dat fotchin' prime critur, but he done tuck on so, we couldn't lay to disapp'int de li'l fellah, nohow."

"A little boy in cowboy-leggin's and a straw hat turned up in front?"

"How'd yo' know, honey?" asked the woman, startled, her eyes rolling big and white. "Dat's him, sho' 'nuff—a mite ob a tad got up regar'less. An' wahn't he de pow'fulles' pooty man, though, wid his blue trembly eyes an' wispy-corny yaller haih! He gib us a fi'-dollah bill foh de dawg.

" 'Nashun lucky we had de change. We don't us'ally hab change befoh de cotton am all picked heah 'bouts. Gits all our things frum de store in Perkins, we does, an' sence the kunnel come back, we gits credit frum Kunnel Chel'sfo', too, daown de Township way.

"But heah yo'," she said to the old man. "Stir yo' stumps, gran'daddy, an' fotch out dat fi'-dollah bill foh de young genl'man." The old man disappeared with glad readiness into the cabin. "It ain't menny niggahs has a fi'-dollah bill," the woman added as though in explanation and proud justification of her command.

Suddenly she noticed something over near the rickety leather-hinged gate.

"Drot yo', Teddy Roosenfelt, drap dat bottle!" she called sharply to a young roly-poly pup who had stolen the bottle of milk from the piccaninny and, with it between his paws, was sagaciously sucking at the rag stopper.

The pup dropped the bottle incontinently, and the baby rolled over and retrieved it with pudgy fists. The baby sucked, the woman went on smoking. And then the old man reappeared, holding a greenback proudly in his two shaking hands. As though studying it wisely, he bent his woolly head and lensless glasses over the paper money—and there was in his attitude a curious childlike awe.

"We don't off'n gits to handle papah money daown heah," he said. "Dis am a pow'ful fotchin' new bill. Me oh my! hear it crinkle, though. Not menny niggahs has a fi'-dollah bill!"

"Which way did the little feller go with the dog?"

"Dat way, daown de road, honey," instructed the woman.

"An' I 'speck he sho' made a bargain, too, dat li'l tad," the old man called wistfully after him. "Dah ain't menny dawgs lak dat li'l quality dawg. But den it ain't lak we got on'y six or seben houn's lak some niggahs—we got plenty houn's."

The Frisco Kid continued on along the road. From the top of a rise he saw, far off, the old Mississippi. It was fully a mile wide in this section, of the color of an Autumn leaf, and hedged on one side by high levees and on the far side by green-jungled banks.

And there was a sternwheeler, white and tiny with distance, coughing up the river and zigzagging from shore to shore like a hapless chip, as it shaved the greenery on the opposite bluffs and then skirted the earth of the levees, in seeking the sleeping water near the banks and along the bars.

Ahead, the Kid came to a fork in the road and, quickly deciding to take the wider stretch yet fearing to lose the trail, he thought to stop and inquire his way at the next farmhouse.

The next farmhouse he approached proved to be a one-storied rambling, dilapidated frame-building in the flat of a small valley. It was flanked by numerous whitewashed outbuildings—chicken-roosts, barns and cow-sheds. Under some scantily-leafed trees alongside the road, a number of corn-cribs stood.

As the Frisco Kid drew near, a huge brown woodchuck darted from the bins, streaked along the road in a little hot white puff of dust, and then disappeared into the jimson weeds on the other side of the road.

Boy-like, the Kid reached down for a stone in the road to hurl after the disappearing rodent. And then he saw something on the corn-cribs—something which caused him, forthwith, to drop the stone. On one of the cratings of the bins were the following signs:

⊡ ·⊤·

They were ciphers. They were part of that loose yet covert system of characters contrived, by the great free-masonry of hoboes, for the safe transmission of secrets. Every tramp knows them and their hidden meanings.

In the great free masonry of hobodom, the first meant, "Don't touch! The farmer has some authority in the district"; and the second, "Buckshot! The farmer has a gun and uses it."

The Kid changed his mind about inquiring his way at that particular farmhouse. But, a step beyond the farmhouse in the feather-flecked yard, he saw a man scattering feed from a tin basin to a cackle of chickens—a lanky bewhiskered man in faded jeans and wide-brimmed straw hat, who wore neither shoes nor coat.

There was something so hoboish in the man's appearance that the Kid got a sudden accession of courage. He felt that the man might be a lowbrowed farmhand or a "gay-cat" who had landed a job. He leaned over the fence and called to him.

The man leisurely put down the tin basin of feed, shoved his hands into the pockets of his jeans and approached slouchily.

"Wa-al?" he drawled.

"Yer ain't seen a little kid go by here with a dog, has yer?" asked the Kid. "Or a old blind phoney man?"

The other did not answer immediately. A great bluebottle fly had alighted upon a rock in the road and was industriously cleaning its many legs. The man made a little sound like *ps-s-t!* A jet of amber juice shot from his puckered lips, hit the rock in the road, bathed the fly and swept it off its perch.

"Jeber Socks, yas," the man answered, thereupon. "I bo't thet yaller dorg fr'm thet ol' peddler what passes h'yer onct in a while. Bo't him to watch th' chickens.

"Tied him to th' fence, I did, with a ring 'round this h'yer topmost wire 'nd a string fr'm thet ring to his collar. And all he had to do in perticklar was to run up 'nd down, 'nd back 'nd forth along this fence, 'nd keep the chickens in, 'nd th' darkies out."

The farmer yawned prodigiously and, once again and dexterously, spit a stream of tobacco-juice at the rock in the road.

"And then, by jings!" he continued. "Not a hour gone, who should come up h'yer but a little yunker all togged out in th' beatenest kind o' clothes, 'nd with a cap-pistol, mind you, most as dangersome-lookin' as though it was real. And he offers me a dollar 'nd a half fur him, thet yunker, 'nd I sees whar I was makin' money right aways 'nd easy as pie. I'm no slouch, I hain't, when it comes to downright hard-headed biz'nus.

"'Wa-al, bub,' I says, jest like thet, none too anxious-like, y' understand—'I don't k'yer sech a heap to tuck paper money,' I says, 'but hol', a bargain's a bargain,' I says, ' 'nd the good Lawd will pervide,' I says."

The man thereupon withdrew both hands from his pockets to exhibit in one a five-dollar bill and to stroke with the other, as he studied the bill, his long ragged whiskers.

"I wonder whar he come by this fibe-dollar bill? It's a sight o' money fur sech a speck of a yunker. I wonder—"

He spat, without a care for marksmanship, into the road.

"By Jeber Socks!" he exclaimed. "I wonder ef the paper's good!"

The Kid dug out along the road, very fast. Gamaliel and the dog were only an hour in advance of him, according to the farmer's story, and he must soon overtake them.

Perhaps a half-hour had intervened when he noted, ahead, a little cloud of dust. It was just such a dust-cloud as the scurrying woodchuck had raised, only a deal magnified. Presently, in the cloud of dust, he made out the heavy-legged and tiny figure of Gamaliel, trudging along most nonchalantly and dragging after him by an absurd length of hay-rope, a little yellow drooping-headed dog.

The Frisco Kid emitted a wild whoop of triumph and joy. The little tad turned around. The dog's sharp head came up and, with a yelp of delight, he tore the leading-rope free from the hand of Gamaliel and dashed madly back to the Kid.

The Kid was on his knees, hugging the Gay-cat to him, bending down so that the leaping, joyfully-barking dog might lick his face in an excess of love and happiness.

The Frisco Kid looked up at last, his deep-sunken eyes bright and dewy. And the little tad turned eyes to him that were bright and dewy, too, and that were, besides, wistful, pathetically wistful. With a pout of sweet baby lips, the little fellow gulped:

"Jiminy, yo' keers heaps fo' thet puppy, 'n' he 'pears to keer heaps fo' yo'. I nevah see sich takin's-on 'n' huggin's. Nobody—nobody 'cept ole deef-'n'-dumb Phœbe, my black mammy, mebbe—nobody at all in the world would tuck on so 'bout me!"

V

THE KID AND GAMALIEL MAKE TOGETHER A GREAT FRIENDSHIP

THE FRISCO KID GOT TO HIS FEET and looked down at the wistful little chap.

"Aw, Gay-May!" he said inarticulate and singularly stirred. "Aw, say now, Gay-May! It ain't as bad as that, is it? Jerry Mears, yer father now, he'd take on consider'ble if yer was lost, or stolen like Gay-cat. And the Old

Woman, I'll bet she'd—"

Perhaps it was that the Kid had sounded a wrong note in his attempt to console the little tad; perhaps it was that the little tad already was ashamed of his wistful words; but anyway he burst out fiercely:

"Oh, dad blame it, don't talk to me 'bout them ornery ole rips. Don't tell me Jerry Mears 'ud make ovah me—rot him, he on'y whales me, hides the stuffin' out'n me. He don't keer fo' me, nohow, 'n' nuther does the Ole Woman. Hanged ef I knows why, 'cept mebbe 'cuz he ain't my right pappy 'n' she hain't my mammy at all."

"Not your father! Not yer folks at all!"

The Frisco Kid was shocked. Then, on the sudden, he remembered the phoney man's story of the flood. He remembered the dead woman in the floating house. And he said with a sympathy almost incoherent:

"I know it's kinder tough, Gay-May, but then it might be worse. Lookit me. I'se got a mother 'way over in Californya, what's old and what's waitin' for me all the time. But I can't seem to go back. There's somethin' in my blood, somethin' what keeps me movin' on always. I donno," he added pensively, "I don't understand it at all."

He hastened to change the disquieting subject. He asked—

"Where was yer to meet old Jerry again?"

"Down t'other side o' Perkins Landin'."

"Well let's go on to Perkins. We won't go beyond it to meet Mears. I'll throw my feet in Perkins and get somethin' to eat for bofe of us, and Gay-cat too. I'm beginnin' to feel all empty inside. I didn't have no scoff this mornin', I was so feverish 'bout Gay-cat. And Perkins now, it ain't so far, is it?"

The little fellow shook his sombreroed head.

"No; not sich a mighty ways. Jis' 'round t'other side o' thet hill ovah thar. Thet hill, it war a bluff on the ole Mississipp' wunst, they say, when it went a-boomin' along heah, 'n' it war called the Jumpin' Off Knoll.

"But it seems a purty longish stretch off to me, bo. I's done some powerful tall walkin' this mawnin', I cal'late, 'n' I's kinder all wore out. I ruther wish I could rest heah a spell."

The Frisco Kid was hungry. He looked along the white winding road and, through the glare of the early afternoon, he could see no house at which he might batter the back door.

Perkins Landing was, to all appearances, the nearest place at which he might secure food. Yet the little fellow pleaded that he was too tired, just then, to hike the distance to the town. The Kid, wanting to be generous yet urged by hunger, found himself in a predicament.

But unexpectedly, as Gamaliel sat down in the jimson weeds, the Kid noticed the heavy chaps on his legs.

"Gee whiz!" he exclaimed. "No wonder yer tired, Gay-May! I'll bet, if

I had to foot it with them hairy heavy things on my legs—I'll bet I'd be jes' trimmed down to nothin', and ready to drop right now. Why don't yer take 'em off? It'll lighten yer up a bit, and I'll pack 'em and we'll make Perkins and a feed as easy as flyin'.'"

"Hain't thet the bangest thing! Why I nevah thought of it!" And the little fellow smiled delightedly.

The Frisco Kid knelt down in the dust on one knee and helped the little fellow unbuckle the leggings. As one legging came off, he hefted it up in his hand.

"Whew, ain't it heavy, though! And dusty—why, I'll bet there's a ton of dust in it. Lookit!"

He shook the legging and beat it vigorously with one hand. Well, as he did, out of it amid a smoke of dust dropped, like so many falling leaves, a number of crisp new greenbacks, fully a dozen of them. He looked at them, mute, his eyes dilated with amazement.

"Dern thet Ole Woman!" swore Gamaliel softly. "So thet's what she meant a-tellin' ole Jerry to tan ole Harry outer me, 'n' tuck off them leggin' things to make it worser! Hain't she the most treacherousest low-down, ornery ole busybody, though!"

Amazement had fled the Kid's wide eyes. His eyes had narrowed, all at once, with suspicion.

"What's the gag, Gay-May?" he asked sharply. "Is these bills good?"

The little fellow was surprised in his turn.

"Good? Wul, say! Is watermelon good? Is 'simmons arter a frost good? Is cakes 'n' candies 'n' ice-cream 'n' pies good? Cos'e they's good 'n' so's this heah money, dad fetch it! None better, ole Jerry himsef says, 'n' he orter know.

"He's wukked a sight o'time fo' the Govamint a-makin' this money— most wore his eyes out, he has, carvin' them steel dies—'n' I jis' s'pose the Govamint hain't powerful proud 'n' mighty obleeged, too, fo' all what he's gone 'n' done! Is this money good, yo' granny! Hang it, why do yo' lay to ast sich kustions?"

The Frisco Kid was fairly browbeaten.

"Oh, nothin'," he returned evasively. "Only I've heard tell of phoney grifters what tried to shill off bum change and got time for it in stir, too, when they was nabbed. Seein' so much money kinder knocked the daylights out of me, and made me plumb suspicious. It's all come of me hobnobbin' with boes and yeggs, I guess.

"I ain't never met up before with a man, like old Jerry, what makes money for the Govamint. But old Jerry, now, he must be a pretty big gee in these parts, makin' money for the Govamint, and makin' heaps of it besides, I guess, peddlin' that phoney stuff to the shines 'round here."

"Sho' he is," agreed the little fellow. "And he's tighter'n a Thanksgivin' turkey with his—Jiminy crickets! heah's some moah o' the stuff!"

Gamaliel, in pulling off the other legging, had shaken out of it, from between the lining and the leather, another dozen new crisp bank-notes.

"Dog my cats!" he exclaimed. "Heah we've got all of twenty er fifty fi'-dollah bills. Most a thousan' dollahs, neahly. Le's skedaddle fo' Perkins like ole Jerry hissef war arter us, 'n' buy all kinds o' cakes 'n' candies befo' ole Jerry cayn fin' us!"

"Ye're on!" said the Kid grimly. "We'll give Jerry a bit of his own med'cine for tryin' to steal my dog and for bein' so tight and stingy with yer."

Gamaliel danced about.

"Oh, won't he be all ovah mad 'n' bilin', though! He'll wanta chaw me up! And it'll be nuts for the ole rapscallion. He'll larrup me to mush!"

The Frisco Kid looked at the little fellow rather sadly, even as though a bit hurt.

"No, he won't. Don't yer worry, he won't harm yer none, the old blind phoney stiff—not if I knows it!"

Gamaliel stopped dancing. He drew near the Frisco Kid and caught his hand. And he looked up at the Kid out of his clear blue eyes that were big and very round with unstinted admiration.

"Yo' sho' tuck the starch outer ole Jerry las' evenin', bo, all right! He jis' couldn't 'pear to git ovah it er fohgit it, nohow. All this heah mawnin', he kep' lookin' back 'n' listening a-skeered yo' war comin'. I raiken ole Jerry won't whale me no moah ag'in, now—rot him!"

The Frisco Kid was stuffing the banknotes back into the leggings.

"Come on," he said hastily, feeling suddenly very big and very good. "I'm so hungry and holler inside, I could eat a dead cat!" And he smiled down at the little fellow.

The little fellow smiled up at him. The Kid took the dusty leggings under one arm. Then followed by the Gay-cat, trailing the long length of hay-rope, his stump of a tail still wagging with happiness, the Frisco Kid and Gamaliel, holding hands like the children that they were, made along the winding white road.

VI

In the Village of Perkins Landing

They rounded that hill which once had been a bluff overlooking the Mississippi and came, under the lee of it, upon the little hamlet of Perkins Landing. It consisted of a number of widely separated houses straggling on either side of the road. Before each house stood some sort of tree and beneath each tree there appeared to slouch some sort of man.

Back from the road, on one side, they came upon a semicircle of poplar-trees. Beneath the trees were a couple of rustic benches upon which half a dozen men sat. Most of them had canes, while one or two wore battered Army service hats.

Just beyond the semicircle of trees a road branched off from the main artery toward the river—a road which must have been built since the river swerved away from Perkins Landing and which had been constructed to all appearances, by private enterprise; for swinging across the road was a white toll-gate.

At the junction of the two roads stood a trim solid-looking house, a story and a half in height, made of brick and cobble, with two white windows in front and, over the door in the sloping red-shingled roof, a small dormer window from which swung a sign labeled—

"Perkins Toll-House, Post-Office and Gen'l Merchandise Store."

Toward this building, the boys made.

As they did, a man came out of the tollhouse—a small, old, straggly-whiskered man with a sightless left eye, sunken and lidded, and one very bright ferocious eye. He crossed the road, thumping heavy and solid on the heels of his high boots. The old men under the trees seemed to liven at his approach and the two in the service hats saluted, hands to brim.

"Evenin' Capting."

"Howdy, Ebenezer."

"What's the latest news in the *Weekly Chelmsford Mississippi Bugle*?"

"Wal, Jedge Dickinson," the ferocious-looking new arrival returned to the last speaker, "I see by the papah thet Hank Glover's half-sister, Angela, wah unite in holy wedlock las' Thusday night with Jarge Rutherfo'd, the overseer o' Kunnel Chel'sfo'd's plantations.

"An' Missus Chel'sfo'd wah at the chu'ch in the fust light-cullahed dress she's wore sence hern baby-gal wah lost, er stoled as the story has it. She looked reely han'some the papah says, only kind o' saddish, Missus Chel'sfo'd.

"An' Dunc' Jenks, he's got his app'intment approved from Woshington as the Deputy Revenuer daown thisaways. Ole Dunc', I raiken he'll be all swelled an' uppish naow—put on a power o' side an' try to lay it all ovah us, same as ef he *wah* same somebody. But holy Moses, he needn't tuck on, enny. Warn't I, Ebenezer Tuttle, the Deputy Revenuer h'yer'bouts, back f'o year ago, whin Kunnel Chel'sfo'd wah Revenuer Agent fo' the hull Fed'ral deestrick?"

Gamaliel, the Kid and the leashed dog went across the road. Entering the store, they found themselves between two long counters heaped up with a disarray of notions, food-stuffs and hardware.

There were shoelaces and boxes of hairpins upon a round of cheese; there were sewing articles in the same glass case with a number of home-made pies; while from the box-laden shelves on the walls hung crinkly new gingham and calico frocks, starchy sunbonnets and straw hats, large and round as gigantic mushrooms.

Near the doorway was a raised portion of counter, grilled and marked "Post-Office." Behind the grille work, a white-haired sweet-faced old woman sat knitting. She hopped up at the boys' entrance and shoved her horn-rimmed spectacles up upon her furrowed forehead, her little eyes sparkling.

"Laws-a-mercy!" she exclaimed. "H'yer am strangers shore, sez I, the moment I clapped eyes on yeo'. An' this leetle fellah h'yer—ain't he the cutest leetle chap an' all dyked out regar'less! Laws-a-me, how I wish my Ebenezer mought see yo'! My Ebenezer, he's a case, that man. Allus moseyin' acrost the road, he is, to that pow-wow o' ole uns ovah thar at Lee Circle. No head fo' bizness at all, but shore the longest head fo' memorization I evah struck.

"I of'n sez, sez I, 'Ebenezer, yo' shore missed yo' vocation, man. Yo' sartinly would huv made the primest sma'test parson, suh.' He cayn read the papah an' repeat it all jist like a singin' lesson. An' the Good Book—lan', he knows that from kiver to kiver!

"But deary me," she broke off, with a sheepish little smile, "h'yer I am a-runnin' on an' on regar'less, an' yo' pore leetle uns jist plumb tuckered out an' most-like starvin' right beneath my eyes. What did yo'-all 'low yo'd like, naow?"

But the purchase proved a matter of some moment. The Frisco Kid selected a creamy-yellow custard pie and a great round frosted cake fairly oozing red juice and strawberries, and then Gamaliel pointed out with a dirty greedy finger, any number of "all-day suckers," "jaw-breakers" and "hot roasted Southern peanuts." A bit fearfully, the Kid tendered in payment one of the five-dollar bills.

The old woman lowered the spectacles over her eyes and very circumspectly examined the greenback. Then she nodded, went behind the grilled "Post-Office" and from a drawer extracted a woolen sack, swelled and jingling with money.

"My golly smoke, yo' got a sight o' money!" ejaculated Gamaliel, his sugar-coated lips smacking together. "I raiken now—I raiken yo' could cash twenty sich fi'-dollah bills er—er fifty, huh?"

The old woman beamed.

"Law bless yo', yes!" she returned quite proudly. "I 'low we has got consid'able money nowaday. Most all the darkies h'yer 'bouts, they bank thar money h'yer. Some new law o' the Govamint, my Ebenezer sez, what makes pos'-offices plain ornery savin's-banks.*

"I 'clar to glory, thar's no stannin' these h'yer darkies. Yo' jist watch an' see. Pooty soon one uv 'em 'll be tryin' to be President, shore's yo're born!"

---

* The Postal Savings Bank Bill of 1910.

She counted out the change and the boys, pocketing it and with effort gathering up in their arms the many purchases, left the store, recrossed the road and seated themselves with their backs against two of the poplars of the Circle.

They ate pie and candy, cake and peanuts indiscriminately and, as indiscriminately, threw bits of it to the dog. Behind them, as they munched, the old men still were talking. In the warm listless afternoon, the talk sounded monotonous, drowsy, like the heavy droning of bees.

"Wal, I see'd by the *Bugle*," the one-eyed Ebenezer was saying, "thet a cullahed buck daown the taownship way wah was conwicted uv makin' moonshine. He had a cabin 'mongst the vines an' sassafras o' Baggerly Islan'. An' the papah says he done fixed up the ole still what Sol Baggerly himsef used fo' year agone, and what Kunnel Chel'sfo'd done busted all to pieces thet time he wah Revenuer Agent."

"I reckerlec' the time, 'Nezer. But what war the black's name?"

"He wah named Fayette Williams—he's some sort o' far-off relative o' Scheeherazadee Williams, Dunc' Jenks' scullery wench. An' she wah daown fo' to see the wuthless lot, an' whin she wah in the store this-yer mawnin', she wah bitter as' simmons on the kunnel. Said he wah puttin' his fingah inter everybody's pie an' thet he kerlected all the evidence—"

"But Chelmsford's not a Revenuer any mo'."

"I knows; I knows thet, Jedge Dickson. But thish-yer Williams gal, she says as how the kunnel's naow in the Secret Sarvice—"

"Secret Sarvice yore granny! I 'low we don't need no Secret Sarvice daown heah, an' what's moah, Capting Tuttle, I 'low Kunnel Chel'fo'd hain't nohow the kinda man to jine up with sech a hidin'-out sneakin' sorta outfit."

"Right yo' air, Zeke. Thar hain't a better man this side Orleans, I cal'late, than the kunnel. Looky what he done fo' the nigger chillen daown the Taownship-way, 'nd the yunkers o' the pore whites—"

"But 'twah sho' a cryin' shame the way ol' Solermun Baggerly done sarved him," interposed another. "I allus held an' I allus will hold thet 'twah ol' Sol what done tuk his leetle Celestie, arter the kunnel had bruk up his still an' shoved him neck an' crop outer the country. An' thet's the low-down why the kunnel done raired up thet school—outer sad an' sorrerful memory uv his baby-gurl—"

The boys slept. Surfeited with all they had eaten, their heads had tilted farther and farther forward until at last, with a final sag, their chins had rested on their chests and they were asleep.

Even the Gay-cat was asleep, lying coiled and yellow in the sun between them, the hay-rope from his neck held loosely in the Kid's hand. Once he roused to lift his sharp yellow head and to look about him querulously.

But that which had disturbed him proved only to be the old men marching off along the road, their gossip and arguments left to be continued the following day. The dog yawned, licked his candy-sticky chops, slid his head between his forepaws and then again to all appearances, he was dead to the world.

The grind of wheels on the dust of the road and the sound of a man urging on a horse awoke the boys and dog. It was dusk. In the diffused light of the gloaming, the whole world seemed wrapped in a gold-sprayed dust that made everything, near and far away, very vague and beautiful—the white road, the reach of trees on either hand, and the brick-and-cobble toll-house opposite, with its sign-board creaking and its white-framed windows glistening in the last rays of the sun.

The boys sat up and guiltily rubbed their eyes. The dog yawned and looked questioningly and a trifle impatiently at them. The sound of grinding wheels and heavy hoof-beats neared, and a man jogged into view on a two-wheeled cart drawn by a grotesquely ponderous horse with long hair on its fetlocks.

He was the lanky bewhiskered fellow of the jeans and straw hat whom the Kid had spoken to early that afternoon. At sight of the boys, he jerked the ponderous horse to a standstill.

"By jings!" he ejaculated, "h'yer air yo' two got together! And th' dorg along, too! By Jeber Socks! ef thet hain't th' bangest thing evah!"

He looked at them sharply, a growing suspicion in his eyes.

"Say, yunkers," he called out, after a moment, "whar did yo'-all git thet custard pie yo've part et, 'nd thet candy whose wrappin's is lyin' all about?"

At the man's inquisitiveness, the Kid remembered, all at once, the fellow's suspicion of the greenback that afternoon. He motioned Gamaliel to remain quiet. But Gamaliel seemed filled with a sudden pride.

"Why, we bo't it. We had a greenback, jist like the one I guv yo'," he rejoined, "an' yo' betcher, too, we got plenty moah!"

Whereat he reached into the chaps under the Kid's arms, ere the Kid with a greater caution lent by experience and fear could stop him, withdrew from between the lining and the leather a fistful of bills.

The man's eyes fairly bulged. He took off his hat and scratched his bald head in deep perplexity. Then from a pocket of his jeans, he drew out the five-dollar bill Gamaliel had given him for the dog that morning. He eyed it as though with a strengthened suspicion, and looked from it to the bills in the boy's hand.

Suddenly he spat neatly between the horse's ears and said, ingratiatingly:

"Waal, yunkers, I'm gwine into Chel'sfo'd Township 'nd I'll give yo' a lift. I would 'a' ben thar by now on'y Alice Baabar h'yer, he cast a shoe three mile down th' road, 'nd I had to turn back home 'nd make a new un 'nd put it on mysef. But thet's no nevah mind. I'll give yo' a lift to th' Township, ef yo' say. Want a lift?"

The boys looked at each other. Presently Gamaliel shook his sombreroed head vigorously, a kind of fear in his round blue eyes.

"No," he said, suddenly subdued. "We'd like to ride with yo' like everything but we cayn't. Jerry Mears, the ole rapscallion, he's ahead along the road som'eres, 'n' he'd ketch us. We don't want fo' to meet him at all, no moah."

The man nodded, spit, and scratched his head again.

"By jings, I'll tell yo' what yo' do," he said at last. "Yo' is gwine to hang around h'yer a spell, eh? Waal, yo'-all go down to my house at the fo'k o' th' road ternight, 'nd stay tell mawnin'. Tell' em Dunc' Jenks, th' new Depooty Revenuer—thet's me—sint yo'. I'll be back 'long toward midnight, I cal'late."

"All right," said the Frisco Kid.

"Thet'll be candy fo' us," agreed Gamaliel.

Both were so happy at receiving promise of shelter for the night that, with childish innocence, they never thought to question the motive actuating the man's offer. They did not realize that he wanted them to stay overnight in his house in order that he might be able to lay hands on them forthwith, should the greenback he had received prove spurious.

Quickly the night darkened. A reflecting kerosene lamp was lighted in the tollhouse and the light streamed out of the two lower windows and open door, and lay across the road like the three white fingers of a mangled hand. The bats came out and flew back and forth across the lighted spaces in a bewildering game of tag.

The boys could see the old man leaning against one counter, an old brown fiddle beneath his chin. He drew the bow tentatively once or twice across the strings, and then began playing and singing, and tapping time with his foot:

> She's my Juliana Feebiana Concertina Brown,
> > She am the prettiest gal was evah in the taown.
> She has eyes so bright an' feet so nice—
> > She wears a numbah nine—
> She am the fairest queen uv all along the line!

And then, as they lay there, heads nodding to the melody, they heard the sound. It was a dull sound in all that soft music of fiddling and singing; yet was it a distinct, staccato and strangely familiar sound—*tap, tap, tap!*

VII
"AN' YO' HAIN'T GWYNE-A LEAVE ME NEVAH NO MOAH?"

THE DOG SCRAMBLED AFOOT, trembling nervously in every leg. Gamaliel scrambled afoot. He was in a panic of dread. He was about to run away when the Kid said:

"What yer 'fraid of, Gay-May? It's only the blind phoney man a-stompin' along on his stick. He won't hurt yer none. Yer jes' stay here by me. I'll fix him for stealin' my dog!"

There was more than threat in the Frisco Kid's voice. In the Frisco Kid's voice was a mighty tone of bravado. Before the little frightened boy, he felt very big and very strong then.

The blind man's seedy stoop-shouldered form took shape in the night. His large silver-rimmed glasses, outstanding and peering, glimmered in the light from the tollhouse. As though guided by some random sound of their whispers, he headed straight for the poplar tree beneath which the boys waited. He asked in his singsongy whine—

"Is thet yo', Gamaliel?"

"Yes, Jerry," the little fellow answered tremblingly; then added, in a brave afterthought, "Sho', yo' ornery ole pirut!"

Mears said no more. He came on, a quiet smile on his lean brown face. He got quite close to the boy. It was shocking, then, that vehement change which swept over him. Unexpected and nimble as quicksilver, he reached out one lean bony hand, and caught the boy by the shoulder, and raised over his head the heavy knobby stick.

"Yo' thankless little runt!" he said. "I'll larn yo' to keep me waitin'!"

The stick descended, but the Frisco Kid, leaping in, caught it on an interposing arm.

"No, yer don't!" he cried. "You drop that stick! There ain't gonna be no beatin' of kids 'round here, not while I knows it!"

The phoney man stepped back, shocked, chagrined, and terribly angered.

"Yo' heah? Yo' heah, yo' measly dod-rotted bum!"

He whirled on the Kid. But abruptly all his surprise and anger fled. He lowered the stick and hiding his chagrin, became all at once whining and conciliating.

"Why, good evenin', bo, evenin', to yo'. Ole Jerry nevah 'spected yo' wuz heah, he nevah 'spected yo'd be heah nohow. Shore, yo' must be some tall walker, bo! Ten mile hain't nuthin' fo' yo' to traipse, I raiken, now. En thet cute little yaller dorg o' yourn, he's heah, too, heh?"

He felt about with his stick very quickly until he touched the dog. The Gay-cat growled.

"Yeah!" he chortled. "So thar yo' be, yo' elegan' little animule! En I cal'late now, yo' is quite put out, bo, 'bout losin' yo' precious yaller houn'. But I didn't mean fo' to hive him fo' keeps; hones', I didn't. As shore's my name's ole Jerry Mears, I on'y cal'lated to keep him jist long enough to fetch a little money.

"En we done hit, bo; we made a sight o' money, thet pert little articule en the ole blin' man. I'll han' some ovah to yo', wunse we fetch thet shanty-boat; a elegan' new greenback—think o' thet, bo—all fo' yo'sef!"

The Frisco Kid, while a whit appeased by the man's excuses and promises, still harbored resentment enough to feel a joy in contradicting him.

"I can't see where yer made any money on my dog," he said sullenly. "Them darkies said yer paid back more for Gay-cat than they gave yer first, and so did Dunc' Jenks, the revenuer, what I met this afternoon and who passed along the road not more'n an hour ago."

The blind man chuckled. He peered at the Frisco Kid through his glasses, as though nonplused; yet he continued to chuckle. At last he whined:

"Me make money off'n yo' dorg! Dingnations, lad, hain't yo' nevah figgered ole Jerry wuz on'y a-foolin' uv yo', a-foolin' uv yo' all the time, now en afore? Thet's why I tuck the dorg in the fust place. Says I, this smart little feller, he thinks a precious lot uv thet cute yaller dorg.

"I'll tuck the little animule along, jist to fin' out how fon' he is o' him en jist to fool him a middlin' bit. En I done hit, bo," he cackled, "I fooled yo' all holler! But now thet the dorg's back en we're all reunited in one bosom fambly, as the Good Book says, why everythin's jist gaudy en elegan'-like, I raiken—yeah?"

The Frisco Kid said no word. Only, with grave suspicion, he watched the man.

Using the stick as a support, his other hand sliding down the bole of a poplar tree, Jerry Mears sat down. He sat down full upon the partly eaten custard pie. He leaped up. Swearing a blue streak, his thin hawk-like face convulsed with anger, his left hand frantically brushing the custard from the swallow-tails of his coat, he cried:

"Dang all creation! What's this? Custard—custard pie!"

The discovery of the exact cause of his discomfiture wrought a sudden change in the man.

"Custard pie, heh? Ben havin' a feast, no doubt; yeah, a sumchous feast, all gran' gaudy to behold. But won't yo' tell the ole blin' phoney man whah yo' done fetched the money to pu'chase sich a elegan' repast?"—he appealed to the Frisco Kid—"I's jist perishin' to know, bo!"

He appeared worried and a bit nervous. The Kid eyed him and sought for an answer. Suddenly Gamaliel, holding to the Kid's hand, began sobbing brokenly.

"Thar now, Gamaliel, thet's a good little feller. Yo' tell ole Jerry; yo' tell yo' ole man jist whar yo' got all that money."

"Aw," sobbed Gamaliel, despite the Kid's cautioning pressure on his hand—"aw, we found a bunch o' greenbacks, all o' fifty o' them in my leggin's, an'—"

"Found them in yo' leggin's!" repeated Mears, reaching for the chaps and wheezing with excitement. The Kid gave the chaps over into his keeping, and he thrust a hand within one and discovered, between the leather and the lining, the many bills.

"Dad fetch thet Ole Woman!" he said in an undertone. "So thet's what she meant a-tellin' me to tuck off his leggin's. These heah greenbacks in his leggin's! En I nevah knowed! I's come all this way back, en it hain't one tolerable bit safe fo' me to 'pear round thisaways so soon. Dern the Ole Woman fo' a muggins! Why couldn't she speak out straight, consarn her!"

He was truly nervous now.

"Chillen," he said unctuously, "whar did yo'-all cash thet greenback?"

"In the post-office acrost the road," returned the Frisco Kid desperately.

"An' she cayn cash all kinds o' greenbacks, Jerry," said Gamaliel. "She's got heaps o' money, all jinglin' 'n' tied up in a ole woolen sock. All the darkies heah'bouts, they bank thar money with her. Say, why don't yo' try her, Jerry?"

Gamaliel spoke in a manner which indicated that he had been instructed to look for logical places to cash greenbacks.

Mears turned and, his head on one side, peered across the road. The light from the toll-house flashed upon the tarnished rims of his glasses, and pulsed and dulled on the lenses. For a space no word was said. Within the toll-house, they could see the old man fiddling, and the sound of his voice drifted, clearly distinct, to the three on the shadowy road:

> Sum folks say thet a niggah don' steal—
> > An' I'm gwyne-a git a home bimeby;
> But I cotched two in my cornfield—
> > An' I'm gwyne-a git a home bimeby.
> One had a shovel an' one had a hoe—
> > An' I'm gwyne-a git a home bimeby;
> Sho', ef thet ain't stealin', wal I don' know—
> > An' I'm gwyne-a git a home bimeby!
>
> Oh, thet watahmelon,
> > Lan' o' goodness, yo' mus' die!
> Fo' I'm gwyne-a jine the contraband chillen,
> > An' I'm gwyne-a git a home bimeby.

Very quietly and carefully, the blind man sat down. He asked—

"Whar does she keep hern money?"

"In a drawer," answered Gamaliel glibly and guilelessly. "She's got a high ole desk in thar neah the door, what is marked 'Pos'-Office,' 'n' she keeps all that money, a powerful sight o' it, in a drawer uv thet ole desk."

The blind man nodded.

"En did yo' see ennythin' o' a malickous weapon 'round abouts, ennythin' like a gun, now?"

"Shucks! Hain't thet jist like yo', Jerry Mears! Alluz askin' has they got a gun, er a colluhed sarvant mebbe! But my golly smoke, I lay she don't need no gun! She 'n' hern ole man with the shiny eye—"

"Thar's a ole man along, too? Dang it, why didn't yo' tell me thar wuz two uv 'em!"

"Wul, I would 'av, I raiken, ef yo'd 'a' guv me a chanst. Cos thar's two o' them, her 'n' Ebenezer, a ole white-haired dried-up kind o' little feller, what should 'a' bin a preachin', psalm-singin' one-eyed pahson—she done tole us so hernsef. Thet's him ovah thar, a-fiddlin' away 'n' a-singin' like all glory. An' they is the best-naturedest souls—"

"Yeah? Good-natured they be, heh? En mought 'a' ben a pahson, too!"

The blind man nodded his head several times, very slowly. He seemed to be pondering. Presently, he looked up at the sky where the stars were just beginning to peep out. He said, apropos of nothing—

"Thar'll be no moon ternight."

Suddenly he bent over, pressing his stomach and grimacing.

"Law, I's powerful hungry. My innards is all scrunched up en I's hungry as a hawg. By Zachariah, I raiken I'll go ovah thar to thet toll-house en pu'chase a supper. What say, heh?"

He looked quizzically through his glasses at the boys and there was about him then a terrifying resemblance to some great bird of prey.

Gamaliel assented readily. But there was that in all the questions and answers which filled the Frisco Kid with vague misgivings.

"I guess I don't need no supper," he said. "Gay-cat and me, we's plumb stuffed up with all that sweet truck we et today. I think we'll be moseyin' along. We'll go back, me and Gay-cat, to Dunc' Jenks' place for the night."

The blind man said nothing, only turned his head to one side to hide the sudden smile that wrinkled his lean hawk-like face. Not so Gamaliel. He sidled over to the Kid's side, and took his hand, and looked up at him out of great round blue eyes.

"Yo' hain't gwyne to leave me, is yo'? Jist come along, 'n' yo' don't have to eat no moah 'n me—I'm tighter'n a Thanksgivin' turkey mysef."

But the Kid shook his head.

"I'm skeered if yo' go away," pleaded Gamaliel, dropping his voice to a whisper and looking fearfully at the smiling blind man. "I'm skeered ole Jerry'll tan me. He hain't forguv me none fo' spendin' thet greenback. He'll lash the livers 'n' lights out'n me." His tiny hand trembled in the Kid's hand.

The Kid could not resist that trembling hand, that pleading voice. A heritage of dreadful memories rose in his mind, memories of the beatings he himself had received at the hands of Frisco Red. He said quietly:

"I'll go, Gay-May. Come on."

But Gamaliel held back.

"An' yo' hain't gwyne-a leave me nevah no moah, bo—not fo' love o' money?"

The Kid looked down at him. He nodded—he could not speak.

Behind them, very silently, the blind man had got afoot.

"Yo' leave the dorg behind, bo," he said querulously, as though somehow vexed.

The boys swung about, startled at the suddenness and sharpness of his voice.

"Not that I hain't tuck consid'able to thet pert little animule, as I done said," he went on, his voice quickly becoming wheedling again; "but dorgs is dorgs, en sometimes they git 'nation pesky, alwuz about. Yo' tie him to a tree. He's had a-plenty to eat this evenin', I raiken." And he cackled hollowly.

Obediently the Frisco Kid did as he was bidden. The length of hay-rope served to make the Gay-cat fast to one of the poplar trees. Then the Kid and Gamaliel leading the way, the blind man tapping behind them, the chaparejos under one arm, an enigmatic smile upon his shrewd lean face, they started for the lighted store where, once again, the old man had launched into the sprightly chorus:

> *Oh, I feel jist as happy as a big sunflower*
> *Thet nods an' bends in the bree-zes,*
> *An' my heart's jist as light as the winds thet blow—*
> *Thet blow among the tree-zes!"*

VIII
A LODGING FOR THE NIGHT

THE WEAZENED OLD MAN, WITH THE ONE FEROCIOUS EYE, lifted his chin from the fiddle.

"Evenin', neighbor, evenin' to you," began Jerry Mears in his singsongy voice, his blurred eyes blinking in the lamplight behind the outstanding glasses. "The ole man cayn't see so elegan'-like, but he cayn listen right pert. He hearn yo' fiddlin' an singin' when he wuz back the road a piece. Shaw!

thet moosic done drawed him on, like the sweet singin' o' David done the giant, Goliar, as the Good Book says."

"Good even' to yo', suh," returned the ferocious-eyed fellow. "Good evenin' to yo', an' thrice welcome yo' be, jedgin' as I do from yo' talk thet yo' be a man o' sound Christian larnin' an' principul."

"Yeah, sta'wart Christians we be," said Mears—"sta'wart Christians thet has walked a consid'able long ways, this day through a most heathenish country. Sence break o' day, thar wuz nevah a good Samaritan, as the Fo'th Chaptah o' Genesis has hit, to give us a lift er a bite o' somethin'.

"Jidge, we'se powerful hungry. Yo' couldn't set us down to a smack, now could yo'? Law bress yo', I'll pay fo' hit. I've got a bit o' money myself, en food is wuth good money enny day, I cal'late, en menny thanks."

From the chaps under his left arm, he tendered to the old man, with the words, a crisp new bank-note. With Southern instinct for courtesy and hospitality, the old man refused to accept the money. But the blind man, as if with some premeditated object, insisted upon paying then and there.

"Yore a man arter my own heart, Jidge," he smirked; "but jist the same, right is right, en the ole blin' man must be said en led by the principuls thet has shaped his life all these year. Pay fust en eat arter-wards, thet's my principuls."

"Ef I git to glory, them's noble sentermints!" exclaimed Ebenezer, capitulating. "But jist the same, thar would 'a' bin a-plenty o' time fo' yo' to pay, arter yo'-all had eaten yore fill."

He took the five-dollar bill and made for the "Post-Office" at the entrance of the store.

"But speakin' o' principuls," he continued in a manner indicative of giving a confidence—"speakin' o' principals, I must tell yo', on principals, thet I hain't a jedge in these parts at all. I fo't ag'in Geronimo, whar I los' my lef eye, in my young sinful days way back in the eighties, an' some folks has come to call me capting, knowin' next to nothin' 'bout the Sarvice.

"I wah on'y a toler'ble pore corp'ral, but they calls me thet, Capting Tuttle. Folks do have a power o' respect fo' me daown thish-aways," he ended guilelessly.

The blind man's thin shrewd face lighted up. There had come, from the direction of the "Post-Office," the slither of a drawer being pulled out, and then the jingle of money as the old man, to make change, lifted in his hands the woolen sock.

Mears remained as he was, facing the rear of the store; but his head was half turned around and his body all hunched over to one side, his face smiling quietly the while.

Ebenezer, coming back, counted into the blind man's bony hand nine silver half dollars. As Mears murmured an obsequious, "Thankee, Captin'," the old man said—

"Come thish-yer ways."

He then led the queer trio into a tiny cubby at the back of the store which served, from appearances, as kitchen and dining-room in one.

It was scrupulously clean. A large squat stove seemed to take up most of its area and there was, against one wall, a table covered with a blue-patterned oil-cloth. At one end of the table stood a kerosene-lamp, by the feeble light of which the sweet-faced old woman was darning socks. She dropped her work as the door from the store opened and, shoving her horn-rimmed spectacles up on her wrinkled forehead, peered at the newcomers.

"Goodness-gracious-sakes-alive!" she ejaculated, her little sparkling eyes alighting on Gamaliel and the Frisco Kid. "Ef h'yer an't them stranger tads I wah tellin' yo' 'bout, 'Nezer. An' this leetle chap h'yer—ain't he a case though, with all his trappin's an' blue eyes!"

"Yo' mean, Susannah—my kingdom! yo' mean them yunkers what wah in h'yer terday pu'chasin' sweets?"

He looked in bewilderment from his wife to the blind man.

The blind man drew his thin lower lip in between his teeth and a sudden press of blood darkened the brown of his face. Then slowly a forced smile loosened the stiffness of his face and he released his lip, which was savagely red.

"Yo' raikened correckly, Jidge—pahdon the ole man, I mean Captin'. Yo' know I cayn't hep callin' yo' jidge, yo' look en ack so 'nation ven'rable en religjus. But as I wuz sayin— Law! now jist what wuz I sayin'? Oh, yeah, yeah; 'bout eatin', warn't hit?

"Wal, as I wuz sayin', my boys come in heah terday to buy some candy en sich-like truck, en as they wuz gwyne back along the road to meet thar ole man, lo en behold! heah wuz a little du'ty-face' chile, a-cryin' en a-blatterin' like no slouch, I tell yo'. They guv hit a piece o' candy, en it kind o' laid off bawlin' a spell, en up en tole them hits mothah wuz sick—"

"Sick?" repeated the old woman, straightening up from busying about the stove. "Laws-a-me, thet mus' be Missus Rawlins what hain't been feelin' well these menny-a-day. Whar did yo'-all meet the leetle un? 'Roun t'other side o' the hill?"

"Yeah, 'round t'other side o' the hill," agreed the blind man with astonishing quickness. "Missus Rawlins' little gurl—warn't hit a gurl, Gamaliel?"

"Lan' sake, it must 'a' ben a g'yirl," interposed the old woman ere Gamaliel could aid out in the falsehood. "Missus Rawlins, she's got fi' childern, all g'yirls—the pore thing!"

"Wal, hern little du'ty-face' gurl—"

"Thet'll be Hanner, she's allus dirty, of co's'e."

"Wal, Hanner, she done tole the boys thet she en hern fo' sisters, they hadn't nuthin' to eat all day. So what does my boys do but up en guv 'em all thet candy en pie, en the pore boys jist pinin' hungry themsefs at the time—"

"Oh, the darlin' leetle critturs!" burst from the old lady and, for a moment, it looked as if she would hug both little hoboes to her bosom. "But set daown, set daown," she added hastily. "H'yer I am a-runnin' on an' on, an' yo' two leettle chaps jist plumb tuckered out and most-like starvin' right beneath my eyes. Set daown an' have a bite."

With marvelous celerity, the old woman put upon the table a crockery pitcher brimming with rich thick milk, a bowl of brown sugar, a small jug of molasses, heaping platters of corn pone and hoe-cake, and colorful bowls of prune and peach jam, and crab-apple jelly.

All the time she had been talking, she had been busying about the stove from which now arose the smell of catfish sizzling in butter. Quickly but thoroughly she warmed over, in the oven, a huckleberry and a pumpkin pie, some chicken and a number of sweet potatoes. Then serving steaming fragrant coffee to Jerry and large mugs of milk to the boys, she set the repast before them, with the delicious addition of some blackberries and cream.

"What a mouth-waterin' gaudy dinnah!" the blind man could not refrain from remarking as the odors tickled his nostrils.

There was in his voice, for the first time that evening, a positive ring of sincerity.

"All raired up in thish-yer county," said the old man with a justifiable pride.

Now, it is a precept, an irrefragable law of conduct among hoboes, never to pass up a meal.

"Swallow it down if it busts you," is the commandment; "you never can tell when you'll get another."

And this was more than a meal; it was wholesome fare, appetizing fare, such fare as would tingle the palate of even an epicure, a sybarite. Yet the Frisco Kid felt no urge of appetite at all.

It was not alone because he had gorged himself with sweets that afternoon; there was filling his mind vague misgivings regarding the blind man's purpose and, somehow, those misgivings had communicated to the pit of his stomach a rather sick feeling. He could not eat.

Not so Gamaliel, however. As if in truth he had not eaten all day, as if violently hungry, he no sooner sighted the juicy hot pies, smoking chicken, jams and molasses and milk than he started in, with dirty greedy fingers, to help himself. But with one claw-like hand outreaching across the table, the blind man halted him, doffed his shapeless black hat, bowed his head, and reverently said grace.

"Deah Lawd," he prayed, "fo' thet which we air now about to receive en partake uv, heah below, en all out'n Thy bounty en good-naturedness o' heart, we do 'umbly thank Yo', good Lawd."

"Amen," ended the old couple in one voice. They were visibly impressed.

Mears cut into the snow-white meat of the catfish, smeared some crabapple jelly on the sweet potatoes, dabbed a chunk of corn pone with molasses, and began eating voraciously.

"Man alive, what a good fry this heah cadfish done make!"

Ebenezer opened and closed his single good eye in ready agreement.

"Ketched it mysef thish-yer mawnin', I did," he said. "An' thet reminds me—holy Moses, I'd most fo'gotten! But it wah whilst I wah fishin' fo' thet cadfish off'n Milkens' Wharf thet along come Long John Rawlins, the same whose wife am now tuck daown sick.

"An' he up an' tells me that whin he wah out midstream, yisterday noontide, brungin' in some logs to the mill, thar as shore as he wah born, he see'd a mermaid sunnin' hersef on a log! Yes-sir-ee, a mermaid with golden ha'r fallin' daown to her waist, an' big sad eyes, an' the whitest kind o' skin, an' a awful fishy tail beneath! Ef I gits to glory, hain't thet the bangest thing evah?"

"I believe hit," replied the blind man, nodding emphatically to the quick accompaniment of his munching jaws. "Some folks, they don't lay thar is mermaids no moah, but I's not one o' them kind. Mermaids thar be, some sinful creeturs en some as big-naturedes' as the Lawd A'mighty himsef. Don't the Good Book tell o' mermaids?"

He paused for effect. The Frisco Kid sat, gloomy and pensive, eyeing him questioninly, regretfully, over his mug of milk. It did not escape him how oily and fawning was the blind man's tone, how eagerly he concurred in everything the old folk said, no matter how absurd; and the misgivings assailing his mind strengthened almost to the point of conviction.

"Yeah, the Good Book tells o' mermaids, a heap o' times. Thar wuz Moses what wuz chattin' with the bullfrogs in the willers whin he wuz foun' by some mermaids. By Zachariah, it wuz one o' the good mermaids foun' him, a han'some beautjus mermaid, the darter o' a queen, the Queen o' Sheba hernsef, the Good Book says.

"En 'twixt yo' en me, I raiken Moses, he lamed a trick er two from thet mermaid. How else do yo' su'pose he could traipse so easy-like acrost the Red Sea en all them 'Gyptians be drownded, neck en crop? How else, I ask yo' thet?"

The blind man paused to lift his blurred bespectacled eyes and to look about him very triumphantly. Suddenly his eyes halted in sweeping about and peered straight ahead at the wall opposite. It was as if some bright object on that wall had flashed a vision to his retina through the dimness of the crystalline lenses of his eyes.

Said Mears suddenly—

"I see yo' got a gun thar on the wall."

The Frisco Kid from making a pretense of sipping his milk, followed the direction of the phoney man's riveted gaze. There on the opposite wall, its short, well-kept, polished steel barrel scintillating like- star-stuff in the lamplight, was an old-fashioned Springfield rifle.

"Oh, yes, we got a gun, sech as it is," the old man chuckled softly. "Susannah h'yer is afeared to 'low me load it. So thar, empty an' useless, it hangs as a keepsake an' ha'ntin' reminder o' my un-Christian days in the Injun wars.

"But leastways, ef I wah put to it, Susannah says, one sight o' it in my han's would be fitten to keel a evildoer ovah, knock the starch plumb outer him."

Mears put down the chicken leg and wiped his brow with a cotton handkerchief.

" 'Deed en 'deed!" he cackled. "I 'low yo' ole woman is puffeckly correck. Thar's no manner o' sense er use in havin' a vicious weapon lyin' 'bout, loaded, in a hones' Christian's house."

It may have been the odor of food in surfeited nostrils which sickened the Frisco Kid; it may have been the grimly suggestive turn to the conversation; but in either case, the squeamish feeling at the pit of the Kid's stomach became so poignantly distressing that he rose, now, to his feet.

At the sound of the scraping chair, the blind man jerked up his head sharply.

"Whar now, bo?"

"Only outside, Jerry. I feel kinder sick—and I wanter see if Gay-cat's all right and—and if the moon has come out."

The fresh earthly-fragrant air, breathing on the Kid's warm temples and into his lungs, quickly allayed the sick heaving of his stomach. Across the road his dog whined with loneliness, while out in the wide star-coruscating night, a watch of crickets stridulated remote and eerily.

At sight of the Kid in the lighted doorway, the Gay-cat's whining quickened into half-sobbing whimpers, and he strained at the hay-rope harshly tying him to the tree. The Frisco Kid went to him, and patted his muzzling head, and whispered into his ragged ears all his terrifying apprehensions.

Then, looking along the pale ribbon of toll-road which led to the river, the Kid was heartened by sight of a great round orb swinging in the sky. The moon had risen. Now would Mears have to go on!

But of a sudden, out of the eye of the orb lunged a stream of light and the Kid realized then, with a lowering of spirit, that it was not the moon, but the searchlight of some steamboat feeling, head-on, for the dyke and bars on this side of the river.

A spray of sparks coughed up from the steamboat's funnels and it swung its broadside—a row of lights—toward him, and he even imagined he could see the white foam and hear the *swash-swash* of its churning paddle-wheel.

As he reentered the store, he heard Mears saying:

"Shore, I couldn't 'low to rob yo' o' yo' room, Jidge, not fo' love o' money. The spare room upstaihs is plenty good enough fo' sich as us, says I, en I says it moughty thankful. But all the same, I'm dead sot ag'in' stayin'."

"Ef thar's even on'y a inch o' moon in the sky, it's fo' my boys en thar pore ole blin' man to be up en walkin' along the road. Howsomevah—ah, heah yo' be," he broke off as the Kid appeared. "En is thar enny moon at all ternight?"

He peered eagerly at the Kid. The Frisco Kid shook his head.

"Yet it's kinder bright out," he qualified.

"Wal," said Mears slowly, "I dunno—"

"Oh, glory be!" interposed the old woman. "Looky h'yer! This leetle chap is all scrunched up in the cheer an' dead to the world in sleep, he's so plumb tuckered out with all the tall miles he's done kivered this day.

"Have done with all this talk uv gwyne on. Sakes alive, it would be a purty howdy-do, a pizen-mean shame, to make this leetle fellah go on further this evenin'."

The Frisco Kid looked at the piquant little picture of Gamaliel—asleep in the chair, his tiny pouting mouth open and smeared with stains of red from the huckleberry pie and of yellow from the pumpkin one, his large round eyes closed, his sombrero fallen on the floor, and his yellow curls tumbled about his ears. He heard Mears repeat once more—

"Wal, I dunno."

"Oh, go long," said the old woman, shooing them out of the kitchen. "Go 'long upstaihs, the hull kit an' bilin' uv yo'! I'll tote the leetle chap. H'yer, Ebenezer, tuck the lamp an' show the way."

IX
TAP, TAP, TAP!

THERE WAS A RICKETY STAIRCASE mounting from the store into the attic. The old man led the way, the lamp held above his white head; the Frisco Kid followed next; and the woman came after with the sleeping little Gamaliel held snugly in her arms. Bringing up the rear was the blind phoney man, his heavy knobby stick tap-tapping on the creaking stairs.

They entered a little slanting-ceilinged room which was lighted feebly by that dormer window from which swung and squeaked the large sign.

The room was filled by a large four-poster bed. There was a brass-bound trunk against the window, an old-fashioned marble-topped wash-stand in one corner, a horsehair sofa in another, and a rag carpet on the floor partly covered over by several coon skins. Here and there on the papered walls were several chromos of idyllic sylvan scenes, and here and there also bright patches where the lithographs formerly had hung.

The woman laid Gamaliel on the bed and, seeming to have taken a solicitous motherly fancy to him, was about to undress the little fellow for the night when Mears, in an unaccountable perturbation, interposed.

"Let be, let be!" he said hastily.

Then, at the surprised, bewildered expression in the old woman's eyes, he chuckled softly, and singsonged—

"I raiken yo'll have to pahdon me, m'am, but I wuz powerfully afeard yo'd wake him. I us'ally ondress Gamaliel myself. My ole woman, she says I got the lightest touch, lighter'n a fly, she says. En I cal'late yo' folks has done a heap enough fo' us—thar hain't menny would 'a' done as much—en I don't want to put yo' to enny moah trouble. Sho', jist leave a light heah fo' us, en we'll git along scrumpchously."

The old woman nodded that she understood and lighted a candle which stood on the wash-stand beside the crockery pitcher and bowl. Then, bidding them good-night the old couple went creaking down-stairs.

But Mears did not undress the little fellow. He went to the door and looked after the couple, harkening to their retreating footsteps; then closed the door softly again and came back to the bed. He removed Gamaliel's shoes and covered him over with a comforter. He took off, from beneath his shiny green swallow-tail coat, the heavy yellow oilcloth packs.

"Yo' sleep on the sofa," he said to the Kid.

The Frisco Kid stretched himself at full length on the sofa. He watched Mears take out one of his home-made cigars and extinguish the candle, and then he could see him sitting on the trunk, his back to the dormer window, his unkempt head and stoop shoulders in silhouette, and the lighted end of his cigar glowing and dying in the dark.

The Kid could not sleep. He was distraught, a prey to fears and dreadful imaginings. Below, very faintly, he could hear the old couple talking together.

All at once, outside, a prolonged mournful cry shattered the night and soared upward, shrill and vibrating, as though to pierce the remote stars. It died away sobbingly and a second cry rushed up, spearing the stillness like a sharp javelin. It was the howling of a dog. It sounded frightful, hideous, like the keening of a lost soul.

"Somebody's gwyne-a die ternight," said Mears somberly from the dark. It was as though he were talking to himself.

The Kid sat up, shivering.

"It's my Gay-cat," he said.

"What? Is yo' awake, bo?"

"Yes, Jerry, and I think I'll go down and see what's the matter with my dog. I never heard him howl like that before. It's kinder creepy."

The blind man mumbled something, but did not openly object. As the Frisco Kid left the room, the thought appulsed on his brain that perhaps Mears did not want him to come back. He went down the creaking stairs.

The store still was open, and lighted by the rays from the oil-lamp glancing through the partly ajar door of the kitchen. Across the road was the Gay-cat, up on his haunches, his nose lifted to the unapproachable stars and the howls mournfully ululating up through his throat.

"S-sh, Gay-cat!" admonished the Kid.

The howling broke off into a quick succession of plaintive pleading whimpers. The Kid turned away. A sudden, desperate if vague plan had burgeoned in his brain. He approached the kitchen.

The old man and woman were seated about the table. They rose up as he entered. They were on the point of saying something when, significantly, he put a finger to his lips.

Nervously he glanced about, and now his eyes rested longingly on the gun on the opposite wall and now they were raised fearfully to the ceiling, as though he dreaded lest the peddler might have his ear to the flooring above, or be looking down through some crack at him.

"What is it?" the old man asked in a shaking whisper, feeling the contagion of the Kid's nervousness.

The words stuck in the Kid's throat. Finally, with effort, he stammered inarticulately:

"Thet gun over there. You'll load it, won't yer? Aw, I wish yer would! I'm skeered somethin's gonna happen tonight. Don't ask me, I don't know what for sure. But you'll load the gun—you'll load the gun, won't yer, mister?"

The old man looked from the Kid to his wife, quickly, in bewilderment, and with something of telepathically induced fear. Just then, outside, the dog set up one prolonged piercing wail. Their teeth went on edge. The wail was thin as the scraping of a nail on a glass pane.

"See," said the Frisco Kid. "My dog, he knows. And he's a-warnin' of us. You'll load the gun, won't yer, mister?"

"Wal, I dunno," said the old man.

He looked almost pleadingly with his one bright eye at his wife. She nodded.

"Yes, yo' will, Ebenezer. Come to think on it, we've got a sight o' money h'yer tonight, more'n we've had in a long time; an' I don't like no dogs howlin' nights, nohow. It's a sartain bad sign. I'm most sho' we'd better load the gun fur this once, Ebenezer."

Mutely, with his deep-sunk eyes, the Frisco Kid thanked her. He tiptoed out of the room to the foot of the staircase. He listened. There was no sound overhead. Even his dog, out in the road, had quieted. It was as if the precaution he had caused the old folk to take in loading the gun had averted some fell fate.

At the top of the staircase, the Kid bumped full into Jerry Mears. He leaped back, terribly affrighted. Had the blind man overheard?

But Mears only asked—

"Has they bundled off to bed?"

"No," gulped the Kid.

"Wal, they orter soon," murmured Mears.

The Kid lay down on the sofa again, and this time prepared to sleep. A certain calmness had entered his mind. Yet for a little, he could not sleep. He watched the cigar in the blind man's mouth pulse and dull by turns, and he listened to the grind and squeak of the sign swinging outside the window. He heard the old man walking through the store below and then, as he locked the front door, the rattle and grate of a bolt being shot.

From far off, above the constant fritinancy of the crickets, he caught a sound as of negroes singing and the thrumming of banjos. And once, from the direction of the river, there came a loud boom as though a gun had been fired or a bank had caved in.

He was falling into a doze when the phoney man whispered—

"Is yo' asleep, bo?"

"N-no," he answered sleepily, and the next moment wished he hadn't.

For he realized, in that moment, the significance of the blind man's question and he thought that, had he not answered, he might have had opportunity to observe what the blind man purposed to do.

Mears swore.

"Dad blame it, why hain't yo'?"

"It's yer cigar. It bothers me, it looks so much like a openin' and closin' red eye."

Mears said no word to that, but stood up and ground the cigar under foot. The Kid saw his form move from the window into the darkness of the room. There was, from the straw-tick on the bed, a dry sound as of rustling papers, then the creak and groan caused by some deposited weight, and then all was still.

Long moments snailed by, the while the Kid listened on tenterhooks. He had been stirred into a new wakefulness. He wanted to hear the sound of deep breathing from the bed; but from the bed there came no sound at all. The singing of the negroes, the stridulating of the crickets out in the night, had died away. Everything was ghostly still. Even the squeak of the swinging sign had dulled.

He heard the cough of the steamboat, once again starting up the river and, as he counted the coughs, so still it was, he began to imagine he could hear the jingle of the small bells down in the hold. The last thing he remembered was the prolonged hooting of an owl.

An odd sound awoke him. For a single breath-fraction of time, so abrupt and startling had been the transition from sleep to harkening wakefulness, he was confused. He thought that the Gay-cat was outside, scratching and softly thudding at the door with his paws. It was a sound just like that, a strangely familiar staccato sound—*tap, tap, tap!*

He remembered then. It was the blind man! He was stealing along the dark hall. He was walking down the rickety staircase. He was stealing down to rob the post-office!

X
AND THE KID MOVES ON

THE FRISCO KID SAT UP.

"Gay-May!" he called softly, and again: "Gay-May!"

There was no answer. He got afoot and went to the bed and felt all over the straw-tick. The little fellow was not there. He was gone. He was leading the blind man!

All his fears flooding back on him, the Kid stood in the center of the floor, listening. The creaking resounded from the rickety staircase, but the *tap, tap* came at longer intervals as though the blind man were feeling each stair carefully with his stick. The Kid knew, then, that Gamaliel was not leading the blind man. Were Gamaliel leading, Mears would not need to tap out his way with the cane.

No; Gamaliel was holding back in fear! He was being dragged along! He was to be used, later on, as a lookout or, perhaps, in finding the cash-drawer!

Like one in a dream the Kid listened and understood all this, and yet, as in a dream, he could not move. For an intolerable time he stood where he was, riveted to the spot, powerless to do aught but hearken.

There was, all at once, the echoing *crang!* of a rifle, and the stairs creaked loudly as under some falling weight, and a kind of moaning breathed its soft painful monotony through the dark.

The Frisco Kid, galvanized, leaped for the door.

"They's got him!" he ejaculated. "They's got Mears!"

A frightening hurly-burly of sound stopped him. He stood nonplused, one hand on the knob. From below there came a frenzied arpeggio of *tap, tap, tap!* The stairs creaked and squeaked as under a foot hurrying down. Came the voice of Mears, shrill, shaking with ferocity:

"I'll wring yo' neck, yo' —— one-eyed pahson! Let me git my han's on yo'! Wheah is yo', wheah is yo'?"

A second rifle *crang!* and the stairs shrieked, and for an eternity continued to shriek, as though some one were somersaulting down their whole length. A concluding and particularly heavy thud, and then silence—silence dark and uneasy, silence broken only by the dull sound of moaning. The signboard outside the window flapped and fretted.

The Kid pulled open the door and hurled himself into the hall. Now he knew who made that low moaning. He dashed down the stairs. Almost at the foot of the stairs, he tripped over a soft form and only a hand on the balustrade saved him.

He became aware, as he drew up, of two things. The Gay-cat was barking outside and there was a loud knocking on the front door of the store. That knocking echoed peremptorily through the house.

He picked up the soft form at his feet. It was Gamaliel. He was moaning dull and brokenly as with pain, and his side was damply wet. The Kid felt that wet on his hands and, a great fear clutching his throat, he rushed with the boy down the remaining stairs.

There was a tremendous crash from the front door. As the Kid reached the bottom of the staircase, the door burst in. A long finger of light streaked from that shattered doorway down through the store. It illumined the form of the old woman hurrying, in white night-robe and slippers, between the laden counters toward the door.

It lighted upon the old man, in hastily donned trousers and shirt, the old-fashioned Springfield rifle in one hand, bare feet wide apart, backed against a glass case at the foot of the stairs and gazing, with horror chiseled on his face, at something which lay upon the floor before him. And it came to rest upon that something on the floor—the sprawled-out figure of Jerry Mears, head twisted unnaturally under him, the cane still clutched in one talon-like hand as if when he fell he had been about to strike, and the swallow-tails of his coat spread out like the lifeless wings of some dead bird.

The Kid stopped at the bottom of the stairs, Gamaliel moaning and bleeding in his arms. He could move no farther. The sprawled and strangely built form of the blind man lay in the way. The finger of light moved about like a trembling digit of suspicion, and then came forward as a number of men entered.

"Thet's him," said a voice. "Thet's him on th' floor. An' thet's his yunkers stannin' thar above him. By Jeber Socks, we'se shore got them co'nterfitters trapped!"

Shaking all over, the old woman lighted the reflected kerosene-lamp of the store. The man who had spoken stood pointing a ragged whip at Mears and the Kid. He was that Dunc' Jenks, in straw hat and jeans, who had ridden to the township some hours before.

Behind him were several men. The one just alongside of him, holding the flashlamp, was a tall frock-coated man, in the middle thirties, with the clean-cut aquiline features of authority. He asked—

"What's happened heah, Ebenezer?"

"I shot him, Kunnel Che'msfo'd. He wah a-tryin' to rob us an' I shot him. An' I nevah shot a white man in my life afo'. Oh, my God!"

The old man was aghast at that which he had done. But quietly the colonel came up to him and took the rifle away, as one might take an object away from the hands of a wax figure.

"It's not so bad as yo'-all think," he said with decision. "This fellow's a counterfeiter and we're after him, been after him for some time. We heard the shots. We were just gwyne on to Dunc' Jenks' place where we thought they'd put up to-night.

"Jenks had invited them to stay ovah at his house just to hold them theah, while he went to town to determine if their phoney greenback was good. We broke in when we heard the shots. He can't be dead. Hear that moaning?"

"But it ain't Jerry Mears moanin', mister," burst out the Kid. "It's this little boy here in my arms. He's been shot and there's blood all over—"

"A little boy!" ejaculated Colonel Chelmsford.

"Shore a little boy!" returned Dunc' Jenks. "This co'nterfitter, has a hull raff o' childern a-wukkin' off his ol' bills fur him."

"Oh, I've kilt the fathah uv a fambly! An' I nevah kilt ennythin' more'n an Injun in my life afo'. Oh, my God!"

"He ain't our father. I jes' met him yesterday and this little feller, Mears picked him up in the flood four years ago, and he's hurt, mister, hurt bad. Won't you save him? Save him, mister, and then yer can 'rest us afterwards."

The colonel motioned the old woman to take the conscience-stricken Ebenezer into the kitchen. Then he stepped across the body of Mears and lifted Gamaliel from the Kid's arms. There was a peculiar staggered look on his face.

"Come heah, Rawlins," he said.

Followed by a tall man with a beard under his chin, he carried Gamaliel into the old couple's sleeping-room.

The Frisco Kid waited with his heart lumped in his mouth, wondering whether Gamaliel was seriously wounded or not, desiring to follow the two, yet afraid to step across the body of the blind man. Some of the men lifted up the body now, and dragged it full into the light of the store lamp.

As they did, something warm and furry darted against the Kid's legs, and whimpered up at him in commingled fright and joy. It was the Gay-cat.

The Kid dropped down on his knees and whispered into those ragged ears:

"It's all my fault, Gay-cat. I tole Ebenezer to load the rifle, and he did, and now he's killed Mears and wounded Gay-May, I dunno how bad. Mebbe— mebbe he's dyin'!"

It was a horrible thought. The Kid rose up and turned toward the closed door of the sleeping-apartment in the rear through which Rawlins and the colonel had disappeared.

As he did, one of the men in the store, Dunc' Jenks, said:

"Looket thet beam in his eye. I nevah remarked it perticklar whin he had his specs on, but I'll be hornswoggled, it does look powerful familiar, naow. Who was it I once knowed had a beam in his eye?

"By Andy Jackson, I know who had a cast in his eye 'nd in the right eye, too! But I nevah thought uv it afore coz he's ruined his eyes altogether, most gone bat-blin' makin' steel dies fo' his ole co'nterfit money. It wah Solermun Baggerly!"

The men ejaculated in astonishment—

"The moonshiner?"

"Baggerly, the kidnaper?"

"Law, I nevah would 'a' knowed him with his glasses 'nd stoop, 'nd his wrinkles!"

The door in the rear was flung open, at that moment, and the colonel burst forth, his face white with some great emotion.

"Men, men!" he called as though distracted. "It's not a boy, it's a girl! It's she—Celestie! Drive down to the house some one and tell my wife! Bring her heah—oh, my God!"

There was a rush toward the room in the rear, a sudden hesitation, and then, shouting incoherently, the men plunged out into the night.

The Frisco Kid stood stupefied amid the whirl of events. Dimly he knew now, of course, that Gay-May had found his folks. But something else was doggedly worrying him.

"Is he—is he bad hurt, mister?" he asked.

The colonel looked at him. The colonel looked at him for a long moment, as though trying to place from what particular crack in the floor he had sprung. Suddenly, as the light of recognition leaped to his eyes, all sublime joy fled his face.

His face stiffened and became swiftly engraved with bitterness. It was as if all he had suffered, since he had lost his child, was congealed in resentment and acrimony at that moment upon the features of his face.

"You!" he snapped. "What do yo' want to know fo'? Yo' stole her away from me, yo' and Baggerly theah four years ago, and now yo've nigh brought her to her death. I know what I did to Baggerly—I broke up his illicit whisky business and caused him to slink into hiding—but as God is my judge, I don't know what I evah did to yo! Yo' clear out of heah. Baggerly's dead and yo'd better clear out, right now, yo' thief, befo' I arrest yo'!"

The colonel stepped forth threateningly. The Frisco Kid slunk away, quite crestfallen and fearful, the dog hugging his legs, the tragic stump of tail snuggling his back. But altogether suddenly, Long John Rawlins appeared at the colonel's side and laid a restraining hand on his arm.

"She wants fo' to see him—thet youngster thar."

"She? Celestie? Why?"

"Beats me. But she's a-beggin' to see him an' his dorg."

The colonel stood aside, utterly astounded. Rawlins motioned the Kid to enter. But the Frisco Kid did not enter. The fact that Gamaliel had proved to be a girl upset all his philosophy of action. Were Gamaliel only a little boy, he would have entered that room with the manner of an elder brother, as one to whom such admittance was not only natural but due.

But Gamaliel wasn't a boy no more! She was a girl, the colonel's daughter, and the colonel was looking on, none too pleased. The Kid felt like running away.

And then, at that moment, sounding like music in his ears, Gamaliel's voice lifted in the room beyond.

"Dern it all, yo' lanky son-o'-a-steambo't-whistle, why don't yo' let him in? He hain't got nuthin' to do with thet pirut Mears. I tell yo' ole Jerry war 'nation skeered o' him 'n' hated him like pizen. Didn't he save me from a tannin' yisterday 'n' agin terday? Why, my golly smoke, he stuck up fo' me like a frien', 'n' he *is* my frien', 'n' now yo' won't lemme see him!"

The child's voice broke in a kind of fretful sob.

"Dad blame yo' all fo' ornery ole rapscallions 'n' Lemuels!" she added fiercely, with all her old manner. "Secret Sarvice er nuthin', yo' let him in, consarn yo'!"

An odd quirk twisted the colonel's lips, as he listened, and he smiled. He smiled down at the Frisco Kid in a new sympathy. Then, with a sudden warmth of feeling, he put his arm about the diffident youngster's shoulder and so, encouraging, drew him into the room.

Gamaliel was propped up in the bed, a pillow at her back, the red bandanna still knotted about her neck, cowboy fashion, and her yellow hair brushed away from her round blue eyes and curling about her ears. Her face was very dirty where she had knuckled her damp eyes with grimy hands. At sight of the Frisco Kid, a glad light broke through the misty storm of those eyes.

"Hullo, yo' ornery ole tramp," she greeted him. "Whar in tarnashun is yore puppy?"

The Kid held the Gay-cat up in his arms. The girl reached over to pat his sharp yellow head, winced suddenly as with pain, and thereat, at her inability to move, grinned bravely.

"Is yer hurt bad, Gay-May?" asked the Kid solicitously.

"On'y a toler'ble light scratch on the side. Hit war the blood what skeered me most, mainly. Jiminy crickets, I thought I war kilt!"

"I jest knew somethin' 'ud happen tonight, Gay-May, and so did my dog.

If Gay-cat hadn't howled and I hadn't tole thet ole man to load his gun, yer'd never 'a' been wounded—"

"Nor nevah 'a' foun' my folks, nuther. Thet's my pappy ovah thar, bo, what's a high-muckamuck in the Secret Service, 'n' my mammy, too, she'll be along in a breaf, they tells me. Hain't this bin the bangdest night evah!"

"Gee, I should say!" echoed the Kid. "When Gay-cat howled this night, the phoney man said some one was a-gonna die, but he never thought it 'ud be hisself at all—"

"Naw. I raiken he 'lowed he'd go on fo'evah, stealin' money 'n' dorgs 'n' kids right 'n' left."

Thus they talked. Then, of a sudden out in the store, there was the sound of quick pattering footsteps, the swish of a dress, and in rushed a handsome young woman with the same glorious hair as Gamaliel's and the same blue trembling pools of eyes. And there was about her eyes, too, that delicate tracery of shadows which comes from many sleepless nights of sorrow.

With a low inarticulate moan of joy, she picked up the child in her arms, and hugged and kissed her again and again. She was Gamaliel's mother.

The Frisco Kid backed out of the room. Something about the tenderness and joy shown by the father and mother, but especially the mother, brought a choking lump into his throat. He could not stand to watch it. Memories rose in his mind—poignant memories of his own little mother standing at the gate near the bush of white marguerites and waiting all these years for him.

He went out of the store, followed by the dog. It was dawn, cold and wide and gray. High in the heavens a few stars fought against the growing light, twinkling brightly and strangely, like make-believe stars in the scenery of a stage. As his body drooped to the long walk, the Kid said to the dog at his side:

"Always movin', always movin' on. Gay-cat, when we gets tired of bein' boes we'll go back to the valley and surprise my ma. But I guess"—with a wistful smile—"you and me'll never get tired of bein' hoboes. We're blowed-in-the-glass stiffs, we are, and it's in our blood."

Adventure Mid-July 1924 Vol. XXX No. 2

CHILDREN of the ROAD

A COMPLETE NOVEL by Patrick and Terence Casey

I
THE PORTUGEE KID'S PUSH

IT WAS A NIGHT OF SUDDEN WINTRY GUSTS. Off along the railroad embankment an empty kerosene can went rattling away with tinny clamor. Down in that famous hangout or jungle, The Willows, pillared high and writhed low among soughing trees, the naked gladness of two hobo fires. Around the one fire eleven tattered figures sprawled; about the others two moved restlessly, gathering wood-chips and broken willow branches for their more meager blaze. There was a presage of rain in the uneasy dark.

The two fires were widely spaced apart. It was significant. That wide interval, the isolation of the lazy many from the toiling two, marked a difference. It was a difference old as the clan. It began when first was fire and the Neanderthal fire-owner clubbed out of his private circle of wood-heat and wolf-frightening light those less than he in strength and weapons and not of his immediate cave. To the lonely two the popular blaze was tabu.

These twain were fake hoboes. Off beyond their scantier fire bulked a covered wagon, lettered in black and crimson, "Bigley's Circus and Congress of Wild Animals"; more remotely, among lanky trunks of willow, a horse could be heard crunching and stamping.

The two were poster men preceding a wagon-show. They worked. That was the disgrace, the stigma. They lacked altogether the efficiency in living without work which marks the blown-in-the-glass stiff, the true hobo article. They were that sort scorned by all good rodeos. They were gay-cats.

The eleven about the popular blaze were most diminutive hoboes in man-sized cast-offs. They were like a pigmy people. There was a curious gnome-like spryness about such movements as they made.

They were road-kids. They were runaway boys who had wandered into hobodom and found its ways sweet. It chanced that they were all one push or following. Their leader and instructor in hobo ethics was a fifteen-year-older called the Portugee Kid. The youngest was Crybaby Kid, nine years of age.

There are many similar road-kid pushes. The boy victim of the *Wanderlust* drifts almost immediately into a certain one of the three categories of road-kids. There is the youngster who hoboes in the company of an older vagrant and in return for his protective strength and sundry lessons in the hobo trade begs for him both money and handouts. Another sort is the lad who unites with other boys and thus becomes numerically strong enough to keep from being preyed upon—so strong in fact as to be able to prey upon others in turn. The third category comprises such as have graduated from either of the two previously named schools and go hoboing masterless and primitively on their own.

It was only on the grudging sufferance of Portugee Kid's push that the two gay-cats were allowed to jungle up in The Willows. The gay-cats were hulking figures, greater in stature and strength by far than any one of the road-kids. But the road-kids had the strength of numbers; they were a pack; and road-kids traveling in pack are vicious as a gang of rats. Gay-cats are as a matter of truth the road-kid's wonted prey. A gay-cat is likely to have money because he works, and that money makes him good pickings for the little Tatars.

A push of road-kids on the trail of a chosen gay-cat is not a pretty sight. Hunting together like a pack of cub wolves, they close in upon their man in some district of vacant lots or in an alley among warehouses. Small boys leap upon him from all sides.

If he resists stubbornly, some kid springs upon his back and applies the dreaded strong-arm. That is the road-kid's standby. A kid upon a man's back, his knee to the man's spine, one arm under his chin—and an irresistible leverage is in operation. A puny youngster applying the strong-arm scientifically can lay a full-grown and husky man flat and gasping upon his back in almost the flutter of an eye.

There was a clattering of displaced stones and then a crashing among fallen leaves. Rushed precipitately down the railroad embankment and well into the circle of road-kids the little ragged-eared yellow dog, Gay-cat. Wise small head cocked to one side, a foreleg raised and slightly bent, mouth open and expectant-eyed, he abruptly halted among the eleven and stood motionless as a tawny metal statuette.

The boys lifted on elbow and greeted him with startled whoops of delight. They knew the dog.

"Ef it ain't the Gay-cat 'n' no foolin'!"

"Hello, youse, ol' hobo, Gay-cat; where's the Frisco Kid?"

He came slowly into the bland firelight. He too wore overlarge cast-offs. The trousers were rolled up bulkily at the bottom; the coat sleeves hid his thin-wristed and dirty hands as in a pair of muffs. He was a meager-framed fifteen-year-older with sun-tanned, childish face in which were deep-sunk tragic eyes, the blue of the gipsying Celt. He had all the seeming of a much younger road-kid, but already had he been graduated by one of the preparatory schools of hobodom. He was a free road-kid.

"Hello, Frisco," greeted the Portugee Kid. "Which way youse headin'?"

The boy nodded round the circle and went at once toward the smoke-blackened kerosene can steaming fragrantly on the fire.

"Headin' north, Portugee," he answered. "Upper Illinois and Chi is on me line of travel."

"Better keep outer upper Illinois, Frisco."

The Kid lifted a moist nose from the open top of the kerosene can.

"Why the orders?"

" 'Cause upper Illinois ain't safe fer road-kids nohow. The roads is all guarded by sheriff's depooties and rubes with shotguns. Me and me push is drillin' south on the double."

"But what's the idee? Is every one turned horstile to boes?"

The Portugee Kid snorted.

"Boes, nothin'! Me and me push shoved through Joliet from Chi yisterday on the C. & E.I., and there was all kinds of excitemint round the State prison—sireens a-blowin' and men all along the railroad tracks a-watchin' with Winchisters. It's some guy wot made his gitaway from stir. Better keep outer upper Illinois, Frisco."

Full strong in The Willows was Portugee's push that night. The Frisco Kid sniffed rapturously the sticky odors from the kerosene can, then directed a look of deferential inquiry toward Portugee. The Gay-cat, dogging the Kid's steps, turned also his little black eyes in wistful interrogation. Crybaby Kid intercepted the mute appeal. He said grandly:

"He'p yerse'f, Frisco. We-uns has scoffed some time ergo."

Portugee Kid spoke a short word to the Crybaby Kid. Crybaby got up from his railroad tie thereat and searched in the litter of old newspapers and empty cans until he found two cardboard biscuit cartons. These he slit down one side and spread out into flat improvised plates.

The Frisco Kid appropriated the railroad tie vacated by Crybaby. The

Gay-cat climbed upon the tie also, putting his pipe-stem forelegs upon the Kid's lean shank and lifting himself almost upright thereby the better to watch Crybaby, his quivering nose going now to the right, now to the left, as he followed attentively Crybaby's every move.

With a flat stick Crybaby heaped one cardboard plate with the meat, potatoes, onions, carrots and bread of the "combination" stewing in the can. He carried it to the Frisco Kid. The Kid sat up and, balancing the smoking mess gingerly upon his knees, fell to eating without thanks or other ceremony. Inelegantly, quickly, greedily, he gorged himself.

Crybaby placed on the tie beside the Frisco Kid a plate for the dog. Curtly and voraciously the Gay-cat attacked the hot food. With low moans of joy he bolted whole potatoes and lengths of carrots and chunks of meat big as a man's fist. Great puddles and spills of gravy vanished at a hurried flicker of his red tongue.

"Say, Frisco, thet's some cute li'l dorg, thet Gay-cat puppy," said Crybaby suddenly.

He was standing over the Kid's tie, watching with serious thought the happily moaning Gay-cat.

"An' wot a gorgeus appetite fer sech a li'l feller! Say, has he ever had the blue ribbings?"

The Kid did not pause in his eating. He shook his head.

"Well, I'll bet now he's had the pedergee; eh, Frisco?"

Again the Kid shook his head. But he felt there was something in all these questions to which he had to answer no, which sounded derogatory to his dog.

"No, he ain't never had the pedergee that I knows of," he admitted; then proudly, "but he had the mange somethin' fierce last summer!"

"I knowed it, Frisco; I jes' knowed he had somethin'. He's some dorg all right. An' smart, too. I'll bet yer couldn't lose a dorg like him. I'll bet yer could sell him an' he'd git away somehow an' foller yer like a good hobo buddy, noseyin' yer out clear acrost the country. A dorg like him oughter be wo'th a heap o' money, don't youse think?"

The Frisco Kid paused in the engrossing business of eating. He looked slowly round the circle of fire-tinged eyes that were watching him with an attention oddly canine and sober. His gaze fixed at last on Crybaby.

Nine-year-old Crybaby was a tiny tad in overalls, faded to an oil-stained cream color, and blue denim shirt open at the babyish sun-burned neck. He had left his ragged cap and man-size coat reposing beside the tie the Frisco Kid had appropriated to his own use. His bright hair was yellow as a new broom. In the leaping play of the terra-cotta flames his face, despite a certain artful assumption of manliness, looked very soft-curved and winsomely infantile.

"Aw, Crybaby," objected the Kid. "What yer beefin' about anyway?"

"Jes' this, Frisco," said Crybaby, leaning over, his large brown baby eyes dull and smoky with covetous desire. "Yer don't wanter sell thet Gay-cat to a stiff like me, does yer? Jes' fer a week er two. I'll git yer real money fer him. An' then he'll come back to yer like I says, noseyin' yer out clear acrost the country."

"Aw, say now, Crybaby. Lay off thet stuff, will yer? I couldn't think of partin' with Gay-cat. Not for no money—not for all the money in the world!"

At that positive answer Crybaby looked as if he were going to live up to his moniker, or road-name. His round baby face showed an utterness of woeful dismay.

The Frisco Kid suddenly softened. He felt the acute stab of sympathy. He saw himself but a few months since, ere the Gay-cat had come to gladden his life, the yearning counterpart of poor Crybaby Kid. Hastily he explained:

"Yer don't understand what Gay-cat is to me, Crybaby. I used to be the kid of Frisco Red. He was a big fat husky stiff, but so lazy and shif'less he would 'a' starved but for me beggin'. He snared me to the hobo life when I was a measly little shaver of twelve.

"For three year, up until a coupla months ago when Gay-cat shoves along, I begged jack and handouts for that stiff. I used to keep him in drink-money regular, 'cause when he was full of booze he laid off some on beatin' me. He were a wonder for givin' beatin's, Frisco Red. I used to ermagine how it 'ud feel without no black-and-blue marks from his shoes all over me. And then along comes Gay-cat.

"He were a measly mongerl that hadn't had nothin' but wind-puddin' to eat and kicks and punches moster his sweet life. He was the leeriest, scariest, most horstile hobo dog I ever seed. He was sich a 'fraid-cat he wouldn't take even a handout from me without scrunchin' down in the dust and whinin' sick-like and thinkin' I meant to hit him, when all I wanted to do was hug his or'nary ol' hobo head. But I snared him into likin' me, and he lost his leery ways, and I erdopted him for my buddy.

"But Frisco Red thought Gay-cat 'ud a-hurt me beggin'. He beat me up somethin' tumble 'cause I let Gay-cat drill right along and didn't try to lose him. He tried to croak off Gay-cat by drowndin' him in a covered hoss-trough near Sac in Californy.

"I turned horstile against Red then; but I never could 'a' had the nerve on'y for Gay-cat. I went at Red like I was crazy with alky. And Red with a razor, too, wavin' it around and hollerin' he'd carve me up.

"First thing, I got that razor. Then I got Red. It were the Gay-cat that changed me and give me the guts to do it. I'd still be a-beggin' and a-slavin' for Red if Gay-cat hadn't come drillin' along. But Red, I sure surprised that stiff. I gives him the strong-arm. I curled him gaspin' for air upon his back in the dirt. All the bums with our push seen me done it.

"Now I ain't no beggar for nobody but me and Gay-cat. I'm a free road-kid and so's Gay-cat, and we likes the life. I wouldn't sell my buddy; no, not for no money. Why ever did yer ask? Yer must be bug-house, Crybaby. Why did yer think yer could buy Gay-cat off'n me?"

Answered Crybaby surlily—

"Aw, I thought I'd git a thousand bullets in good solid jack fer him, thet's wot!"

"A thousand dollars?" repeated one called the Swede Kid, his tow-head silvery and oldish-seeming in the flickering cast of tawny firelight. "How youse talks! Yer mus' be one o' them millionaires er somethin'!"

Asked another, Cigaret Jimmy, significantly—

"Wot brand o' forty-rod does youse most fill up on, Crybaby?"

"Don't youse laff at me, yuh fellers!"

The Crybaby Kid's lips were petulant and beginning to tremble.

"I never meant no hurt to the dorg. I thought mebbe I could buy Gay-cat from youse, Frisco, an' then sell him to Miss Heffernan fer a thousand dollars. She's sold dorgs fer thet much—she tole me so herse'f—and I thought mebbe she'd buy Gay-cat, er else sell him on commission an' hand me the cash, see? I never meant no harm, Frisco an' fellers. I jes' wanted to make some jack, jes' wanted to—"

At length and broken-heartedly the Crybaby Kid began to cry. The derisive grins and continual snickers had been too much for him.

No one noticed, in the sudden chill embarrassment caused, by that faux pas in road-kid etiquette, that one of the two gay-cats about the other blaze had risen to his feet. He was a big slouch-shouldered fellow, smudgy-faced with a week's stubble of red hairs. Stooping as if engaged in the business of gathering wood for the fire, he drew near the circle of road-kids as if to overhear what was going forward.

II

AN OLD ACQUAINTANCE

THE PORTUGEE KID GAVE THE ROAD-KIDS the "office" to lay off the rough stuff. Crybaby was making his whole push look like a regular kindergarten. A cold flash of command out of amber Iberian eyes traveled from face to face and abruptly quieted the boys, even Crybaby, who dared thereafter only an occasional woebegone snuffle. Portugee then turned to the Frisco Kid.

"Don't mind Crybaby," he apologized, a dark flush on his face. "He's on'y been with me a coupla months an' hasn't had much chance ter learn."

"But this Miss Heffernan," queried the Kid. "Who's that dame?"

Portugee was visibly surprised.

"Don't know Miss Heffernan, Frisco? Why, where yuh been doin' yer boin'? I thought every stiff this side o' the Mississipp 'nd specially road-kids sure knew her!"

The Frisco Kid felt a trifle uneasy at his social slip in displaying ignorance. All at once he heard, from far down the railroad embankment, the deep thrumming of an approaching train. On a slap of wind came the spine-tingling shrill of its whistle. He felt glad for the momentary interruption.

Above The Willows, from around an abrupt curve, a headlight burst out like a blazing eye. Ponderously the locomotive thundered along the embankment, shaking the earth, shooting fire between its grinding wheels. Came a long line of dust-raising coaches, shifting with breath-taking rapidity, clacking by in endless persistence; then the observation car, as sudden as the headlight, and a lady in green and a little golden-haired girl looking down over the gilded handrail; and then the train was a fast dwindling beam in the gusty night.

Thick, oily-smelling smoke fell like soot about the boys huddled around the fire. Presently they heard the shrill grinding of brakes as the train slowed down for the water-tank where the massive locomotive would slake its thirst.

Said the Frisco Kid, with an effect of ease and knowledge, at this first opportunity to make himself heard:

"Oh, Miss Heffernan—she's some rich dame then. Must be when she can give a cool thousand for a single measly dog."

"Naw, she ain't so rich; jist comfortable-like," returned Portugee. "She's a ole maid wot lives in Middletown a coupla dozen miles up the track. But she's good ter hoboes. A stiff don't have ter batter no back doors all over thet town ef he knows where she lives. Why, there's boes thet has gone fifty 'n' a hundert miles off'n their line o' travel jist ter throw their feet in her direction. Say, Frisco, how's it no one guv yer the office ter panhandle her when yuh headed this way?"

"I dunno; but she sure must be a good meal-ticket all right, Portugee. Setdowns, I s'pose."

"Yuh betcha. Setdowns in the dinin'-room, waited on by herse'f an' her nigger cook, Mammy Selina. An' sich setdowns—reg'lar farmhouse horspertality! But she don't allow no grown bums ter sleep over in her house. On'y road-kids.

"Tell yuh wot, Frisco, she's plumb crazy 'bout road-kids. She has a iron bed in a li'l rag-carpeted room up under the roof jist fer road-kids ter pound their ear in. Many's the kid wot has flopped there fer a night. Slep' there myse'f oncet, an' so's most o' my push. One o' the bunch was up there on'y last week."

"Thet was me," spoke up Crybaby Kid between snuffles. "I was on me own then; the push ditched me jes' south o' Chi. I made a bee-line fer Miss Heffernan's on a freight headin' south.

"She done treated me royal, all right. Chicken 'n' dumplin's 'n' marmalade on ginger cookies, an' a whole special chocolate layer-cake jes' fer me. I stayed two nights in thet ole whitey bed. An' breakfast in the mornin's— creamy mush 'n' hot cakes 'n' ham an' eggs 'n' three cups o' java afore I blew back to pick up the push.

"She didn't like none to see me go, Miss Heffernan. Kinder hinted round as she wanted to erdopt me.

"Yer see, she'd jes' made a big stake sellin' a year-dale dorg she raised hernse'f to a big gee in Chi. Thet guy must be plumb loco 'bout dorgs 'cause he guv her a thousandy roundy dollars fer thet year-dale. Thet's why I wanted to buy Gay-cat—to git to thet big gee fer mebbe a thousand more. I tole the push all about it when I came back, but the push, they wouldn't believe it.

"Miss Heffernan showed thet thousand right afore my eyes, an' I even seed where she kept it hid. But I ain't coughed none o' thet to the gang 'cause she said she done trusted me. I'm afeered kinder thet ef I tole the gang some kid 'ud blab to the wrong party, like a yegg er strong-arm guy on the road, yer know."

"But this dame don't keep that money hid in her own house, does she?" asked the Frisco Kid, dismayed for her. "She must be a little queer up-stairs."

"Oh, she's queer up-stairs all right," affirmed Portugee Kid. "But she's the nicest, queerest up-stairs person I eversee'd. She lives all alone with about thirty er forty dorgs on the road outside town, an' because she's horstile ter everybody but boes the rest o' the townies look on her sorter like a witch. But they're a mean ornery crowd o' skinflints as 'ud set the dorgs on yuh, while she takes yer in an' feeds yer steak smothered in onions."

"She don't keep them forty dogs in her house, same as her money, does she?"

"Yuh betcha she don't! There's a kinda buggy er hoss-shed runs around behind the house, like the place was oncet a road-house, an' thet hoss-shed is all fenced up with wire screenin' an' the dorgs behind, barkin' like a bunch o' dern fools whenever a stranger comes. Thet's how she makes her livin', raisin' them dorgs; perlice dorgs an' year-dales, mainly.

"She's a queer un, all right. Thet's why she hides her money in the house. Lost some in a bank-failin' oncet, an' she don't trust money out of her sight no more."

The Frisco Kid chanced to turn his head, in flipping away the butt of a burned cigaret. Midway between the two hobo fires and so near that he could overhear every word uttered by the boys was the big slouch-shouldered gay-cat. It was difficult to distinguish the fellow; his outline was dimmed and blurred by reason of his position, remote from either fire in the shadow of the willow-trees.

But the sound of rattling leaves had not come from him. He was standing perfectly motionless, not even making a pretense of gathering wood-chips. As the Frisco Kid glimpsed him, he was cocking his bulbous head to one side in an attitude of harkening.

The rattle of leaves underfoot persisted, and into the jungle, in single file, slouched spinelessly three newcomers. Evidently the trio had arrived on that clamorous passenger train, having ridden the blind-baggage cars or rods beneath until they had been ditched when the train halted at the water-tank.

They were full-grown and husky fellows, all three. Each had a bleak-edged, emaciated, remarkably sallow face, the typical hobo face.

Unlike the road-kids, they were not clad in ill-fitting cast-offs. The forlorn rags of the road-kid are part and parcel of his efficiency. They give his piteous song and dance—his begging story—a certain poignant note of realism, most appealing to the hearts of large-bosomed women at the time of crucial need.

These full-grown, bleak-faced hoboes cultivated another sort of efficiency. It was not for them to look travel-dusty and out-at-elbows. The nearer they resembled in cleanliness and respectability of attire the folk they panhandled, the better for their stomachs.

Each wore black overalls outside trousers and close-buttoned coat. Neckerchiefs were wound about their throats, and on their heads were tight-fitting dark caps. One wore over his overalls a blue trainman's jumper. At the first farmhouse or community to be battered for a handout the overalls that protected trousers from oil-stains and dust of railroading, the neckerchiefs that kept cotton shirts clean, and even the blue jumper, would be sloughed off and cached away beneath a bush or rock-pile.

Forth would they emerge as from so many drab chrysalides, white of shirt collar, clean of trousers and coat. To the suspicious eye of the housewife and even to the cynical eye of patrolman or constable there would be naught to mark them as anything but respectable workmen overtaken by temporary hard luck.

They made at once for the fire of the push. To the road-kids, they nodded greeting with an odd civility that was almost deference. But they had every right to join Portugee Kid's push in common community and to help themselves to the road-kids' stew, as they quietly proceeded to do. No gay-cats, these, to be ignored, isolated and tabooed. Here were three blown-in-the-glass.

The Frisco Kid looked quickly at the gay-cat eavesdropping in the shadows. But the burly fellow had become aware of the Kid's surveillance. Stooping and picking up wood-chips and twigs, he was moving circuitously back toward his own fire. Perhaps the appearance of the three blown-in-the-glass stiffs had added to his caution.

"Who's them bums over at that other fire, Portugee?" asked the Kid suddenly.

Portugee made a grimace of loathing.

"Gay-cats!"

"An' they'd better keep their distance, them measly scissor-bills," spoke up Cigaret Jimmy, as if he too had noticed the eavesdropper. "I ain't got no use fer them gay-cats. We ought never ter allowed 'em ter jungle-up here anyways."

"Well, it was on'y because one o' them bums used ter be a blowed-in-the-bottle as good as yuh 'n' me," explained Portugee.

"But he's gone ter the dorgs now," persisted Cigaret surlily. "He's travelin' with a sure enough gay-cat, an' wot's more he's woikin' like a gay-cat hisself. He's bill-postin' fer Bigley's Circus. See thet hoss an' wagon off ter one side?"

"Which of the two no-accounts do yer mean?" asked the Frisco Kid. "That one I jes' catched inchin' up here, tryin' to git an earful 'bout Miss Heffernan an' her thousand-dollar year-dale?"

"Was he listenin', Frisco? I thought as how he was pickin' up chips."

"Was he listenin'? Aw, say now, Portugee! He were snoopin' round on the edge of the firelight, and his ears was big as cauliflowers an' hangin' out a mile.

"Listenin'? Why, he had his mouth gawpin' open like he was catchin' flies! But he got me when I give him a nasty look, and he pussy-foots it right back where he belongs and no foolin'! That ain't the gay-cat yer mean—the big fat stiff?"

"That's him," Portugee nodded. "The fat one, the strawberry blond."

"What's his moniker?"

"Dunno, Frisco. Haven't hearn his pal call him any yet," said Portugee. "But I'm sure I seen him some time ergo, some place. I know his face, but I jist can't place it. But I'll lay money thet when I seen him last he was travelin' hobo fashion as a real blowed-in-the-glass. How'd I 'a' noticed him otherwise?"

"Mebbe he's some old-timer wot has lost his kid," spoke up the Swede Kid sagely, "an' has growed too fat an' lazy, wot with easy livin' off his prushun beggin', to git by as a hobo alone."

"Er mebbe," was Cigaret Jimmy's conjecture, "he's a old-timer wot has toined horstile ter everybody an' gone in fer gun-work. He's got a ugly face, an' his graft don't look no good ter me. Bill-postin', huh! There's somethin' crooked underneath."

"He looks kinder familiar to me, too," said the Frisco Kid thoughtfully. "Think I'll give him the once over and clost up."

The burly gay-cat who had been eavesdropping sat hunched before the chattering blaze in a gloomy attitude, chin cupped in hand. But under his heavy brows he was watching the Frisco Kid as he drew near, the dog at his heels.

The man's face looked coarse and bloated from the stubble of red hairs on his cheek. His nose was fatly bulbous.

The Frisco Kid recognized with a start that nose and bloated face. So did the Gay-cat. The dog backed away, hair bristling along his spine, a low growl rumbling in his throat.

"Hello, Frisco Red."

The man that had formerly been the Kid's hobo-master did not look up. Morosely he studied a red wood-ember that had been spewed out at his feet.

" 'Lo, Kid," surlily in a voice that throat-trouble or a liking for strong whisky had thickened into an unbelievably hoarse bass.

"What yer doin' nowadays, Red?"

"Can't youse see?"

"What—that tethered hoss an' wagon over there? Workin', eh? But what's behind the bill-postin' job, Red; what's the graft?"

The man put out a heavy brogan and viciously kicked the ember back into the many-tongued exuberance of flame. He looked up at the boy, his small pig-like eyes tinged red by the firelight.

"Wot d'yuh mean, graft? Can't a bloke woik an' play it straight? Where'd yuh git thet stuff, Kid?"

"Oh, no harm meant, Red. I was jes' wonderin', old-timer. Kinder funny to see yer workin', that's all."

Frisco Red grunted sourly. He was quick to change the subject.

"Still got the dorg, I see, Kid," he said in his whisky voice, a leer far from affable upon his red-stubbled face.

"Yuh betcha," was the proud rejoinder. "We're some buddies, me and Gay-cat. We've hoboed some since we left yer, Red."

"Hoboed?" snorted the man scoffingly.

He looked up at the boy with deep calculation in his piggy eyes.

"But yuh ain't never hoboed back to the walley, has yer, Kid; yuh ain't never gone back to yer ma, the leddy in the shawl, wot? I hear she's been a-waitin' fer yer ever since thet day three year ago when yer joined out with thet circus."

The Frisco Kid did not answer. Musingly, with deep-sunk eyes, he stared into the fire. It was not often he thought of home; but this night the long explanation to Crybaby and now this meeting with his old hobo-master had filled his mind with memories. In the red leaping flames of the fire he could see the little cottage clearly.

It was sweet where he was born. Whenever he thought of it, it was the same—always as it had been in the morning when the air was crystal and the marguerites near the picket fence had no dust on their whiteness.

It was up in Grass Valley. Before the damp had got him his father had been a workman in the mines. His mother always gave setdowns to hoboes. Year after year she did that. All the hoboes knew the white-faced little woman.

"The lady in the shawl," they called her.

Always she asked them, in return for her kindness, to look for her baby who was out there among all those lost boys and men.

For him every night she kept a lamp lighted—an oil lamp in the window. That was his room. A hundred road-kids had slept for a night within the pink-papered little cubby. They had told him.

But the Kid did not go back. He felt he never could go back. He knew that when the train shrilled high up on the side of the valley and the sounds dropped down, he would go as he had gone before. He never could stay on.

An urge was in him. That urge had drawn him out of the arms of his graying mother when he was twelve, and after a circus train that had dipped into the little valley to extract its tribute of quarters and the irretrievable tribute of boys. That miserable urge kept him moving—moving to find peace. It was the accursed *Wanderlust*.

A low whine rose from the Gay-cat and the boy shivered out of his dream. Some change in Frisco Red had frightened the dog, for he had retreated behind the boy's legs.

The Kid looked at the tramp. The fellow was sitting up rigidly, his little eyes wide, a startled light in their red-tinged depths. Red was staring as if at something behind the Kid.

The Frisco Kid turned round. Another hobo had entered the jungle, was moving with sharp certitude of stride toward the road-kids' fire. He also must have come in on that recent train. He was garbed with the calculated forethought of the true blown-in-the-glass—black overalls, neckerchief and cap. The cap this man wore was a large affair turned inside out, the yellow silk lining exposed.

He carried under one arm a roll of clothing, the "bindle," tied compactly with a bit of hay-rope. He was hardly a head taller than the Frisco Kid; he stood about five feet eight or nine; but the Kid, watching him from behind, noted the suppressed violence of hip-swagger and arm-swing that told of hidden strength, of vigorous and brisk nerves and muscles acting together in perfect coordination.

The Kid turned to Red with surprise. There was naught about this newcomer to cause alarm; he looked merely the sturdy blown-in-the-glass. Red, he found, had shifted his position. He sat with his back squared to the road-kids' fire, his body hunched forward and head sunk on chest. It was much as if he were striving to conceal himself from the view of the newcomer; at least, by thus huddling, to render recognition more difficult.

In a mixture of feelings, not the least of which was an inordinate curiosity, the Frisco Kid moved rapidly across the shadowy interval between the two camps. He noticed, as he drew near under the flame-burnished willow branches, that the faces of the boys had all gone blank and dismayed. The road-kids were huddled together, exchanging whispers in great seriousness and stealth. The Frisco Kid sat down beside Portugee.

III
STRONG-ARM

THE LATE-COMER WASTED NO TIME in greeting the road-kids or the other three hoboes; nor did he stride directly to the kerosene can to help himself to the remainder of the stew. His brutal, unfinished-looking gash of mouth was set as with a grim purpose.

He cast the bundle of clothing upon the ground within the circle about the fire. Then rapidly, with strong stubby fingers, he began to unbutton the black overalls worn over trousers and coat.

He was a peculiar and rememberable-looking man. His face was not so swarthy as muddy-hued. His nose was short, the cheek-bones high, and his brows formed of very black, distinct hairs.

His eyes were remarkable. They were almond-shaped and of an odd cast of blue, an almost greenish-blue. It was startling, those green-blue eyes in that muddy, black-haired face. They were eyes instinctively to be distrusted. In their green-blue depths were profounds of weakness as well as power. They were the eyes of a religious fanatic, of the cold-blooded criminal for a Cause.

The Frisco Kid leaned close to whisper a question in Portugee's ear. The fellow, as he did, slipped off the overalls and kicked them viciously against the bundle of clothing. He unbuttoned and tore off his coat.

"A strong-armer!" breathed the Kid in a cold whisper of awe.

Beneath the man's left armpit, over the vest, was slung a shoulder-holster. There was a revolver in that holster. Its muzzle set deep and snugly into a round of leather; across the gleaming metal handle, holding it firmly in place, was snapped a springy whalebone. The revolver was high under the man's armpit. But one jerk with his right hand and that revolver would slip out from under the snapping whalebone.

"Sure, a strong-armer," returned Portugee in a cautious whisper. "Thet's the Black Finn, Strong-Arm hisself. I didn't expect him ter blow along, er me an' me push 'ud never 'a' jungled-up here. He's a bad *hombre*, Strong-Arm. He's a ole Ref boy, an' youse knows how hard an' wicious them Ref boys is."

Yes indeed, the Frisco Kid knew. In all his railroading he had met no more case-hardened, brutal and depraved specimens of humanity than those finished products of State reform schools, the old Ref boys. They are like men congenitally perverted to crime. During their most susceptible years, confinement in reformatories causes them to be companions and comrades of older and more vicious boys.

Because most of the older boys have been in lesser jails sometime and because the discipline and restrictions of the schools are so similar to those of penitentiaries, it becomes a matter of pride for the boys to imitate convicts and seize greedily upon prison slang. In a reform school, as in a prison, all guards are "screws" and all clever criminals "good people." The world beyond is "the outside." The boys are forever aping the "real thing," the "one or two time losers," the "zebras in stir."

Small wonder then that when these perverted youths are sent forth into the world, knowing naught else but depravity, brutality and crime, they become the dread of older criminals as well as the police. Older criminals, who have not had the benefit of their institutional education, fear them and their wanton savagery and flee them on sight. The whole tramp world looks askance at each and any of them as at a dangerous lunatic abroad with a sharp knife.

"What's this Ref boy's special line?" whispered the Frisco Kid cynically. "Highway robbery or merely croakin' guys jes' fer fun?"

"Dunno fer a fac', Frisco, but of course Strong-Arm's got his own pertic'lar line. He's a gun-man, yer kin see; but he's kinder quieter and less wiciously murderous than most. I've heard him called various monikers—Strong-Arm, an' the Black Finn, an' even the Big Sab-Cat."

"What! A Wobbly?"

Portugee began a nod. His eyes glued to the thick-set man near the fire, however, he thought better of it.

"Sure," he whispered guardedly; "an I.W.W. I think he's a quick-limer er a bomber fer the Wobblies. I've noticed, whinever I've met up with him, thet most boes an' even other old Ref boys is scared stiff of him. He's no gun to monkey with; jist take thet from me, Frisco. Tell yer wot; I'm jist waitin' my chancet ter give the push the office, an' then we'll all pussy-foot it outer here without him noticin'. Yuh better beat it, too, Frisco."

The man had thrown his coat upon the bindle tied with hay-rope. He had opened his vest. He busied himself morosely, unbuckling a very new and gaudily stitched pair of suspenders. He tied the two long elastic plaits together so that the metal clasps bulged from the knot like knuckles from a fist. Then he took firm hold of the suspenders by the end farthest from the heavy knot. The suspenders were an impromptu instrument of punishment, an improvised but cruel knout.

"Wot's become of thet kid as used ter do Strong-Arm's beggin'?" asked Cigaret Jimmy in a stealthy undertone, as if struck with sudden thought at the man's ominous preparations.

"Who—Chick? Dunno, Cig. Mebbe he run away."

Strong-Arm raised his head. He looked between the trees toward the outer confines of The Willows. A boy cowered there in the shadows. That boy was watching him with a fixed and poignant interest. He had watched him since he approached the road-kids' fire.

That boy never for a moment remained still. Flitting from tree-trunk to tree-trunk with an uncanny restlessness, standing on one leg at a time, rubbing the calf of the used leg with the toes of the other and forever nervously shifting legs, he watched the man with great peering eyes, stark as an animal's with fear.

"Yuh won't do it, Chick?"

There was in the calling voice a tone that showed the man had asked the question before. There was in that voice, also, a certain note which showed he would not ask that question again.

The boy cringed beneath the voice as if beneath a blow. He turned as if to run and hide deeper in the shadows. Then, as if drawn and compelled by the question, he came slinking to the edge of the firelight, his legs dragging as if heavily weighted.

He was about ten years of age. His body was pitifully scant and scrawny. He wore only a thin, faded, red sweater and knee-trousers; and, although it was still April and the weather biting and wintry, he was unshod and bare-legged.

His was the face of a baby, small, inchoate of feature, the great childish eyes red-rimmed from much recent weeping. He might have been brother to Crybaby Kid, the two were so infantilely alike.

As with most children, he was not of a strongly pigmented order; he was straw-colored of hair and wan of complexion. Just now a path of pallor was upon each tear-streaked cheek like a coating of thick rice powder, and his eyes were enlarged and strained-looking with a sickening, abject fear.

"Aw, I can't, Strong-Arm!" he answered in a shaky, fluttering, thin voice. "Yer knows I'd love ter do ut, but I—I jes' can't. I'm too leery. Honest, Strong-Arm, I'd love ter; but I'm leery; I'm scared stiff!"

"Come here!" said Strong-Arm with saturnine finality.

He spread his legs and waited, the suspenders dangling from an idle hand.

Sundry significant whispers and glances had passed between the road-kids of Portugee's push. Without ado, with indeed a stealthy precaution, Crybaby Kid got to his feet and slid out of the huddled circle into darkness. A moment after another road-kid vanished.

It was like a game of niggerbaby. Still another road-kid tiptoed away, and then there were eight. The Swede Kid went next and then there were only seven.

One of the burly, bleak-faced hoboes noticed the Swede Kid soft-footing it out of camp. His eyes followed that slouching little figure as if he, too, should like to steal silently away. But he was more fearful than the kids to move. He was afraid of Strong-Arm taking sudden alarm or anger and maliciously using his gun.

Between Portugee and this bleak-faced blown-in-the-glass sat the Frisco Kid, the ragged-eared yellow mongrel between his knees. The Kid knew that the boy skulking on the edge of the firelight was about to be whipped unmercifully. Why that boy was to be whipped he did not know, nor did any one else save and excepting that man with the fanatical almond-shaped eyes, waiting there so quiet and saturnine. But that was all sufficient.

The branches of the willows soughed overhead. The acrid sharpness of the wood-smoke edged every gust of wind.

The boy came slowly into the bland firelight. He walked stiffly; wooden, brittle of stride. Walking, with him, was arduous labor; he seemed about to fall at every step. He halted once and retreated in sudden panic.

One could see the terrific inward struggle on his quivering, white face. Instinct told him to run away; he wanted, dearly wanted, to run away; but reason and many past experiences told him that to run away would only add tenfold to the severity of the beating he eventually would receive. He came on at a snail's pace, his stiff legs dragging and clogging progress.

The man with the cold green eyes waited. He made no move.

The boy did not look at the man. His wide baby eyes were rigid in a terrible fascination upon those knotted suspenders dangling idly but portentously by the man's side.

Once his abject eyes fluttered up to the Russian eyes of the man. A low plaintive whimper escaped his pouting lips. He stood rooted, unable to inch on a step. He whimpered again and his leaden-hued baby face worked and contorted with the agonized endeavor to struggle nearer those knotted suspenders. He came on at last obliquely, circling forward like a cringing dog.

He halted within striking distance of the suspenders. The man raised his arm; the boy cringed lower in affrighted anticipation of the blow; the knotted suspenders whistled through the air.

The Frisco Kid flinched himself at the weight of the blow. The knot on the suspenders weighed them down and caused them to curl tightly round the boy's bare legs. The boy shook with pain in every fiber of him. He squealed aloud.

The elastic in the gaudy strands stretched with the weight of the knot, then contracted quickly as the strands curled round the boy's legs. When the suspenders lifted again in the air, the flesh showed white where the suspenders had curled, then red where the elastic in contracting had torn away the skin.

Again the suspenders zipped through the air; again the savage red welt sprang up on the boy's thin legs. Five times. Then the boy began to dance about in his agony and scream shrilly in that thinness of voice common to the very young.

The Frisco Kid clutched the dog to him. The little mongrel was trembling; he himself was breathing hard. He knew what that screaming, dancing boy was suffering. Had he not been beaten, often and inhumanly, by Frisco Red when slave to that brutal hobo?

He looked, in a kind of plea, at the Portugee Kid beside him and at Cigaret Jimmy just beyond. They were all that were left of the push. Portugee's swarthy face was stiff with poorly restrained emotion, his amber Iberian eyes dark with anger and an excess of fear. There was a dangerous curve to Cigaret Jimmy's thin lips. He was raging inside and growing more recklessly furious each moment.

As the Frisco Kid noted his working lips, he saw Portugee reach over and tap his hand. Portugee nodded jerkily toward the darkness beyond the fire. In implicit obedience Jimmy rose to his feet and slid out of the firelight. But he paused once to look back over his shoulder at the vicious Ref boy and to place a daring and contumelious set of fingers to his nose.

The Kid's eyes sought, in further plea, the full-grown hoboes about him. The bleak-faced fellow alongside, who had followed the Swede Kid's departure with fearful longing, was rolling a cigaret as if to keep sight of the beating from his eyes, as if indeed pondering deep thoughts. Another was looking on with a dull, almost bovine interest, as if for lack of something better to watch. The third, however, was evincing a real and visible pleasure in the sight.

His wide-spaced eyes were pretty bright, and he was nodding his head at each cruel blow to lend encouragement to Strong-Arm—as if, to tell truth, that old-Ref boy needed any one to egg him on in his brutality! Perhaps the fellow hoped thus to curry favor with the strong-armer.

The Kid knew. The hoboes stood in mortal dread of the Black Finn. Not one of them would interpose to save the boy. He knew he could do naught himself to interfere. Those three blown-in-the-glass about him would not allow him to interfere.

The boy, Chick, belonged to the man who was beating him. He was

Strong-Arm's road-kid, his prushun. It was the Law of the Road that the man should beat him whenever he so minded, however cruelly he desired, and that no one should step in between.

Besides and above all, the brute who was administering the whipping in this case was a notorious and vicious strong-armer. Plain to see, under his left arm, was that revolver in its shoulder-holster. The hoboes about the Frisco Kid were afraid of that man, and especially of his gun. In fear for themselves they would not suffer the Frisco Kid to interfere.

Suppose they were to allow the Kid to interfere, what could he do? Strong-Arm was little bigger than the Frisco Kid, true; but Strong-Arm had a gun. The Frisco Kid knew his type. He would use that weapon at the first show of interference from any one of them. The chances were, if the Kid interposed at all, he would slug him over the head with the gun, then return with redoubled vigor to the beating of the boy.

The boy was screaming continually. He was dancing about, leaving thick, dark spots on the ground where his feet touched. But the man did not follow him around, nor even attempt to curb his backward leaping, to herd him with blows.

The man stood still. When the boy danced out of range, he lifted the suspenders and waited until the boy danced, screaming, back into striking distance.

Once Chick did not dance back quickly enough. The suspenders lashed his tiny face. A streak of white showed full across small nose and cheeks, to change rapidly into a red line of swelling where blood oozed in many pinheads.

IV

THE JOB

SHOCKED OUT OF ALL CAUTION by the fiendish barbarity of that blow on the face, the Frisco Kid made at that to rise. But the bleak-faced fellow alongside him, who had finished rolling the cigaret, shoved him down, a hand on his arm.

The hobo said no word, but he used more strength than the occasion demanded to shove him down. He used that strength to instill into the Kid's mind a sense of fear of himself. He was prepared to back up Strong-Arm. It was dog eat dog. He was afraid of Strong-Arm and his gun and, to protect and safeguard himself, he would attack the Frisco Kid.

Portugee looked at the Kid, his amber eyes blank with a vast and utter surprise. All at once his swarth face broke out into a thick sweat. It was as if he were shocked and altogether shaken by the Frisco Kid's foolhardiness. He turned over abruptly and, on hands and knees, went creeping stealthily away into the darkness.

Chick's frail, quivering legs were pulsing blood from the red welts that stood out like so many malignant boils. Strong-Arm suddenly paused in his inhuman pursuit, the suspenders upraised menacingly.

"Yuh'll do it now, Chick," he insisted.

The boy did not look at the man. He danced from one foot to the other and his screams broke into soft, choked squeals of agony. He could not speak. But he nodded his tiny straw-colored head.

Strong-Arm threw the discolored suspenders upon the ground. He reached over and picked up the bundle of clothing.

"Yuh know what's wanted," he said through the unmoving gash of mouth.

He handed the squealing boy the rope-bound bindle.

"Git there before the twenty-fifth. Slope!"

The boy started off among the trees. As he limped away, he whimpered like a whipped dog.

Strong-Arm wiped the sweat from the back of his neck and from his brow. He felt in the right hand and seemingly unconsciously, for the shoulder-holster under his left arm. Then he looked round at the three hoboes and at the sole remaining road-kid, a challenge in his almond-shaped, cold green eyes. No one said a word nor made a move. Only the Frisco Kid held tightly to his trembling dog.

"Gimme a smoke," he demanded.

He approached with sharp certitude of stride the hobo alongside the Frisco Kid who was proffering the sheaf of papers and small muslin sack of tobacco. But he did not take the makings. There was an uncontrollable gulping behind him. He slewed round, one hand under his left armpit, his almond eyes suddenly narrowed into semicircular slits. The boy, Chick, stood there on quaking legs, the bindle of clothing under one arm.

"Oh, Strong-Arm, I—I can't; I can't," he gulped. "I—I'm scared!"

The red welt across tiny nose and cheeks showed with startling vividness the ghastly pallor of the little face. He looked up at the man, a hideous terror stretching his baby eyes—the distracted terror of an indescribably driven child.

Strong-Arm said no word, but his almond eyes widened with cold malignant light and his brutal, unfinished-looking gash of mouth curved into a frightful snarl. He reached down for the suspenders upon the ground. Once more he curled those suspenders round the blood-streaked, frail and quivering legs of the screaming boy.

The Frisco Kid made an inarticulate sound in his throat. He could not help it. Here was cruelty cutting into cruelty's wounds!

The discolored suspenders dropped from Strong-Arm's hand as if afire. He whirled round. His right hand was again under his armpit, his eyes once more narrowed into semicircular slits.

"Who's coughin' now?" he vociferated through the snarling gash of mouth that never moved.

"It was the dorg, Strong-Arm," spoke up the bleak-faced fellow who had offered him the makings.

"Dorg?" repeated the old Ref boy incredulously, the snarl to his mouth deepening. "Dorg nothin'. Ef any o' youse bums think yuh wanter jump in here, step up. Come on. I'll give yuh the kid's beatin' an' then some."

The challenge, pregnant with vicious threat though it was, sprung the Frisco Kid to his feet. Ere any of the hoboes could stop him, even if they had the courage with Strong-Arm looking on, he was on his feet and making with grim defiance toward the man. He hardly knew what he was saying.

"Lay off that kid, Strong-Arm. I can't stand to see him beaten up that way. I've seen too much of it. *I'll* take his beatin'."

Again Strong-Arm said no word. He stooped and picked up the discolored suspenders. The snarl to his mouth was set as if done in granite; there was cruel calculation in the curving slits of eyes. He swung the suspenders, and the metal knot caught the Frisco Kid full on the face. The dog rushed forward, snarling in turn, hair bristling, fangs bared savagely. He kicked the Gay-cat into a yellow bundle that sailed, whimpering, through the air.

The boy, Chick, for whose sake the Frisco Kid had interfered, looked on at the beating, his puny harassed body shaking with unrestrainable sobs. There was in his red-rimmed eyes such an empty blankness that it was as if the blow across the tiny white face had shocked the nerves of those baby eyes out of all power of expression.

The truth was, his eyes were wide with dumb astonishment, blank with an inconceivable and incredulous wonder. He could not understand why the Frisco Kid had interposed; why any one, in fact, should interfere. He never had expected it.

In the few years he had been on the road, never had the like happened before. He could not believe it true and real until he saw the malignant bruise on the Kid's face where the metal knot had struck and wounded.

The Frisco Kid bent his head between lean shoulders and huddled there under the lashing. He uttered no scream; he did not even dance; but his shoulders burned where the suspenders furrowed his back, and his trousers clung damply to the calves of his legs. He cringed, bit his lower lip, clenched dirty hands and sweated in grim martyrdom.

The suspenders lifted and bit, lifted and bit with a monotonous and cruel persistency. The wide nostrils of Strong-Arm's short nose fluttered visibly in and out with the exertion. At last Strong-Arm tired.

"Had enough?" he snarled.

"Naw," returned the Kid, giving meanness for meanness. "I kin stand it as long as you can."

A momentary flicker of stinted admiration fired the man's narrow eyes like the gleam of steel striking steel. He lifted the suspenders. He'd give this boy all he wanted! But bravado was yeasting strongly in the Kid.

"What yer so horstile about anyway?" he challenged. "What yer want yer kid to do? I ain't a-scared of yer dirty work."

The suspenders dropped to the man's side; his eyes widened and his heavy jaw slackened in a real and sharp surprise.

"Wot!" he exclaimed, and for the first time his uncouth lips moved with the sound. "Yuh'll do the kid's job?"

He eyed the boy with cold, green calculating eyes—eyed him up and down as if judging and weighing his fitness for the task at hand.

"You hearn me, didn't yer?"

There was no warning other than a sharp noise, like the sound of a twig crackling in the fire or the sudden snap of a springy whalebone. The old Ref boy slewed round on the three blown-in-the-glass about the fire. There gleamed in his right hand, as he did, the metal of a revolver. He menaced the hoboes with the weapon. His voice exploded in command—

"Slope, yuh gay-cats!"

Hastily but spinelessly the three got to their feet. Said he who had gloated over the beatings, plaintively:

"But we-uns ain't no gay-cats, Strong-Arm. We'se blowed-in-the-glass."

"Blowed-in-the-glass?" echoed Strong-Arm, a withering scorn in his voice. "Why, there ain't one o' youse has the spine of a fish. It took this road-kid here ter show yuh all up. Blowed-in-the-glass, nothin'! From now on ye're gay-cats, an' youse calls yerselves gay-cats, see? Now, slope!"

The three hoboes shuffled out of the firelight, up the railroad embankment and southward into the gusty night. Strong-Arm watched them go. He wheeled slowly round and, looking between the willow trunks under the flame-burnished foliage, scanned carefully the whole jungle.

The Kid, following his eyes, noted all at once that there where the embers showed the former fire of Frisco Red, there was no longer a covered wagon and tethered horse near by nor any sign of the two poster men. With a quietness come of fear, the two had harnessed the horse to the wagon and driven away. They had been frightened off by the appearance in the jungle of Strong-Arm.

"Here," said that dread personage to the Frisco Kid, sure they were alone, his greenish-blue eyes blazing strangely. "Take thet bindle o' clothes from me prushun, Chick. Today's the twentieth. Drill through Illinois an' up to Joliet afore the twenty-fifth. No stallin', kid; git there by the mornin' o' the twenty-fifth an' be darn sure yuh do!

"Give the bindle to the furnace trusty o' the warden's mansion. The mansion is jist outside the stir. It looks like the commandin' officer's shack in a military reservation—all flower-beds an' shell-walks.

"Yuh'll find the furnace trusty down in the basemint, tendin' the fires. Jist give him the bindle o' ole clothes; he'll know wot's wot. Youse got yer orders. Now slope!"

The Frisco Kid went to the boy and took the bundle of clothing from his hands. The boy rubbed his blank baby eyes; he seemed altogether stupefied by the turn of events. The Frisco Kid was really going to perform the job he so feared! He watched the Kid, a great admiration in his thunderstruck eyes.

The Frisco Kid came back to the waiting man, the rope-bound bundle under his arm. He looked steadily up at the malign eyes.

"Thet furnace trusty must be a pretty thick friend of yourn."

"Wot's it to yuh!" snarled Strong-Arm.

He added rancorously:

"Wot matters to youse is ter git this job done, an' done right. By the twenty-fifth, remember, either deliver the goods er take the consekences. Yer asked yerself in on this deal so ef youse tries any phony play er falls down on the job, yuh'll hear from me. I knows youse, Frisco Kid, an' I'll look yuh up ef yuh acts anyways funny. Besides, I ain't the on'y gun interested in this little stunt. Now last an' final orders—slope, an' slope sudden!"

The Frisco Kid called to the dog slinking round the other side of the fire—

"Here, Gay-cat!"

Then, the dog at his heels, the bundle of clothing under one arm, he went through the trees, up the railroad embankment and northward along the rock-ballasted ties toward Joliet. Behind him, in The Willows, Strong-Arm and his prushun, Chick, were along in possession of the hangout.

V

JOHNNY TINPLATE

IT WAS MID-AFTERNOON OF THE FOLLOWING DAY. The April prospect was chill and gray beneath vague curtains of falling rain. Since that gusty black nocturnal hour in The Willows, when Strong-Arm had beaten so cruelly the boy Chick, the rain had been threatening. It thrummed down now with a brooding, cosmic patience.

There was a brown, dreary road going somewhere through black, empty, rolling fields. As he walked the road the Frisco Kid's worn shoes squashed with sucking noises and spouted tiny jets at each down-put of his feet.

The boy no longer carried under one arm the bindle of clothing bound with hay-rope. Instead he wore two of everything—two coats, two vests, two pairs of trousers, each kind of garment superimposed over the other. One pocket of the outside coat bulged where within he had stuffed a green cap.

That the Frisco Kid should bethink himself of the device of wearing both his own suit and the suit he must bring to the furnace trusty at Joliet was no stroke of original genius. The stunt of wearing two of everything is an old hobo trick, a traditional favorite with the confraternity of blown-in-the-glass stiffs. Besides, the day was sleetily chill.

The little cur, Gay-cat, was as wet and woebegone as the boy. He streamed water from each wire-like spike of dirt-pasted yellow hair. At times the dog dropped wearily behind the boy; at other times he drew a little ahead to point up a quivering nose to the boy and worriedly question him with patient, loving eyes. At one of these times the Kid said:

"Don't take on so over a little rain, Gay-cat, old hobo; jes' keep a-drillin' a coupla miles more. I didn't think it 'ud take us so long—most of last night an' all of terday; Portugee said it were on'y a coupla dozen miles on. But everything will be jake oncet we hit this burg I'm tellin' yer about. It's sure to be the nex' burg, Gay-cat, an' its moniker's Middletown.

"And we won't have to throw our feet all over that burg in the rain. No, siree, bo; we won't even have to toot a ringer or batter a back door. 'Cause that's where Mis' Heffernan lives, Gay-cat, old-timer!"

A whitewashed barn bulked up through the vagueness of rain to one side. The Frisco Kid halted and gave vent to a little whistle of surprise. There was a vividly colored circus poster on the whitewashed boards. It was the depiction of a family of aerial gymnasts, the men in green tights, the women in pink, some hanging by their knees from high trapezia, others leaping from hand to hand through the air. Over the top of it was labeled in crimson letters:

THE SEVEN SCOBOLOFFS
Poland's Premier Aces of the Air

Beneath the lithograph on a wide strip of paper appeared:

**Bigley's Mammoth Wild Animal Show,
Two-Ringed Circus and Congregation
of Twentieth Century Wonders**
Middletown, Friday, April 22

The circus poster, the Kid noticed, was brilliant and glossy with newness. The rain had not yet torn off hanging segments and Irish pennants. It could not have been pasted in place many hours previous to the downpour.

"Frisco Red!" ejaculated the Kid. "That stiff headed straight this way as soon as he wiggled outer sight of Strong-Arm's gat. An' he's beatin' our time, Gay-cat. I'll jes' bet he hit it up along the road in that bill-postin' wagon for all his old hoss was worth while we was countin' them ties."

The boy stood in the streaming grayness, one thin-wristed hand holding the turned-up collar of the outer coat tightly about his reed-like neck.

"But I wonder why Red's in sech a rush to git on. I never knowed him to be so chipper for work afore. Of course, that circus will be here tomorror; but I wonder has he some business in Middletown, some graft what he's pullin' under cover of that bill-postin'."

The downpour boomed a melancholy accompaniment to the Kid's sudden and suspicious train of thought. He was starting on, picking a careful way between rain-lashed puddles that brimmed the ruts of the road when on the sudden he was hailed from a window in the whitewashed face of the barn—

"Come back here, young feller."

The oddly official tone of the command disquieted the Frisco Kid. He saw the huge door of the barn slide open and two men appear. As they stumbled forth, they were adjusting upon their heads gunny-sacks that had been flattened out and then knocked into pointed hoods. It was a protection from the rain for both head and back.

Often the Kid had seen country-folk wearing sack cowls and often had he availed himself in wet weather of similar protection. But of these two men only one was palpably a countryman. He was a hulking fellow in blue jeans and heavy brogans. He carried a shotgun.

The other man, who walked first and who hailed the Kid, was garbed in a conflicting assortment of garments. He wore brown leather puttees and khaki Army trousers like an equestrian or motorcyclist, and faded cutaway coat, hard-boiled collar and black string tie like a Southern colonel. He clutched in one hand a vicious-looking, sizable automatic. Upon the coat sleeve of that right hand, at the wrist, was a large nickel-plated star which threw dim flashes in the rain like a broken piece of mirror.

"The sheriff hisself!"

The Kid's lips fluttered dryly and his spine tingled with unreasoned fright. He swung round to flee. It was a reflex impulse altogether mechanical. Subconsciously motivated, almost instinctively, he felt the desire to run.

The Frisco Kid was a hobo, an outcast. He had learned, through many harsh contacts and disillusioning bitter experiences, to put small faith in the law and justice of that world from which, as a hobo, he was cast out. The appearance of the law in a physical guise was to him like the crack of the starter's pistol in a race. It was the signal for him to take to his heels, to get quickly hence.

The man with the star saw the boy turn. He sensed the subconscious process. He grinned appreciatively through drooping-tailed mustaches.

"No you don't!" he barked. "No use trying to beat it, bo. I've got you dead to rights; and besides the roads are all patrolled up yonder where you were heading."

He raised the snub-nosed automatic.

The Frisco Kid froze in his tracks, standing stiffly upright and paralytically still. He watched the sheriff and the deputy saunter up with eyes that were alone alive in a blanched, bruised face—eyes that were shifty and wary as a frightened animal's.

"A hobo kid!" ejaculated the sheriff, turning to his deputy in surprise. "Why, I thought it was some little runt of an old-timer trying to run out on me."

His eyes came back to the boy and he reached over and, with the snub-nosed barrel of the automatic, lifted aside the flap of one coat.

"Traveling rather heavy, aren't you, kid?" he asked with sudden suspicion. "Not thinking of meeting up with any one along the road, are you, and swapping a suit?"

There was swift guilt in the boy's deep sunk eyes. But he answered stoutly:

"Naw; this is me winter outfit. I ain't changed yet; not till I git south."

"Well, that's the way you're going to head," returned the sheriff significantly.

He looked round at his countrified deputy.

"What do you think of him, Josh? Shall we turn him back the way he came, or slap him as a suspicious character in the Middletown hoosegow for safe-keeping? You see, he's wearing two suits, and he's heading north. That looks queer to me. Say, I have a great mind to vag him. Maybe he's not so innocent as he seems at first look."

The deputy shook his gunny-sack-hooded head vigorously.

"Aw, wot ef he has two suits, sheriff! It's cold enough, I'm here to tell yuh. Walkin' in the rain, he sorter needs two suits anyways. Besides, he can't git fu'ther no'th than Middletown, account of all them citizens guardin' the roads. Jest bundle him back the way he came. He's only a kid, Sheriff Kummer, an' can't be put up to no power of harm. Jest head him so'th, says I."

The sheriff turned to the Frisco Kid without any trace of discomfiture at having his suspicious theories gainsaid.

"You heard, kid? Well, those are your orders. Beat it back south. Upper Illinois is dangerous for your kind. It's the back track for you, boy. Now drill along."

Slumped into the typical hobo slouch, the Frisco Kid retraced his steps. The two sack-cowled ones watched him through the misty curtains of rain until he was far down the road.

Then the Kid reached a point where another road swung in. He turned promptly on his heel and pursued this other fork north again. From the moment he had received his orders he had had no intention of keeping south. He had a job to do and a certain time limit in which to do it.

He had lost perhaps three good hours by meeting with the Johnny Tinplate. It was now coming on evening and a dull wintry dusk. The black, empty rolling fields continued on either hand, and the road was of a fellowship in dreariness with the first he had walked.

The rolled-up bottoms of the double thickness of trousers dragged mud at his heels with every step. The two coats, heavy with soaking, slapped their moist tails against his knees, and wearied and smarted his shoulders, raw from the lashing of the previous night.

The dog dragged wearily behind him as if at the end of an invisible thong. All about, the vague curtains of rain draped the world, and dimmed and toned everything to a chill, dreary gray.

A dog commenced barking ringingly on a remote rise of hill. The sharp clamor, breathing from afar over black, empty fields, was as the voice of inhospitality, speaking of dog-guarded kitchen doors. The Gay-cat halted in his tracks and gave back instant defiance.

"*Ssh!*" warned the Kid, struck with swift fear. "Do yer wanter start somethin', Gay-cat? That old Johnny Tinplate said as how he had men with dogs an' guns all along these roads. Better put the muffler on, old-timer."

Answered from the rise of hill a whole chorus of harsh and challenging dog voices. There were commingled the shrill yelping of terriers and the hoarse baying of some sort of hound. Somberly the throaty explosions rose and fell and then rose again in the intolerable cosmic persistence of the downpour. Browbeaten and heedful at last of the Kid's warning, the Gay-cat put wet tail between legs, and cringed and was silent as the two drew wearily onward.

Uncontested by any sound from the cowed Gay-cat, the barking pulsed dejectedly away. Boy and dog topped the rise of hill. Before them, down the slope, they saw a scattering of red-roofed houses and whitewashed outbuildings squatting low to earth beneath the streaming curtains of rain.

From somewhere far off they could hear a kitchen screen-door banging and banging. Behind certain windows the first lights of evening were blinking up, one by one. Otherwise there was no show of life in the little community of Middletown.

To their left and very close at hand the dogs commenced chorusing again. There was a whitewashed boarding paralleling the road. From behind, the uproar of barking seemed to explode.

They followed the line of fence. As they did, the boarding shook and sagged and resounded with the impact of leaping dogs, as if behind that fence dogs padded along with them, an unseen but tumultuous escort. They came to a graveled driveway above which hung a signboard, the golden letters of which shimmered faintly in the gloom:

Middletown Police-Dog and Airedale Kennels
Rose Lydia Heffernan, Prop.

The Frisco Kid studied the sign.

"Here's the place where our meal-ticket lives, Gay-cat, old-timer."

He proceeded down the driveway which was palisaded by yew that was black as ink in the thickening dark. Through the great rents in the disheveled hedges he could make out a succession of wire-meshed fences walling in a row of sheds at either hand. In those sheds many vague, agile shapes moved restlessly and barked.

At the end of the yew alley was a dimly white building with peaked roof and many tall, lean windows barred by heavy shutters. The house did not look like an old family mansion. What with its sequestration from the road and semicircle of former carriage sheds it had the appearance of an obscure road-house long run to seed.

There was a deep-alcoved entry and an old-fashioned pull bell. Far within the depths of the house the bell jangled remotely at the Kid's behest.

There was a long pause. The Frisco Kid and the Gay-cat stood shivering with damp and cold, and nervously harkened.

The door opened in their face. Said a small feminine voice from the darkness of the hallway—

"You're not Jerrold, are you, naow?"

There was strangely wistful inquiry in that thin, taut voice from out the gloom. The Kid stepped back to the brink of the stairs, his spine tingling with unreasoned fright, his whole being quiveringly disquieted. The moment was suddenly dynamic.

The Kid wet his lips and strove to answer. He wanted to say that he wasn't the Jerrold she seemed to be expecting; he was just a road-kid, only the Frisco Kid and his dog, Gay-cat. But the grip of the unexpected and unexplained was upon him, and he could not speak.

VI
A SETDOWN AT MISS HEFFERNAN'S

"LAWS, NO; YOU'RE SARTAINLY NOT JERROLD," broke out the small voice more freely. "I see that plain naow. You're too little."

The Kid, his eyes become accustomed to the dark, could make her out in the gloom of the hallway. She was a little old lady, her scanty white hair smoothed primly back from her forehead and tied in a compact knot. He glimpsed gold-rimmed spectacles and had the impression of rather bitter and challenging eyes studying him sharply through the coldly gleaming lenses.

The Frisco Kid was an expert moocher. There never was a better hand at battering a back door and begging a handout. But he was wet to the skin, chilled to the marrow with cold, hungry and very tired. He was in no condition to give a song and dance—that is, a good begging story. He tried, but all he could say was:

"No, m'am. I ain't Jerrold. No, m'm."

The truth was he was too taken aback. Her greeting had nonplused him; and now her appearance—those bitter and suspicious eyes behind gold-rimmed glasses—filled him with the heart-sick feeling that he had come to the right door but the wrong person.

This was not the Miss Heffernan he had pictured to himself. Her mouth was pursed in an uncompromising button; she looked the tart schoolmarm type; certainly not the Miss Heffernan so good to hoboes. He hugged the soaked coats more tightly about him and began to shiver anew in formless but bitter disappointment. The Gay-cat retreated behind his legs with a low, miserable whine.

But, as if she had not heard him, the woman went on:

"Little? Why you're only a road youngster. My, but you're drenched. And that little mongrel too, just a-dripping water. Land sakes, child! How did you ever get yourself so wringing wet? Come in, come in! You'll be catching your death of cold."

She spoke rapidly in a sharp, high-pitched, petulant voice. But the Frisco Kid and the Gay-cat did not mind that. Behind those gold-rimmed glasses an odd, soft brightness had appeared in the bitter eyes. It was wonderful. That light in her eyes softened and made strangely tender the thin, faded, austere face. Forgotten was the severity of her tight-bound hair and pursed mouth; she seemed altogether a new Miss Heffernan.

The dog ceased whimpering. To the Kid it was as if somewhere doors had opened to expose a warm fire blazing upon a cheery hearth. And—strange—it was as if his own graying little mother stood upon the threshold, wrapped in her shawl and beckoning him within.

"Don't stand there, a-gawping at me and shivering your little jawbones off. Come in, come in," repeated Miss Heffernan hastily. "But do be careful of tracking your muddy shoes over my nice hall carpet that I swept myself this very day. Oh, dear! And I raiken that silly little dog of yours will be messing things generally, too.

"Couldn't you 'a' thought to tote yourself and that little animule around to the kitchen door in the rear? Most trampers that have been here before and all my little road youngsters come that way. Laws-a-mercy, child, but you're soaking wet. Let's hurry up-stairs and get you skinned out of those damp things."

She took complete possession of the two at once. Ere the Kid could fairly grasp the meaning of all that had occurred he had been personally conducted up the hall staircase to the second story and thence up a narrower staircase into a room. Miss Heffernan lighted the kerosene lamp on the bureau. He saw he was standing near a neat green-painted iron bed in a rag-carpeted room up under the sloping eaves.

Here, from a maple bureau, clean, dry woolen underwear was laid out for him by the quick-moving Miss Heffernan, who talked and talked at a furious rate. From a closet were produced a pair of knee-breeches, a Norfolk jacket and a little shirtwaist such as small boys wear. Also, a crimson neckerchief.

The Kid wondered vaguely at all the preparations. Said Miss Heffernan handing him two crash towels of generous size:

"Here, dry yourself thoroughly with one of these after you've skinned out of all those wet and dirty garments. My lands, but you're dressed heavy. What on earth are you doing with all those clothes on your little body, child?"

"This is me winter outfit, Miss Heffernan," lied the Kid shamelessly. "It's purty cold out on the road, nights."

"Well, well; so it is indeed, pore child. Naow here's the other towel for to rub off that little drowned rat of a dog of your'n. I've heard of your dog from ragged youngsters like yourself who've come to me from time to time.

"Oh, the boys that come and go!" she exclaimed pensively. "Often I think how their pore mothers must be praying for them, and they out tramping the lonely roads."

It was uncanny, the vision that flashed before the eyes of the Kid as Miss Heffernan sighed. The flame of the kerosene lamp seemed to go out; the rag-carpeted cubby with its maple bureau and green-stilted bed vanished as into darkness. There rose before his eyes a bush of white marguerites, clean of dust and sparkling with dew.

Behind it shaped the cottage, and on the doorsill a pale, little, shawled woman. He could see the dimmed plaid of the shawl about her thin shoulders. Her pale face was so near and distinct that he could see the blackness of her once brown eyes.

She looked over the marguerites along the road. She stretched out her arms to him, white arms, pitiably thin. Then she faded from sight. The white marguerites faded. Miss Heffernan was speaking:

"But your dog's quite a renowned character, isn't he? What's his name naow?"

"Gay-cat, ma'am," gulped the Kid, turning his head away a trifle to knuckle secretly one deep-sunk eye.

"The Gay-cat; that's it. Well, you will both feel much better when you are dry and cozy from the skin out. These clothes of Jerrold's may be ruther smallish for you, but—"

"Yer expectin' him tonight?"

The woman looked at him oddly. She seemed suddenly and profoundly alarmed. It was as if he had surprised her in some close-guarded secret.

There was a panicky moment of guilty flushes and fluttering hands. Then her mouth pursed up and she regarded him sharply through the gold-rimmed glasses. Once again was she the challenging school-marm type.

"Who?" she snapped.

"Aw, I didn't mean no harm, Miss Heffernan; honest, I didn't. I jes' thought mebbe yer was expectin' Jerrold ternight, that's all."

She seemed somehow relieved.

"Yes, I was," she admitted.

She nodded reminiscently and her challenging eyes flooded once again with that wonderful motherly softness.

"Every night I'm expecting him, but the years go and he never seems to come. He was only a youngster when he went away; yes, just a wee bit smaller than you be—my pore dead sister, Corra May's only child. Maybe I was hard on him; but Heavens knows it was for his own good. There's nothing like schooling nowadays, child. But run off with a circus when he was only fo'teen, he did, ruther than go to school, and I've been waiting and waiting ever sence."

The Frisco Kid nodded. He understood. Had it not been that way with himself, and was not his own little mother waiting for him up in Grass Valley and, with the wait, slowly graying in her shawl?

He saw clearly that here was why Miss Heffernan was so good to road-kids. In every child of the road that came to her she saw Jerrold as he was when he ran away. She was waiting for Jerrold to come back to her. She was waiting and hoping as the Frisco Kid's own pale little mother had been waiting, for three long years, in the cottage up in Grass Valley where the marguerites were always fresh and white.

"Oh, I clean forget to get you dry stockings. And naow you'll come down as soon as you're ready, won't you, youngster? My old mammy cook, Selina, has been tuck with the grippe and has gone into town to her darter's house for a spell, so you will have to eat in the kitchen, it's so late naow. But there will be plenty to eat, never fear. There is another tramper down there, and I have dinner already on the table."

"Who's him—this other bo?"

"Oh, just a man off the road that is walking to Chicago to get work there, pore fellow. And naow do hurry, child, or all the juices will be cooked out of the food I shall save in the oven for you."

As in her hurried yet prim way she swished out of the room, the Kid went over to the dry clothing laid out on the bed for his use. Curiously he examined the various articles of apparel: the Norfolk jacket, the knee-breeches, the childish blouse, the crimson neckerchief. Panic seized him. As he fingered each garment with dirty, hesitating paws, he muttered:

"Aw, say! What's eatin' her anyway? Aw, say now!"

What flattened him most were the knee-breeches. The Lord Fauntleroy blouse and neckerchief were bad enough; but knee-breeches on the Frisco Kid, a blown-in-the glass, a comet and a hobo royal! Better to eat wind pudding that night and pound his ear against the hard turf behind a bill-board out in the wind and the rain!

He fished, from a bandanna-wrapped parcel of valuable odds and ends in an almost dry pocket, the sheaf of wheatstraws and little muslin sack of tobacco. A cigaret was most necessary to the moment. He drew long breaths of the fragrant smoke into his lungs and exhaled them pensively. The rain thrummed monotonously upon the wooden roof overhead and streamed down the window-panes.

Gradually he assumed a more philosophic viewpoint toward the trials and tribulations of a road-kid's life.

After all, who would see him in the Clarence fancy-dress but Miss Heffernan and that other bo? That other bo was, to judge from Miss Heffernan, only a shiftless no account who worked and hence dared never poke his low-caste nose into the hangouts and jungles where congregated the real aristocracy of hobodom, the blown-in-the-bottle stiffs to which order the Frisco Kid belonged and whose good opinion he cared not to lose. They take the word of such a gay-cat against the stout denial of the Frisco Kid?—any time! Besides, the other suits would be dry in the morning and he could change ere taking leave.

Ten minutes later slowly and hesitatingly he descended the narrow staircase from the attic room. The Gay-cat, foolishly skittish after the rub-down, went with him. But the Kid did not feel skittish. He was too uncomfortable and abashed in the tight-fitting Fauntleroys of Jerrold.

However, as he went down the dark, spacious hall of the former road-house, certain subtle aromas of well-cooked food wafted pleasantly to his nostrils and made him forget a bit of his mortification. Sniffing deeply, his empty stomach beset by quickened sharp pangs, his nose drew him steadily on toward a door that stood slightly ajar.

As he put hand on knob, there assailed his ears the hoarse tone of a man. Either throat trouble or a liking for strong whisky had thickened, and coarsened the man's bass into what has come to be termed a whisky voice. To the Frisco Kid those gruff tones were unmistakable. It was the voice of his old hobo-master, Frisco Red.

VII
FRISCO RED SHAKES HANDS

THE FRISCO KID PAUSED, HAND ON KNOB, and gave ear. Within, in the sulfurous brightness of the lamplighted kitchen, Red was saying:

"I calls yer leddy friend a real calkylatin' an' cute kinder dame—parding the woids, ma'am, but I'm a rough sort, bein' left a orphing werry young an' not given no school in pertic'lar. But thet leddy friend o' yourn is sure wise not ter trust no banks. Banks ain't safe nohow. Oncet I knowed a expert shoplifter name o' Detroit Mamie thet was Mis' Johnny Hep, like thet. She didn't trust no bank safes none, havin' been pals with too many good petermen. No safe kin stand against them electric drills an' the more gineral use o' high explosives nowadays. Money is better tuh home."

There was the rattle of a pot being placed upon the stove.

"That's the very way this friend of mine raikened," spoke up the sharp voice of Miss Heffernan. "She noticed that every time a circus came to town some bank was robbed. " 'My goodness,' she thought, 'sech a state of affairs can't last.'

"Fust thing she knew the banks would all be bankrupted by these robberies, and what little she had would be lost."

"It's me wot knows them circuses, Miss Heffernan, mum. Take this one wot will be here termorrer. There's allus travelin' with them backwoods wagon-shows a lot o' cheap crooks an' some real dyed-in-the-wool criminals. They goes with them shows inter little hick towns an' breaks inter the keester o' the bank safes an' gits away with all the stored-up jack of all them reubens round about."

"But what I can not understand, I declare, Mr. Red, is why these bad men are not captured by the perlice."

"Oh, thet's easy, ma'am. Yer see, these mobs o' crooks is four er five strong. They would be spotted first thing ef they tried ter move round the country on their lonely. Youse knows how one stranger in a hick town makes all kinds of excitemint on Main Street o' a week-day arternoon? So they travels under cover o' the circus. In all thet crowd with a circus, who's gonna spot three er four safe-crackers wot is woikin' as razor-backs er ticket-butchers er the like? A coz, the job's on'y a blind."

"I raiken I understand what you mean. But still it seems to me, Mr. Red, that the constable should be able to detect and capture them in the very act."

"Thet's true, very true; but them crooks play too deep a game fer most cornstables, ma'am. They us'ally has a pal wot travels ahead o' the show two er three days, mebbe as a phony jool'ry man, er on'y as a plain bindle stiff er somethin' sech. This gay-cat spots the fat banks 'n' swell mansions an' draws plans jest how ter rob 'em, an' sends all thet infermation back to his mob. An' then 'bout a couple days later along comes the main push with the circus, an' the last night the circus is in town they pulls the job an' gits away clean in the cold o' the next mornin'."

"Land sakes! That's the same name as the little hobo dog's got up-stairs. Why, here's the teeny Gay-cat naow, dry as toast and his tongue a-drooping with hunger! Go right on eating, Mr. Red; I'll tend to him with a pie-plate full of victuals here beside the wood-box. But, doggie, where's your little master?"

The smell of food had proved too much for that blown-in-the-glass hobo, the Gay-cat. He had waited for the Kid to swing open the kitchen door, until he could wait no longer. Thinking probably the Kid had lost his good rodeo sense, the dog had slipped in through the door, which was slightly ajar, while the boy's attention was engrossed in listening.

It was too late for the Frisco Kid to retreat. He swung the door more fully open and stepped into the kitchen. The bare flooring was sandy white underfoot with the many times it had been energetically scrubbed. The kitchen itself was a spacious high-ceiled and scrupulously clean room. There was a squat, shiny, nickel-plated range in one corner. Adorning the green-painted walls were a loud-ticking clock, a richly lithographed calendar and the yellow-flamed kerosene lamp in a gilded bracket. There in that navy-neat kitchen, seated in the sulfurous lamplight at an oilcloth covered table, elbows squared and coat doffed before many steaming dishes of food, was Frisco Red.

He sat facing the Kid; but he was not looking at the boy. He was looking back over one shoulder toward where in the corner Miss Heffernan busied herself with the Gay-cat. The disheveled red head, the bulbous nose and stubbled lantern jaw were in profile to the Kid. A laden knife was raised in one hand—that knife which alone did service to convey food—and his mouth was open like a fly-trap in a complete and blank surprise.

Wiping her moist forehead with the back of a very clean blue apron, the white-haired old lady lifted from stooping over the dog, turned and saw the boy.

"Sit right down, youngster," she said. "There's a place set for you opposite Mr. Red's plate. Sit right down while the food is hot, and don't worry none about your dog. He's eating here in the corner just like all git-out."

Frisco Red turned cumbersomely. The Kid slid into the indicated seat. The man gave the boy one surly look. Then with dexterous knife he busied himself in shouldering his way through the meal. It was quite palpable that the unexpected appearance of the Kid and the dog had dum-founded his slow wits.

As grimly he gorged himself he glanced from under heavy brows every now and then at the boy. The Kid knew that in his sluggish brain he was morosely turning over the whole situation. Perhaps he wondered just how much the Kid had heard.

There was no sound for a space save the quick munching of two busy jaws and the steady tick-ticking of the clock on the wall. By the time Red topped the dinner with coffee and biscuits, however, he had fairly recovered himself. He looked full at the boy, a malicious leer on his broad red face.

"This yunker here, mu'm, he ain't yer neffee be enny means—the long-lost Jerrold I've hearn so much about?"

"Oh, no, indeedy, Mr. Red, though I do wisht he were, he's so pale and wis'ful like. My Jerrold would be quite a man by naow. It's all of twenty year sence he run away."

"Twenty year! Thet's a long time, ma'am. An', ma'am, I begs yer parding fer remindin' yer of yer sadness; but this young feller is so beatin'ly gotten up I jest thought he must be some relashun o' your'n. He does look fine an' handsome now, if yer don't notice thet bruise on his face."

The Frisco Kid squirmed.

"A very natural mistake, Mr. Red. Those are Jerrold's clothes he's gadding in. Jerrold was a handsome boy, with sech eyes he should 'a' been a girl."

"But you were a-saying as how these bank burglars prepared their robberies, Mr. Red, and how the man that went in advance was called the gay-cat. Naow I should like to know why this youngster here ever gave his dog sech a or'nary, lawless name."

Frisco Red in his turn was confused. His small eyes glanced quick and worriedly at the boy. He did not care to talk of bank robberies and yeggmen while the sophisticated Kid was present. He tried to dissimulate.

"Oh, thet dorg's name is hobo slang. Thet's quite different from crook slang, ma'am. But my, he's a cute, spry little feller, thet dorg; an' wot a fine yaller color! A dorg like him makes a good buddy, don't yer think, Mis' Heffernan? I'll bet now thet dorg an' this magnifercint stranger here hit it off purty thick on the road tergether."

"They are a picture, pore dears," sighed the old lady.

"I'll bet now yer couldn't buy thet dorg from thet kid fer love er money. He's all wrapped up in him, I says ter myself at first glance. I guess he's wo'th all o' a thousand dollars ter thet kid."

"I shouldn't wonder a bit, Mr. Red."

Mr. Red turned round from the table and, throwing one knee over the other, said with a boorish attempt at finesse—

"They tell me, Mis' Heffernan, ma'am, thet yuh sells dorgs fer thet much—all o' a thousand dollars!"

The woman looked at him askance, her eyes sharp with quick alarm, her hands fluttering palely.

"Why, yes," she hesitated confusedly. "Only last week—"

She broke off. Her spectacled eyes went to the clock ticking on the wall. Perhaps it was a subtle hint that now he had finished dinner he had stayed long enough.

"Oh, surely," she began again, withdrawing her eyes hurriedly. "I can sell any of my registered Airedale terriers for a thousand dollars and more."

She glanced again at the clock, removing her eyes only with evident effort. She rose to her feet and, still nervous and agitated, began hastily to clear the plates from the table.

"All o' a thousand dollars!"

Red seemed fascinated by the hugeness of the sum. He too glanced at the clock. The ill-concealed excitement of Miss Heffernan increased alarmingly as she noted the direction of his gaze.

The clock was shaped like a heavy-topped figure 8. The upper circle contained the hands and numeral-ringed face of the clock; in the lower and smaller circle swung the gilt pendulum. Save for a circlet round and small as a dollar, the glass of the lower circle was frosted and opaque. The pendulum could only be seen, every regular now and then, as it swung back and forth past the round clear face. Red appeared to study that swinging pendulum.

"All o' a thousand dollars!" he repeated with great unction, at length dropping his small eyes from the clock to the very obvious relief of Miss Heffernan. "Wot a stake! But here, it's gittin' on ter eight o'clock. I better be a-hikin' toward thet job in Chi."

He got to his feet. It was as if, seeing Miss Heffernan about to wash the dishes, he decided to go, fearing work to do. He put on his coat, which had been drying behind the range, and his shapeless and stained black hat.

Then with an odd and uncharacteristic politeness, he commenced to thank Miss Heffernan fulsomely for her charity. It was a terrible massacre of the English language. He ended with an uncouth parade of hobo gallantry, bowing low and scraping one foot awkwardly.

He turned to the Frisco Kid then, an inexplicable expression upon his red-stubbled face.

"Young stranger," he said, "I wishes yer good night. Yer reminds me o' them days when I was young myself an' wore fine feathers sech as yuh got on now. Good night, young feller; I leaves youse in kind hands, an' very charitable."

Before the Kid could gather his intention he had reached out, grasped the boy's hand in a huge hairy paw, and was shaking it slowly and solemnly. The Kid did not know what to think. His lifeless hand was pumped up and down.

Then suddenly he understood. Red gave him the office. With his index finger he tapped on the back of the Kid's hand twice. It was the secret crook signal, meaning—

"I want to talk with you alone."

Abruptly Red turned then and went out by the screen door into the rain.

VIII
A MENTION OF GIPSY FRANK

Outside, in the night-enveloped open, the rain drenched the world with great, brooding persistency and a far, dull, booming cry. Within, inside the green-painted walls of the kitchen, the kerosene lamp pulsed up wildly and almost flared out as the screen door banged behind Frisco Red, then burned steadily, casting yellow beams over range and table, and pondering boy and woman. The range sang whirringly, and the clock on the wall deliberately ticked as if heavily adding up a sum.

The Frisco Kid abruptly broke the pensive spell. As if his mind were at last made up he shrugged himself and said:

"It's too bad, Miss Heffernan, that Mr. Red must walk the road in all the rain. Don't yer think he could linger in one of the sheds behind till the stormin' stops?"

The woman seemed to start out of profound reverie.

"Why, yes; yes, indeed. I had clean forgot about it raining. I'll call out the screen door to him."

But the kid was before her.

"Lemme go, Miss Heffernan. I'll run after an' tell him. An' I kin tie up Gay-cat for the night out in the shed at the same time."

The screen door banged behind the Frisco Kid. The dog under his arm, he groped through the rain toward where the shaft of light through the screening of the door showed out dimly the carriage sheds in the rear. Behind him he heard Miss Heffernan call:

"That shed right yonder is tolerably empty, only for some straw and a few boxes of dog-biscuits. Tell Mr. Red he can make himself comfortable there until the weather clears off. You make a bed in the straw for the dog, youngster."

The Kid entered the blacker gloom of the shed. Off in one corner he made out a pin-point of light that glowed and waned. It was a cigaret.

"Thet yuh, Kid?" came the hoarse whisper of Frisco Red.

Quietly the boy put the dog upon his feet on the straw-covered flooring.

"Yes, Red."

The man must have been sitting upon one of the invisible boxes of dog-biscuits. There was the scrape of feet. He drew near the Kid.

"What's the lay, Red?"

The boy tried to peer through the darkness up at the man.

"Aw, yuh knows well enough, Kid. I'm gonna rob thet Miss Heffernan ternight. She's got all o' a thousand bucks stowed away in the house. That leddy-friend business was all the bunk. I've got a strong hunch thet thousand bucks is all stowed away, neat as pie, in the pendulum-box o' thet clock. I'm wise, Kid; I'm jerry.

"Wot d'yuh say? D'yuh wanter come in on it? A thousand bucks wot we'll split fifty-fifty. Wot say, Kid?"

"What yer want me to do, Red?"

"Jest lay low in the house an' flash me the office when she goes ter bed. It'll be dead easy, Kid. All yuh gotta do is light the lamp up in thet room under the roof. I kin see the winder from here. Then I'll know everything is jake, an' steal inter the kitchen an' cop thet thousand."

"But she locks up at night, most likely."

"Thet so? I never figgered thet. Let's see."

The cigaret glowed in the darkness; the rain tattooed echoingly upon the thin roof overhead.

"I gotcha, Kid! Yuh kin come downstairs in the night, makin' no noise, an' open the back door fer me. It's the real McCoy, thet idee. Yuh'll be on the spot then when I nabs the pile, an' we kin split right there, fifty-fifty."

The Frisco Kid sensed the deep guile of the man in his persistent repetition of the way they should share. Were Red ever to get his hands upon the money the boy knew he never would share with him, nor any one. To show forth a bit of the clumsy duplicity of the fellow the Kid said very quietly:

"But what will yer mob say, Red? What will they do when they finds yer double-crossed 'em?"

There in the thrumming darkness, the man started in surprise and a little fear.

"Wot mob? Who's double-crossed? Say, wot d'yuh mean, Kid?"

"Oh, I hearn yer ternight, Red. That was a neat ghost story about yegg gay-cats an' petermen, but I knowed yer graft as soon as I cotched two words. Yer gay-cat for a bunch of circus yeggs yerself, Red."

The lighted end of the cigaret in the man's mouth formed slow up and down streaks in the blackness, as thoughtfully the fellow nodded his head.

"Thet may be," he admitted sourly. "But they don't know nothin' about this Heffernan money. I was sent ahead ter look over the hick bank here. They'll come up with the circus termorrow.

"They'll never know I threw the skids under them. Before they gits here, we'll have copped, an' be skeedaddlin' along the road an' outer sight. They'll think I'm jugged som'eres, most like. It's plain as day. Wot d'yuh say, Kid? A thousand bucks, fifty-fifty."

"It sounds like the money all right, Red, but I dunno."

The Frisco Kid was playing his cards. He knew this man with whom he dealt. Had he not been his road-kid for three long, sorrowful years? He knew how sluggish of brain the burly fellow was, how innately cowardly of soul.

"Wot's the idee, Kid; wot's a-botherin' yuh?"

"Nothin' much, Red; on'y why don't yer cop one of them year-dales and sell it yerself!"

"An' have all them dorgs a-yawpin' like blue murder, fit ter rouse the town, an' mebbe git bit in the barg'in! Not me, Kid. Yer knows I hates dorgs. I don't monkey none with dorgs when I kin help it. No; this other stunt's easier. It's a dead cinch, Kid. All yuh gotta do—"

"I wisht it was, Red; but I dunno."

"Aw, wot's the idee; wot's eatin' yuh, anyway? Tell yer ol' buddy. Red'll fix it up, Kid; yuh kin depend on ol' Red."

The man's tone was wheedling. Said the boy most seriously:

"Well, it's like this, Red, old-timer. When I came up to the front door ternight, Miss Heffernan, she says—

" 'Ain't you Jerrold?'

"Them's her very words, Red; the first words she says to me."

"Wal, wot o' thet? Didn't she arsk me the same question, too, come ter think on it? Say, yuh don't make ennything outer thet; do yuh, Kid? Yuh don't think now she was kinder expectin' some one along like?"

Red was suddenly very dependent upon the boy and most anxiously interested.

"That's jes' what's botherin' me. She is expectin' Jerrold ternight. And he ain't no kid any more, Red; he's a big fat stiff, she said so herself. I don't fancy none tacklin' a big fat stiff like her Jerrold, now."

The man was quiet, the cigaret pasted on his lips. The raindrops pelted down overhead, sounding loud in the black silence as if pelting on tin. The dog huddled against the boy's legs and whined softly.

"And that ain't all, Red. But right after yer left, Mis' Heffernan, she says to me—

" 'I hates to see Mr. Red a-walkin' the road in the rain, but Jerrold will be here ternight and he don't like them trampers hangin' round a little bit.' "

"Ternight?" the man repeated blankly. "Did she say ternight, Kid?"

"Them's her very words, Red, old-timer. An' that ain't all by any means. She wouldn't let me keep Gay-cat in the house.

" 'Jerrold don't like dogs none,' she says. 'He calls 'em pesky critters an' can't stand 'em around nohow.'

"So I say as how I was comin' out here for to put up Gay-cat for the night, when all I really wanted to do was to see yer.

" 'Yuh better hurry,' she calls after me kinder anxious-like. 'Jerrold will be here any time now.' "

The man made a swift movement in the blackness as if casting from his mouth the dead cigaret. He stepped out through the shed to view the house once again. The house squatted darkly massive before him save for the bright rectangular band of yellow light filtering through the screening of the kitchen door.

"Wot d'yuh think, Kid?" he whispered hoarsely back to the boy. "Yuh jedge it too risky?"

"Risky? I'll tell yuh what, Red. I wouldn't hang round here one second longer than I had to, ef I was yer. I'd beat it while the beatin' was good."

Slowly the man nodded his shapeless-hatted head.

"Mebbe ye're right. I'm sorter skeered, Kid. But I hates ter split with the mob; I'll only git a quarter divvy ef they pulls it. I wish I could go it alone. But it's too dangersome a job fer one man. I guess I better flash back the dope ter Gipsy Frank an'—"

"Gipsy Frank—who's him, Red?"

"Oh, a mugged gun, the leader o' the mob. He's a bad guy, the Gipsy, but a darned good peterman by all accounts. Knows all the good people, he does; has worked with some o' the best yeggs o' this country. He kin turn off a safe like it was a seegar-box, an' jimmy a winder quicker than look at him. An' plan! I never seed a gun could plan a job like the Gipsy kin. It'll be a cinch fer him ter cop off this place."

The Kid was silent. He could see white-haired Miss Heffernan moving to and fro behind the lighted screening, and there came to his ears above the drumming of the rain the homely rattle of plates. All in a heap and most acutely he felt very sorry for the poor old lady. Try as he would to save her, she seemed doomed to be robbed.

Frisco Red's mob would be in Middletown with the circus the following day. There were at least three other crooks in that mob. What could he do to prevail against such odds and such black fatality? Peering through the darkness, glumly he watched Frisco Red, slouch-shouldered and shuffling-legged, go on round the house in the rain.

He felt a sudden itch in his throat. He coughed violently. Then he bent down over the dog hugging his legs.

"Yuh stay here, Gay-cat," he whispered, his voice sounding unnaturally thick in his ears. "An' if any one comes ternight—if yer notices anything unus'al, old-timer—yuh jes' lift up yer voice an' howl. Yuh'll git a lot of company quick enough, Gay-cat, 'cause there's all kinds of dogs round here."

IX
THE SPIRIT OF HIS ORDERS

THE FRISCO KID WAS COUGHING AGAIN as he opened the screen door and reentered the kitchen. But despite the racking seizure he noted that behind the gold-rimmed spectacles the eyes of the old lady were red and swollen-looking as from recent weeping. She pushed the spectacles up upon her furrowed brow, and, wiping her eyes with the blue apron, exclaimed:

"Laws-a-mercy, child, it's jest as I feared! You've catched cold from all that wetting. Sit right down on the cheer here and skin off those shoes and stockings. I'll brew up a hot mustard foot-bath to drive the cold from your head. And then a little hot camphorated oil to relieve your chest, and you can bundle right quick to bed."

Little old Miss Heffernan, for whom he felt so anxiously sorry, proceeded then to mother the Kid as if he were small and frail as nine-year-old Crybaby Kid himself. The water coming to a boil upon the purring stove, she poured it into a little foot-tub and, kneeling down upon the white flooring, tested it with a bony elbow lest he scald his reed-like legs therein. She draped a towel from his knees over the sides of the tub to hold in the sharply pungent steam. Then with gentle hands she propelled his legs up and down in the medicinal bath, admonishing him:

"Wo'k your feet up and down. That'll cause the mustard fumes to rise and soak through your chilled limbs. And tomorrow you'll feel brash and chipper as a new penny."

She nodded her bowed head slowly.

"Tomorrow," she repeated softly. "And tomorrow you will be out again and walking the long, hard roads, you and the dog. Wouldn't you like to stay here with me, youngster, just for a little?"

She looked up at him, a velvety brilliance in her red-rimmed eyes.

"After a spell you might come to like it here, and then p'rhaps you would go to school and grow into a fine l'arned man."

The Kid understood. She wished to endow him with the old ambitious dream she had held for Jerrold. He did not answer. He could not tell her of the errand he was in duty bound to execute. And yet, constantly reminding him of that errand and of his temporary thralldom to Strong-Arm, he saw whenever he looked that way, his two suits drying behind the stove.

When he had come down to dinner he had left those suits lying in a sodden heap on the rag-carpeted floor of the little bedroom up under the eaves. She had climbed the dark stairs and fetched down the soaked clothing during the interval he was without in the carriage shed, listening to the black villainy of Frisco Red. It was only another of her sweet and motherly kindnesses. But it was what those two suits poignantly symbolized, the mission he had obligated himself to perform, which put it entirely out of the question for him to linger here.

Besides, even had he no errand to execute, he knew he never could stay on in one place. He could not explain to himself the urge for moving, let alone any one else; but thus it had always been since he was a little tyke of twelve and first had heard the call.

But Miss Heffernan seemed to understand!

"It's always that way," she sighed, smiling sadly and yet indulgently. "Boys come and stay a brief spell and then grow res'less as little dogs to move on. In twenty years haven't been able to hold a one. Oh, the mis'able *Wanderlust* that draws the teeny wayward feet!"

The Frisco Kid looked down at the bowed head of the little lady, as she knelt there at his feet and gently aided in moving his legs up and down beneath the towel. He could see the pinkness of the scalp through the thin threads of white hair tied severely at the back in a compact knot. He felt, all at once, as if he would like to hug that old head, so thoughtful of his needs, so motherly to care. He said in a hoarse but gentle voice:

"Yer been cryin', Miss Heffernan. And I hates to see yer cryin'. It's nothin' I done; it's not 'cause I can't stay on; now is it, Miss Heffernan, honest?"

The old lady smiled wanly and shook her head in negation.

"What a child; what a funny little fellow! You shouldn't mind me, youngster. Tut! It is nothing at all; jest the plain carrying-ons of a old woman."

She rose hastily to her feet and went toward the range. In a saucer she heated some oil of camphor for the Kid's chest.

"I thought," persisted the boy, "that mebbe yer expected some one ternight, an' he didn't come, an' it kinder hit yer hard. Yer didn't expect Jerrold ternight, now did yer, ma'am?"

She turned quickly from the stove, fluttering with dismay, as if once again and with uncanny surety he had surprised her in her close-guarded secret. She stood, suspiciously watchful, flushing guiltily, in a constrained silence. Then, as if suddenly determined to trust him with some knowledge which seemed extremely difficult for her to keep from his prying young eyes, she advanced swiftly toward him, saying:

"Why, yes, child; so I did. But not necessar'y tonight; just around this time tolerably, either tonight or tomorrow or p'rhaps the next day. But, laws, it beats me how you l'arned all that, child."

The Kid coughed a little. The sweet, clean smell of the heating oil was pervading the room and tickling his nostrils.

"Well, when I first came to the door, yer asked me was I Jerrold. I thought then yer expected some one, and now when I come upon yer cryin' I thought it was 'cause of somethin' I done, or else 'cause he hadn't showed up."

"That's true; I did ask you that when I opened the door. You see, I have been expecting him for a week naow. And I'm so all over trembly and feverish I jest don't know what to do."

"But how do yer know he's a-comin' home? Has he written yer?"

"No; that's jest it. I don't quite understand; I can't make it out nohow. But men who have come along the road have told me that he should be here this week."

"Men? What kinder men? Mebbe they've been stringin' yer, ma'am."

"Oh, I can not believe that. These were good men, but pore and walking. They were trampers. One came to me about a month back and asked for something to eat; and then after he had done eating he says:

" 'Miss Heffernan, you haven't had word from your nephew in many a year. Well, I have met up with him. I saw him arrested. He was put in jail for another man's felony. He wouldn't expose the other man because that man had been his friend once.

" 'He's a fine fellow, Miss Heffernan; you have reason to be proud of Jerrold. And I wouldn't feel badly because he's in jail. He will be out very soon naow. He's got many a good friend on the outside.' "

"And did he?" asked the Frisco Kid, strangely interested. "Did he git away from stir?"

"I think he did, child, 'cause two days back another tramper came by and said as how Jerrold had got out from Joliet, and—"

"Joliet!"

"Why, sartainly, child; the prison upstate a ways. Why do you ask? Why you so su'prised? Have you heard something, youngster?"

There was sudden burning excitement in her old eyes.

The Frisco Kid fidgeted. His brain was glowing with illuminating surmises of which he never before had dreamed; but, none too certain of his snap judgment, startled himself by the vivid connection between the events of Miss Heffernan's story and those of his own life during the past twenty-four hours, he wondered how much to divulge.

He feared to raise the motherly old lady's hopes lest he should prove wrong and all her hopes be cast down later. He feared more to tell all he surmised, lest he disclose thereby some secret of Strong-Arm and incur that dread personage's ire and vengeance.

"No; I didn't hear nothin'," he stalled.

The poignant disappointment which sharply engraved her old face swept him with pity. He decided all at once to tell a bit of what he knew.

"On'y last night," he added almost glibly, "in a hobo hangout called The Willows where I jungled up with Frisco Red and a whole gang of road-kids, Portugee, the leader of the push, guv me the office as how upper Illinois was dangerous 'cause a loser, a convict, had jes' escaped from Joliet. An' this afternoon the sheriff of the county hisself came outer a barn with a gun in his hand an' shooed me back on a road clost by here. Tol' me to keep outer upper Illinois, he did, an' head south. So I jes' knowed right off he was lookin' for that zebra what had made his getaway from stir."

The woman did not notice that the Frisco Kid had said he had been with Red the previous night. She was too excited to notice such a detail. She hovered over the boy, trembling like a humming-bird over a honey-brimming blossom.

"That'll be Jerrold!" she exclaimed. "He has escaped and is on his way back to me, jest as that last tramper said. Oh, I do trust he has done nothing very wrong in leaving the jail! But the truth is he never should have been put in jail. What a world, what a troubleful world this is! Naow I shall have to have some git-up to myself. That last tramper said I was to hide Jerrold and give him clothes if he needed them.

" 'But he'll prob'ly have changed from his prison suit before he comes here,' the tramper said."

The Kid was silent. He looked down somberly at the knickerbockers and Norfolk jacket on his lean frame. But he did not see those Fauntleroy trappings. He was thinking of the extra suit of clothes and the cloth cap that Strong-Arm had given him in The Willows the night before. That suit and cap were meant for Jerrold. He understood now. He was to bring the suit and cap to the furnace trusty of the warden's house, and that trusty was to give them to Jerrold.

But Jerrold was no longer in Joliet. He had made good his getaway. He was coming to his aunt, Miss Rose Lydia Heffernan. Would it be wise for the Kid to continue on toward Joliet to carry out his orders to the letter and by so doing probably miss Jerrold wide; or should he stay here at Miss Heffernan's, and, fairly certain that Jerrold would arrive in a day or two, be prepared to give up the suit to him then?

"Miss Heffernan, ma'am," he asked cautiously, "has yer got a suit all ready for Jerrold?"

She shook her head.

"No," she confessed. "I'm so tied down here with the dogs, and naow with Selina sick and gone, I haven't been able to git to town."

"Well, if yer don't mind, Miss Heffernan, I'll give yer one of my suits. I've got two of them, yer know, ma'am, and the outside one will fit Jerrold to a T, I'm thinkin'. Yer'll be su'prised, Miss Heffernan."

"Oh, you little muggins, that's so good of you! There are the two suits jest a-steaming behind the stove. But you're sure naow you won't need both suits? It's cold out of night, you said."

"Oh, that's all right, Miss Heffernan, ma'am," said the Kid magnanimously. "It's comin' on fine weather and I'd be changin' soon anyways."

The Frisco Kid was decided. He would remain with Miss Heffernan a few days to see that Jerrold got the suit and his orders were fulfilled. He was taking no chances with Strong-Arm.

From all he had heard that evening he judged Strong-Arm's mob to be a large and powerful one. They had aided Jerrold's getaway from Joliet. They had sent men along the road to prepare and make easy his escape.

He did not believe Jerrold had suffered for another's crime. That was a ghost story built expressly for the old lady's ears. Jerrold was, he judged, only another yegg member of Strong-Arm's mob.

Another thing decided the Kid. Miss Heffernan was to be robbed, he felt sure, by Frisco Red's mob the following evening—the evening of the circus' one-night stand. If he should remain with her he might be able in some way to save her from Frisco Red and that greater menace, Gipsy Frank.

"Miss Heffernan," he said quite boldly, "I think I'll stay on with you here jes' for a while. Once Jerrold comes yer won't mind so much, and then I can be a-movin' along, me and Gay-cat."

She was placing upon his chest a red flannel cloth, warmly damp with the camphorated oil. Convulsively she hugged him to her.

"Oh, you pert little muggins!" she exclaimed. "To think of staying on jest to keep a old woman company! You're a dear, child! Maybe if you do stay a spell you may want to stay all time, for ever and ever. And then I will be so glad and proud!"

Despite all her experience with road-kids, her wistful old eyes flooded with longing and fond hope.

But the Frisco Kid knew he never could stay on. An urge was in him. That urge had drawn him out of the arms of his graying mother when he was twelve, and after a circus train that had dipped into the little valley of home to extract its tribute of quarters and the irretrievable tribute of boys.

That miserable urge kept him moving—moving to find peace.

It was the *Wanderlust*. The accursed *Wanderlust* would never suffer him to remain here.

X

A ROKERBEN IN ROMANY

SHORTLY BEFORE DAWN THE FRISCO KID was awakened by a great commotion among the Airedales and police dogs. Yelping shrilly or exploding in throaty rumbles according to their species, the dogs were stewing and milling round and tumultuously flinging themselves against the walls of their carriage-shed kennels, the groaning of boards and the metallic clash of wire netting adding to the hubbub. The Frisco Kid sat upright in the little green-painted iron bed, his heart in his throat, his eyes wide and dull with fear.

Had Frisco Red already fetched Gipsy Frank and the others of the mob, and come back at this early hour to break into the house?

In sudden craven panic the Kid cowered deep beneath a small mountain of tightly clutched bedclothes. And then as he lay there hushed and unbreathing there came creeping through the frenzied uproar to his ears a heavy undertone of sound from far off. There were the creaking of straining axles and the rumble of heavy wagon wheels, the dull padding of horses' hoofs and the sharp crackling of drivers' whips. A considerable caravan was laboring near along the road.

The Frisco Kid was out of bed and at the window in a jiffy—that small dormer window through which Red had wanted him to signal. Outside it had tired of raining. The sky against the window-panes showed as yet no streak of silver or glow of soft rose announcing the nearness of daybreak. Without, the whole world still swam in a misty sea of blacks and dim grays.

By standing to one side and peering out obliquely, the boy could look down above bulking gray carriage-sheds and black yew hedges upon a short section of the road. He knew it was the road because, snailing along it, he could make out the lights of a covered touring-car followed by a procession of heavy van-like wagons drawn by straining pairs of horses. It looked like the early morning parade of vegetable wagons into a large city.

Each bulky covered wagon bore under the driver's footboard a stable lantern to illuminate the way and another lantern, swinging from the rear axle, to point the path to the fellow next following. By those swaying yellow flares the Kid could see that the vans were all painted crimson and ornately gilded as to cornices and wheels, and that they were driven by high-perched, slouch-hatted and shadowy figures, swathed in blankets, and slumped and swaying over the reins as if dead asleep.

There were barred black openings in the sides and rears of some of the vehicles through which came occasional throaty explosions, deeper than those of the excited hounds, and yelps so shrill as to put to shame the Airedales. In an interval between the wagons there slowly lurched along on massive pads of hoofs three elephants, looking stupendous in the flaring yellow lantern-light and rolling at each stride like ships in a rude sea.

The Frisco Kid made out, at that, the dim letters of gilt below the ornately carven cornices of the wagons: "Bigley's Circus and Congress of Wild Animals." The circus was coming to town!

The old fascination swept through the hobo boy. It was as if he were once more back in Grass Valley and the circus train had rumbled high up on the side of the mountain and the sound dropped down, calling to him, beckoning and urging.

He dressed hurriedly. His own clothing and that extra suit were drying out behind the range in the kitchen. He dressed in the knickers and Norfolk jacket. But he did not mind the Fauntleroy regalia. He was thrall to a compelling glamour. The circus had called to him with its pied-piper voice; and, caring not at all how ill-becoming was his costume, heeding naught, he must answer that alluring call.

The house was silent, the long halls dark, with a feeling of cold. Stealing down the creaking stairs and out of the kitchen door, the Kid went to the carriage shed in the rear and called softly to his dog. The Gay-cat was padding back and forth, sniffing with prolonged questing breaths under the shed door, restless and nervous over the many strange sounds and smells in the night. Noiselessly the Kid swung open the door.

As he went down the graveled driveway to the road he thought he glimpsed the vague, wistful face of Miss Heffernan looking after him from a second-story window. Then, the Gay-cat romping and frisking about him in the moist freshness of the rosy daybreak, he followed the wagon-show into town and on through the town to the farther outskirts.

It dawned a glad April day, the sunshine bright and warming, a fresh, sweet tang exuding from the damp, black fields, birds chattering in the rose-bushes of the old-fashioned gardens and grasshoppers snapping up out of the tangled weeds of the waste lots. On their way through town the Frisco Kid and the Gay-cat were joined by other youngsters and dogs. When at length they reached the circus lot every small tad and terrier in town was on the scene.

Such a scene! What bawling of coarse voices, what cursing and ordering about! What rush and flurry! Roughly garbed men howled frantic commands, thick-studded with oaths, at gangs of ragged negro roustabouts, and these latter rushed this way and that with huge tent-stakes and rolls of canvas, or bent their sweating backs to arduous digging and lifting and pulling on myriad ropes.

The lot was a place of mad excitement and uproar. There seemed no order to anything. Yet rapidly, almost magically, a canvas city raised up out of the chaotic odds-and-ends to confound the lovely Spring morning.

The Frisco Kid watched the white city come into being—poles raised, stakes driven, guys clamped and tautened, canvas spread over all. The smell of the damp canvas, of sweating human beings and of axle-grease, even the animal odors so inseparable from a circus, were sweet to the boy's nostrils. He reveled in kicking up the sawdust spread underfoot, in peering into the barred cages of leopards and hyenas and monkeys as each was backed by its caretaker and driver into place in the newly erected menagerie.

Though razorbacks cursed him roundly and sought to drive him away with threatening tent-stakes the Frisco Kid was in a seventh heaven of delight. Round and round the circular tiers of plank seats in the Big Top he raced, pursued by the excited, happy dog. It was wonderful. The Gay-cat thrilled to the circus as much as did the Kid.

The boxes that served as ticket-officers were hastily put in place; the faded, gaudy banners of the side shows swung down from tall poles on either hand of the midway. Their short hour of frantic endeavor over, a crowd of negro roustabouts engaged in a boisterous game of craps behind a black top, while others lay outstretched in the shadow of the motion-picture tent, their coats spread over them, asleep.

There was a constant coming and going of greasy, unwashed-looking performers. Now and then one glimpsed spangles and tights under long cloaks as glassy-eyed and tangle-haired women issued from the wagons where they had spent a jolting night and sauntered over to the small dining-tent for breakfast.

"Hi s'y! Hi there, me young toff with the yaller dicky-bird!"

He was a pasty-faced, skeleton-framed, thin-haired young fellow in a cheap-looking check suit, a cap and celluloid collar without a tie. He issued from the shadowy entry of a "kid tent" or side show and, beckoning, thus hailed the Frisco Kid.

From his aspirated and nasal accent, the boy knew him to be a "limey" of some kind. Approaching, the Kid was informed that the cheap-jack wanted him to run to the bar of the village hotel for some beer.

"Four or five bottles, s'y. I'll p'y ten cents to ye when yer bring back the byer. I'm thet dry inside I bally well feel like I m'y go off with a puff if I sh'd light a cigarite. An' the Gipsy needs a few swigs, too, or he cawn't go on with his ballyhoo this arfternoon."

"Yer'll be here when I come back?" asked the Kid, accepting the currency note from the man.

"Sure; I'm ticket-butcher fur this bloomin' kid-show. Arsk fur Anzac Pete or the Austrylian, if yer like thet better. Or arsk fur Frank, the ballyhoo blokie, if ye don't see me. Hurry now, me cove, an' I'll give yen ten cents fur to buy lollies. The forenoon parade will be startin' soon and I'll have to be off without me bloomin' drink."

Not until he was trotting back with the parcel of four bottles from the village inn did it strike the Frisco Kid that in referring to the Gipsy and Frank, the ballyhoo man, Anzac Pete had meant none other than that peterman, Gipsy Frank, the leader of Frisco Red's mob. Quickly he made up his mind to ask for Gipsy Frank and not the Australian, once back in the circus lot, in order that he might get a good view of that yeggman.

But pacing back and forth in the midway and thirstily awaiting his return was Anzac Pete. Perforce the Kid could try no such shrewd subterfuge as he had planned, but must hand over the beer to the Australian and glumly receive his commission.

Anzac Pete popped out of the dark interior of the side show a few minutes later. The Kid stuck to him like a brother amid all the hurlyburly of preparation for the forenoon grand parade. Through the offices of the Australian he got a seat in the band-wagon, riding back and forth through town in close company with the music and immediately behind the clowns.

There were seven comical cut-ups in the parade, but only two were really hired as clowns. Anzac Pete, for instance, always marched in the parade dressed as a clown in order to make the circus appear to have a larger aggregation of talent than it really had. Whether Gipsy Frank marched as an acrobat, bareback rider or clown, the Frisco Kid did not know.

All in a blaze of glory the Kid and the Gay-cat came back to the lot as the morning drew on into noon. The boy did not leave the glamorous circus to return to Miss Heffernan's for lunch. He appeased his hunger and that of his dog with peanuts from the shrilling roaster. The peanuts were in payment for another errand; he had run up the main street for paper bags for the peanut butcher.

He munched and listened to the shell workers talk singsongingly of the elusive little pea. He watched the phony grifters wide-eyed as they short-changed and swindled the gathering townsmen.

Time came for the opening of the afternoon performance. The grounds filled with uncomfortably garbed men, and women in sunbonnets, who dragged by the hand awed, gaping children in starched, crinkly dresses. Wary lest any roustabout catch him in the act, the Kid dived under a flap of the main tent; the dog curved his back under and after him; then both clambered up between two lower tiers of seats and sat on the hard boards through the marvel and splendor and surprises of the show.

There were the glittering colorful trappings of the grand opening concourse; the irresistible horseplay of the clowns; the daredeviltry of the aerial acrobats, flying from one giant swing through the air to the other; the dexterity of the Japanese tightrope walker who slid down from the very tent-top. Through the succession of astonishing wonders and spine-tingling thrills, boy and dog watched in fascinated breathlessness, never closing a mouth, unblinking of eye, bewitched, ecstatically transported.

The side shows were in full swing when the Frisco Kid came out after the performance. Followed by the dog, he went slowly down the midway between the two rows of features, missing naught, pausing at each in turn.

He paused finally before that side show which flaunted on a glaring banner the painting of a long-haired, dark-skinned man with enormous blocks of wood in his ears and a severed head upheld by its forelock in one hand. The banner was entitled, "Sabu-Suva the Head-Hunter." There was a platform built out in front of the tent, on one end of which was a box where sat the ticket-seller, none other than Anzac Pete. About the platform strode the ballyhoo man, singsonging loudly:

"Sabu-Suva the Head-Hunter, capshured in the wilds o' Su-mar-tra! The wilds o' Su-mar-tra, ladies 'n' gents, where the teak an' banyan trees grow by the mile. Now on exhibisshun on the inside. On the inside, inside! Ten cents. Ten cents ter see Sabu-Suva the Head-Hunter, a king an' a sultan an' a raja *muda* o' Su-mar-tra. Come one, come all.

"Sabu-Suva the Su-mar-tra Head-Hunter. Carries a shield wot he calls a *kliau*, all decorated with the hair o' all them men an' womens wot he's killed an' scalped. Have yuh seen Sabu-Suva, the Head-Hunter? Now showin' on the inside fur the first time. First time, first time! Step right up, ladies 'n' gentlemin. Ten cents. Ten cents is all we charge."

The spieler was a big, heavy-set man with a broad face of a peculiar swarth hue. His eyebrows met over the nose in a straight black band. He wore no coat. He was garbed in a very pink shirt, black corduroy trousers, high boots and a bandanna round the neck. His hair, beneath the slouch hat, was short and inky black. The Frisco Kid knew him at once for an American Gipsy. He thought him to be that Romany yegg-man about whom he had heard so much—Gipsy Frank!

What puzzled the Frisco Kid was something hauntingly familiar about the man. Somewhere before the Kid felt certain he had seen that broad dark face; somewhere before he had heard those gruff, heavy tones. He strove to place the fellow.

The Frisco Kid as a hobo was an intimate of those other rodeos, the Gipsies. Often had he stayed overnight in some Romany *hatsh* or camp, and traveled a space along the road in the *wardos*, those large covered vans.

He knew the Black Men of Zend, their life and tongue and different ethnic traits. He knew that in the whole country there were only about a dozen distinct families. This fellow he judged to be one of the Hares or the Lovells because the men of those clans are usually broad-faced, dark and thick-chested.

"It won't make er break yuh," ballyhooed the Gipsy. "Ten cents. Ten cents is all we asks, ladies 'n' gents, ter see Sabu-Suva the Head-Hunter. Kilt all them men an' womens with his *sumpitan*, he did, a long bamboo wot he blows arrers outer. A deadly weapon ladies 'n' gentlemin. Have yuh seen Sabu-Suva with his turrible blowpipe?

"Yer last chance, folks; yer last chance ter see a real live blood-thirsty head-hunter from the wilds o' Su-mar-tra. The race is almost distinct 'n' wiped out. Sabu-Suva is the on'y one left o' his kind an' he's showin' now, fur the first an' last time, on the inside. On the inside, inside!

"Step right up, ladies 'n' gents. He wot hesitates is lost. On'y a dime admisshun. Ten cents, folks. Ten cents ter see Sabu-Suva—Sabu-Suva the wild man o' Su-mar-tra!"

The Frisco Kid noticed of a sudden a man in the crowd who seemed trying to attract the spieler's attention. This fellow was obviously a Gipsy: He wore the black corduroy trousers and velveteen jacket, adorned with white shell buttons, so uniform with his race. On his head was a moleskin cap. His hair fell in long, black, unkempt strands over his ears, and pendant from each ear was a heavy gold ring. In one hand he carried a bandanna-wrapped parcel. In his eyes was that stare so peculiar to the Zincali.

Presently the ballyhoo man got the office from him. As he finished the spiel and the come-ons stepped to the ticket-box and on up the runway to start off the crowd he came over to the edge of the platform near the other Gipsy.

"*Latcho divvus, pal,*" he greeted in Romany.

The Frisco Kid sidled toward the two through the hesitating crowd. From his haphazard association with the people of Cales he could understand that gibberish called Romany. He knew that the ballyhoo man had said—

"Good day, brother."

"*Tu shan o didakai jin* as Gipsy Frank?" asked the other. "You are the part-Romany known as Gipsy Frank?"

The ballyhoo man nodded.

"*Mandi shan yek o Lavells,*" he answered in his gruff voice. "I am one of the Lovells."

"*Mandi shan lasho lees o Romanitshel. Mandi av rokerben from o gorgio, Frisco Red,*" the other introduced himself. "I am Louis Lees, the Romany. I come with a speech from the gentile, Frisco Red."

The Frisco Kid understood. The newcomer was a Gipsy of the Lees family who had met up along the road with Frisco Red. And Red had given him some verbal message to fetch back to Gipsy Frank. According to the ethics of the road the man was in duty bound to carry that message as from one hobo to the other. The fact that the message was to be given to another Gipsy made the duty something ethnically sacred and covenantal.

Speaking in their little known language, neither Gipsy worried lest they should be understood by some one in that throng of country folk. Jabbered the newcomer:

"*Besh alay* with Frisco Red *adre o ketchema. Yov pen ratti sig. Jaw te rawni* Heffernan's *apre o drom* outside *o gav. Rawni* has a *dukkerin*—one thousand dollars—*adre o* clock *apre o* wall. *Yov pen* all's *kushto*, but *te* watch out *jukels ta* a *gorgiotshavo. Yov pen yov* thought it wise *te* carry a *swegler ta* be *del-apre te maw.*"

The Kid comprehended. Translated literally, the man had said:

"Sat down with Frisco Red in a road saloon. He said tonight early. Go to lady Heffernan's on the road outside the town. Lady has a fortune—one thousand dollars—in the clock upon the wall. He said all's good, but to watch out for dogs and a gentile son. He said he thought it wise to carry a pipe or gun, and be ready to kill."

"*Del o del bakk!*" exclaimed Gipsy Frank in a kind of grunt. It was the Romany, "Good luck!"

The Cale known as Louis Lees starred away through the crowd.

The Frisco Kid lingered no longer.

"Here, Gay-cat!" he called softly to the dog scratching the earth under the platform.

The man above started perceptibly at the Kid's incautious call, and looked sharply down at the boy. He saw the yellow Gay-cat whisk into view. Then he watched boy and dog zigzag off through the crowd thronging the midway.

"The Frisco Kid!" he muttered savagely. "I'd never knowed him in thet fancy rig ef he had not called the dorg. But wot's thet kid doin' round here? I wonder," he added somberly, "I wonder ef his ole buddy Atlanta Slim's anywhere about."

There seemed cause for fear in his sudden strain of thought. But abruptly he chuckled.

"Wot's the matter with me?" he ended. "Here I'm goin' off my nut 'bout a gun wot's safe in stir fur a stretch o' twenty years!"

XI

THE TALK IN THE GULLY

IT WAS COMING ON EVENING. The smoke of supper-time lifted lazily from scattered chimneys among willows and old oaks. This was the hamlet of Bedford, fourteen miles up the railroad from Middletown.

In a grass-soft gully between the level crossing and the town Frisco Red was brewing coffee in a lard-can over a tiny fire. He had removed from his slouch shoulders a new serge coat and, folding it carefully, had deposited it upon a disheveled clump of grass. No gay-cat fellow-posterman was with him in the dingle, nor covered wagon nor stamping horse. He was altogether alone, cooking his eventide "java."

A passenger train lumbered near from the south, hallooing disconsolately for the level crossing through the hush of the evening. Came a sharp rattle of wheels and the pounding of hurried hoofs on the wooden bridge spanning the gully. Red looked up with bovine interest, to see a two-wheeled cart racing for the crossing, a black-garbed, preacher-like figure standing beside the driver and signaling wildly with a greenish umbrella.

Down by the flag-station that alone put the town of Bedford on the railroad maps the agent threw over his block signal; the locomotive shrilled several times and jerked to a steam-hissing halt; and the preacher clambered out of the dog-cart and dragged a cumbersome carpet-bag toward the nearest dusty coach. With the same precipitation with which the preacher boarded the train, two figures dropped down from the forward platform of a baggage-car and came hurrying back along the opposite track toward the smoke of Red's fire.

The one was a man in overalls, black neckerchief and cap turned inside out, the yellow silk lining exposed. He was medium-sized, deep-chested, solid, built like a boulder. The other was a diminutive shadow in faded red sweater and knee trousers. There were savage welts on the boy's bare legs and a red rise across tiny nose and cheeks. The two were Strong-Arm and his road-kid, Chick.

They paused on the ballast gravel to look down into the dingle at the blowsy hobo and his tiny fire. Red was somberly busy just then, lifting the lard-tin between two sticks from a spot where the embers had grayed to another place where the embers glowed red and hot. But Strong-Arm recognized with a shock of surprise that red-smudged, bloated face. He turned quickly to the bare-legged boy beside him.

"It's inter town for yuh, Chick. Bang the screen doors fur some handouts. We'll chow here in this holler with our old frien', Frisco Red."

Strong-Arm purposely raised his voice as he ended, and the words carried through the still, vaguely gold air to the tramp below in the gully. Frisco Red straightened from bending over the fire. He looked up. The charred sticks dropped from his hands. He stared at Strong-Arm above there at the top of the gully, as if at some fearsome apparition that had risen from the grass-roots.

Chick started off briskly along the track for the village among the willows and old oaks across the bridge. With sharp certitude of stride Strong-Arm came down the grass-slippery side of the dingle, the suppressed violence of hip-swagger and arm-swing telling of hidden strength, of vigorous and brisk nerves and muscles acting together in perfect coordination.

Red stooped for one of the charred sticks and made to straighten the lard-tin in its bed of embers. But his hand shook so that he spilled some of the brownish contents with a loud sizzling, and only saved the can from entirely upsetting by letting the stick remain where he had poked it under one end.

Strong-Arm came close. He removed the inverted cap, and without a word seated himself upon the serge coat Red so carefully had folded and placed in the grass. Red turned around, gulping hard in desperate effort at casual greeting. He saw that Strong-Arm was sitting on his valued property. But as if he failed to notice that, as if indeed he saw Strong-Arm for the first time, he quavered in his hoarse whisky-voice—

"Ef it ain't—the Finn Kid hisself!"

"Strong-Arm's me moniker," corrected the man on the coat evenly. "I outgrowed thet Finn Kid handle years ago, Red, when I quit bein' a beggin' kid for yuh. But it's funny thet me an' yuh should meet up a'gin arter all this time. I guess it's all o' twelve years; eh, Red? Funny, don't yuh think?"

He chuckled mirthlessly as if at some hidden joke, his gash of mouth unmoving, wooden-lipped. Red, watching him with fearful nervousness, forced a laugh also; but there was in that laugh little of ease and naught of pleasure.

There followed a painful interval of silence. The coffee boiled over. Red dug up two short sticks and gingerly lifted the smoking can off the embers.

He fished out a scrap of newspaper from a trouser pocket. Winding this about the lard-tin to save his fingers from being burned, he tilted the piping-hot, brownish liquid into two tomato-cans he had set near by.

"I wonders," spoke Strong-Arm abruptly—"I wonders does my kid, Chick, ever have the notions I used ter have when I begged handouts fur yuh, Frisco Red?"

Red's fingers slipped from the lard-can; he looked up sharply. Strong-Arm was gazing down the road where a cloud of gold-brown dust hung beneath willows and old oaks. He seemed speaking more to himself than to his apprehensive listener.

"But no," he added. "Chick's too chicken-hearted an' babyish. He's scary of his own shadder."

The oblong, greenish eyes turned full on Red, and, recalling himself, the man chuckled.

"It's funny," he explained, "the idees I git, seein' yuh here an' thet kid dodgin' inter them trees. It all comes back to me now, how I used ter feel when I was yer prushun, Red, twelve long years ago."

"Aw, Strong-Arm, I wasn't so wurser!" expostulated the other hastily. "Me, I was allus half-skeered o' youse, even though yuh was on'y a yunker. It was yer eyes, Strong-Arm—them queer, greenish eyes. Thet's why I had ter beat youse up so—I didn't want yuh ter git wise I was afeered o' youse.

"Youse was a queer un," he went on guilefully, as if desirous of changing the subject by gradual means to more pleasant topics. "Yuh was allus listenin' with open mouth to them soap-box spielers an' then comin' blabbin' back ter me about the Cap'talist System an' Indoostrial Freedom an' the Abolitiun o' Wage Slavery, when, needer me nor yuh never held no job more'n a week at a time."

He laughed shakily.

"Youse was a queer un, all right, Strong-Arm," he ended.

Strong-Arm's almond-shaped eyes widened a trifle as if Red had surprised him with light on a forgotten side of his character.

"It's not thet I'm thinkin' on, Red," he said. "No, not thet a-tall."

He went on grimly:

"When I was a measly kid and yuh used ter beat me up black an' blue, Red, I used ter dream of growin' big an' strong overnight and, jist when yuh reached out to grab me, turnin' round sudden an' manhandlin' yuh a-plenty. I had every step of them manhandlin's doped out pretty. And I used ter stand afore them second-hand pawnshops when youse and me was panhandlin' the main drag of a town— Gee, how I longed to git my fins on one of them guns in the winders! Then, at the first kick or blow from yuh I'd have cooked yuh sure.

"And here we be, all met up ag'in," he pointed out. "And I could beat youse up proper if I wanted to, or croak yuh with the gun I've got under me arm. It's like me old dream come true, Red."

The older hobo sat down suddenly. Under the red stubble his face had gone gray.

"Aw, Strong-Arm!" he gulped. "Aw, say now, Strong-Arm, all them's bygones. Youse ain't got no idee o' thet terday! Me, I'd think yuh'd be sata'fied, the way yuh scared the livers an' lights outta me thet time we parted comp'ny back twelve years ago.

"But here," he added jerkily, producing from a hip pocket a small flask of colorless liquid. "Let's fergit all them bygones in a good cup o' coffee royal."

"Alky!" exclaimed Strong-Arm. "Gee, I've been thirstin' fur a drink o' alky ever since I hit these horstile parts."

"But coffee royal's better, Strong-Arm," said Red, solicitous as a salesman. "There ain't nothin' stronger in the booze line than pure alky mixed with jamocha."

He got to his knees and emptied a goodly portion of the flask into the steaming coffee in the two tomato cans. By his swift production of the alcohol he felt he had staved off imminent peril. He handed Strong-Arm one of the tins. The two sipped the hot, brownish admixture with loud sucking sounds. It was surprising how quickly an alien glow came to their eyes.

Strong-Arm lowered the tin from his gash of mouth and began slowly revolving it between stubby fingers the better to mix the ingredients. A dark flush was sweeping the muddy complexion of his face. There was in the heightened green of his eyes an odd and somehow loose quizzical expression.

"Say, Red, old boy," he remarked. "However did us two part comp'ny? I've clean forgot. Yuh say I scared youse. How come thet, an' me on'y a kid?"

An exaggerated look of disquietude and deep chagrin engraved the older hobo's red face. So the timely appearance of the alcohol had not entirely shifted Strong-Arm's thoughts from the past. He was a deal taken aback. But he had made the break and he felt he must go through with it. He took another sip.

"Well, it was the last night we was tergether as road-kid an' jocker. It was on the Santa Fee som'eres in New Mexico, one o' them hot nights thet was clear an' still as a Sunday. At a place called Jarales thet day I had give yuh an all-round good whalin' 'cause yuh had got a setdown from one o' the waitresses in a Harvey House without comin' back with no handout fer me.

"We was holdin' down the decks an' bumpers of a freight, an' the shacks was sure horstile; the hull train-crew was on the jump ter ditch us off. At each stop—an' thet fool rattler slowed up fer every water-tank an' cluster o' adobes—we was forced ter dodge about from cow-catcher to caboose an' run ahead till she swung inter high. Yuh knows it wasn't no fun on a hot night. An' the worst of it was it was so blamed bright an' moonlighty them brakies didn't need to carry no lanterns ter smell yer out, but could sneak up on yuh without a sound.

"I remimber at one water-tower I was purty near corralled between the engine-crew runnin' down from for'rd an' the shacks comin' up from the caboose. I crawled under a cattle-car as ef ter try the rods fer a change. But I was afeered the crew had seed me, which it toined out they hadn't, an' I kept goin', oncet I was under, until I climbed out t'other side. Jest as she started clackin' on I grabbed an iron ladder alongside and swung up an' decked her.

"But I didn't stay put on the top o' thet hoss-car; not me. I was afeered them shacks had glimmed me. I wint crawlin' for'rd an' was jest gonna dive to the nex' car ahead when I see'd yuh, the Finn Kid, ridin' down below between them two cars, yer legs spread out on the two bumpers. I don't know why I didn't holler ter yer, but mebbe it was 'cause I was so scared o' rousin' them shacks.

"The shacks must 'a' passed yer by, they was so hot arter me, and besides yer was so small an' shaddery—yuh was on'y 'bout fourteen at the time. I flattened out an' looked down at yer over the edge. An' all ter oncet I seed yuh take out from yer overalls pocket a iron couplin'-pin yuh must 'a' jest picked up at thet last stop, an' a piece o' cord yuh must 'a' got, I don't know wheres. But I couldn't 'a' hollered then ef yer paid me, 'cause I began ter git a awful hunch wot yer was up to.

"Yuh tied one end o' thet line to the eye in the couplin'-pin an' then yer paid it out, down between the bumpers till it was jouncin' about right beneath the rods of the car behind, where yuh thought I was ridin'. Back an' forth yuh paid it, lettin' the roadbed an' the speed o' thet rattler bounce it up 'n' down. I could hear it bangin' the wooden bottom o' thet cattle-car an' makin' all them hosses inside stamp an' snort with fright. Ef I was where yuh thought I was, ridin' them rods, it would 'a' sure mashed me to a quince jelly.

" 'Thet's how I sarves youse, Frisco Red, fer all the beatin' yuh've giv me!' I hearn yuh say. 'Take a little mashin' yerse'f, you lousy bum!'

"To my last day I'll never fergit yer words nor the cool way youse played with the line on thet bangin', smashin' couplin'-pin. It seems ter me now thet I glimpsed yer eyes, an' they was cold an' green an' kinder fishy. An' yer was on'y a little shadder o' a kid at the time!

"But me, I see'd the no-good badness was in yer an' I was hep yer sure was no road-kid fer me to be travelin' with chummy. At the nex' stop down I crawls real quiet-like from the top o' thet cattle-car an' without no last handshake nor *adios*, off I beats it as fast as I could hike from thet train an' youse."

It was noticeable, as he finished, that the visualization and recital of the uncouth incidents had had a sobering effect upon Frisco Red. He paused as if astounded at his own temerity in relating the story and studied Strong-Arm from under unkempt brows as if wondering with some dread just what the result would be on that personage.

Strong-Arm finished his drink in one long quaff.

"I remember now," he said, an alcoholic, malicious leer widening his gash of mouth. "And I remember too thet when, months later, I l'arned yuh was alive and kickin' an' hadn't been under thet hoss-car a-tall, I was so plumb disapp'inted I jist sat down an' bawled me eyes out."

"Aw, I wasn't so worser!" repeated Red almost plaintively. "Me, I was mighty sorry youse toined ag'in' me as yuh did. Yuh wouldn't 'a' fallen inter bad comp'ny an' been sent to the Ref to l'arn real badness, Strong-Arm, if youse had stuck to ol' Red. I tell yuh, I tuck to yuh like glue when youse was the Finn Kid an' my prushun—"

"Cut the bull, Red," savagely. "An' yuh needn't git so scared an' trembly. Me, I'm out arter bigger game than beatin' up an old whisky-soaked bum fur revenge. Remember the kid what used ter gawp at them soap-box orators? Well, he's trampin' out the Vintage o' the Lawd terday, Red, workin' fur the great Day o' Universal Brotherhood to come!"

There was a swift fanatical light in the greenish eyes of Strong-Arm.

"Ye're a funny bloke," said Red shakily. "Sometimes yuh spiel like a sky-pilot er a Galway. Yer ain't—yer ain't toined Salvationist, has yuh, Strong-Arm?"

In Red's quavering voice was strange hope.

The other swore. The alcohol he had imbibed seemed rather to have fretted than smoothed the natural bile in the man.

"Me, Strong-Arm, the Big Sab-Cat, out fer the choich, the product an' bulwark o' the System!"

He laughed harshly at the idea.

"I'll tell the cock-eyed world I ain't! I'm out for the One Big Union, the Greatest Thing on Earth, the Industrial Workers of the World!"

Something of drunken braggadocio had entered Strong-Arm. Red looked askance at him out of the ends of his small, piggy eyes.

"A Wobbly, Strong-Arm?"

"Sure, a Wobbly, an I.W.W., a carrier o' the red card thet will yet be the flag o' industrial freedom fer the world! There's no White Cat about me, no quick-limin' of the boots of scissor-bills what don't know enough about their own welfare to jine the Union, an' sech small sabotage as thet. I'm done even with the Black Cat stuff, the Big Sabotage of the Wobblies, with pencils of sulfate fur the hay-ricks in the sun and blocks o' phosphorus fer the wine-cellars an' munition plants an' places sech-like thet are a bit damp. Me, I'm the Avenging Angel o' the Wobblies!"

It was a dramatic statement. Frisco Red wet his dry stubbled lips.

"The Avengin' Angel o' the Wobblies!" he repeated in a thick whisper of awe. "Strong-Arm, wot's thet?"

Strong-Arm leaned closer to the blowsy, red-bearded hobo. His long, greenish eyes looked bloodshot in the dying firelight.

"Listen, Red," he confided. "The Govamint is makin' up a list o' all the stool-pigeons in the Wobbly ranks. The idee is fer all the private detective agencies in the country to toin in the names of the snitches they has workin' amongst us. Yuh knows there is a number of stools—I seen some as high as secretaries of locals—an' they is usu'lly the wurst Reds of us all. They has ter be to keep their hands dark an' ward off suspicion. But they egg on the others an' then toin them in fur the rewards.

"The govamint knows this. It wants to hold down them stools somewhat, but mainly it wants ter be able to put its finger on the snitches whenever anything starts in any part of the country. Then the snitches kin toin up the real Reds.

"Now somewheres there's a list of them stools bein' made up. Thet's what I'm workin' on. I wanta git hold of thet list.

"Doublin' Bob—yuh know, the old nearsighted chemist an' bomb-maker o' the Wobblies—holds thet the list ain't in the headquarters o' the Secret Sarvice in Washington. He says thet somewheres, in some town like Orleans or St. Louie, far from Washington, there is some quiet slick old man livin' alone. A secret agent, but nobody knows thet, not even his sarvant, an' nobody visits him. He don't receive no telegrams nor letters. But every mornin' he comes out to his front door an' picks up the bottle o' milk an' the mornin' paper waitin' outside on the porch. Inside thet paper, within the wrapper, Doublin' Bob claims, there is sometimes a number o' names to be added to the list of snitches. The old man is makin' up an' in persession of the entire list. Thet's Doublin' Bob's idee.

"But me, I don't put much stock in thet. I believe there is a safe somewheres, mebby in Washington itself in the very inner rooms o' the Secret Sarvice—a safe containin' the names of all them stools—a safe to crack.

"And I got the man ter do the job! Red, d'yuh know this zebra what escaped from Joliet? He's one of the two slickest petermen in the hull country. Me, Strong-Arm, ingineered his gitaway from stir!"

"Youse, Strong-Arm!" gasped Red.

"Yes, me. An' the hull Wobbly crew is behind me. This escaped gun is the little old sandpaper-fingered boy what'll break the keester fur me and git them names. Once I put hands on them names, Red, won't there be a cleanin' in the House o' the Wobblies!"

Strong-Arm's muddy-complexioned face was flushed with passion; his red-tinged greenish eyes were glowing wildly.

"It'll be work to do, Frisco Red—cold, bloody, nasty work! But the

House o' the Wobblies must be swept clean o' all them blood-fattened spiders an' their dirty webs. Strong-Arm, the Black Finn, the Big Sab-Cat o' the Wobblies, has elected hisself ter be the Avenging Angel o' the Cause. Direct action, Red; direct action!"

XII
A DISCOVERY

TO RETURN TO THE FRISCO KID. Hanging round Bigley's Circus through the day, the Kid had learned considerable about Gipsy Frank's mob and inferred from that a deal more. He felt sure that Anzac Pete, the ticket-butcher, was the third member of the mob. If there were any others they were undoubtedly side-show grifters also.

As side-show workers the men must attend to their ostensible business at peculiar but certain hours. It was a rule of Old Man Bigley that the kid shows should not distract trade from the bigger show. They must ballyhoo and draw the crowds whenever the main tent was empty and dead, and discontinue operations entirely whenever the performance was going forward in the Big Top.

Therefore Gipsy Frank, as ballyhoo man, and Anzac Pete, as ticket-seller, would not be released from work until the main performance started at eight o'clock. They would have to return at eleven, when the feature show was over. Between the hours of eight and eleven while off duty they must pull their burglarious attempt. It was the best time of the day at that, for always during those hours, in whatever town or countryside they showed, the inhabitants and guardians of the spotted houses and banks were engrossed in enjoying the popcorn and blaring trombones and spangles under the Big Top.

One thing the Kid dearly wished, and that was that he might originate some dodge whereby he could shoo Miss Heffernan safely away from the house before the time when Gipsy Frank and his mob were due to attempt the burglary. He didn't trust the yeggmen. He cared not to picture the rough treatment they might mete out to the sweet old lady should some outburst upon her part excite or otherwise arouse them.

A clock, towering above the composite town hall and lock-up, boomed out the hour of seven as the Frisco Kid, leaving the circus lot behind, went through the straggling village of Middletown. He counted the deliberate strokes with an increasing frown and a panicky sinking feeling. Seven o'clock already! He quickened his step and called to the Gay-cat to hurry.

Perhaps it was seeing the village lock-up which made him think for one brief instant of informing the Middletown constable that the house on the hill was to be robbed that very night—within two hours by his strict computation. But the Kid was a true hobo. Hobo ideals were his ideals; and hobo ideals are strange ideals. He had all the true hobo's dislike and fear of the forces of the law, and to work in with those hated forces by informing the constable savored too much of peaching on his own kind, of acting the despicable stool-pigeon.

Besides he had all the sneering contempt of a blown-in-the-glass stiff for countryside police officers and rural guardians of the law. In his eyes constables, sheriffs, country judges and such ilk were ludicrous, blundering bumpkins, wearing horse-blinders, and grass-green in all the larger wisdom of the world. What use to tell that sort the burglarious plan of such resourceful criminals as Gipsy Frank and Anzac Pete? Better to trust to his own powers of ingenuity to put one over on Gipsy Frank and company.

Besetting his wits for a dodge by which to trip up the crooks, the Frisco Kid mounted the rise of hill toward the rambling former road-house among its kennels and yew hedges. What a surprise! Coming down the slope with hurried, tiny steps, he saw the small, spare figure of Miss Heffernan clad in her going-out clothes—a rusty black silk of an old-fashioned pattern and antique Basque effect, and a black, snug little bonnet. She seemed out of breath, what with her quick-step haste, and altogether astounded at seeing him.

"Oh, lan'!" she gasped. "I raikened I never should see you ag'in. I thought you had up in the dead of night and left me for good and all."

"Aw, say, Miss Heffernan! Aw, say now, ma'am; I wouldn't take no run-out powders on yer that way. I jes' was a-hangin round the circus all day, that's all."

"The circus? Oh, to be sure. I had forgot it was here today. But I'm so all over nervous and excited I don't know jest what I am a-doing."

"Has Jerrold showed up then?"

"No; more's the pity."

She shook her black-bonneted head.

"But I jest had word that pore old Selina, who has been with me these long thirty year, is very low and sinking fast. It were the influenzy she had 'stead of the grippe, though she never called it anything but jest the plain miseries; and naow her little black gran'son says as it's turned into the double pneumony.

"Pore soul, what shall I do without her? Sech a help in raisin' my thoroughbreds, she was; and the elegantest cook! She should 'a' been born white!

"But you go on up to the house, child, and don't mind me being gone a little. You'll find some cold meat laid out for you in the pantry and some jelly for your bread. There's an apple-cooker, too, that I baked myself this morning 'case you really did come back to me.

"Help yourself, child, and go to bed at nine like a good boy, and don't set up for me 'cause I may be gone all night. I'll stay with Selina to the last, pore soul!"

Not mind her being gone! And this after he had wracked his brain all the way from the circus lot to devise a plan whereby to get her safely out of the house! He could hardly resist a great whoopee of glad relief right in her troubled face. Decidedly the first round belonged to the Frisco Kid.

She was watching him in a hesitant, nervous manner.

"Anythin' else, ma'am?"

"Well, if any one comes—you know, if Jerrold comes—you give him the suit you promised me you'd let him have, and tuck him out of sight up in your room in the attic. Or better, here's the key to what was once the barroom of the house when it was the old South End Inn. I use that barroom naow for a lumber and odds-and-ends room. You stow him in there and lock the door all snug-like. I'll be back jest as soon as I possibly can."

She handed him the key and then was off down the hill in a little quick-step run. The Kid whistled to the dog. He felt wildly elated that Miss Heffernan was out of the house for the evening. Had not Frisco Red given Gipsy Frank the word to carry a gun? The Frisco Kid feared violence. He feared lest in some resentful or panicky moment the strong-arm men might harm or even kill the sweet old lady. How he himself might be treated, alone with them in the rambling house, he did not care to think.

He found the screen door in the rear unlocked. He went through the kitchen into the dining-room. It was an immense room with high, dark wainscoting and a large open fireplace in one side, set with old-fashioned massive andirons. There was a lonely small table in the center, draped over with a red cambric cover.

He went into the pantry between kitchen and dining-room. On a cleared space of shelf, where food had been set out, he found dismaying signs. The platter had been swept almost bare of cold meat; the bottle of milk was empty; and there were crumbs of bread and apple-cake, and dabs of jelly all over the frilled oilcloth-covering of the shelf.

He recalled Miss Heffernan's words. The meat and bread, milk and cake and jelly had been set out expressly for him. He knew then. Since Miss Heffernan had left the house, only a short while before, some one had been here and had eaten. He looked quickly and a little fearfully about.

"Who can it 'a' been?" he asked himself. "Jerrold? Frisco Red?"

Remembrance of the latter made the Frisco Kid hurry back to the kitchen, place a chair against the wall and, standing a-tiptoe upon it, open the frosted face of the pendulum box of the clock to ascertain whether the money still was there, if it ever had been there. Surely enough therein in a compact bundle of ten one-hundred-dollar bills was the one thousand dollars.

The Kid returned the money and swung shut the frosted face. As he stepped down to the clean white flooring he suddenly remembered having noticed, tagging out of the top of the flour-bin in the pantry, a dirty-looking inch of white cloth, like a soiled shirt cuff. It struck him, now, what an unsanitary and incongruous place the flour-bin was wherein to secrete soiled garments. He resolved at once to investigate.

The flour-bin pulled out easily on pivots on either side of the bottom. Within was a flour-whitened roll of clothing. The Kid picked at the garments gingerly, lifting them out one at a time, the flour in which they were smothered whitening his hands and the front of his Fauntleroy garb. There were two garments of coarse material, a jumper and trousers. Across the breast of the blouse was stenciled in large black figures the number 7292. They were the black-striped shoddy garments of a convict.

"A zebra suit!" breathed the Kid in a cold whisper of awe. "Gee, it must 'a' been Jerrold!"

He saw that one of his own suits, drying behind the range, was missing. It was the suit Strong-Arm had given in his charge. It was that suit intended for Jerrold.

"Well, if it *is* Jerrold, everything's jake. But I wonder where he's gone to. Has he flown the coop, or is he still hidin' about som'eres?"

XIII
FRISCO RED DRIVES A BARGAIN

THE BOY, CHICK, CAME SLOWLY through the thickening twilight from the direction of Bedford. Down in the gully, in the flickering red glow from the embers of the puny fire, Frisco Red was moving about, pouring the remainder of the coffee in the lard-tin and the alcohol in the flask into the two tomato-cans which served as cups. Strong-Arm, half-reclining on one elbow upon the folded serge coat, was watching the older hobo with brooding thoughtfulness. The boy came close to his enslaver and wordlessly held out to him a small newspaper-wrapped parcel.

"Is thet all?" bit out the man, sitting up.

Frisco Red swung about his bloated, red-stubbled face and looked at the bare-legged urchin, a tomato-can poised in one hand. Chick lifted the bottom of the faded red sweater where it bulged in front and, twisting one dirty little hand underneath, produced several bulky paper-wrapped packages. Partially unwrapping the treasures, Strong-Arm placed them before him upon the grass. He seemed to perk up a bit in spirit.

"The eats is on me, Frisco Red!" he exclaimed. "Yuh got a setdown, didn't yuh, Chick? I thought so—youse allus fares better'n me. Well, Red, there's enough fur two, an' yuh kin take yer pick—beef sandwiches, egg er bacon sandwiches an' a hunk o' angel cake. There's no reason why we should live on jamocha royal alone when we kin be cap'talists an' exploit the beggin' ability o' a kid like Chick. It's the System o' the World, on'y on a smaller scale."

Red's free hand, thick with sun-hairs, reached out for a sandwich; but his eyes remained fixed in peculiar scrutiny upon the puny boy. He took a noisy swallow of the brownish admixture, tore off a huge chunk of sandwich and then, his mouth filled and widely chewing, he mumbled:

"That's some kid youse got there, thet Chick. Looket thet mess o' eats— sand'iches enough fer a dozen an' variety fit fer a kink! An' here I've been livin' on nothin' but java fer the larst two days 'cause I dassent poke my nose near the screen door of a single solitary farmhouse. I tell yuh, Strong-Arm, I'm plumb leery o' bein' shot in the back by some o' them rubes with shotguns wot mistakes me fer thet escaped con—"

"I know," agreed Strong-Arm thoughtfully. "I came near gittin' vagged myself jist afore I boarded thet train down south. Thet yegg wot I helped make his getaway from Joliet sure has stirred up this hick country. It's pretty bad, all right."

"Bad?" munched Red thickly. "I tell yuh this is no-good country fer boes the likes o' me. Why, I'm thet scared I'm throwin' up a fat job wot I cottoned to with Bigley's Circus on'y a short time ergo, and which I allowed I'd never pass up till I croaked, it was so soft an' easy. Ternight I'm takin' my walkin'-papers o' me own accord, an' I'm leavin' fer parts safer fer my kind, a few links from Illinois. I'm on'y lingerin' hereabouts ter git my divvy o' a little deal wot I pulled as a side line to the bill-stickin' spiel."

"What was it—crackin' the keester of a village bank or jist plain house-breakin'?" asked Strong-Arm wisely.

"Well, I ain't tellin' everybody, but youse bein' an ol' friend—"

"Aw, I don't care nothin' 'bout it!" broke in Strong-Arm as if incensed at the fellow's boast of friendship. "If ye're doin' gunwork keep it to yerself. On'y I didn't think youse had the guts ter play the yegg. Me, I'm off gunwork fer good."

" 'Nd so youse kin!" exclaimed Frisco Red, not only strangely undaunted by the other's show of anger, but even with something of elation in his voice as if he had gained a point in the discussion. "So youse kin, Strong-Arm. Say, youse ain't got no kick comin' at all, even in this horstile neck o' the woods. A fat an' soft life youse kin lead ennywheres with a swell beggin'-kid like Chick along. A lazy, easy life wot beats all-holler bill-postin' er even gay-cattin' fer a bunch o' circus sharpers!"

He leaned toward Strong-Arm, his small piggy eyes dull and smoky with inordinate desire, his bulbous face working with eagerness.

"Say, Strong-Arm, yuh don't wanter sell thet prushun, does youse? Me,

I'd give three dollars fer him—I'd give anything I got fer ter own a wis'ful beggar-kid like him, now!"

"Feed yer face 'n' shut up!" snapped the Wobbly. "The kid ain't fer sale. He's too babyish 'n' scary a sort, spineless as a white rabbit. He'd go plumb bughouse ef I sold him ter youse, Red—yuh've got such an ugly mug."

The blowsy older hobo affected to be surprised and deeply mortified.

"Aw, he don't need ter be frighted o' me, Strong-Arm," he fawned. "A kid wot's a good beggar has a soft time with ol' Red. Youse knows me, Strong-Arm. I'm too lazy o' nature to be real orn'ary. Fact, I'm a kinder tender hand with kids."

Strong-Arm studied the fellow with narrowed, green eyes. He seemed astounded by his blunt effrontery, even hotly indignant. Yet as he spoke his voice was cold:

"Frisco Red, I knows yuh. I knows yuh too —— well. An' I'm tellin' yuh somethin'. Chick ain't fur sale."

The food he had eaten steadied Strong-Arm, though his brain still worked rapidly with the after effects of the pure and potent alcohol. He turned to the boy with sudden thought.

The little fellow had seated himself in the disheveled grass a space away from the two men. He was making for himself a cigaret from his own sheaf of papers and small muslin sack of tobacco. Throughout the conversation he had not looked up, but it was noticeable now as he rolled the paper tube that his dirty little fingers were trembling.

"Chick," said Strong-Arm, "did yuh see any sign of him—either him or his dawg?"

The head that was hatless and of the color of straw snapped up. Chick shook his head.

"No, Strong-Arm," he gulped. "Notta sign."

And he bowed his head swiftly over the engrossing cigaret. He had not once looked at Frisco Red.

That personage, meanwhile, had showed quick interest at the mention of the word, "dawg." Now with a bovine attempt at off-handedness he said:

"Who yer lookin' fer, Strong-Arm? Yuh can't be any chance mean the Frisco Kid an' his dorg, Gay-cat."

Strong-Arm's black, distinctly haired brows lifted in stupefaction.

"How'd yuh know, Red? Who tole yuh?"

His muddy face darkened, and he snarled—

"Has thet kid peached?"

Red chuckled at the other's swift emotion.

"I ain't sech a bad C.O. Dick; wot yuh think, Strong-Arm? No, the Kid never said nothin' to me. I guess he wouldn't anyways 'cause he used ter be me prushun a coupla months ergo an' there ain't much love lost between us.

I jest jedged who youse was arter when yer happens to mention the dorg. Whenever anybody says, 'Dorg' to me I thinks immedjit o' the Frisco Kid an' his dern yeller cur, Gay-cat."

"Used ter be yer prushun, eh?" repeated Strong-Arm significantly. "Say, Red, what have yuh got ag'inst him? Has he played yer fer a sucker? Tell me, Red; what d'yuh know about the Frisco Kid?"

"Know about him?" iterated Red vehemently. "Why, I got the hull low-down on thet Kid! I've been right on his heels sence thet night he met up with youse, two evenin's ergo, in The Willows."

Strong-Arm exhibited sharpened interest.

"Say, Red, what's he been doin'?"

"Well, when he left The Willows he hit straight fer Miss Heffernan's house on the hill back o' Middletown, fourteen mile below here. Yuh hearn tell o' Miss Heffernan, Strong-Arm?"

"Oh, sure. She keeps a clearin'-house fer boes." The Wobbly was watching the older hobo closely, eager for his every word.

"But it's road-kids she's real sweet on," Red resumed. "Well, I ditched the poster wagon an' Sammy, the gay-cat wot drives, in Middletown an' ambled up there about supper-time. This Miss Heffernan dame, she comes to the screen door in the back an' says—

" 'Ye're not Jerrold, is youse now?' Me, I didn't know wot ter make of it an' opens my mouth like a dummy, gittin' a swaller o' rain thet made me cough. An' then I thinks mebbe it was a stall er somethin', so I says:

" 'Naw, I ain't Jerrold, mum, but I'm Jerry all right, ef thet's wot yuh mean, 'cause I sure knows this is the right place ter come fer a setdown.'

"She gives a shrilly yelp an' pulls open the door like she was gonna throw herself at me neck.

"But she lamps me auburn mug all to oncet an' draws back sudden, like I was a rattler.

" 'I thought youse said yuh was Jerrold an' was comin' to the right place,' she says, real disapp'inted-like. 'Wot does yuh mean? Youse can't deceive eyes as good as mine, Mister Man. Youse don't look like my neffee Jerrold one little bit!'

"I thought she'd shoo me away quick, so I tries to explain thet I meant on'y I was Jerry—Johnny Hep; wise, yuh know.

" 'Well, I'll give yuh somethin' to eat,' she sighs, 'but I don't mind tellin' yer thet youse give me the fright o' me life, 'cause I was expectin' my neffee Jerrold wot run away—' "

"She said thet—she was expectin' her neffee Jerrold?"

Strong-Arm's muddy-complexioned face flushed darkly with some great inward excitement.

"Sure; an' she says the same to the Frisco Kid when he drills along later.

Say, wot ails yuh, Strong-Arm? Youse don't know this bloky Jerrold, does yuh?"

"Shut yer old cow-face! This ain't none o' yer bus'ness. Jist yuh tell me this an' tell it straight: Did the Frisco Kid meet up with Jerrold?"

"How do I know? Thet Kid scared me off afore Jerrold arrived home. Yuh see, it was this way: Miss Heffernan, she had a thousand bucks hidden cold in her kitchen clock, an' I wanted the Frisco Kid ter come in on the job an' help me, and I'd split fifty-fifty. O' course I never meant ter split with him—"

"And he knew thet right off, yuh bet. I see now why youse loves him, Red. Thet Frisco Kid ain't no dummy be any means."

Frisco Red turned to Strong-Arm, a ludicrous expression of woeful dismay etched on his bloated, red-stubbled face.

"Was—was thet why he toined me down?" he gulped. "Here I been stewin' about thet all day, worryin' my fool head off ter explain why he wouldn't come in with me. So that's the reason! The foxy varmint, the slick little gunsel! Why, he was plannin' all the time ter rob her hisself, an' tellin' me bold as brass an' lookin' straight up at me honest-eyed as a preacher:

" 'No, Red, I'se too leery. I'm scared ter try ut. She says Jerrold will be home ternight, in a coupla hours, an' Jerrold's a big fat—' "

Strong-Arm reached over abruptly and got Red by one thick, hair-coated wrist.

"Red!" he cried. "Did he say thet—thet Jerrold would be to home in a coupla hours? Yuh sure the Frisco Kid wasn't stallin'?"

"Aw, lay off the rough stuff; will yuh, Strong-Arm. My arm ain't no iron pipe. I'll cough up—yuh don't have ter force me. Thanks, Strong-Arm."

And Red nursed his released but crushed wrist.

"Aw, youse is too excitable a guy fer me, Strong-Arm," he complained petulantly. "Why git so riled up? Yuh'd think youse was this Jerrold bloky yerself."

"Spiel!" snapped the Wobbly. "Come on; shoot what yuh knows. Was thet Kid stallin'?"

"Gee, Strong-Arm, ol'-timer, thet's jest wot's a-botherin' me. It struck me like a bu'st o' lightnin' a while back when I put the java on—mebbe thet Kid *was* lyin' jest ter scare me off an' nab all the swag hisself."

"But ye're not sure, sartain! Supposin' he warn't lyin'—did he meet up with Jerrold? Did Jerrold arrive to home last night? Did yuh see him? Did the Kid continue on this mornin'? What—"

"Hold up a momint, Strong-Arm. I can't answer all them custions. I don't know nothin' more'n wot I tole youse. Me, I ain't never seed this Jerrold guy. I don't know who the stiff is ner wot it's all about. I got skeered off too soon, I tell yuh, by thet —— Frisco Kid."

Strong-Arm gave vent to his disappointment in a vile oath.

"Aw, I thought yuh said youse knowed all about the Frisco Kid," he ended angrily.

Abruptly he fell silent, looking into the graying embers with morose thoughtfulness. Red watched him for an appreciable interval, then turned round to view once again the boy who sat and smoked some distance apart from the men. Presently Strong-Arm raised his head and in his wonted passionate manner burst out:

"Devil take all these Johnny Tinplates an' sheriff posses an' rubes with shotguns thet are gone offn their nuts 'cause a single lonely loser escaped from stir! I jist gotta move round this country on a little bus'ness—I wanta git down Middletown way an' see jist what thet Frisco Kid's done—an' I can't fer fear o' gittin' nabbed as a suspicious character. —— all these scared forces o' the law!"

"Youse got a little bus'ness hereabouts?" questioned Red with strange eagerness. "Yuh'd like ter nosey round Middletown quiet-like 'n' not git nabbed?"

In his small, piggy eyes there was a peculiar look, a wise, calculating look.

"Yuh heard me, didn't yuh?" snapped Strong-Arm with morose surliness. "But what kin I do—a sab-cat fur the Wobblies with a record fer wise work an' certain results? Me git by these minions o' the law in these days when they're so leery of Bolshevism spreadin' over here an' with them partic'lar wild over this zebra hidin' somewheres about? No, I can't risk gittin' vagged an' then rekernized from them private dick dodgers. Not me of all men. With me railroaded on some fake charge who's gonna clean house fur us? Who'll be the Avenging Angel o' the Wobblies? No, it's too risky; I got too much work to do fer the Cause! I'll have to grab the next south-bound rattler an' git outta here ternight."

"Say, Strong-Arm," began Red suddenly.

"What? What d'yuh want?"

"I got it, Strong-Arm. I was gonna offer yuh three dollars ag'in as an inducemint ter sell Chick ter me, but I jest thought o' somethin' better'n a three dollars, better'n three hundert dollars!"

He leaned toward the Direct Actionist with an air of great secrecy.

"It's a paper, Strong-Arm. Thet paper will make yer glad ter sell Chick ter me, an' it'll git youse around this country jake 'n' fast, an' with no danger a-tall from the perlice an' sheriff's men. It'll make them take off their hats to yuh an' pass youse on like a hot pertater. Youse kin go to Middletown an' see Miss Heffernan an' find out all about the Frisco Kid, an' no trouble—"

"Let's see it," interrupted Strong-Arm. "Quick, Red. What paper you got?"

Red rose to his feet.

"Git off thet coat a momint, Strong-Arm," he said.

His request complied with, he lifted the serge and fished in an inside pocket. He drew out a folded sheet of heavy writing-paper. Spreading this out between dirty-gnarled fingers, in the halting voice of a schoolboy in his second reader he began slowly reading what was written therein:

" 'Warden's Office, State Penitentiary, Joliet, Illinois.' Thet's the headin', Strong-Arm."

"Go ahead, man!" exclaimed Strong-Arm, getting to his feet with excitement and coming up behind Red. "Who's it addressed to?"

" 'Mr. Jarge Kummer, Sheriff o' Middlesex County, Middletown. Dear Kummer:—This is ter introduce to yuh Abraham Powers, who has been employed as a guard at this prison fer the last seven years an' who knows the escaped convict, Number 7292——' "

Strong-Arm snatched the paper from him. He could no longer wait, in his agitation, on the other's halting rendition. With eyes far more accustomed to the printed page he read the letter quickly to himself.

"Why, this is jist the thing! Fine!" he ejaculated after he had done. "Evidently Sheriff Kummer asked the warden fer the assistance of some one what could identify the escaped zebra at sight, an' the warden sent along this man, Powers. Lissen to this, Red."

Strong-Arm read aloud:

" 'I hope now, with the aid of Powers, yuh will be able to capture our man and secure fur yerself the $1,000 reward offered by the State as well as the standin' reward of the American Bankers' Association. The escape, yuh know, is a notorious safe-cracker.' "

He looked up at Red with sudden wonder and suspicion.

"Say, old-timer, however did yuh come to git yer hands on this paper? Why, this is valu'ble!"

The blowsy, slouch-shouldered hobo fidgeted from one foot to the other. But he felt rather proud of himself. He said:

"Well, me an' a Gipsy name o' Louis Lees met up on the road below here around noon terday an' wint inter the Six-Mile House to git a beer an' transack tergether a little matter o' private bus'ness. Whilst we was havin' the second schooner o' suds, in blows a guy wot has shed his coat, account o' the heat, an' is wearin' on'y a white west-cut with a big gold chain acrosst. He is a large, pink-faced, comfor'ble-lookin' *hombre*. We gives him a good day, at which he invites us ter have a drink, not likin' ter drink alone.

"We has beer an' he has red-eye. I was some su'prised when Lees buys another all around. But when I treated, as in dooty bound, I begins ter gather, 'cause the Gipsy gives me the office, an' then dopes the baby-faced gent's whisky whilst the barkeep ain't lookin' an' the big feller is busy gassin' with me.

"Thet dope in the forty-rod hits him all ter oncet. He begins rollin' round on his legs an' talkin' like a crazy loon. Says as how his rig's outside at the hitchin'-post, an' thet he's driven down all the way from Joliet an' has ter make Middletown thet night. We helps him out real friendly-like to the little summer shack outside an' leaves him sleepin' peaceful as a infant.

"Lees gits his gold watch an' heavy chain, and then we jumps inter the buggy an' hits it out south. Lees is happy as a clam in high water. He says the baby-faced guy won't wake up till the middle o' the nex' day. He tells me how he plans to dope up thet buggy with a new coat o' paint an' fix the hoss with a pair o' shears an' a brandin'-iron so yuh couldn't rekernize neither of them. But me, I don't like this hoss-stealin' stunt nohow, knowin' it's a prison offense, an' I says the same ter Lees.

"He's none displeased, Lees ain't, bein' a Gipsy an' thinkin' nothin' o' stealin' hosses an' sech. Besides, he sees the chance o' not havin' ter divide with me the profits o' the rig. I takes as my divvy the feller's coat, a new serge wot he had left in the rig 'count o' the heat. Thet's it wot yuh've been settin' on, Strong-Arm. I likes thet better 'cause it's on'y petty larceny. Lees goes south with the rig an' I hops off an' comes by a roundabout way up here. I finds three dollars in bills in the coat an' this paper—"

"It's jist the thing, Red; jist the thing I needs. I kin go anywheres with this—to Middletown, Miss Heffernan's, anywheres. And the sheriff will be back of me, behind all my actions, every move. It's fine, Red; jist the thing!"

Red looked at him with bright, furtive eyes.

"An' yuh'll sell Chick fer thet paper; wot, Strong-Arm?"

Strong-Arm stepped back in a complete surprise, as if he had not heard the idea broached before. There, in the grass-disheveled gully, in the fire-tinged dusk, the two hoboes looked long at one another. Hungry hope, smoky desire, and a deal of craven fear crowded Red's piggy eyes. Strong-Arm's face grew arrogant with contempt, his eyes mere greenish slits. Quietly he folded the paper and shoved it into an inner coat pocket.

Red's small eyes moved with mechanical jerkiness. They watched Strong-Arm stealthily a trice, darted away and then came furtively back again. He feared that Strong-Arm would say him nay and pocket the letter without payment of any kind. What could he do then?

But suddenly Strong-Arm smiled, an odd smile for that brutal, unfinished-looking gash of mouth, a peculiar cat-and-mouse smile. He nodded his head as if in answer to some unspoken thought.

"Well, seein' that's the barg'in," he said with wooden lips, "yuh kin take Chick, Red; I'll take the paper. It's a go. I'll stand by the deal."

XIV
AND PAYS THE PRICE

THE BARE-LEGGED BOY, CHICK, gave an incoherent scream, leaped afoot and, rushing to Strong-Arm, clung with tiny dirty fingers to his coat-ends. His pouting, baby lips quivered; the welt across little nose and cheeks glowed scarlet against the ghastly pallor of his face. Stretching wide the baby-blue eyes was such terror as to turn one sick, an inconceivable terror, full of vague but grisly horrors. Frantically, in the thin sexless voice of a child, he begged not to be sold.

Roughly Strong-Arm cast him off. But when he spoke there was not so much anger at the boy in his voice. It was almost as if such resentment as he felt were directed against himself for having been roped into such a despicable bargain. He said not unkindly:

"Chick boy, don't yuh want me ter sell youse to this bo, Frisco Red? He's a old-timer, Chick. He's over forty, an' he's growin' weaker every day with booze 'n' laziness. His hand ain't' as strong as mine fer beatin's, Chick."

"Aw, Strong-Arm!" pleaded the child, rushing to him again and tearing distractedly at his coat-tails. "Aw, please, please, Strong-Arm, don't sell me to him. He's too—too bad-lookin'."

It was a wail of poignant terror. The boy shuddered away from the bulbous-nosed Red with squirmings of unspeakable loathing. He had no love for Strong-Arm, but Strong-Arm he knew to his most brutal depths. This old, bloated-faced, altogether disreputable-looking hobo he did not know. He feared in Frisco Red depths of cruelty to which the harsh, tempestuous but clean brutality of Strong-Arm might be as nothing.

Strong-Arm laughed bitterly.

"Youse see, Red. He's kinder sweet on me—me bein' thet good-lookin' an' so thoughtful of his needs."

Red fawned.

"Aw, he don't need ter be frighted o' me. I knows I got a hard an' onhandsome mug—I scares the farmers' wives at the screen doors all the time—but I got a big heart. Youse knows me, Strong-Arm."

And he winked at the other over the wailing, clinging boy.

"I'm a tender hand with kids. Why, I wouldn't think o' liftin' my fist to a child."

There was that in Frisco Red's words which exasperated Strong-Arm. He shoved the clinging boy from him. The little fellow staggered dizzily; the trembling, red-welted pipestems of legs gave suddenly, and he fell on his face in the grass, weeping desperately, torrentially. The Wobbly turned on the older hobo.

"G'wan, Red!" he growled savagely. "Take the kid. I'm done. He's yourn."

Red advanced with a proprietary air upon the wailing boy, smirking complacently.

"Thet's talkin', Strong-Arm. I jest knowed yuh was a stiff arter me own heart."

The boy lifted his straw-colored head. He saw Red coming toward him, the satisfied grimace on Red's bloated face. He shrieked despairingly, lifted to his knees and scrambled hurriedly toward Strong-Arm.

"Aw, Strong-Arm!" he wailed. "Fer Gawd's sake, Strong-Arm!"

The hairy paw of Frisco Red clapped down on the boy's shoulder and brought the frantic crawl to a stop.

"Yuh will, will youse! Run away from Red, eh? Well, I'm yer new jocker now, an' I'll soon l'arn youse wot's wot. Quick, git to yuh feet, er —— yer hide I'll lick the daylights outta yer."

Red's fingers dug into the cringing flesh of the boy's frail shoulder. He made to lift the child bodily by the shoulder to his feet. He felt all at once a heavy hand upon his own slouch shoulder. With an unusual and vehement show of anger, an aroused righteousness, Red released the boy, snapped erect and swung about.

Frisco Red looked into the eyes of Strong-Arm, not three inches from his own. He could see the veins standing out, blue and swollen, on Strong-Arm's quivering, dark-flushed temples. He became on the instant servile, abject, cringing.

The eyes of Strong-Arm held him as in a spell. Those eyes were like deep green pools rived by a fury of lightning.

"Yuh've guessed it," said Strong-Arm coldly between set, wooden lips. "The barg'in's made an' I'll stick by it; but, Red, I owes youse somethin' else, somethin' more. Yuh reminded me of it yerself, Red. Yer hand on Chick's shoulder, yer last words. I owes youse somethin' fur all the beatin's yuh gave me when I was on'y a kid like Chick. Yuh made my life one hell o' misery; yuh had no mercy on me; an' I'll have no mercy on youse now!"

Under the heavy hand on his shoulder Frisco Red shook like a wet dog.

"Gawd, Strong-Arm!" he cried. "Yuh don't mean—"

A harsh fist crashing against his jaw stopped the cry, mashed his lips, filled his mouth with teeth and blood. He reeled away, spitting out teeth as if they were seeds. His right hand whipped round to a hip pocket. When that hand came back a razor glistened in the dull play of firelight. That razor was opened and doubled up backwards in the crotch between thumb and forefinger.

Strong-Arm saw Red's move. But he did not reach for the revolver hanging in the shoulder-holster under his left arm. Altogether contemptuous of Red's vicious weapon he advanced on the man with unswerving intensity of purpose, with grim certitude.

All at once, his muscles tight, Strong-Arm bounded from the ground, fanged out one long arm and grasped the wrist that held the weapon. It was the leap of the panther, quick, not to be resisted. Strong-Arm's stubby, strong fingers closed like steel pincers about Red's wrist; there was a sharp snap; the razor dropped from Red's hand like a hot coal and that hand fell to his side, loose, inert and useless. Frisco Red had paid for his perfidy. The ulna bone was broken. In the sudden darting agony of the shattered wrist Red screamed hysterically.

The blood mania was seething in Strong-Arm. Boy and man, he had been brewing venom in his veins against this old, brutish taskmaster. The sweaty contact of struggling bodies, the fleshy thud of blows, the treachery and screaming of Red stirred up all the poisonous rancor within him, intensified his lusting haste. His knotted fists shot out like barbed pistons and hammered mercilessly the quivering stomach, heaving torso and messy face of his old master.

Frisco Red could not see. There were folds of discolored flesh swelling over the sockets of his small eyes. Crouched, one arm covering his face, he backed down the gully toward the reed-overgrown creek, the breath wheezing asthmatically through his lungs.

He stumbled, his leaden legs entangled in the reeds of the shallow creek. His mind, as he felt himself slipping, blazed up with a grisly fear. He feared the *coup de grâce* of the Road, that dread stamping and finishing act—the boots of Strong-Arm. He forgot the excruciating pain of his broken wrist to clutch wildly with both hands at the air. He screamed bestially, hideously— the yelp of a stricken animal being dragged down to the kill.

The scream was choked off; his head rocked loosely on his neck and his whole frame shuddered convulsively under a swift, deadly blow from Strong-Arm. He fell with a loud splash, broken and senseless, into the water. And the clatter of the creek sounded suddenly and preternaturally loud as it eddied about his still form.

Strong-Arm, well-nigh unmarked, the muscles outstanding on his short, thick neck, the knuckles of his right hand lacerated and bleeding where they had impacted against the teeth of Frisco Red, kicked the inert body, spraying up the shallow water. His lips were twisted with savage glee; in his long, greenish eyes burned fiercely an unholy triumph. Never had he performed a more complete man-breaking.

"I've broke yuh, Red," he panted, looking down at the result of his handiwork. "When I was yer beggin'-kid years ago I longed fer some one ter do this to yuh, but no one never did. But yuh got yers now, Red—yuh got yers now."

He turned to Chick, who had been standing aside and watching it all with a thorough comprehension but in protean terror. He reached beneath his left armpit; there was the snap of the springy whalebone of the shoulder-holster; and out in his blood-damp hand gleamed the steely revolver. Into Chick's astounded and fearfully hesitant fingers he forced the weapon.

"Take this," he snapped imperiously. "Yuh is Red's road-kid now, Chick. He done me a good toin with thet letter, so I won't go back on me barg'in with him. But I ain't through with him yit. I can't myself git paymint in full fer the way he used me when I was a measly kid. Youse seed me do what I could—manhandle him. He deserves more, much worse. But I can't cook him myself. He's too spineless, leery, yaller. He won't fight back, an' I can't croak him in cold blood.

"But youse, Chick boy, youse is elected by me ter pay him back in full. Yer weak an' scary o' yer own shadder, spineless as a white rabbit; but ye're a kid, an' it's a little 'fraid kid what should kill Frisco Red. It's me dream, Chick, me old dream o' vengeance thet I had when I was his prushun, years ago.

"Listen, Chick. Ye're to stick with Red an' be his beggin'-kid; ye're not to leave him till he's done fer. But at the first kick or blow from him ye're to pull this stick-up gun an' cook him good.

"Them's my orders, Chick. Fail me in this, leave him before thet time, come back ter me 'n' try to beg off, and I'll croak yuh myself as sure as me name's Strong-Arm. Yuh got them orders, Chick?"

"Y-yes, Strong-Arm."

Strong-Arm turned thereat and moved slowly away, going toward town. He was protected and armed by that paper he had secured from Frisco Red—the letter to Sheriff George Kummer from the warden of Joliet—and he feared no longer the sheriff's deputies, roadside guardians with shotguns, or any other forces of the aroused law.

Long after he had gone the little barelegged Chick stood as he had been at the cruel and fateful parting, the huge revolver held in two puny, shaking hands, the fingers stiff with fear, and great, slow sobs shuddering through his whole childish frame.

Once the broken, appalling figure of Frisco Red stirred slightly among the reeds and groaned in dull agony. A scream of fear rose in Chick's throat to be hushed immediately by a fear still more acute and awful.

Of all things he dreaded that Red should return to consciousness. Chained by invisible yet weighty gyves to the senseless body, unable to leave the plagued spot because of the orders given and that deeply instilled fear he had for Strong-Arm, the child remained. In his wide-stretched baby eyes was the despair of an unwilling soul damned to an everlasting torment. Thus the night found him there.

XV

THE ROBBERY

MEANTIME, IN THE FORMER ROAD-HOUSE on the hill above Middletown, the Frisco Kid, having discovered in the flour-bin the prison suit stenciled 7292, paused in the pantry and harkened for any noise which would show that the escaped convict still was hiding in the house. But there was no sound from overhead, from any part of the rambling structure.

He recalled Miss Heffernan's words about the disused barroom. On tiptoe then he went through the dining-room and out into the spacious, gloomy hall. The Gay-cat trotted knowingly before him. Suddenly he noticed the Gay-cat sniffing with prolonged, questing breaths at the crevice between a certain door and the sill. It was as if the dog caught the taint of some human being behind that door.

It was the door just across the hall from the dining-room. Softly the Kid tried the knob. But the door did not give. He thought at once that this must be the former barroom. He tried the key Miss Heffernan had given him, but still the door refused to open. He realized then that the door was bolted from the inside. There was, indeed, some one within that room.

Again he listened. No sound breathed from the room. He thought to call softly through the keyhole. As he bent down, it struck him to peer through that keyhole. But he could see nothing. Whoever was within that room had had the forethought to hang a cloth of some kind over the doorknob, entirely covering the hole and preventing sight into the room.

Abruptly the Frisco Kid lifted erect. His usually pale face was ashen, his eyes seemingly deeper sunk than ever. Now whether to whisper or not he did not know. The precautions taken by the man in the room had caused with smashing force a primitive fact to impact upon his comprehension, changing his purpose, giving him sudden pause.

That man within was as a hunted animal. For several days he had been bayed and hounded down. He was likely to be armed. Certainly he was nervous and inimical, at a final ditch of desperation. Should the boy merely whisper through the keyhole, the man within might fire at him through the door in panicky alarm.

While he hesitated, undecided, the Kid held pressed against his breast with one flour-whitened hand the suit of coarse convict shoddy. What should he do with those black-striped, telltale garments? Hide them certainly; but no nook seemed secretive enough to conceal them securely. They were like an armful of hot embers in a powder-plant. But at last he decided upon the huge open fireplace in the dining-room. Standing in the gaping mouth of the fireplace, upon one of the massive old andirons, he shoved the garments far up the soot-lined chimney.

He came back to the kitchen on tiptoe to ponder over the whole jumbled state of affairs. He did not think to eat; he was too overwrought. He glanced at the clock. It was five minutes to eight o'clock. How time shrieked by! Gipsy Frank would be along very soon now; and here was he, the Frisco Kid, doing absolutely nothing to forestall the burglars, only moving round in futile circles like a dog chasing its tail.

He noticed, in glancing at the clock, that the frosted face of the pendulum box, insecurely shut, had swung open. The money was in plain sight. He got afoot to close the frosted face and thus conceal the money when, like a blow, the long looked for inspiration struck him. Why not hide the money elsewhere and thus lay the yeggs by the heels?

There was the plan! He would ransack the house, turn it over from top to bottom for valuables, gather all those valuables in a sack or something, and cache them outdoors under a yew hedge or in one of the carriage-shed kennels crowded with dogs. He would leave all the valueless stuff from the ransacked drawers and closets scattered about the floor, the drawers open and in disarray, the chairs and chests turned topsyturvy. Thus when Gipsy Frank's mob at length broke in, the house would have the cyclone-struck appearance of having been already fine-combed for valuables, turned inside out, completely gutted.

The Frisco Kid became at once feverishly active. He banged out of the kitchen and into the carriage shed where he had housed his Gay-cat the night prior. There surely enough on top of an unopened box of dog biscuits he found a gunnysack. He brought it back.

He took down the bundle of bills from the pendulum box. He thought as he did so of the convict clothes up the flue. Surely that was no safe hiding-place. To make certain they were well concealed he would cache those clothes with the money. He fished the sooted, shoddy garments down from the dining-room chimney, wrapped the bills within, knotted the black-and-white sleeves securely about the bundle and placed all in the bottom of the gunny-sack. He left the frosted face of the pendulum box swinging open.

He returned again to the dining room. He pulled open drawers and cast silver knives, forks and spoons clattering into the sack. He left each drawer, as he had done with it, open and in disarray, the discarded contents streaming out upon the carpet. It struck him that in taking everything of value he was again forestalling the burglars. Finding the money gone, they might have thought in their turn of stealing anything else of worth. He would cache the gunny-sack of valuables under one of the yew hedges.

He opened a tall window in the side of the room to clamber out upon the lawn.

A noise halted him. He was not certain that it came from the barroom on the other side of the hall or from the kitchen behind him. He looked hastily about.

He missed, of a sudden, the dog. Some one was approaching; the Gay-cat had probably gone to greet the newcomer; he could hear quick footsteps. He must conceal the sack of loot. There was the place—under the table where the red cambric cloth draped down to the rug on the floor, hiding even the polished legs. He swung the sack under the table. It was completely out of sight.

He was rearranging with a quick hand the trailing cambric cloth when he heard a gasp behind him. He turned. There in the doorway, her austere face pale and grim, a bitter light in the eyes behind the gold-rimmed spectacles, stood Miss Heffernan! In one sweep she took in the open and disordered drawers, the obvious robbery. She clutched the jamb of the door.

"Oh, you little thief!" she burst out at him. "You o'nary little thief to rob a lone woman! In twenty years this is the fust time that any one has turned against the bread that he had eaten. What ingratitude and treachery! You mean, low o'nary little thief!"

The Frisco Kid was struck dumb. She had spoiled all his plans by coming back so soon. How could he begin to explain. The cards seemed stacked against him.

How long he stood and stared slack-jawed at the little old lady he never knew. But suddenly she shivered a little, and then came quietly into the room. She bent down over an open drawer and began silently to straighten its disarray. The boy watched her, hope and pleading crowding his deep-sunk eyes. But she did not look at the boy. She cried to herself, softly.

"God'a'mercy!" she murmured very low. "I shouldn't take on this way. It's not the pore lad's fault; it's all come of his upbringing. I mustn't lay a power of blame on him; he don't know any better, pore thing. I must be less harsh and not too strait-laced and goody-goody, and lead his little wayward feet back into the right path."

She looked up at the boy, her eyes red from tears and piteously pleading.

"You don't want to keep all them stole articles, naow do you, child? That would be very, very ungrateful and wrong. You will give them all back to me and be a tolerable good boy from naow on; won't you, pore dear?"

The Kid still stood as she had found him.

"Aw, say, Miss Heffernan! Aw, say now, ma'am, I didn't mean no harm, honest I didn't. But I can't give them back to yer right away. I'm a-scared, ma'm. Aw, say, Miss Heffernan, I can't tell yer now. I—I jes' wisht I was dead!"

The little old lady snapped erect, her eyes sharpening with suspicion.

"Why, child, why do you talk thataway? What do you mean?"

But truthfully the boy could not explain. If he should return the sack of valuables under the table she would only be robbed of them, shortly and for good, when Gipsy Frank's mob appeared. He could not tell her of Gipsy Frank's mob. She would be too terribly affrighted. She might even think he was a member of that mob himself.

He quailed under the suspicion deepening in her eyes. He was in a real and fearful extremity. Nervously he racked his brain, looking for an out. Suddenly he remembered the man locked in the barroom. He made a little jerking motion of the head toward that room. He gulped—

"He's in there, ma'am."

She started, took a deep, audible breath. She was swept through and through by strong emotion.

"Who? Tell me, child! Who's in there? Jerrold?"

The boy nodded, then abruptly cut short a nod to stiffen into an alertness of harkening. Miss Heffernan, uncontainably excited though she was, noted his sudden rigidity of attitude. She was about to dart toward the barroom; she saw the dog standing tense and bristling in the doorway to the kitchen; she halted dead. Then she, too, listened. The sound came again. The kitchen screen door was slowly and cautiously creaking open.

There were footsteps in the kitchen, a muffled exclamation of anger in a man's gruff voice. The Kid realized that Gipsy Frank was in the kitchen. He had noted the open frosted face of the pendulum box of the clock. He knew that the money was gone.

The dog, growling rumblingly in his throat, was retreating from the doorway. The Kid rushed across to the old lady, suddenly panicky with fear for her.

"Yer better go, Miss Heffernan," he pleaded, seeking to hustle her across the room and out of the doorway into the hall. "Yer better go quick. They's liable to git rough with yer when they find I beat 'em to it."

But she mistook his motive. She stiffened into the bitter schoolmarm type. She rallied against his pushing hands, flaming with abrupt hostility.

"Go?" she exclaimed in a voice that broke the silence with unusual loudness. "Me go! Oh, you incorrigible little thief! You ungrateful, treacherous imp—to think that you were conniving all the time with these bad men to rob pore me! Oh, you—"

She paused. Crowding the doorway into the dining-room were three men. Gipsy Frank, in pink shirt and black corduroy coat and trousers, bulked large and evil in the lead. Behind him were two other men, in one of whom the Kid was quick to recognize the pallid-complexioned, thin-haired ticket-butcher, Anzac Pete.

XVI
GIPSY FRANK AND COMPANY

UNDER THE STRAIGHT BLACK BAND OF EYEBROWS Gipsy Frank's eyes were darting quickly about the disheveled room. He looked from the Frisco Kid to Miss Heffernan. He noted the antagonistic, almost pugnacious attitude of the little old lady. Sharply he glanced again at the boy. He seemed visibly to start as he did, and his mouth curved into a cruel, animal-like snarl.

"So this is yer game, eh, Frisco Kid!"

The Kid looked at the man in a complete and utter surprise. Gipsy Frank knew him! It was true then that somewhere, in some Gipsy *hatsh* or *wardo*, he had run up against the fellow. But exactly where?

The Kid thought quickly, the gruff voice ringing hauntingly in his ears. All he could tell, however, was that there was something strangely familiar in that broad, dark face, that thick-chested frame, that heavy-lipped, snarling mouth.

"So this is yer game," repeated the Gipsy, as if striving to get a grip on himself, fighting for time. "Stickin' up a' ol' woman wot has been a friend ter every road-kid in the country. Wait till some o' the kid mobs around the states hear tell o' this, Frisco Kid. Yer life won't be worth a nickel."

He stepped boldly into the room, as if suddenly sure of himself.

"We've been on this kid's track fer a long time, ma'am," he said, addressing the little old lady with marked deference. "I jedge now yuh nabbed him in the act. Where's the loot? Did he cough up the swag ter yuh?"

She shook her head, still snugly bonneted, and glanced with quick anxiety about the room.

"I don't know what he's done with the silver and money, sir," she returned in a trembling whisper of voice. "But who are you-all?"

The man feigned to be surprised.

"Me?" he asked, lifting the straight black band of eyebrows. "Yuh mean ter say, ma'am, yuh don't know me?"

The two men behind were watching him closely, a thin grin of understanding and perverse admiration slowly growing on their rough faces. The Frisco Kid saw through the game. The Gipsy was preparing a ghost story for the old lady—a story which would explain with some plausible reason why he and his pals were there and place all the blame and odium of larcenous intention upon the Frisco Kid.

"Me?" repeated the man once again. "Why me, I'm Frank Lovell, chief detective o' Bigley's Wild Animal Show an' Circus. An' this here is Anzac Peter—I mean, thet's wot we calls Pete 'cause he's a' Australian."

He indicated the pale-faced ticket-seller.

The fellow immediately leaped into the rôle. He scraped the cap from his thin-haired scalp.

"No bally wowser, mum," he smirked in a nasal voice. "An Australian detective, mum."

"This other man," continued Gipsy Frank, indicating the third member of the mob, an undersized sallow-complexioned individual, "is known as Sabu-Suva, the Head Hunter, 'cause he acts thet part in a kid show o' the circus,

but he's reelly Charley Small, the famous Burns man. We're all dicks fur the
Bigley Circus, Miss Heffernan. Mostly we has ter cop off the strong-armers
an' stick-ups an' grifters an' dips an' other ringtails wot pester a circus; but of
late fer a long time, as I says, ma'am, we've been on this Frisco Kid's trail.

"He's been trackin' along ahead o' the circus, bustin' open the keesters
o' post-office safes an' robbin' pore widders and orphings along the road. It
makes it bad fer the circus havin' this kind o' crook runnin' ahead o' us an'
sp'ilin' our good name. We three was hired jist ter run down sich criminals,
an' partic'lar this kid.

"We hearn he was gonna break in here ternight. So we up afore the evenin'
performance an' laid low in the bushes outside until we was sure yuh had
nabbed him red-handed. We knowed we could git in ter help yuh out afore
thet kid could pull any rough stuff. But I wasn't none too easy-like about it.
Ther kid's a bad actor, ma'am, ef yuh'll berlieve me. See; he was all ready
ter git away outer thet open winder there with all the loot!"

He pointed at the open dining-room window, which he himself had but
just noticed.

"Oh, he's hard-boiled, thet kid," he insisted. "I guess we oughter know,
ma'am. We've been on this kid's trail a long time. He's been workin' with a
nortorious yegg afore this, an' I don't wonder any but the two o' 'em were in
on this job. Yuh didn't see anything of another yegg, did yuh, ma'am—a yegg
name of Atlanta Slim thet by all right an' reason oughter be safe in stir?"

The Frisco Kid's mouth fell open. He was absolutely astounded. Atlanta
Slim! It was months since he had seen Atlanta Slim. At that time Slim had
been captured by the Hindoo hop-pickers working on J. Curtis Haines'
ranches out in California. He had cracked the safe in Haines' office and
had been captured through the treachery of the stoolpigeon, Scar-Face Mike
Hagan. It was not a sweet memory to the Frisco Kid. Slim had been his
buddy and his friend. And Slim had been sent to prison.

But how did this man, Gipsy Frank, know of Slim and the Kid as buddies
together? The Kid had thought that only two persons had known of his
joining out with Slim. One was that member of Slim's mob called Yorky; the
other was the snitch, Scar-Face Mike Hagan. This man before him bore no
shadow of resemblance to either of the two.

Yorky had been morbidly white-faced at the time from several years'
confinement in Sing Sing. Scar-Face was built like a policeman, with a
quarter-inch white scar clefting his beefy red face from left eye to overly
strong chin. This man was black-banded of eyebrow and dark as any of the
Black Men of Zend. He was a breed Gipsy. How then did he know?

The Frisco Kid eyed critically the other men. He dismissed quickly and
altogether the pseudo head-hunter, Charley Small. Pete, the ticket-seller,
however, might easily have passed for Yorky on account of his pallid-

complexion had not the Kid heard his nasal voice and aspirated accent.

The Frisco Kid noted, as he observed the two men, that a look of bewilderment was slowly etching their faces. It was as if they were unable to follow Gipsy Frank in this abrupt tangent about Atlanta Slim. That part of the ghost story seemed not only new, but very surprising and puzzling to them.

"Yuh say yuh don't know nothin' about this other yegg, ma'am," he heard the gruff voice of the Gipsy saying. "Well, let it ride. The thing ter find out now, ma'am, beggin' yer pardon, is where's the loot. We've got the kid here. Now either he's got thet loot hid som'eres about, or else thet pal o' his, Atlanta Slim, got away with it through thet open winder there.

"—— it!" he exploded sharply, a rush of blood darkening his swarth face. "I'll bet thet one-time loser has beat me to it agin!"

Over the top of her spectacles the little old lady looked at the boy as if astounded at the extent of his perfidy. So this tiny, pale, wistful-appearing road-kid, whom she had fed and mothered and taken into her house as one of her very own, was really a case-hardened criminal, the boon companion of a notorious yeggman! It seemed almost past belief.

"My pore sinning boy," she pleaded with him, "why are you so teetotally bad? I never thought this of you; it's so simply turrible! But I'm only—only too willing to forget and forgive all, if you will just forsake this wicked life—"

"An' return yuh the stuff wot he stole. Don't fergit thet, ma'am," insisted Gipsy Frank.

The Frisco Kid looked at the man. He was beginning deeply to hate and fear the fellow. He knew his game. The Gipsy wanted to learn where the Kid had cached the money and silver in order to make off with it himself.

"Yuh better leave him to me, ma'am," suggested Gipsy Frank. "We'll make him cough up in short order. He'll tell where Slim boy went with the swag, or else where he's got it hid. Yuh leave him to us, please ma'am, an' go inter the kitchen an' rest quiet a bit. We circus dicks has ways o' makin' these hard-boiled crooks talk."

The Frisco Kid sensed the ugly threat in the last words. He shivered. He knew what it was to be tortured. Had he not suffered often at the hands of Frisco Red and once, unforgettably, from Scar-Face Mike Hagan, the stool? He looked up at the little old lady, an extremity of distress and pleading in his deep-sunk eyes.

No woman could have refused that look in the Kid's eyes. Quickly Miss Heffernan shook her white head.

"No," she said quietly; "I think I'll stay right here."

The man called Gipsy Frank uttered a choked exclamation of anger. He stepped toward the Kid. He nodded Charley Small, the sometimes Wild

Man, over toward him. He got the Frisco Kid by the wrist. Interposing his burly frame between the boy and the old lady, he vised his big paw about the Kid's wrist and began slowly and covertly to turn. Charley Small crowded close like a pickpocket's stall, helping thereby to conceal the actions of the other. Meanwhile Gipsy Frank talked in a smooth if gruff tone:

"Better tell, Kid. Yuh knows you'll have to. Here, yuh Anzac!" he called, half-turning round to the Australian in the doorway. "Look through this room, will yuh, an' see ef yuh kin nose out the swag? Wot d'yuh say now, Kid? Gonna beef where it's hid? Gonna squeal ef Slim boy's got it or not? Say, I knows all about Slim, Kid, so yuh may as well spill.

"Yuh knows, Slim was ter be sent up in California. But them hog-globmers had gone on strike an' fired ole Curt Haines' hop-vines on the very same night as Slim cracked the Haines' peter, so the authorities was afraid them labor unions out West 'ud think Slim was one of 'em an' start soup in politics jist ter save him. The Chi National had a strong case against Slim boy, so they extradited him ter Illinois an' shoved him through on the bank-breakin' charge.

"Where'd yuh meet up with him ag'in, Kid? I thought he got twenty year. Must 'a' made his gitaway somehow, though I ain't heard none about it. Where'd yuh meet up with him, Kid? Where's Slim boy now with the swag?"

The Frisco Kid bit his lip. He bent over, contorting with pain as brutally the Gipsy twisted his arm more and more. The sweat started from his forehead; tears of agony showed in his eyes. Yet with all the pain, it sounded odd to him that this man should know so much and be so manifestly interested in Atlanta Slim. Indeed, there was something in the Gipsy's attitude very reminiscent of Scar-Face Mike Hagan, the stool-pigeon.

The Kid remembered that night when, down in the little yellow shack among the burning hop-fields, Atlanta Slim had cracked the Haines safe and stepped out into the arms of the onswooping Hindoos. He remembered how Scar-Face had wanted him to be a witness in the trial of Slim. Scar-Face had dragged him down in the tar-weeds when he would have gone to Slim there among the ragheads. With a hand on each frail shoulder, Scar-Face had held him down as in a crushing, terrible machine.

Scar-Face Mike Hagan wanted to earn the large rewards offered for Slim. He proffered the Kid a road-stake of one hundred dollars if the boy would tell all he knew about Slim.

But Slim had fed the boy and named him the Frisco Kid and taken him as his buddy; yes, him and his dog as buddies. He had promised to share with the Kid on this safe-cracking job—the last of his yegg life—and then he and the boy and the dog were to go shanty-boating together down the old Mississippi. Slim had stirred deeps of the Kid's being never plumbed before. He had been altogether good to the Kid. The Frisco Kid could never tell on Slim!

Scar-Face, hearing that, had jerked out a revolver from where it was concealed under his padded vest. He had put one foot upon the boy's chest and held him from squirming off into the weeds and the dark night. Point-blank at the boy he had fired the revolver, but the gun had proven empty. Scar-Face then had kicked the boy. He had kicked the boy until the boy could no longer feel those brutal kicks.

"Wot d'yuh say now, Kid?" insisted the Gipsy in that deadly tone. "A bit more an' yuh won't have no arm in yer socket. Better tell, Kid."

The Frisco Kid gnawed his lips in effort to contain his agony. He wanted to scream but he feared to scream. He feared to alarm Miss Heffernan. Were she to become aware that he was being tortured, there behind the concealing bulks of Charley Small and the Gipsy, she would instantly know what type these men were. She would see through their game. And the Kid was fearful lest, thoroughly aroused, she might roundly accuse the men and they, realizing their game was up, might then turn like cornered rats and inflict on her the violence they were even then using on him. Had not the message from Frisco Red said that they were to go armed and be prepared to kill?

Interruption came from an unexpected source. There sounded through the room an ominous and prolonged growling. It came from the Gay-cat, yellow hair bristling, lips drawn menacingly back over sharp fangs. The dog hurtled forward and snapped at the Gipsy's high boots.

The man swore resentfully. He gave the dog a savage kick that propelled him, sliding as on ice, over the rug and well under the dining-table. He gave also, as he kicked, a sudden sharp wrench to the Kid's twisted arm. Suffering horribly, the boy exclaimed aloud.

Instantly the little old lady was between the Gipsy and his victim. The agonized cry of the boy had apprised her, for the first time, of the fact that he was being tortured.

"Let go! Let go that boy, I say!" she cried, and she pounded frantically upon the Gipsy's broad chest.

Immediately the man, still playing his part, released the Kid's wrenched arm. The boy nursed that arm.

"So that's the kind of detectives you be!" she added scornfully. "Torturing a pore little weak youngster!"

She looked at Gipsy Frank, an odd suspicious light behind the gold-rimmed glasses.

Suddenly that member of the mob called Charley Small made a sound in his throat like the guttural exclamation of a head-hunter. He pointed toward the dining-table. Underneath was the Gay-cat. In being kicked under that table the dog had become entangled in the trailing ends of the red cloth cover; in trying to extricate himself, he had only made matters worse. Now, a ball of red, squirming life, he backed out from under the table, carrying the cloth cover entirely away. There, exposed to full view under the table, was the gunny-sack of valuables, the open mouth showing the silver spoons the Kid last had put in!

Gipsy Frank darted for the table. He pulled out the sack. He dug his hand into the mouth. He was wildly excited. He rattled the silver spoons and knives and forks. He was digging for the money.

Suddenly he withdrew his hand. He looked wide-eyed at what he held in that hand. It was the black-and-white striped shoddy of a convict.

"Atlanta Slim!" he exclaimed, his dark face almost black with pounding blood. "He's escaped from stir as I thought! He's out—an' he's been here! He's been here!"

"Jerrold!" burst shrilly from Miss Heffernan. "It's Jerrold! That boy wasn't telling fibs; it's the truth, thank God! Jerrold's home!"

The little old lady became all at once very pale and slumped back against the wall as if seeking support.

For an appreciable moment the Gipsy looked at her with a peculiar wildness in his stare. His hand clenched tightly about the clothing as if with some inward tension. He felt the bills, crisp and crinkly, within. He jerked at the zebra sleeves and exposed the ten one-hundred-dollar notes. His voice boomed out like a foghorn:

"Here we are, guns! Here's the money! One thousand hicks! Come on; let's go!"

Forgotten was the old lady holding herself up by the wall; forgotten the Frisco Kid, whom they were supposed as detectives to be apprehending. The three men started in a rush for the open window, Gipsy Frank in the lead, his heavy boots pounding the flooring and shaking the house.

With supreme effort the old lady gathered herself together.

"Thieves, thieves!" she shouted at the top of her sharp voice. "You are the real thieves! I see it all now. That boy was only trying to save the money by hiding it from you. Robbers! Thieves!"

The Frisco Kid stood helplessly by. He could do naught to stop the men. He was overwhelmed by his own impotency. Yet he thought he heard, above the thunder of the Gipsy's boots, the sound of a bolt being sharply slid in its iron brackets. That grating sound came from the barroom.

XVII
GIPSY FRANK SHOWS HIS TRUE COLOR

CAME, AT THAT CLIMACTIC MOMENT, an unthinkably abrupt interposition of solid flesh and bone. It did not come from the direction of the barroom, however. A man bulked up outside the open dining-room window. In one hand, pointing at the three onrushing crooks, was clenched a bulldog automatic; on the sleeve of that pistol arm, at the wrist, a plated star gleamed ominously. The Frisco Kid recognized in this drooping-mustached, cutaway-coated and slouch-hatted man the sheriff who had forced him to retrace his steps the evening previous.

"No, you don't, Gipsy Frank!" said the sheriff quietly.

Gipsy Frank, in the lead for the window, made a sharp swerve toward the doorway into the kitchen.

"No use, Ballyhoo," said the sheriff laconically. "I got you covered, and I've got a coupla men waiting for you at every door. Put up your hands."

The last was an explosive command. Gipsy Frank, swerving again, had made a sudden vicious movement toward the vest under his corduroy coat. The Kid, startled at the movement, so reminiscent of Scar-Face Mike Hagan, was instantly aware of the Gipsy's intent. The breed had indeed come armed. Beneath that vest was a revolver concealed.

But Gipsy Frank's hand never reached the vest. Two men, clad in blue jeans and wearing the stars of deputies, were poking rifles through the doorway from the kitchen; two others had appeared, with the suddenness of jacks-in-the-box, in the entrance from the hall. The three crooks stopped dead, their hands flung overhead, their jaws slack with an utter and sickly surprise.

"Come on, Powers," said the sheriff as if to some one behind him.

He leaped upon the sill of the window and dropped down on the rug of the dining-room.

A man in a garish plaid cap appeared behind him at the open window. He gripped the sides of the window and swung himself with apelike agility nimbly into the room without touching foot to the sill. He was a short man of quick, lithe movements. He had a rough-chiseled, high-cheekboned face of a peculiar muddy color; his eyes were almond-shaped and oddly greenish-blue in hue; and his mouth was a brutal unfinished-looking gash.

His feet had no sooner bounded resiliently upon the rug than he reached his raw-knuckled right hand under the left armpit of his coat; there was a distinct snap; and his hand reappeared holding a police-special, short-barreled .38.

"Strong-Arm!" breathed the Frisco Kid, astounded and bewildered. "Now what's that old Ref boy doin' here?"

The sheriff was waiting for Strong-Arm. He asked—

"Any of these crooks the escaped con we want, Powers?"

With his slow, greenish eyes the Wobbly looked the three men over. He shook his head.

"No, Kummer," he returned. "None of these fuzzy-tailed prowlers is thet mugged gun, Number 7292. But you'd better frisk 'em, sheriff. I don't trust them cheap circus crooks none."

The sheriff acted promptly on Strong-Arm's advice. It seemed almost as if he were under orders to the Wobbly. He strode at once to Gipsy Frank and, jerking open coat and vest, exposed a revolver hanging in a cloth sling under the vest. It was not a large revolver; its barrel had been sawed down. On either side of the cloth sling the vest was padded deeply. That was to round off the bulge of the revolver. It was to lessen, if not wholly conceal, the outlines of that revolver. The sheriff relieved Gipsy Frank of the weapon and snatched the currency from his upheld hand.

Strong-Arm stood behind the sheriff at the open window, legs spread apart and police special in hand, his greenish, oblong eyes roving the room with an acute interest. He noted the old lady pressed against the wall; the boy beside her, dressed in Norfolk jacket and knickerbockers. He looked away to the deputies crowding the doorways. They all were watching absorbedly the sheriff search the burglars. Quickly thereupon Strong-Arm's long, greenish eyes leaped back to the boy in the Fauntleroy garb.

The Frisco Kid was watching him rigidly in perplexed wonder and no little fear.

Strong-Arm raised his left hand and covered with four fingers his brutal, unfinished-looking gash of mouth, coughed slightly as if clearing his throat and then, sure of the boy's attention, winked furtively a wink of recognition and secret fellowship.

It was the crook office. It told the boy that he had nothing personally to fear from Strong-Arm. Because it was done covertly it told further that neither the sheriff nor his deputies were at all in-the-know; to them, the Wobbly was merely Abraham Powers, a guard delegated by the warden of Joliet to aid the sheriff in the search for the escaped convict. Strong-Arm, however, had some deep scheme afoot. He, the Frisco Kid, was supposed to hold his peace and await events.

The sheriff was feeling the bulges and pockets of the other two circus crooks. In the hip pocket of Charley Small he found a billy of lead. Anzac Pete was armed with a razor.

The sheriff pocketed the various weapons with a grunt as expressive as "I thought so!" He stooped to pick up, from where Gipsy Frank had cast them, the numbered black-and-white striped garments. He approached the little old lady.

"Here is your thousand dollars, Miss Heffernan," he said politely, handing her the bills; then, his manner growing suddenly constrained and official—

"Now you will tell me, please, how these came here."

He held up the convict suiting.

The little old lady did not look at the zebra garments. Her fingers searched her dress for a pocket in which to place the currency, the while nervously, evasively, her eyes darted here and there behind the gold-rimmed spectacles.

"Oh, don't ask me, Sheriff Kummer," she pleaded. "I can't tell. I'm not sartain. I—I don't know!"

The lie came with a distinct wrench. Yet was she the inevitable woman, fighting for her own flesh and blood—her nephew hunted and cowering there in the barroom.

"No?" returned the sheriff, his voice rising with incredulity. "You don't know? Well, then, what did you mean, Miss Heffernan, when you said—

" 'It's Jerrold's!'

"Oh, I heard you. I saw the whole little act with my eye to that sill there; I heard you through that open window, and so did my deputy, Abraham Powers here. Isn't that right, Powers?"

The sheriff appealed to Strong-Arm with marked deference in his tone. The sab-cat nodded.

"I know a thing or two, Miss Heffernan. This blouse is numbered 7292. Convict 7292 escaped from Joliet four days ago. He was seen in these striped clothes heading this way a coupla hours gone. That's why I'm here; George Kummer ain't no fool. We were right on the heels of that escaped gun until he shook us off only two miles from this house. Where is 7292 now? Just explain a little, will you, ma'am?"

His voice sharpened sarcastically.

The little old lady, still bonneted as for the street, trembled in an extremity of fear and helplessness. Her worn hands sought the wall behind her, the fingers nervously picking.

"Oh, I can't; I can't, sheriff," she exclaimed piteously. "I 'clare to goodness, I'm not sartain. I—I don't know what it is all about. Oh, do believe me, sheriff."

"Well, we'll soon find out," harshly snapped the representative of the law.

He turned around on his deputies.

"Here, Josh Spiers and the rest of you fellers, herd this fancy bunch of cheap crooks out into the kitchen. I'll sweat 'em one at a time in the dining-room here. I'll call you, Powers, if I need you. I'll soon git the low-down on this little prize-puzzle, or know the reason why."

He stepped up behind Gipsy Frank, the last of the trio of crooks to enter the kitchen. He said sharply, close to the man's ear—

"What'd yuh mean—Atlanta Slim's made his getaway from stir?"

He trusted to the abruptness of the question to startle the fellow into committing himself. It is a favorite third-degree trick.

But the man called Gipsy Frank only swung his broad, dark face slowly round, looked full at the sheriff a tense moment and then quickly closed his left eye and jerked his head back toward the dining-room.

The Frisco Kid was following behind the crooks, aiding the trembling old lady. He saw the wise exchange. He knew from it that Gipsy Frank wanted to see the sheriff alone in the dining-room. He wanted to be the first to see the sheriff alone in the dining-room.

The sheriff stepped back.

"Just a moment, Gipsy Frank," he said. "I want to see you in here."

Gipsy Frank turned, his black band of eyebrows lifting as if in surprise. He stepped out of the herded line and with seeming dejection walked back into the dining-room. The sheriff promptly closed the door behind him.

There in the tidy kitchen the deputies stood guard over the quaking old woman, the Frisco Kid and the two circus crooks, while the rumble of heavy voices rose and fell in the other room. The dog, Gay-cat, put stump of tail between legs and slunk in a roundabout way to the Frisco Kid. The Kid lifted the dog and hugged the round yellow head against his scrawny neck. Gay-cat tried thereat and most solicitously to lick his left cheek and the tip of his nose.

"He jes' wanted to git the sheriff alone," whispered the Kid into the dog's ragged ear. "I'll bet he lams that Johnny Tinplate over the head with a chair and makes his escape. He's a bad un, that Gipsy."

He turned to look for Strong-Arm, alias Abraham Powers, in order to convey by eye-flash his suspicion of Gipsy Frank's intentions. What a surprise! Strong-Arm had left the other deputies; was standing by the closed door through which throbbed dully the indistinct voices, his right ear glued to the crack between door and jamb. Those other deputies might surmise as they pleased—he was eavesdropping to the conversation going forward in the dining-room with an utter disregard for their opinion, with a complete recklessness and bravado.

All at once Gipsy Frank's gruff tones swelled in volume as if some statement he had made had been refuted or doubted by the sheriff and he thought by thundering to down all argument, force belief. Amid the rumble of his voice his words could be heard in the kitchen with fair distinctness.

"I'm tellin' yuh the straight, Kummer," he was saying. "Why, I've worked fer the govamint fer years as an elbow and fer the Burns people too. Who nabbed Chi Blondy in thet post-office job down in Simpson jist below here, about ten months ago? Thet was me as a govamint dick. Did yuh ever hear o' Whitey Horn, the sab-cat? Thet's me when I'm noseyin' fur the Jugel Agency among the Wobblies—the I.W.W.'s. Lemme—"

"For the Jugel Agency, was it!" hoarsely muttered Strong-Arm on the other side of the door.

Swiftly he reached out his left hand and flexed his stubby fingers about the doorknob; the other hand brought up the police special to the level of his tumultuously heaving chest. He took an abrupt step forward as if to burst into the dining-room.

But on the sudden the insensate fanatic heat fled his oblong greenish eyes. He snatched his hand from the door-knob as if that knob were a scorching live coal. The police special came down with a jerk to his hip. He retreated from the door as from a threatening calamity, precipitantly, an aghast and foolish expression overspreading his muddy face.

"What's the matter with me?" he muttered shakily under his breath. "This ain't house-cleanin' day yit."

From the other room, loud upon surprised ears, boomed the voice of Gipsy Frank:

"Lemme ast yuh somethin', Kummer. Who was it got all the dope on Atlanta Slim, alias Swaggerin' Bob, out in Californy—"

The sheriff uttered an exclamation. It was the name—

"Atlanta Slim!"

Then he could be heard to say:

"And that's who I'm after now. Broke out of Joliet, he did, four days ago. Nobody knows how; it's darned queer; but every sheriff in the state is on the trail, and the prison warden and all kinds of deputies and posses. He was here tonight. I know; I got the dope straight; and that's his suit numbered 7292. Say, what do *you* know about Atlanta Slim?"

"Me? Me know about Atlanta Slim? Why, I knows all about him! Who was it follered him fer months clear acrosst the country from thet peter job in the First National o' Hartford an' the big haul on the Chi National? Why, I knows all about him; yes, siree; all about him, 'ceptin' this new gitaway stunt. Broke from Joliet, eh? Why, there'll be dodgers sent all over the states about Slim boy an', man, wot a heapin' reward! Sheriff, from now on I'm out after Atlanta Slim myself."

Dawn was breaking on the listening Kid. Yet how could it be? Gipsy Frank had not the beefy red face of a policeman. There was no quarter-inch scar streaking with hideous whiteness the red health of that face from left eye to overstrong chin. Truly, Gipsy Frank had a large jaw, a heavy-lipped, snarling mouth and a broad face; but that face was dark as any of the Black Men of Zend and the eyebrows met over the nose in a straight band of inky hairs.

The Frisco Kid looked in profound perplexity at Strong-Arm, backed away from the door. Strong-Arm's head was thrown back and his lips were drawn away from the strong white teeth in an animal-like snarl. In his long, half-closed, greenish eyes was a cold, gloating light. It was as if, having overheard all that Gipsy Frank had to reveal, his fanatic brain had gestated a swift plan that would require only watchful waiting to move it inevitably to its crashing and fateful denouement.

The Kid turned to the two crooks of Gipsy Frank's mob. They too were listening in a strange fascination of harkening, their eyes upon each other, a terrible realization growing in those eyes. He saw the man called Anzac Pete swallow nervously, his throat-apple bulging up and down.

Unexpectedly the door into the dining-room swung open. The sheriff looked into the kitchen.

"Give me a basin of water," he ordered, "and a piece of yaller washing-soap."

Miss Heffernan tremulously poured into a tin basin some water from the kettle upon the cold stove. The sheriff carried it into the dining-room. He seemed to forget to shut the door behind him. He placed the basin upon the table.

The Frisco Kid watched bepuzzled. The while he listened acutely for some sound from the barroom. He thought once he heard a remote creak, as if a sash or door were being opened somewhere in the reaches of the house.

He saw Gipsy Frank take off his corduroy coat, roll up the sleeves of his pink shirt and step to the basin as if about to wash his face. And that was exactly what the fellow proceeded to do! He bent down, and rubbed and scrubbed, with the water and coarse washing-soap, at the skin of his cheeks and the hair of the eyebrows over the nose.

When at last he lifted up, puffing, the hair streaking water down his face, the skin of his face was no longer the swarth hue of the Gipsy. It was flaming red from the scrubbing, beefy red as a policeman's. And there was no band of black brows across the top of the nose. The eyebrows were separated as widely as the far-spaced, brutal eyes.

"Mike Hagan, the stool-pigeon!" exclaimed the sheriff as he looked at the man's dripping red face. "So it's really you, you slick blackguard!"

The Frisco Kid stiffened and congealed in every limb. He could feel the pulse pounding crashingly in his ears.

"Scar-Face!" he breathed in a cold whisper of terror.

Now he knew! Just as Gipsy Frank had scrubbed off the pigment that had dyed his skin to the swarth hue of a gipsy, just so, back in the tar-weeds of California after he had kicked the boy into insensibility, had Scar-Face rubbed off the paint of his faked-up hideous blemish, that jigger across chin and cheek which had given him a certain identity among crooks. The kid was aware at last where he had heard before that gruff, snarling voice. Gipsy Frank was Scar-Face Mike Hagan, the stool that had peached on Slim and sent him up, months gone, to Joliet.

Some one brushed by the Kid and stood swaying in the doorway, clinging weakly to the frame. It was little old Miss Heffernan.

"Jerrold!" she cried in a quavering voice. "It's you, Jerrold, after twenty years! But good laws!" in a sharp frightened gasp. "Then that man hiding in the barroom isn't Jerrold at all!"

The world seemed to reel, the whole rambling old house to quake and stagger as in a seismic shock. The deputies, their hangdog captives, Strong-Arm,

Sheriff Kummer, the Frisco Kid—all looked in dazed unbelief from Miss Heffernan to Gipsy Frank, *alias* Scar-Face Mike Hagan. But it was indeed true. All could read that plainly on the face of Hagan himself.

What a sorrowful moment for the little old lady so good to road-kids! This utter scamp was her long-awaited and long-prayed-for nephew, Jerrold, the runaway boy of more than twenty years gone—this thief in the night who had stolen into her home and under the sheltering roof of his babyhood had tried to wrest from his own aunt her pitiful store of wealth. Fate had never played a crueler trick than it had played so unmeritedly upon Miss Heffernan!

A deep and moving pity smote the Frisco Kid, and the salt tears blinded his eyes so that he could see no longer her unforgettable tragic face. Even the sheriff and the circus crooks, once the wild look of unbelief and consternation smoothed from their faces, became suddenly grim with sympathy for her.

But abruptly, with smashing-impact, the sinister significance of her last words penetrated the shocked intelligence of Sheriff Kummer.

"The man in the barroom," he repeated, slewing round to her again, his mouth open and exposing under the drooping mustache much gold work. "You mean the owner of this zebra suit?"

She nodded dumbly, too shaken and overwrought by all that had happened to speak.

"Here, Abe Powers, watch these circus crooks," shouted the sheriff. "Come on, you others; we'll break into the barroom. We'll get that Atlanta Slim."

XVIII
STRONG-ARM STARTS HOUSE-CLEANING

THE FRISCO KID GAVE A TORTURED, INCOHERENT CRY at the sheriff's words, and hugged his Gay-cat to him so tightly that the dog squealed once like a trap-nipped rat. The Kid's face had turned a sickly gray; his distended, agonized eyes burned in his dead face like two great woeful stars. How he hated to see his former buddy, Atlanta Slim, taken there before his eyes!

But he could do nothing, only watch the sheriff and his four deputies clatter out of the dining-room. As the men turned their backs to him in gaining the hall he could see their free hands wrenching electric torches from their hip pockets. Strong-Arm, *alias* Abraham Powers, alone remained in the dining-room to keep an official eye on Mike Hagan and his circus grifters.

Sheriff Kummer and his deputies effected an entrance into the barroom without any difficulty. Atlanta Slim had left the door unbolted since that time when, just before the appearance of the sheriff on the scene, he had been about to burst out to the assistance of Miss Heffernan. The men disappeared into the darkness of the room, spraying the ghostly beams of light about and calling sharply upon Slim to surrender to the law.

The Kid found himself dragging his cold, squeamish body on stuttering legs toward the barroom and peering, as into a tunnel, into that place of strange glooms and lunging lights. The blood was pounding in his ears with the fever of his pulse. Any moment he expected to hear a shot or else the voice of the sheriff yelping in triumph.

But no such pealing outcry came. The Kid sickened with the suspense. The febrile state of his nerves robbed his eyes of their functioning power; but still he could manage to hear as from a great distance the curses of the searching men, the sounds of their stumbling against boxes and over old lumber.

How long after it was, he never knew; but there came a tremendous bang, like the report of a pistol or the thud of an opened shutter. His brain cleared miraculously. He heard the sheriff bellowing:

"Here's where he got out! He's flew the coop, the slick rat! While we were gassin' in that other room like a bunch o' the Ladies' Aid he shoved through this window and then jammed the shutter tight behind him so's we wouldn't notice it being open. Looket that broken yew-hedge where he dropped down!"

The Kid's heart began suddenly to pump at a surprising speed, leaping like a live wild thing, filling his whole chest and choking him. He hugged Gay-cat convulsively to him and whispered hoarsely into one ragged canine ear:

"He's got away, Gay-cat, old-timer! Slim's got away!"

What a brave and reckless fellow, that Atlanta Slim!' Like a yeast rose within the boy all his old unquestioning admiration and faith in his glorious buddy!

He looked up sharply, sensing that some one was staring at him. He caught sight of Miss Heffernan standing in affright and bewilderment against one wall of the dining-room, her bespectacled eyes riveted upon the barroom door through which Sheriff Kummer and his four deputies had disappeared.

Beyond her was Strong-Arm leaning against the jamb of the kitchen doorway and swinging his police special from the two crooks within the kitchen to Mike Hagan standing, spread-legged and expectant, near the open dining-room window. Strong-Arm's head was turned back over one shoulder and it was he who was staring at the Kid. Though the Wobbly surely must have heard what the sheriff said and hence fully realized that Slim had made a getaway, the Kid could still read in his long, greenish eyes an acute question.

The Frisco Kid gave ready answer. There was no mistaking that emphatic nod of the unkempt head, that light of epic victory on his glowing face. Atlanta Slim had got away! A look oddly incandescent swept through the muddy complexion of Strong-Arm's face; his face lighted up with satanic triumph. He stepped out of the kitchen doorway and toward Mike Hagan.

From the barroom came the voice of the sheriff barking out orders:

"We're wasting time, ——— it! Out the window, a coupla you fellows, and see if you can pick up that zebra's trail."

Strong-Arm was close to Hagan. His cold, green eyes on Hagan's wide-spread ones, he leaned forward and whispered. The Frisco Kid could not hear what he said; not even Miss Heffernan, who was nearer him, could hear what he said; but what he said was:

"So yer Whitey Horn, the stool fer the Jugel Agency among the I.W.W.'s, eh? Well, does yuh know who I am? Me, I'm Strong-Arm, the Avenging Angel o' the Wobblies."

Mike Hagan must have heard of him before. He gave a short, hoarse, strangled cry. He flung up one arm as if to ward off a blow and fell back toward the open window, his beefy face blanching with terror.

"Yuh will try ter break fer thet open winder!" yelled Strong-Arm abruptly, theatrically.

He jerked up the police special and blazed away at the retreating pink-shirted chest, once, twice, three times.

Hagan's upflung arm dropped like a slug of lead; his jaw sagged, his tongue lolled out, he slumped to his knees; and then his head and trunk shot forward on the rug for all the world as if he were striking out into water.

Sheriff Kummer and his two remaining deputies rushed into the room. They found Miss Heffernan pressed against the wall, white as a fresh towel, her eyes bulging with horror; Strong-Arm, heavy of face and morosely somber, standing near the dining-table, revolver in hand; and before him, flat on his face upon the rug and altogether dead, the stool-pigeon, Jerrold Michael Hagan.

"Good Lord, what's this, Powers?" asked the sheriff.

"His us'al tricks, Kummer," returned Strong-Arm grimly. "He tried ter make a break through thet open winder an' I got him, the ——— stool."

The Wobbly had played his subterranean game skillfully. No one could contradict him, for of all those present, not one had heard his whispered words to Hagan. He held out the police special, grimy from usage, to the sheriff.

"I s'pose I'm under arrest, Kummer; what?"

"That's the formality, Powers," nodded the sheriff. "It's too bad, Abe, but it was in the line of duty. You'd better keep the gat, though. You'll need it for that Slim party before the night is out, I'm thinking."

XIX
Strong-Arm's Chick

For two days past the house on the hill had been crowded with folk who had not crossed that threshold in years. There were gray, spare farmers' wives who had ridden in on buckboards and flivvers from remote pockets and corners of the county; there were stout bovine women from right next door in Middletown, the wives of prosperous merchants of the township. Both sorts had been girl and girl and skipped to school with Miss Heffernan in the long ago; but only a death in her house and that the death of the motherless nephew she had raised from a babe caused them to recall that friendship and feel for the "queer upstairs" old maid in her tragic bereavement.

There was one mercy to the lugubrious ceremonial. So busy was Miss Heffernan recalling names to fit faces and in listening to awkwardly put words of condolence from strangers, dimly remembered, that she had no time to think about the loss of those gilded illusions which had kept her going almost half her years, which had caused her to be so good to road-kids.

But now it was the third night, and the rambling old structure upon the hill was suddenly hushed and empty. They sat in the tidy kitchen, Miss Heffernan, the Frisco Kid and his dog. The Gay-cat was outstretched upon the boy's lap, his sharp little head turned sidewise in the crotch of the Kid's arm and his brown canine eyes closed in sleep.

Miss Heffernan sat opposite in an oddly crouching attitude in her rocking-chair. She looked very frail and beaten, her pale, fragile hands clasped quietly together in her lap, her eyes strangely dull; for she was facing facts now, the most terrible ordeal any one may undergo in this vale of sorrows called living.

Outside it was a wide, hollow night, starless and very black. Through the screening of the kitchen door came nervous little gusts that caused the yellow flame of the kerosene lamp to blink in its wall-bracket like a sleepyhead batting his eye. The figure 8 o'clock ticked heavily as if adding up a hard sum, and its hands climbed slowly toward nine o'clock and bedtime.

There sounded a sharp tattoo like the rapping of knuckles on the door and then on the heels of it, in a sudden wintry gust, the light of the lamp wafted out. The Kid gave a hoarse, strangled cry as if some one had him by the throat. He sat there unable to move, in a complete funk, believing in all the weird and supernatural stories he had ever heard, too dismayed and rattled to think of digging in his pockets for a match to strike a light. The rapping sound came again.

Miss Heffernan rustled by him and the next moment was talking in whispers with some one in the blackness beyond the screen door. The door squeaked open and then two shadows moved vaguely back into the kitchen.

"Won't you light up the lamp if you've a match in your pockets?" asked Miss Heffernan of the Frisco Kid.

She seemed to turn back to the shadowy visitor.

"The lamp blew out real mysterious-like, just as you knocked," she explained in a shaky voice. "It's given us both the uncanny creeps."

"Us both? Who else is here with yer, Miss Heffernan, ma'am?"

The voice of the stranger shook like a twanged guitar string, as if its owner also felt frightened. It was not the voice of a man; it was the thin, sexless voice of a child, shrill now with deep consternation.

At the sound of it the Frisco Kid began once more to breathe. He leaped afoot, spilling the suddenly yelping Gay-cat headfirst out of sleep and sprawling upon the floor.

"If it ain't Chick, Strong-Arm's Chick!" he exclaimed. "And here's me so badly skeered I had the belly-ache with thinkin' all the time you was Strong-Arm come back again, or maybe the ghost o' Mike Hagan hisself!"

"That you, Frisco Kid?" answered a relieved voice from the dark. "Miss Heffernan here never tole me you was in the house. I warn't expectin' to meet up with any bo, least of all good ol' Frisco."

The Kid had dug out a match from among the odds and ends crowding his pockets. Nursing the feeble flame between his hands, he climbed upon a chair and, removing the swiftly cooling glass chimney, ignited the wick.

As the kitchen leaped into warm yellow glow he turned round to face Chick. The little ten-year-older stood near the screen door, his pipestem legs bare to the knees and coated with the brown dust of the road, his soft, pouting, infantile face oddly pale beneath its disheveled mat of straw-colored hair.

"What yuh doin' here, Chick?" he asked. "Where's Strong-Arm?"

It was sickening, the abject look of terror that suddenly distended the baby blue eyes of Chick and caused them to glance this way and that as if jerked by strings. The boy's strained glance fell at last upon Miss Heffernan and became fixed there, the starkness of terror dimming into the graciousness of peering wonder.

Miss Heffernan had slumped into the rocking-chair before the stove. She appeared to have entirely forgotten about the advent of this tiny tad in faded red sweater and knee trousers. Her eyes once again were dull and remote.

The Frisco Kid got quietly down from the chair.

"She's away from herse'f, Chick," he whispered. "She's had a death in her fambly and she's gone plumb queer-upstairs with all the sorrer of it. You can go ahead and spiel, Chick, without her hearin' one word."

Chick reached out and got the Kid by one of the straps of his Norfolk jacket.

"You tell me, Frisco," he pleaded, his tiny lower lip starting an uncontrollable trembling. "Good ol' Frisco, you'll tell me, won't yuh? I'm jist achin' to find out. Where's Strong-Arm?"

The Kid was surprised.

"Did he ditch yer?" he countered.

Chick gulped and lowered his eyes.

"Me, I ain't shootin' off my face," he said surlily, "until yer tells me all the latest news about Strong-Arm. Frisco!"

He looked up suddenly.

"I'm skeered to death of thet Wobbly!"

A shiver ran through his pitifully frail body.

"Aw, Chick-a-biddy!" was wrenched from the Kid.

He put his arm about the little fellow's shoulder. He looked over toward Miss Heffernan, and, keeping his eyes upon her, went on:

"I seed Strong-Arm last jest three nights ago. He was here. *Ssh*, Chick! She don't know nothin' about him an' I don't want her to find out. But you don't mean ye're skeered of Strong-Arm 'cause yuh run out on him, does yer?"

"Naw. He run out on me. He sold me to yer ol' jocker, Frisco Red."

"Frisco Red—hmm! But where'd yuh meet up with that whisky bum? Where's he now? Did yuh ditch Red too, Chick?"

Chick nodded and in low tones related the story of Strong-Arm's meeting with Frisco Red up the railroad near Bedford.

"So that's how it was," interposed the Kid. "Here I've been wonderin' how Strong-Arm got to workin' hand-in-glove with the sheriff. He got the official docket from Red, eh?"

"Yes," said Chick. "An' after he beat up Red onmerciful, as I tole yuh, Strong-Arm he toins to me. He hands me his own pussonel private gat.

" 'Take this shootin'-iron,' he says, 'an' stay here with Red. Them's my orders, Chick. When Red comes to and starts to beat yuh up, you jist plug him proper. I allus dreamed that it was a little 'fraid kid like youse, Chick, what should croak me ol' jocker, Frisco Red!' "

The incident had made a deep mark on the child's soul.

"I sha'n't ever fergit them words of Strong-Arm, not till I die," he said, his lower lip once again starting its ungovernable trembling. "I wanted to do as Strong-Arm ordered, an' again I didn't. Most of all I wanted to run away an' lose myse'f where neither o' them two vicious stiffs 'ud ever find me. I didn't know which way to toin—"

"So yuh stuck; eh, Chick boy?"

"Yes; for more'n an hour, long after it was dark. Every time Red 'ud groan as if he was comin' to, I'd give a yell and 'most jump outer my boots. But Red, he never seemed to git any more wide awake, so I finally got the spunk to slope. And I'm still beatin' it, Frisco, tryin' to find a place to hide until both them guys is outer these parts fer keeps."

"Aw, yuh don't need a be leery of Red, Chick. That old bum ain't worth a hill o' beans nowadays; he's soaked up too much whisky in his time."

"But Strong-Arm, Frisco. I'm skeered to death of Strong-Arm. I dream nights; I'm jumpy o' my own shadder. He tol' me to plug Red an' I didn't!"

"Aw, Chick-a-biddy, there's no use yer cryin'!" burst out the Frisco Kid at sight of the tears welling in the child's eyes. "Strong-Arm, he'll never come here again. He'll be afraid to."

He dropped his voice, glancing toward Miss Heffernan.

"It was him, Strong-Arm, what made her like that," he whispered. "He was here three nights ago an' he caused the death in her fambly. But don't ask me no more about it, Chick. She might hear and feel all thet sorrer over again."

"She 'pears to have plumb fergotten about me," remarked Chick, his voice suddenly woebegone. "I guess now I'll git no setdown like she promised me at the screen door."

"Aw, Chick!" reproved the Kid. "That's no fault of hern. She's all bruk up about that death in her fambly, like I done tole yer. You never had a death in the fambly, I'll bet, or yuh'd know. Why, if it wasn't fer me she wouldn't 'a' eaten anything these last three days. I've been Chinese cook an' Portugee bottle-washer round these diggin's all that time; an', say, she's even forgotten about *me!* Yes, an' Gay-cat here what has stuck to her through it all like the thick-'n'-thin scout he is.

"But I'll give yer a setdown, Chick, a splendiferous setdown: baked beans what's warmin' in the oven, white bread, an' coffee 'n' pie. I got the pie myse'f down in Middletown today."

As the Kid went over to the stove to put on the pot of coffee and remove from the oven the warm crock of beans, Miss Heffernan looked up at him, her old dull eyes brightened and she said very tenderly:

"What are you fussing so about, Jerrold, dear? Isn't it 'most nine naow, time my boy should be abed?"

The Kid halted upstanding, suddenly sober. He struggled to speak, but could only make queer little noises in his throat. It was not the first time she had called him "Jerrold." She had addressed him by nothing else but that name for the past three days. She continued to look up at him now with a gentle smile on her thin lips.

"Aw, a-a-auntie!" he stammered at last. "Jes' a little while before bedtime, please. And I'm not fussin', r-r-really. I'm merely rustlin' up some warm beans an' bread 'n' coffee fer this little hungry Chick here. Ain't I doin' right, a-a-auntie?"

The soft brightness in her eyes mellowed into a wonderfully proud and possessive glow. Smiling on as if in some serene dream, she nodded.

"Of course, Jerrold, dear! Give him all the beans he can eat, pore child, and don't forget there's apple pie in the pantry. And have him sleep in your little bed with you, that's a good boy."

The Frisco Kid came back to Chick at the kitchen table, the crock of beans in his hands.

"She called yer Jerrold," whispered the urchin. "What does she mean by that?"

The Kid put a warning finger to his lips.

"*Ssh*, not now! We'll have a real honest-to-goodness gabfest up in my room later. I'll tell you all about it then."

After they had tucked themselves in, within the little green-painted iron bed up in the attic room, the Frisco Kid fully explained to Chick the tragedy that had befallen Miss Heffernan. Chick returned the confidence by relating how he had come to direct his steps toward the house on the hill. After running away from Frisco Red he had met up along the road with a certain bold *rodeo* called the Crybaby Kid.

"I knows him," said the Frisco Kid. "He's a member of Portugee Kid's push—the youngest member."

"But no more, he isn't," qualified Chick. "He was pitched by Portugee 'cause he was makin' the whole bunch look like a kindergarten. Leastwise that's what I gathers. But he don't care none, he tol' me; says he's sorter glad to be on his own. But he's sore at 'em all jist the same, 'cause he's sure toined horstile to everybody. He's goin' in fer strong-arm work, he claims, an' he offers to lemme join out with him.

"Me, I toins him down cold, tellin' him how I'm fixed. He sees I'm jumpy o' my own shadder even though I've got a gat, so he offers to give me the low-down on a good hidin'-place providin' I'll pass over to him the big shootin'-iron of Strong-Arm's I'm totin'. He can use it in his rough work, he says. Myse'f I'm on'y too glad to get rid of the weapon. So then he ups and tells me to come here.

" 'You go to Miss Heffernan's,' he says. 'She'll take you in an' feed yer on dumplin's an' cornstarch puddin' an' jamocha cake, and let yer sleep in a little whitey bed up under the roof. She's allus been good to road-kids, an' she'll be 'specially good to a little 'fraid-cat like youse.

" 'An' you stay with her, Chick boy!' he says. 'Stay at Miss Heffernan's an' git off the Road. It's diff'rent with a tough kid like me, but the Road is no place fer a jumpy, shiverin' shrimp like youse. What you wants is a home, and that's jist what this Heffernan dame will give yer—a home with mush an' milk o' mornin's an' pancakes that 'ud knock yer eye out! She'll fall fer you right off. She'll wanta erdopt you soon's she sees yuh, you see if she don't. Why, she tried to erdopt me myse'f some time ago, but it warn't no use with a hard-boiled kid like me.' "

Chick was singularly talkative. He went on to say that he had never known a real home before. He had been raised in an orphan asylum in St. Louis. About the asylum were high stone walls which hid from view thoroughfares for street-cars and automobiles and sundry strollers. The boys of the asylum had come to know that these things lay beyond through acting the role of "peeping Toms."

There was a great door in one wall which was clear a few inches of the cement walk. On Sunday afternoons when the "orphs" were loosed in the front yard they used to take turns, so many at a time, lying flat on their stomachs and peering under that door at the passing mysterious shoes and wheels of the outside world. Many a long Sunday had Chick spent with his nose and eyes in close proximity to the cold pavement. Indeed, with the habit the outside world had become so fascinating that finally he had been led to steal furtively from the asylum one dark night, climb the great door and plunge into the glamour and mystery of the beyond.

Chick's words came more and more drawlingly until finally he began a sentence he was never to finish, heaved a prodigious sigh and fell to breathing slow and regularly. Beside him, in the little bed, the Frisco Kid remained stark awake, gazing up into the darkness. He could not sleep.

He remembered how they had filed out of the kitchen that night. Chick in the lead, Gay-cat next and last of all himself. He had paused beside Miss Heffernan's rocker to bid her good night; he had found himself stooping down and kissing her. It was a shamefaced boyish kiss, a quick, birdlike peck, entirely unpremeditated; but what bothered him insistently now was how she had smiled over it, a mist flooding her old eyes.

"Poor Chick-a-biddy!" he breathed to the dark. "No fambly or nothin'! Gee, somethin's got to be done to make this his real honest-to-goodness home! Why, she hardly noticed him all evenin'!"

XX
A CRISIS

THE WEEK WENT BY WITH NO VISITORS, either hoboesque or otherwise, calling at the house upon the hill. The Frisco Kid continued to do for himself and his Gay-cat, for little silvery-haired Miss Heffernan and the tiny Chick. Then one day came a step on the gravel driveway, and while Chick fled into hiding up the attic stairs the Frisco Kid opened the kitchen screen door to Sheriff Kummer.

The moment he saw the official, the Frisco Kid guessed what was up. It proved to be exactly as he had surmised. The real Abraham Powers had finally appeared in Middletown and explained how he had been given "knockout drops" and been robbed of his paper of identification. Then Sheriff Kummer had hunted about for the man who had called himself Powers and who had killed Jerrold Michael Hagan; but that fellow had parted from the sheriff in the search for the escaped convict and all trace of him had been lost.

But the fruitless search had convinced the sheriff of several things. He believed that the false Abraham Powers had been instrumental in assisting Atlanta Slim to his getaway and also that there had been a hidden motive behind the slaying of Hagan. Finally Kummer had bethought himself to climb the hill and question the inhabitants of Miss Heffernan's clearinghouse for hoboes.

He was inclined to be rather sharp and high-handed in his quizzing; but the Frisco Kid proved too much for him. He thrust himself before the apathetic old lady and artfully answered all queries. He seemed at that to know only half as much as the sheriff already surmised; he talked a great deal but in reality told very little. The sheriff finally banged out of the kitchen, disgruntled at the meagerness of what he had learned.

The Kid watched him walk round the house to the road. He could hardly contain himself from giving a great whoopee of delight. The sheriff had practically admitted, in the nature of his questions, that Atlanta Slim had successfully escaped and also that Strong-Arm had vanished completely from that part of the state. The Kid was on the point of darting from the kitchen to tell Chick that he need fear no longer the reappearance of Strong-Arm when Miss Heffernan called him to her side with the tenderly enunciated name—

"Jerrold!"

"Yes, auntie," he replied as he stood before her, respectfully waiting.

"I don't see that little road-youngster who has been here this past week. Has he gone off with the sheriff?"

"Aw, Miss Heffer—I mean, auntie! Why does yer say sech a thing! Chick hasn't left the house at all; he's up-stairs hidin' in the attic room. He's on'y ten, and he's been awful meanly treated, and he's leery of strangers comin', that's all. He don't intend to leave yer ever. He wants to stay on here with you an' me an' Gay-cat."

"But I can't afford it, child."

Her listlessness dropped from her; a bitterness leaped to the eyes behind the coldly gleaming glasses; once again was she the tart schoolmarm type.

"I can't afford to feed three mouths besides my own with the little I earn from my dogs."

The Kid looked at her with frightened, terrible eyes, not knowing what to say. She bowed her head beneath his gaze, and her frail shoulders shook as if with soundless sobs.

"Oh, God 'a' mercy, what have I said!" she murmured. "I'm ashamed. I never was so mean-spirited and raspy before. But I guess"—and she lifted her thin, white face and smiled wearily at him—"I guess I must be getting stingy of you and Gay-cat. I want us three to be alone here together."

The Kid understood. But it appalled him. He thought of the tiny tad hiding up-stairs, and he could say nothing, only wet his lips and gulp. He heard a low, miserable sobbing. Miss Heffernan had bowed her head again and he could see the pinkness of her scalp showing between the white, thin strands of hair. But the sobbing did not come from her.

He made across the kitchen toward the door into the dining-room. A clammy coldness was sheathing his limbs. He flung open the door. There, crouched on the threshold and sobbing as if his little heart would break, was the orphan, Strong-Arm's Chick. He had heard every cruel word spoken by Miss Heffernan.

"I wish I was daid," he sobbed out. "No fambly, no home, no nothin'. Oh, Frisco, I wish I was daid."

"Why—why—what's the matter?" stammered Miss Heffernan, suddenly aware of the presence of the little fellow and accordingly confused.

"It's Chick, ma'am," spoke up the Frisco Kid in a queer, gruff, oldish voice. "He overheard what you said. He wants to know why he can't stay on here forever—why you can't come to love him jest like you does Gay-cat an' me."

"Aw, Miss Heffernan, ma'am!" broke out Chick wailingly. "I didn't mean no harm, honest I didn't. I never would 'a' battered yer back door if I thought yuh wouldn't 'a' wanted me. But Crybaby Kid, he tol' me yer would erdopt me soon's you saw me, an' I came on quick as a shot.

"But I guess it's all no use now, Miss Heffernan, an' no hard feelin's. You can't fall fer me 'cause you've already fallen fer Frisco an' his dorg; I see thet plain. But if yer don't mind, ma'am, I'll stay on fer one more good meal an' then I'll say *adios*, an' not bother you no more."

It was a crisis; a crisis which had been brewing ever since the appearance of Chick in the house; a crisis for which the Frisco Kid was unconsciously prepared. Now, his face very pale, the Kid reached down under the kitchen table, drew out Gay-cat by his stiffened forelegs and gathered the dog up in his arms. Not looking at Miss Heffernan or the sobbing Chick, he started across the kitchen for the screen door, his eyes glassy with a kind of desperation.

But the little old maid got in his way. With a half-stifled cry of anguish she sprang afoot and barred his progress with outflung arms. The Kid stopped and seemed to cringe.

"Aw, lemme go, Miss Heffernan, ma'am!" he begged in a hard, metallic voice. "Yer been awful good to me—to me an' Gay-cat—but it ain't right fer us to stay."

"Name o' goodness, child, what harm can have happened! Why act so tarnation queer and or'nary?"

He looked up at her, his face flaming crimson.

"Aw, can't yer see, ma'am? It's me was to blame fer all this sadness—

yes, me what brought all this sorrer home to yer—me, the Frisco Kid, that was never nothin' but an unlucky mascot to nobody."

"Tut, tut, child! What could you, a sweet-natured little—"

He turned on her fiercely.

"Aw, cut it, will yuh, ma'am! It's me what done it, jes' as I says. I knew all the time that Strong-Arm—I mean, Abe Powers—was a hard sort of guy an' had it in fer yer nephew Jerrold. I could 'a' told Sheriff Kummer on Strong-Arm an' saved yer nephew from gittin' murdered. But I didn't. I worked in with Strong-Arm to do yer harm. Oh, I'm a hard-boiled an' or'nary kid, I tells yuh. I seed the mischief cookin' up an' I did nothin' to stop it."

It was all out. With the confession the Kid felt certain he had killed whatever of love Miss Heffernan might have cherished for him in her heart. He started forward again, stooped over his dog, circling round her toward the screen door.

She watched him go by her, arms at her side, seemingly unable to know what to think or do. She was sadly baffled. Then as he put hand on the knob of the screen door to leave her forever, a flush of blood suddenly suffused her thin, austere face and with a tiny squeal of joy she darted after him, gathered both boy and dog in her arms and hugged them tightly to her.

"Oh, you pert little muggins!" she exclaimed. "You *would* try to paint yourself black and bad in my eyes so's you could leave the field entirely to pore Chick. But 'tain't no use, child; I see it all naow; and Chick baby can stay on with us here and we'll make together one happy little family. Isn't that what you want, dear?"

The Kid hid his head in the crook of her arm. He was suddenly overcome with shame at having his motives thus quickly perceived. But manfully in muffled voice he asked:

"Aw, will yer, Miss Heffernan, auntie? Will yer adopt Chick along with us, the same as Crybaby said?"

"Will I!"

Miss Heffernan put the Kid upon his feet, darted over to the little, startled Chick, threw her arms about him and kissed his wan, tear-streaked, baby face. For the second time since his initial meeting with Chick the Frisco Kid had acted toward the tiny tad the role of savior. Like most rôles in life, that of savior demands more and more of sacrifice. The Frisco Kid had but just begun his task.

XXI
THE ULTIMATE SACRIFICE

CAME THE LAST DAY OF ANOTHER WEEK, SATURDAY. As had become his wont, the Frisco Kid bathed his dog in the briskness of the sunny April afternoon and then in the evening himself. After which he stood by and assisted little Chick in his weekly tubbing. Then the two boys appeared in the dining-room for Miss Heffernan's inspection, attired in the miniature bathrobes which the sweet old lady had purchased just for them in Middletown.

Miss Heffernan pulled down the spectacles from her forehead and carefully examined the Kid's ears and scrawny neck for unwashed places and soap-rings. Dutifully the Kid stood by her chair until she had done, then smiled with glowing pride at her sweet, warming words of commendation.

He leaned over and, unbidden, kissed her good night as he had done one memorable evening before. Then he motioned Chick forward to go through the same Saturday-night ritual.

Miss Heffernan smiled rather whimsically at the hesitating little Chick; her eyes became fixed on his pale, tiny, inchoate face, so full of shy curves and so pouting about the pure, babyish mouth. His mouth was open and innocent as a flower. She seemed to grow dismayed at the fascination its frail trusting loveliness held for her. She made a great effort, withdrew her gaze and pretended to give him as careful a looking-over as she had the Frisco Kid. Naturally, such was her effort, she overdid the thing.

"Law, laws, this will never do!" she cried in a shaky voice. "To see this pore child's neck and here behind the ears, one would think he'd never been in the tub at all!"

Chick trembled like a little, fearful dog.

"But there, child, we'll let it pass this time," she smiled quickly. "Only it's plain I can't trust you to young Jerrold any more. I'll have to wash you myself from now on or else you'll be a disgrace to me among all the folk of Middletown.

"Surely," she added with sudden thought, "no one can breathe a word of scandal about the old maid a-scrubbing you; you're only ten and but the teeniest, darlingest baby. Now kiss me good night, you trembly little dear."

The Frisco Kid was not fooled the least bit. He knew it all for the most arrant sort of stall; for hadn't he himself washed Chick's ears and neck, and rubbed and scrubbed so there wouldn't be the slightest possible chance of the little fellow getting in wrong with Miss Heffernan on this, his first Saturday-night inspection?

The Kid's face glowed incandescently with joy. At last and in heaping measure Miss Heffernan had fallen for the tiny white-rabbity Chick!

Very soon then all the kerosene lamps were out and the woman of the house was asleep in her starchy white bed, a happy little smile on her thin, austere lips. Up in the rag-carpeted room he shared with the Frisco Kid and Gay-cat, Chick talked on and on in a uniquely buoyant way, telling things that had occurred to him before he climbed the spiked gate and ran away from the "orphing" asylum in St. Louis.

But finally his words came drawlingly, his sentences grew disconnected, and there were long, drowsy pauses. At last one pause became so prolonged that the waiting Frisco Kid lifted his head. Chick was breathing slowly and regularly in deep sleep.

The Kid got up then from the little green-painted iron bed and dressed himself in his old hobo clothes—those overlarge cast-offs which he had worn before he had met up with Strong-Arm and become invested with the change of garniture for Atlanta Slim. In preparation for this night's adventure he must have secretly hidden away, several days before, the newly cleaned and pressed suit.

He went over to the box, padded with old clothes, where Gay-cat slept like a top. Stooping, he gathered up the dog in his arms so gently that Gay-cat only waked sufficiently to sense it was his buddy, then cuddled on his chest with his cold, wet nose against the Kid's neck.

"Good-by, Chick-a-biddy!" he whispered to the infantile figure beneath the blankets. "Be good to Miss Heffernan, little feller, an' she'll be adoptin' you in no time, now that we'se gone."

Something seemed to snap in the boy's throat. Huddled as with cold, the dog tightly held to him, he hurried down the stairs and along the dark, damp hallway. He came to a pause before Miss Heffernan's bedroom door. He leaned against that door, and not in his usual voice but in the hoarse broken tones of a weary old-timer murmured:

"Good-by, Miss Heffernan, ma'am. You've been awful good to us and I hates to go away like this, without no word of *adios*; but you'll be wise to why I did it an' on'y love Chick baby more! Good-by fer keeps, Miss Heffernan, ma'am—ye're an angel—but it's best fer you an' Chick."

Presently as the Kid opened the squeaking kitchen screen-door the briskness of the starry night roused the dog on his chest into life. The Gay-cat squirmed over the boy's arm and dropped softly to the flight of rear steps. As the Kid turned the corner of the shadowy old building and walked on stealthy toes by the dim line of wire-meshed carriage sheds the dog bolted ahead, a vague rushing streak, wildly exultant now they were free of the house and once more on the go.

He was always that way, the Gay-cat, mad with Gipsy delight whenever they started roaming. The long road was calling him now, and there was the irresistible allurement of brisk spring mornings and sultry afternoons under drooping poplars beside languorous, green-bordered streams.

Gay-cat seemed to feel the urge of the accursed *Wanderlust* even more than did the Frisco Kid. For the boy went with lagging, leaden feet down between the black yew hedges and, once out under the dim white sign, paused to look back.

When he turned about to continue on, the Kid experienced a great sinking of heart. For here, in the bald road, there awaited him no open-mouthed, eager Gay-cat questioning with wagging tail and uptilted nose which way to take. The dog, in his incontainable exuberance, had lost himself somewhere ahead in the dark.

Suppose the little yellow mongrel should leave him some time for good and all, just as that very night he was abandoning Miss Heffernan and Chick without one honest open word of farewell. Ah, that would be too much after all the Kid had suffered in his hoboing through the world!

And then the dog was back like a stone from a catapult, leaping up and upon the lad, biting at his hands, entangling himself in his legs, acting altogether the darn fool of love. The long withheld tears started from the eyes of the boy and rolled slowly, one after the other, down his lean cheeks. How his Gay-cat loved him! His own attachment to the dog was as nothing to the dog's terrible love for him. There was no one in the whole wide world who loved the Frisco Kid with the heart-breaking ardor of Gay-cat—no one, that is, excepting—

The Frisco Kid turned bleak. He felt suddenly empty inside. For all at once he remembered a wistful, pale face framed in a shawl, a frail figure standing by a bush of white marguerites near a gate of picket-paling. While he watched her in the strange mind-picture she stretched out her yearning arms to him and called a name. That name was not "Frisco Kid."

It was his mother he saw, his little, graying mother up in Grass Valley. She had been waiting for him all these years.

He spoke a word to the Gay-cat in a husky tone that instantly quieted the dog's ardors of love-making. Then together the two started down the hill toward sleeping Middletown. They drilled along in true hobo style, their shoulders slouched forward, their heads bent to the ruts in the road. But in the brain of the boy were unwinding distressful thoughts.

Suddenly he slackened his pace, and partly to himself, more to the dog, he said:

"Always movin', always movin' on. Gay-cat, when we gets tired of bein' boes we'll go back to the valley and surprise my ma. But I guess"—with a wistful smile—"you and me'll never get tired of bein' hoboes. We're blowed-in-the-glass stiffs, we are, and it's in our blood."

He looked up, on the sudden, from the dog and the ruts in the road to the stars overhead. The two, boy and dog, had paused almost at the bottom of the hill, and perhaps it was because the shadows were deeper here in the hollow that the stars overhead seemed so white and near. Indeed, one bright star there was that blinked like a tear-dimmed eye, and seemed to speak to the boy.

The Kid knew then. He was wearying of wandering. He would go back surely and soon to Her, to his little, pale mother waiting forever by that bush of white marguerites. The bright and tender star had told him that. There in the wide and empty night, he felt a great warming glow of pride that a star so high and radiant should send a message of heart's peace to one so lowly and so beaten.

Glossary

Herewith is appended a glossary of flash language, that peculiar argot or slang of the thief and hobo. It is as old as history and has been used as a means of safe communication in public for years. How many words this lingo contains it is impossible to tell absolutely, but it is believed that over three thousand separate and distinct expressions are in use in this country today.

Ace-spot, or bullet: One dollar.

Baldy: An old man.

Ball: One dollar.

Ball lump: Sandwiches, cake, etc., handed out to a tramp, wrapped in paper.

Batter: To beg.

Beef, cough, snitch, spill, or squeal: To give information to the police.

Beefer: One who squeals on a fellow-tramp or criminal.

Be George or hep: To be wise. "Hello, George," said when meeting a bo is tantamount to meaning, "I'm a bo, too."

Black-top: Moving-picture tent.

Blanket-stiff: A tramp who carries his blankets with him; a Western tramp.

Blind-baggage: Baggage-car behind engine, the front end of which has no door.

Bloke: A fellow; same as "stiff," "mug," "bum," etc.

Bloomer: A failure.

Blowed-in-the-glass stiff: The higher caste hobo; a trustworthy professional tramp; a true "pal"; also, blown-in-the-bottle stiff.

'Bo: A hobo.

Boomer: A hobo who solicits subscriptions for magazines, or engages in clerical work or anything high-toned while he is on the bo.

Bracelets: Handcuffs.

Brakey: A brakeman.

Bughouse: Insane, crazy.

Bull: An officer.

Bundle: Stolen goods; plunder from a "job"; pillage.

Buzz, or mooch, or work the main drag or stem: To beg or bum along the main street.

Cash a rush-in: To breeze up to the proprietor of a restaurant after having had a meal ordered for you by some good Samaritan and, when the latter has left, say: "I've got my gut full already. I don't want anything to eat. That was a fall guy what led me in here. Just knock down to me twenty cents out of that quarter he gave you." Usually the restaurant keeper jews the tramp down to ten cents, and they part, well pleased, and both ahead of the game.

Chew: To eat.

Chew the rag: To talk.

Chi (pronounced "Shi"): Chicago.

Cincie: Cincinnati.

Con: A conductor; tuberculosis, or one afflicted with tuberculosis.

Cooked, or croaked: Killed.

Cooler: A prison-cell. Usually, the dark cell.

Cop: To win; a policeman; to be "copped" is to be arrested.

Crib: A bar-room or gambling-joint; a hang-out.

Crisscross: To swap a benefactor. One tramp gets a setdown; he meets another hobo who has also been fed; they explain where they have eaten and each goes to the other's benefactor for the next meal.

Crocus: A doctor.

Crook: A professional criminal.

Dead: Reformed. A "dead" criminal is said to have "squared it"; he has quit the road or the game through discouragement or a kind of reformation.

Deuce-spot: Two dollars.

Dicer: A hat. Synonymous with "lid," or "beany."

Dick, or Elbow: Detective. "Dick" is probably a contraction of the word detective. "Elbow" comes from the detective's way of elbowing through a crowd. A whispered warning that there are "elbows" in the crowd always sends a shiver down a crook's spine.

Dip: A pickpocket. After lifting a pocketbook a "dip" quickly "weeds the leather," that is goes through it hurriedly.

Ditch, or be ditched: To fail in an undertaking; to fall into trouble. The term is also applied to being put off trains and being locked in cars.

Dope, The: The Baltimore & Ohio Railroad. Drug of any form.

Doss: To sleep. As a noun—sleep.

Doss-house: A lodging-house; a place to sleep.

Drill on: To walk on.

Dump: A lodging-house or restaurant.

Electric-flash: Electric hand-torch.

Finger: Policeman. From the policeman's method of fingering and frisking the arrested hobo.

Fence: A receiver of stolen goods.

Fin: Hand.

Flatty: A policeman; a "bull."

Flagged: When criminals permit a likely victim to go unmolested it is called "flagged."

Flicker: A faint; as a verb, to faint or pretend to faint.

Frisked: Searched by the police.

Front: Appearance; clothes.

Gag: A trick used to assist in begging; a fake story.

Galway: A Catholic priest.

Gay-cat: A fake hobo; a tramp who peaches on his mates; the scorn of hobo aristocracy; a hobo who works.

Gee, guy, gun, mug, plug, stiff, etc.: A fellow.

Get your orders: To be met by a Johnny Tinplate, or constable, and be told to leave town by a specified time.

Ghost story: A fake story; a gag; a story of tramp life told to young boys.

Give a man the boots: To kick and stamp on a man.

Go mitted or heeled: To go armed.

Graft, spiel: Line of business; method of begging. "What's your spiel?" asks one hobo of another.

Grafter: A pickpocket. The Swell Mobs or Good People are the pick of the dips and pickpockets, of the second-story men and of the safe-crackers. By good or swell is meant that they make crime pay. A pickpocket's companion, or confederate, is called a stall.

Grease-joint: A restaurant where one gets a grab, such as a cup of Java and some sinkers or doughnuts.

Grifter: Short change swindler, or swindler of small caliber.

Grubbing: Money, but not in large quantity. The more common term is kale, or jack.

Hand-out or poke-out: Same as a ball-lump but without the wrapping of paper.

Hangout: The hobo's rendezvous along the road.

Hit the road; turf it: To tramp; to be on the bum; to hobo.

Hoister, or hyster: A shoplifter.

Horstile: Hostile; unfriendly; antagonistic toward hoboes.

Jake: Good; as, a Jake town, a good town.

Jigger: An artificial sore made to excite sympathy. A common "gag."

Jocker: A tramp who trains, and protects a boy from persecution by others, until he is a regular stiff. The act of enticing the boy into the life is called "snaring," and the person doing it a "snare."

John O'Brien, or side-door pullman: A box-car. In refrigerator cars there is a wire screen in the center, behind which on one side the ice is packed, on the other the meat. A hole in the floor, covered by a panel which allows of being shoved back and forth, lets out the ice and water. A tramp may climb through this opening and, should the car prove empty and the screen torn or none too secure, squirm up into the body of the car. Shacks seldom appear to look here for tramps.

Join out: To be hired by or join with someone on the road.

Keester: The strong-box of a safe.

Kip-house: A lodging-house.

Knocking off a peter: Breaking the door of a safe.

Lighthouse: One well-acquainted with the police and detectives and can give warning when they are near, to his pals.

Lump: Eats.

Make a dead fall to someone: To have an instant liking for someone.

Mark: A place "good" for food or clothes or money; a person easy to "touch."

Meal-ticket: A person "good" for a meal.

Moll-buzzer: One who nicks suckers, particularly women.

Mugged: Photographed for the Rogues' Gallery according to Bertillon System.

Mush-fakir: A mender of umbrellas. The mush-fakir makes a practice of collecting umbrellas to mend and of not returning them.

Office: A signal. Often a mere raising of the hat.

On this gag: On this job.

Pennyweighter: Jewelry thief.

Pete, or peter-man: A safe-cracker.

Pound the ear: To sleep; synonymous with "doss."

Privates: A private-dwelling.

Prushun: A tramp boy. Once his apprenticeship is served the boy becomes an "ex-prushun" and "jockers and snares" for himself and for revenge.

Punk and plaster: Bread and butter.

Push: A gang; synonymous with "shove."

Queer, The: Counterfeit money.

Repeater, or revolver: An old-time or professional tramp; a "blowed-in-the-glass" hobo.

Rush-in: Where a good Samaritan, when you buzz him for a dime, rushes you into a restaurant and orders a meal for you.

Salve: A complaint.

Scoff: Food; nourishment. As a verb, to eat.

Screw: A prison turnkey.

Setdown: To put your legs under for a square; to sit down at a table for a meal.

Settled: In jail; imprisoned.

Shack, or brakey: Brake-man.

Shatin' on me uppers: To be "shatin' " on uppers means to be "flat broke"; without money.

Shell-workers: Shell-and-pea men.

Shill through: To go free, as into a circus.

Shover: A man who passes bogus bills; a counterfeiter's pal.

Skee, old man red-eye, hooch, third rail: Whiskey.

Slope: To run away.

Slopping-up: Getting a big drunk; as a noun, a drunk.

Spiel, or ballyhoo: A talk.

Sneak: House thief. A bank thief is called a bank sneak.

Song and dance: Same as "gag."

Spiked: Chagrined, disappointed.

Squealer: One who snitches on the "push"; one who betrays his pals.

Sucker, shut-eye, green pea, fall guy: An easy victim.

Snow: Cocaine. The user of cocaine is called a "snow-bird," and the act of using the drug termed "taking a sleigh ride."

Stake-man: A tramp who works

for a stake—"booze" and tobacco money while he is on the tramp. To "blowed-in-the-glass stiffs" he is a "gay-cat."

Stall: Pickpocket's confederate.

Steeple: Coal-car covered with plates in the form of a steeple. There is one rod beneath the body of these cars, where the car rounds upward. "Shacks" rarely look here.

Stick-up: Strong-arm man who holds one up with a "gat."

Stool: Stool-pigeon or spy of the law who simulates a man of the under-world and reports the doings of the underworld to the police.

Throw the feet: To beg; to walk along the road; to do anything that calls for much action.

Tomato-can vag: The hobo outcast. So called because he empties beer-barrel dregs into a tomato-can and drinks them. Tomato-can vags generally live on refuse that they find in garbage barrels.

Toot the ringer: Ring the bell.

Yap: A farmer; a "rube." As a verb, to tell; to say.

Index

OFF-TRAIL PUBLICATIONS
Specializing in the era of American pulp fiction

THE WEIRD DETECTIVE ADVENTURES OF WADE HAMMOND
By Paul Chadwick
Volume 1: 10 stories, 180 pages, $18
Volume 2: 10 stories, 172 pages, $18
Volume 3: 10 stories, 202 pages, $18
Volume 4: 9 stories, 232 pages, $18

> *The Wade Hammond stories complete in four volumes. In these chilling adventures, all from the classic 1930's pulps,* Detective-Dragnet *and* Ten Detective Aces, *freelance investigator Wade Hammond battles a series of weird enemies. Some of the best of '30s pulp fiction.*

 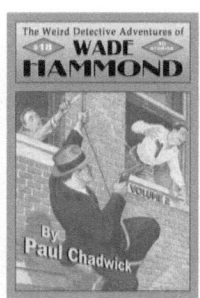  

DOCTOR COFFIN: The Living Dead Man
By Perley Poore Sheehan • Introduction by John Wooley
8 novelettes, 178 pages, $16

> *Weird stories from* Thrilling Detective, *1932-33. A former character actor who faked his own death, Doctor Coffin runs a string of mortuaries by night and fights crime at night. One of the strangest detective series.*

SUPER-DETECTIVE FLIP BOOK: Two Complete Novels
From the pulp *Super-Detective*:
"Legion of Robots" (November 1940) by Victor Rousseau • Introduction by John McMahan •• "Murder's Migrants" (March 1943) by Robert Leslie Bellem and W.T. Ballard • Introduction by John Wooley
2 short novels, 174 pages, $18

> Super-Detective *started as a Doc Savage-like adventure pulp, then changed format to hardboiled detective. The* Flip Book *features a novel from each of the two phases with intros exploring the historical background. Exciting!*

PULPWOOD DAYS: Volume 1: Editors You Want To Know

Edited by John Locke • 180 pages, $16

*Numerous articles from the writers' magazines by and about pulp editors, with ample biographical profiles. Editors include: Frank E. Blackwell (*Detective Story, Western Story*), Ray Palmer (*Amazing Stories, Fantastic Adventures*), Edwin Baird (*Weird Tales, Detective Tales*), and many more.*

GANG PULP

Edited by John Locke • 19 stories, 294 pages, $24

Hardboiled stories of the criminal underworld from the first year (1929-30) of the gang pulps: Gangster Stories, Racketeer Stories, *etc. These violent tales came under immediate censorship pressure; the history is explored in an in-depth essay. "A remarkable work of popular-culture scholarship"—*MYSTERY SCENE, *Fall 2008.*

THE GANGLAND SAGAS OF BIG NOSE SERRANO

Volume 1: Dames, Dice and the Devil

Volume 2: Horses, Hoboes and Heroes

Volume 3: Hell's Gangster

By Anatole Feldman • Introductions by Will Murray

Each: 4 novels • **Volumes 1-2**: 266 pages, $20 • **Volume 3**: 224 pages, $18

The complete Big Nose Serrano novels from Gangster Stories, Greater Gangster Stories, *and* The Gang Magazine, *1930-35. Feldman was the best of the gang pulp authors, and Big Nose was his most inspired creation, the berserking king of Chicago gangsters.*

CITY OF NUMBERED MEN: The Best of Prison Stories
Introduction by John Locke
12 stories, 278 pages, $20

> *During Prohibition, famed publisher Harold Hersey turned America's disintegrating prison system into the hardboiled* Prison Stories *(1930-31). Included are stories from all six issues of this ultra-rare pulp, the startling history of* Prison Stories, *complete cover gallery, and "Harold Hersey: Tales of an Ink-Stained Wretch," the first comprehensive biography of pulp publishing's most colorful character.*

THE MAGICIAN DETECTIVE: And Other Weird Mysteries
By Fulton Oursler
Introduction by John Locke
7 stories, 210 pages, $18

> *Fulton Oursler was one of the great editors of his time, ruling over the Macfadden publishing empire for two decades. But stage magic was his first love, and, in his heart, he remained a conjurer in a black cape and top hat. In this collection of early fiction, Oursler's bewitching imagination takes flight in tales of magic, murder and mesmerizing mystery. Also featured is an in-depth exploration of the astonishing career of Fulton Oursler.*

GHOST STORIES: The Magazine and Its Makers
Edited by John Locke
Vol 1: 19 stories, 256 pages, $24 • **Vol 2**: 15 stories, 272 pages, $24

> *Macfadden's* Ghost Stories *(1926-31) presented haunted tales in every exciting arena: the Western Front, gangland, aviation, the Klondike, the circus, etc. The personnel behind* Ghost Stories *were a fascinating group: poets and scholars, war heroes and war correspondents, adventurers and Bohemians; a few became prolific pulpsters; a few became bestselling authors. And a few led haunted lives. Vol 1 includes the history of* Ghost Stories, *bios of every editor, and every Vol 1 author. Vol 2 includes bios of every Vol 2 author, every cover artist, and a gallery of all 64* Ghost Stories *covers.*